# You Can Have My Back 1

## Minami Kotsuna

YEN
ON

New York

# You Can Have My Back

Minami Kotsuna          ILLUSTRATION BY Hitomi Hitoyo

Translation by Aleksandra Jankowska

This book is a work of fiction. Names, characters, places, and incidents are the product of the author's imagination or are used fictitiously. Any resemblance to actual events, locales, or persons, living or dead, is coincidental.

SENAKA WO AZUKERU NIHA Vol.1
©Minami Kotsuna 2021
First published in Japan in 2021 by KADOKAWA CORPORATION, Tokyo.
English translation rights arranged with KADOKAWA CORPORATION, Tokyo, through Tuttle-Mori Agency, Inc., Tokyo.

English translation © 2023 by Yen Press, LLC

Yen On
150 West 30th Street, 19th Floor
New York, NY 10001

Visit us at yenpress.com
facebook.com/yenpress
twitter.com/yenpress
yenpress.tumblr.com
instagram.com/yenpress

First Yen On Edition: July 2023
Edited by Yen On Editorial: Payton Campbell
Designed by Yen Press Design: Andy Swist

Yen On is an imprint of Yen Press, LLC.
The Yen On name and logo are trademarks of Yen Press, LLC.

The publisher is not responsible for websites (or their content) that are not owned by the publisher.

Library of Congress Cataloging-in-Publication Data
Names: Kotsuna, Minami, author. | Jankowska, Aleksandra (Translator), translator.
Title: You can have my back / Minami Kotsuna ; translation by Aleksandra Jankowska.
Other titles: Senaka wo azukeru niha. English
Description: First Yen On edition. | New York, NY : Yen On, 2023-
Identifiers: LCCN 2023004111 | ISBN 9781975363932 (v. 1 ; trade paperback)
Subjects: CYAC: Fantasy. | Reincarnation—Fiction. | LCGFT: Fantasy fiction. | Light novels.
Classification: LCC PZ7.1.K6828 Yo 2023 | DDC [Fic]—dc33
LC record available at https://lccn.loc.gov/2023004111

ISBNs: 978-1-9753-6393-2 (paperback)
       978-1-9753-6394-9 (ebook)

10 9 8 7 6 5 4 3 2 1

LSC-C

Printed in the United States of America

# Contents

❧

## Lucas
Ionia's schoolmate and the lieutenant general of the Royal Army. He suspects that Leorino is Ionia's reincarnation.

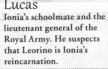

## Ionia
Met Gravis through a strange twist of fate, joined the army, and later died in battle.

## August
Leorino's father. Margrave of Brungwurt. He is concerned about the future of his youngest son.

## Josef
Leorino's childhood friend and bodyguard. His androgynous appearance doesn't betray his headstrong personality.

## Kyle
The crown prince and Gravis's nephew. He has yet to marry. His personality is rather elusive.

## Dirk
Ionia's younger brother. Currently serving as Gravis's adjutant in the Royal Army.

## Julian
Eldest son of the Duke of Leben. He falls in love with Leorino at first sight and pursues his hand in marriage.

# Character Introductions

**Gravis**
The king's younger brother and the general of the Royal Army. He has grown bitter since the death of his best friend, Ionia.

**Leorino**
The fourth son of a margrave. Known for his unmatched beauty, he possesses the memories of the late Ionia.

# You Can Have My Back

# Prologue

To say he was overwhelming would be an understatement.

"…Come, now. Is that all the fight you have in you, Leorino? I may just fall asleep."

"How are you so strong?!"

If Leorino could twist his wrist just a little more, he would be able to break free. But the man's grip around it was much too strong, not giving an ounce of leeway. Leorino struggled with all his might, but it was abundantly clear that for the other man, keeping him bound was mere child's play. The man grabbed his arms with ease and pinned him to the bed again.

"Unf!"

In an instant, the fingers restraining his wrists coiled tighter around his flesh.

"…Stop struggling. You'll only hurt yourself."

With that, the man parted Leorino's legs, slipped between them, and pressed against his slender body.

"Hng…"

It was hard to breathe, which only heightened Leorino's tension.

The man had been right. If he chose to shift more of his body weight onto him, Leorino's delicate frame would be crushed. Unable to properly catch his breath, the young man let his eyes go vacant.

Noticing that Leorino had reached his limits, the man sat back up.

"…Breathe."

Leorino gasped for air like a drowning man.

Then he simply lay there, stunned, his hands still pinned above his head.

"…Leorino."

Blood rushed back to his fingertips, accompanied by a throbbing pain. It wasn't just his wrists. His entire body hurt. He'd struggled so hard the entire time, his body now felt like he was being torn limb from limb. The corners of his eyes twisted in pain, and soon large tears came spilling forth.

The man frowned at the sight. "Ah, I went too far again… I never know when to stop, do I? You're just so *weak*."

With those words, the tears of pain were replaced by tears of humiliation, and those would be even harder to stop.

Leorino knew. This, too, was a sort of kindness from the man. The man was protecting Leorino from himself, ever unable to gauge his limits when he was reminded of their immense difference in strength, struggling until the breaking point. That was the point of the pain. It was meant to serve as punishment for his recklessness, but the man was careful, holding back the full extent of his strength so as not to cause any real damage.

Leorino knew this. And it was the knowing that hurt. Knowing how vulnerable—how utterly dependent on the man he was.

The man furrowed his shapely brows in remorse.

"Don't cry… Did I hurt you? My apologies."

In truth, Leorino didn't want to be seen in such a pathetic state, but once he became upset, he had trouble calming himself down. Choking back a sob, he looked up at the man. "I-if you're going to apologize, then let go of me…"

The man looked at Leorino, who had now been reduced to pleading, with naked pity in his gaze.

"Once you've made up your mind, you never give up… Just like *him*," he murmured with a faint smile on his lips, before moving his hand to the back of Leorino's head and pulling him close.

That perfect beauty of his was so close now, the man's breath nearly caught in his throat at the sight.

"Leorino. Look at me."

"No... I won't."

"Have you forgotten? You don't get to reject me."

"Stop... Mmf."

The man's mouth slowly met Leorino's. Leorino tried to squirm away, but his resistance was completely in vain. Gently, passionately, he surrendered his soft lips. He was helpless to do anything but savor the sweet and sour punishment. As the pleasure continued to fill his body, he began feeling light-headed.

Finally sated, the man pulled away, licking his wet lips. His golden eyes shone with a dangerous gleam. "Now...let's talk about the other matter you've been keeping from me."

Leorino attempted to escape once more, trying to twist out of the man's grip. "I refuse! Let go of me! ...Ow!"

The man had nipped at the fair skin of his exposed throat. Leorino was unused to rough treatment, and the sudden pain in such a tender spot came as a shock to his system.

"...Don't be silly. I've finally gotten my hands on you. You think I'd let you go so easily?"

The man ran his tongue along the bite mark, as if to soothe the trembling Leorino.

"...Y-Your Highness..."

A choked sob slipped from Leorino's quivering lips, which the man was now playfully tracing with his fingertips.

"...Call me 'Vi' the way you used to."

The man's tenderness immediately after teasing him made Leorino's heart feel weak.

"...*The way you used to.*"

How could he not be swayed by the words of the man he loved?

When Leorino shook his head, the man's brow furrowed in a pained expression.

"...Say my name, Leorino... Or would you rather"—the man's voice sounded like an earnest prayer—"I call you by another name...Io?"

Leorino was suddenly overwhelmed by the powerful emotion welling inside him.

Vi and Io.

The names that could only be called by each other—and no one else.

Leorino's violet eyes welled up once more, though these tears were not born of pain or humiliation. He looked up at the man through glossy eyes. He was just as Leorino had remembered him—his wavy black hair, his Prussian blue eyes flecked with gold, which so strongly resembled the night sky. But the man before him was so much more mature now than he had been eighteen years ago.

The man pulled him into a tight hug.

"Io... Ionia, I've missed you so much."

*I've missed you, too, Vi.*

That was the voice of Leorino's *other self* who lived in his memories. At the same time, his heart seemed to scream:

*But I am not Ionia.*

Ionia had died eighteen years ago.
They could never return to the way things were back then.
*Because I can never fight by your side again...not in this body.*

# What Frontier Angels Dream Of

The Kingdom of Fanoren was located in the center of the Agalean continent. Leorino Cassieux was born as the fourth son of August Cassieux, the Margrave of Brungwurt, a territory on the kingdom's border.

Leorino's mother, Maia, had come from the well-respected Wiesen ducal family. She met August—ten years her senior—at a royal ball and, after a passionate romance, married him at the age of eighteen. She blessed him with an heir, Auriano, the following year and with a second son, Johan, one year after that. The two boys looked just like their father, with dark-brown hair, blue-green eyes, and muscular physiques. They were perfectly handsome little boys.

Five years later came the birth of their third son, Gauff. Maia had secretly hoped for a girl, but Gauff was the spitting image of his father, just like his brothers, and was remarkably well-built for one so young.

Maia loved her sons dearly, but with her love for all things cute, she had the poor luck of having three sons, all bulky from a young age and tragically ill-suited to cute outfits.

Six years after the birth of her third son, the family welcomed Leorino into the world. At the time of his birth, the country was fighting with its neighbor, and the ravages of war were approaching the border province of Brungwurt. Maia was happy to have been able to bring new life into the world at such a tumultuous time.

As soon as she had learned this new child was another boy, she was prepared for another clone of her husband. Perhaps she wouldn't be able to dress him in frills, but she convinced herself that as long as he was healthy, none of that would matter.

And yet, when Maia first laid eyes on the newborn, she was enraptured to discover her long-held dream had finally come true.

Leorino Viola Maian Cassieux was practically a cherub, with snow-white hair and extraordinary violet eyes. Twelve years after the birth of her first son, the adorable baby clothes she had prepared saw the light of day at long last.

His pure-white hair gradually darkened with age, until it became a platinum blond that seemed to melt in the light. His violet eyes were like the sky at dawnbreak, the first rays of sunlight piercing though the indigo night. His nose had a lovely ridge to it, and his rose-red lips always appeared to be smiling. All of these features were perfectly placed on his round, doll-like face. There wasn't a stitch of frilly clothing in all the world that did not suit him, such a frighteningly beautiful child he was.

This angel of a baby then grew into an angel of a boy. As the youngest child of the family, he had a gentle demeanor and grew up in good health, loved and protected by his parents, his three brothers, and the people of his land.

From his eleventh birthday onward, Leorino began seeing a boy in his dreams.

This boy was called…"Ionia."

The dream began with him waking up in a modest bedroom. He would stand in front of the washbasin in a corner of the small room and peer into the mirror. Staring back at him was the charming face of a boy with red hair disheveled from sleep and a pair of rare violet eyes.

*Oh…this is me…*

The boy, Ionia, lived in the commoner district of the royal capital. Leorino had never actually seen the capital, but somehow he knew exactly where to find him.

Ionia's family was made up of four people: Apart from him, there was his taciturn blacksmith father, his kind mother, and a newborn baby brother. Their house and his father's workshop were both located in the commoner district, and although they were far from wealthy, they were content.

Ionia was tall for his age and a good fighter, so it was only fitting that he served as the leader of the local children, and he was recognized by his neighbors for his good cheer and mischief alike. Nevertheless, he cared deeply about his family. He would help out with the blacksmith business however he could, and he was often taking care of his little brother.

Ionia also attended the prep school attached to the local church three times a week and was looking forward to entering the elementary school open to commoners.

"Lord Leorino, may I ask what has put you in such a good mood?" Hundert, Leorino's attendant, finally asked, having seen him smiling to himself all morning.

Leorino decided to let him in on his secret. "Recently, I keep having the same dream."

"A dream? May I ask what sort of dream?"

"A very interesting one. I've been having it every night, like a story slowly unfolding before my eyes."

"Why, that is quite strange indeed."

Leorino nodded in agreement.

In truth, it was a very strange experience. Dreams were supposed to be fleeting and hazy, but dreams of Ionia appeared to him almost every night. Moreover, they seemed to follow his life in chronological order.

Leorino couldn't tell if the bizarre dreams were just products of his imagination, but for a boy of noble birth who was living an uneventful life in the middle of nowhere, getting to relive the life of a commoner boy in his dreams for nights on end was the greatest adventure imaginable.

A significant portion of the dreams would fade from his mind as soon as he awoke, but he remembered the most noteworthy scenes. Every night, he went to bed giddy to fall asleep.

"In my dreams, I'm a commoner boy with red hair, but he has the same eyes as me! We're the same age, but he's much bigger than me. He's almost as big as Gauff! Oh, and he's looking forward to going to school."

"Is that so? A boy as strong as Lord Gauff with the same eyes as you, Lord Leorino?"

The servant privately wondered if this dream was Leorino's hidden desire to be as strong as his brother.

"His father is a blacksmith, his mother has black hair, and he has a baby brother. He's adorable!"

His usually quiet master felt especially talkative, his eyes twinkling as he spoke of his dreams. This fact pleased the attendant, and he nodded along with great interest.

From then on, Leorino would dream of Ionia often.

It felt almost as if he would live another life in his sleep, and he could never quite shake off the strangeness of this experience. Leorino, of course, knew that he was Leorino Cassieux. Nevertheless, Ionia's life slowly burned itself into Leorino's memories.

One day, Leorino peered into the mirror and sighed. "Hmm..."

At some point, the reflection staring back at him had begun to feel somewhat foreign—even wrong—to him. Hundert inclined his head at his young master, who had been observing himself in the mirror ever since he awoke.

"...No, this isn't right."

"What seems to be the matter, my lord? Have you noticed something on your face?"

Leorino's countenance was as flawless as ever.

"No, my face is fine. It's just..."

*I inherited my mother's face, and that's all well and good, but why does it look so...soft?*

Puzzled by his master's behavior, the attendant proceeded to show him his two clothing options for the day.

"Which of these would you prefer to wear today?"

His options were a day dress with pastel-pink embroidery or a day dress with a thin light-blue ribbon embellished at the hem.

Leorino finally understood the source of his discomfort.

"...May I ask you something, Hundert?"

"Of course, my lord."

"Um...these are both dresses, aren't they?"

"Indeed, they are."

Now that he thought about it, Leorino had never seen his brothers or Ionia wearing dresses.

"Do boys usually wear dresses?"

"Not typically, no."

Leorino inclined his head. "...Then why am I wearing girls' clothes?"

"Why, because they suit you very well, my lord."

Leorino had been wearing dresses from a young age, per his mother's wishes. Indeed, he had looked so good in them, no one ever gave it a second thought, and Leorino himself hadn't questioned it once until now.

"But...I'm a boy, right?"

The attendant nodded.

In the Kingdom of Fanoren, one became a full-fledged adult at the age of eighteen. At the age of twelve, one was considered "half-fledged" and was gradually allowed to participate in society.

Leorino was fast approaching that tender age.

"Hey, Gauff, I'm almost half-fledged. How much longer will I have to keep dressing like this?" Leorino complained, following his older brother into the stables. He looked down at himself, picking at the hem of his frilly dress.

Gauff stroked the muzzle of his favorite horse, looking at his dispirited brother with eyes full of sympathy.

"…Until Mother is satisfied, I suppose."

"…Stop looking at me like that. I don't want your pity."

"But don't worry—you look good in that! No one minds."

Leorino stomped his foot. "I mind! I don't care if it looks good on me. That's not the problem!"

Gauff hadn't expected that outburst. He had never seen his sweet brother stomp his foot in anger before.

"…Rino, you can't really be considering rebelling against Mother?"

"Please, Gauff! Please tell Mother to stop dressing me this way!" Leorino glanced down at himself with a miserable look on his face.

The light-blue ribbon swayed in the breeze blowing through the stable.

"I want to wear boy clothes like you do!" The boy's heart-wrenching cry echoed through the stables.

One after another, the horses seemed to whinny in sympathy.


Once he became half-fledged, he would enter society and begin meeting new people. Leorino decided that something had to be done before then and finally announced his intentions to his mother.

"Mother, starting tomorrow, I will be wearing clothes intended for boys."

Maia inclined her head gracefully. "And why is that?"

"Because I am a boy."

"Of course, I'm well aware. But what seems to be the problem with wearing clothes that suit you regardless?"

"No, I do not believe dresses suit me at all. Therefore, I will no longer be wearing them."


After that, Leorino did just as he had promised: He tossed his dresses out into the hallway, found Gauff's old clothes, and wore those instead. Throughout Brungwurt, news quickly spread that the angel had entered his rebellious phase.


Both the family and the servants struggled to decide whether to side with Leorino or his mother. Reason would dictate that Leorino's request should be granted. It made perfect sense that a boy nearly half-fledged would want to wear boys' clothing. But as selfish as it might have been, some agreed with Maia's belief that it would be a shame to abandon clothes that looked so good on him. His natural beauty transcended gender, and the luxuriant dresses complemented his appearance perfectly. Leorino was like a white rose blooming in the castle, and his presence alone brought great joy to all.

In the end, the decision fell to August, the head of the house.

"Father, I wish to dress like a boy."

"Yes, Leorino, I understand. However…"

"Father, it's been nearly twelve years since my birth. I recognize that this is sudden, but…I do not wish to wear dresses any longer."

August looked at his youngest son with sadness in his eyes.

"Father? Are you hearing me?"

"Rino… Why don't you call me 'Papa' anymore?"

He was missing the point.

"Father, please!"

Leorino, usually so calm, so soft, and so tender, now stomped his feet, just like he had with Gauff.

"It does not matter what I call you, Father. We were talking about my clothing!"

"Are you saying my feelings don't matter…?"

For the first time in his life, Leorino looked at the father he had respected so much with utter disbelief.

Next, it was Maia's turn to wring the handkerchief she was holding as she stated her case before her husband. "No one thinks twice about gender in this day and age. What's wrong with Rino wearing clothes that look good on him?"

"Hmm, I suppose you have a point…"

Maia pointed at her eldest son, who was watching the whole affair in silence.

"Just look at Auriano. He certainly appears masculine, but look at his white shirt and dark-blue jacket. Don't you find the combination dull? Do you want our Rino to wear something so plain?"

"Dull…? Plain…?" the eldest son muttered to himself. To the casual observer, he would have seemed like a very fine-looking man, but he was no match for Maia.

Leorino nodded in agreement with his mother. "Indeed, my brother dresses rather plainly."

"Hey...," Auriano interjected before he could stop himself.

"Mother, I think your open-mindedness toward dresses and who can wear them is wonderful. But I want to dress like a boy and wear clothes as plain as my brother's."

"Hey!"

"I'm a boy, and I've always been a boy, so I see no reason why I should be denied the right to dress plainly like my brother!"

"Can you stop calling me 'plain' already?!"

Leorino and his mother continued to argue, both refusing to budge even a little.

Leorino's rebellion had involved all of Brungwurt, and in the end, he emerged victorious. August, afraid of antagonizing his beloved youngest son, finally gave in to his insistence. And ever since, Leorino had been wearing the boy clothes he had so desperately longed for. If nothing else, they served to make him look a little more masculine.

The compromise he had reached with his mother involved him wearing shirts with delicate pleats, which weren't nearly as elaborate as the dresses but meant he still looked like a beautiful little angel.

Still, Leorino was satisfied.

He even felt he had become stronger, more like Ionia.

As his twelfth birthday approached, Leorino began to dream of attending school in the royal capital.

"You know, Hundert, I think I'd really like to attend the academy in the capital."

For generations, the boys of the Cassieux family had obtained their higher education in the royal capital after they turned twelve. However, the margrave and his wife had already decided that Leorino would be privately tutored in Brungwurt by a scholar from the capital, even after he became half-fledged. Leorino had never complained about his parents' plans for him, but here he was saying such things.

The attendant broke out in a cold sweat, fretting that he was about to witness a repeat of the dress wars. "Lord Leorino...I believe your parents have already made their decision."

"I know. That's why I want you to help me convince them."

The school was, in truth, a pretext that would get him to the capital.

Leorino wanted to learn more about Ionia. He had been thinking there must be some way of finding out if Ionia was really just a product of his imagination or a real person. He still regularly had dreams following Ionia's life. He figured it must have been fate. That's why he needed to get to the capital.

At the same time, the margrave and his wife had their own reasons for wanting to keep Leorino inside the province. One of the reasons was Leorino's beauty. As the fourth son, Leorino would not inherit his father's title, which meant he would eventually have to find a job and become independent. However, August and Maia already knew that it would be difficult for their youngest son to live a normal life. Living alone without a guardian would likely be impossible, on account of his beauty. Their second and third sons, Johan and Gauff, lived in the capital, but they, too, were title-less and as such unsuited to be his guardians. August couldn't allow young Leorino to reside where his eyes couldn't reach.

But there was another reason, too. Leorino was known as an angel, not only due to his otherworldly ethereal appearance. The Cassieux family, with its long history, was known for its good fortune.

The day of Leorino's birth was a very special day for Brungwurt.

# The Dawn of Hope

The year Leorino was born, the Kingdom of Fanoren was in the midst of a war with the neighboring country of Zwelf.

The cause of the war was the great cold wave that had hit the Agalean continent the previous winter. Many countries located in the northern part of the continent suffered tremendous damage. Fanoren was no exception. In an effort to minimize human suffering, the country took large-scale measures, among them moving its citizens from the north to the relatively undamaged south.

Fanoren was an affluent country, covering a significant portion of the continent stretching from north to south. They were fortunate to have ample stockpiles that allowed them to provide half a year's worth of food for the entire population, which helped in overcoming the crisis.

The neighboring country of Zwelf wasn't as lucky. Because Zwelf was located in the northernmost part of the continent, their people froze and starved to death at higher rates than in any other country. Although Zwelf was rich in mineral resources, the climate was cold and the land barren. Starved and freezing, Zwelf spiraled out of control. Desperate in its poverty, Zwelf turned to the fertile lands of the neighboring Fanoren. When the crown prince at the time, Vandarren, took the throne, he insisted on southern expansion, and Zwelf quickly trended toward war.

The following year, Zwelf invaded Fanoren.

Fanoren had already been informed about the unrest in the neighboring country and was prepared. If Zwelf were to invade, it would be either from the side of the border fortresses of Zweilink through the forested area in the northeast or from the Baedeker Mountains in the northwest. The Royal Army of Fanoren expected the enemy to attack Zweilink first.

Zweilink was a doubly fortified structure built along the border, consisting of separate outer and inner forts. The outer fort, especially, was a huge wall ten times the height of a man and said to be impregnable. However, going through Zweilink was still less dangerous than leading a large army across a steep mountain range still covered in deep snow.

A cutting-edge unit of the Royal Army was dispatched to Zweilink from the royal capital.

The Brungwurt province, which bordered Zweilink, could not sit back and watch. August, the lord of the land, quietly reinforced the Autonomous Army and prepared for war.

However, the Royal Army's prediction that Zwelf would begin their invasion with Zweilink was wrong. Zwelf, to their surprise, entered Fanoren through the Baedeker Mountains in the northwest. The Royal Army had already been marching toward Zweilink and was forced to suddenly change course and deploy its main forces in the Baedeker Mountains. Zwelf's forces were scattered to invade the area. Skirmishes continued endlessly throughout the mountain range. The Royal Army had no choice but to disperse its forces.

But that was exactly what Zwelf had wanted.

Just as the Fanoren army was able to use its geographical advantage and force the Zwelfs to retreat to the other side of the mountain range, a horde of enemy forces invaded the thinly stretched northeastern border fortress of Zweilink. The soldiers in the Baedeker Mountains were a decoy meant to lure the Fanoren forces to a point of no return.

The sounds of war began reaching even Brungwurt.

August took immediate action. He gathered his family and informed them that Brungwurt might be overrun before long. August was forty years old at the time. His wife, Maia, was expecting their fourth child, whom they would later name Leorino. To preserve the blood of the Cassieux family, August allowed his first son, Auriano, to stay, but evacuated Johan and Gauff to Maia's family estate in the royal capital. However, Maia could have gone into labor at any moment, and escape by carriage seemed risky at best.

With a heavy heart, August had his pregnant wife stay at the castle.

It would be at least seven days before reinforcements from the Royal Army arrived. Until then, August steeled himself to somehow withstand the invasion on his territory.

One night, a message from the border arrived in Brungwurt.

《THE ZWELF ARMY HAS RAIDED AND CAPTURED THE OUTER FORTRESS. ZWEILINK HAS BEEN SET ON FIRE, AND ITS GUARD WAS ALMOST COMPLETELY DESTROYED.》

August prepared himself for the worst. The province of Brungwurt was only half a day's ride from Zweilink. If Zweilink fell, the enemy army would reach the castle the following day. Beyond Brungwurt, there was only one major river, and the rest of the country was an expanse of rolling plains leading to the royal capital. If Brungwurt was breached, a large-scale invasion would roll through the country, and disaster would surely ensue.

At that moment, tensions were stretched taut in Brungwurt. Maia went into labor right after the letter arrived. August and his men hung their heads in despair and dread, lamenting the worst possible timing.

A deep darkness hung over Brungwurt Castle. It was almost dawn when Maia's screams cut through the night sky.

"Father! A message from Zweilink!"

Auriano rushed into the great hall with a letter. August took it and opened it with trembling hands. He read the short message, and his eyes widened.

The time had finally come.

Maia's maid rushed out of the delivery room and into the great hall, calling to August: "My lord, your child is born!"

August shuddered. "My god..."

The letter fell from his hand.

Auriano rushed to pick it up and parse through it. His eyes widened, just as his father's had.

《THE TROOPS LED BY THE KING'S BROTHER HAVE RECAPTURED THE OUTER FORTRESS. ZWEILINK HAS BEEN RECOVERED FROM THE ENEMY, AND WE, FANOREN, STAND A CHANCE AT WINNING THE WAR.》

"Father..."

"Yes... His Royal Highness has really done it."

The war was still raging. But for the moment, the crisis in Brungwurt had been averted. The Royal Army had recaptured Zweilink and driven away the enemy.

From far away, a quiet first cry could be heard.

"It's a miracle..."

The long night had ended and dawn had arrived. The first rays of daybreak cut through the darkness.


The birth of a new life and the simultaneous news of the victory at Zweilink filled the province with relief and glee. The baby born that day was beautiful, with violet eyes bearing rays of dawn racing across the indigo. His eyes, which seemed to reflect the firmament itself, knew nothing of the world's harsh realities and were instead brimming with untold potential.

August held his newborn in his arms and wept. "This child is the guardian angel of Brungwurt—no, the guardian angel of our country. He is a miracle."

The baby, illuminated by the morning sun, was the very hope and future of Fanoren itself.

# Memories of Fire

Leorino's twelfth birthday was fast approaching.

The day before Leorino's birthday was an important anniversary for the Kingdom of Fanoren. Twelve years ago, on that very day, the border fortress of Zweilink was recaptured during the war with Zwelf. It was also the day many soldiers lost their lives in battle.

The annual memorial service held at Zweilink would be attended by the royal family, members of the Royal Army, and important officials from the royal court. The Margrave of Brungwurt's castle was the closest to Zweilink and would be hosting and entertaining the guests.

Leorino would turn twelve the day after the memorial service and would be recognized as being half-fledged. He would also be allowed to participate in the memorial service for the first time ever.

As the day drew nearer, Leorino began to be tormented by a strange unease. He figured it may have been guilt. His family loved to remind him of the circumstances of his birth whenever the opportunity presented itself. That day, many soldiers gave their lives to protect Zweilink. As the day broke, Leorino was born just as they received the news of the victory at the fortress.

The family dubbed it a miracle and called Leorino their guardian angel. But every time Leorino heard that story, it came off to him as if someone had to die just so he could live.

That night, Leorino dreamed of Ionia, the way he always did.

Except Ionia wasn't a boy anymore.

*...Ionia?*

Ionia was an adult now. He was wielding a sword and fighting on a battlefield. He felt a dreadful fire at his back and intense pain. Flames lapped at his wounded body. The weight of the sword in his hand. The hot wind scorching his hair. The pain of his wounds. Everything in the dream felt real.

Leorino already knew where Ionia was standing.

*This is a dream of that day...*

A double fortress had been built to protect the border.
The outer fort was occupied by enemy forces.

The attack was carried out under the cover of night. Caught by surprise, the border guards were at an overwhelming disadvantage. Supporting their wounded soldiers, Ionia's men escaped from the outer fort. A fire had been set to the plain. It spread quickly in the dry winter air.

The margrave's Autonomous Army was waiting in Brungwurt. But they could not let the enemy get that far. If the reinforcements from the Royal Army did not arrive in time, if Brungwurt was breached, the country would be beyond saving.

Crossing the burning plains, Ionia fought his way through enemy soldiers to reach the inner fortress. There, he and his men witnessed an impossible sight. In front of the gates of the inner fortress lay a boulder of a size taller than a man. Because of it, the gates would not close.

*We must close the gates immediately.*

As long as the gates could be closed and the inner fortress remained in their hands, they still had a shot at victory. Even if that meant that the people inside, himself included, would not be able to escape. They could wait until the fires on the plains had died down, then seize the outer fortress again. All was not lost.

*I will defend this fort until he arrives. That's the entire reason I'm here.*

Ionia made up his mind. Drawing whatever life remained in him, he set his heart ablaze and worked up his Power. He placed his hands on the boulder and poured all his strength into it. A roaring crack echoed through the fortress. The boulder had split. He used what little life remained in his body to crush the stone into even finer pieces.

*Close them. Close the gates. As long as those gates are closed, we won't be defeated.*

Someone had heard his desperate cry. With a roar, the massive doors began closing. Then someone else's voice rose from beyond the gates.

*He,* to whom Ionia had given his blood, his loyalty, was standing behind the gates. And behind him stood the reinforcements.

He had made it in time. *He* was here now.

*Now we won't be defeated.*

*He* was reaching his hand out now, shouting to Ionia with a look of utter despair on his face.

Ionia shook his head. *I can't. I won't make it.*

The gates were already closing. He knew he would never be able to return to the other side again. But even if he was dying, even if his whole body was engulfed in flames, he could still fight. Ionia swung his sword. And then the gates closed.

*I've done it. I protected his country.*

Suddenly, he felt an impact in his stomach. He looked down and saw that a sword had pierced deep into his flesh. Ionia fell to the ground, and his eyes caught the night sky beyond the red-hot flames and dense smoke.

*Ah, how I wish I could watch that beautiful starry sky for just a little while longer. And please let* him...

Ionia's life was spent. He had prayed until his very last moment.

*Someone, anyone, please tell* him. *Please let him know how I felt...*


Leorino woke up ravaged by a high fever. His body was burning hot. It was so hot, he screamed.

For the past year, Leorino had lived Ionia's life in his dreams, as if sharing his memories. He dreamed over and over of the peaceful, ordinary life of a boy living in the royal capital.

But today's dream made everything clear. Ionia had died young. He had fought in a war, his body had been pierced by an enemy blade, and his flesh had been engulfed in flames. Ionia's death was too much for the young Leorino to relive. What did Ionia want to say in his final moments? And to whom?

Spurred on by his fever, Leorino cried and cried over Ionia's regrets.

# The Turning Wheels of Fate

Leorino had suddenly fallen ill with a high fever but was able to get up just before the memorial service. Leorino asked his father why he had never been taken to Zweilink before. He knew that his brothers had attended the memorial service before they were half-fledged. He wasn't upset about it—he simply wanted to know.

"We did take you once when you were very young."

"You did?"

Leorino inclined his head at his father's words. He had no recollection of it.

"You were very little back then. You must have been no more than three years old."

Leorino felt that he should have remembered something from that time at that age, but his memory turned up nothing.

"Why haven't you taken me to Zweilink since?"

August frowned. "As soon as we arrived at Zweilink, you broke into tears. I held you, Gauff held your hand, Hundert even carried you in his arms and tried to soothe you, but you just wouldn't stop crying."

It went without saying that he had no memory of any of it. Leorino had been a child; he didn't exactly need a reason to react the way he had. But his father's next words shocked him.

"You kept crying, 'Close the gates!' as if someone were skinning you alive."

Leorino wrapped his arms around himself as if trying to hold something back. He could still feel himself being seared by flames.

"Finally, after crying about feeling hot, you fainted. Your unusual behavior sent shivers down my spine, and the same could be said for all the other attendees. No one would have told you, a young child, about the events of twelve years ago, so how could you know such things? ...I genuinely thought you might have been possessed by the ghost of a fallen soldier."

"...I don't remember any of that."

August shook his head. "No, I don't expect you would. After we returned to the castle, you developed a high fever, just like this one. When you woke up, you had no recollection of your visit to Zweilink, nor of your screaming and fainting."

Leorino nodded.

"We haven't taken you to Zweilink since. And now that you're about to return there, you've come down with a fever again. To tell you the truth, I would rather not take you with us."

The previous night's dream and reality slowly fell into place. Ionia must have been a soldier who died in the battle of Zweilink. Leorino's dreams followed the soldier's life from childhood.

*I must go to Zweilink.*

"Father, please take me with you."

"Leorino..."

"I am able to live in peace because of the soldiers who protected the fortress. I want to pray for them. I want to go to Zweilink."

Preparations for the memorial service were well underway. Under the keen eye of Maia, the margravine, the servants were busy preparing to receive the guests.

The dignitaries and their attendants were allocated to rooms in the guest wing, which stretched along the side of Brungwurt Castle. Hosting the event for the twelfth year in a row, the people of the province were well-practiced, and they completed the preparations in an orderly manner.

Among the dignitaries attending the memorial service were Crown Prince Kyle; Chancellor Marzel Ginter; Lieutenant General Lucas Brandt, who was also the acting general of the Royal Army; Deputy Commander Joshua Kern of the Knights of the Imperial Guard; and Archbishop Royce. Finally, there was the Marquis of Lagarea, who was the secretary of the Interior and a close friend of August's.

The first guests would arrive soon. Leorino nervously stood in line to greet them. His brothers had all been made to greet the guests every year, even before they were half-fledged, but this was the first time Leorino was allowed this honor.

According to the announcement, Chancellor Ginter and Lieutenant General Brandt would be the first to arrive. Leorino had, of course, never met either of them.

A slender man with gentle features and a blond man of fine physique emerged from the carriage. The slender man must have been the chancellor, and the man in the military uniform was without a doubt the lieutenant general. Both were imposing men in their midthirties.

Leorino stared at the two men with wide eyes.

Then, when they sensed his gaze, the men's eyes met his. For a moment, the men looked at Leorino, completely dumbfounded. The chancellor immediately clamped his mouth shut, and the lieutenant general rubbed the back of his head with his hand.

*I see you still react the same way you always did when you're surprised.*

It was a silly, impossible thought. Leorino shook his head at this peculiar déjà vu.

It was Lieutenant General Brandt who came to his senses first. He saluted August, the head of the family, in the style of the Royal Army. "It's a joy to see you again, Margrave. I appreciate you greeting me in person."

"We are glad you could come, Lieutenant General Brandt."

Chancellor Ginter thanked August for his hospitality with an aristocratic bow. "I am sure that you, your family, and the people of your estate have worked tirelessly to prepare for the festivities, as you do every year. I thank you from the bottom of my heart."

"Welcome to Brungwurt, Chancellor Ginter."

After exchanging greetings with August, the two began introducing themselves to his family. First, they greeted Maia, then Auriano, the eldest son, followed by Johan and Gauff. Finally, it was Leorino's turn.

"It's a pleasure to meet you. My name is Leorino Cassieux, fourth son of August Cassieux. I bid you welcome to Brungwurt."

Leorino was nervous, but he figured he had done a good job of greeting them. He looked up at his father, who nodded slightly and smiled at him. His brothers were also watching him with smiles on their faces.

The men, however, remained transfixed on Leorino. Leorino worried he had done something wrong.

Then Ginter's and Brandt's grim expressions suddenly shifted as they began heaping praise on Leorino. "But, Lord August, this can't be. I had heard rumors about an angel living in Brungwurt, but I never thought he really existed."

"He is so beautiful it is hard to believe he is of this world. I must congratulate you on producing such a lovely child."

Never before had he received such openly admiring glances and direct compliments regarding his appearance. Leorino's cheeks flushed with embarrassment. Somehow, he found it in himself to thank them without getting too flustered.

August, on the other hand, was frowning, trying to hide his youngest son from the men's gazes. "Thank you for your kind words. My son is still ignorant of the ways of the world, so I would appreciate if you could refrain from speaking of him that way."

Donning a serious expression, August led the two men into the castle. As he departed, he shot a look at Leorino's attendant, who stood behind him. The man smoothly extracted Leorino from the line to the parlor and immediately moved him into the family quarters.

Brandt and Ginter had no untoward intentions for the boy. They were simply admiring the boy's exceptional beauty. At the same time, they were left stunned by Leorino's violet eyes.

"Marzel, did you see that boy's eyes?"

"...Oh yes, I can hardly believe it myself."

They would recognize that unmistakable color anywhere: the moment when day and night met, a ray of twilight shining through the indigo skies.

The boy's eyes looked just like those of a friend they had lost at Zweilink on that very day twelve years ago.

Ginter and Brandt were shown into the parlor. Like most rooms in the historic castle, it had stone walls covered with tapestries, causing it to appear sturdy and solidly built.

After instructing the servants to prepare tea, August dismissed them and his family, then turned to the men. "Lieutenant General Brandt, Chancellor Ginter. Allow me to once again welcome you to the frontier."

"Why so formal, August? I thought we were closer than this. Please call us 'Marzel' and 'Lucas' as you always have."

August brightened at that. Brandt and Ginter had always respected August as a great nobleman who led the Autonomous Army to protect this land, a major strategic point on the continent. This feeling remained unchanged even after the men had achieved their current social status.

"By the way," August prefaced his speech. "Marzel, Lucas... It has not escaped my attention that you have taken an unusual interest in Leorino..."

Brandt and Ginter forced a smile. It was true; they had been struck by his ephemeral beauty—and especially by those violet eyes.

"He really is very young and naive. Please forget about him."

It was Chancellor Ginter who correctly guessed August's concern.

"You have nothing to fear. Your son may one day gain a reputation for his unparalleled beauty throughout Fanoren, perhaps throughout even the whole continent...but we would never harbor any untoward feelings for a child who has not yet come of age." Ginter smiled sheepishly.

August apologized earnestly. "I beg your pardon. The truth is, I'm worried about the future of that child... He's so helpless and fickle, and though he's been improving of late, I'm not certain I should let him out of the castle even after he reaches adulthood."

Ginter would have considered this an undue concern for a son, but after seeing him in real life, he wasn't as certain anymore.

"I can understand the sentiment. I can't imagine letting him out into the world."

If Leorino were a member of Ginter's family, there would be no end to Ginter's worries. The boy was still very young, but when he grew up, there was no question that his beauty would be without peer, transcending both gender and comprehension.

"...Not to mention, that dreamy air of his is very reminiscent of Her Highness Princess Eleonora."

Eleonora was Leorino's grandmother and the younger sister of the previous king.

August nodded. "Indeed, he took after his grandmother. She, too, seems detached from the real world. I can't take my eyes off him. This year we decided to allow him to participate in the memorial service, but as his father, I can't help fretting about exposing him to the world. Once again, I apologize."

"He's becoming half-fledged this year, is he not? He is a beautiful boy, a true angel."

"Indeed. In fact, our province has taken to calling him our angel."

The two men smiled. The father couldn't help but dote on his son.

But August shook his head.

"His appearance is not the only reason he's known as our angel."

Brandt urged him to continue with his gaze.

"...He was born the morning of that fateful day twelve years ago, at the same time as the news of the victory at Zweilink arrived."

All in attendance were shocked to hear that.

"My god... That truly is a miracle."

Brandt's obvious interest in the boy was clear in his eyes. Leorino's unique violet eyes and the date of his birth. It seemed like fate, too perfect to be mere coincidence, to Brandt of all men.

Ginter glanced at Brandt next to him.

There came a knock at the door, and the conversation between the three men came to an abrupt halt. August spoke again only when the butler finished serving tea and left the room.

"Now...I suspect there's a reason why men as busy as yourselves arrived so early."

The two men's faces turned grim as they remembered the other purpose of their visit to Brungwurt.

"Yes, I have a message from His Excellency the general. There is something that I would like to bring to your attention, August."

"Would that mean there is some...suspicious activity going on *over there*?"

Ginter's eyes narrowed. "I see nothing escapes you, August. I would love to know where that information came from."

"Why, it's no secret. Anyone who crosses the border through the gates of Zweilink and enters our territory is strictly screened. After the cease-fire, commercial exchanges have resumed, but you never know what might happen. So Lev has been learning all he can from passing merchants."

Lev was the commander of the Brungwurt Autonomous Army.

Ginter nodded. "That certainly speeds things up. May I first ask what kind of information you have obtained from Lev so that we may compare it with our own?"

"Yes, he claims he heard from the merchants at the local tavern. They've been saying for some six months now that iron from Zwelf is no longer available on the market."

Ginter frowned. "I haven't heard anything about the iron veins in Zwelf running out. If the iron has been off the market for six months now...that would mean that for some reason Zwelf is restricting its iron exports."

August nodded. "Ginter, you always did have a keen eye for detail. They also said that Zwelf nobles are buying up jewels and gold. There was also talk that some of the nobles were fleeing the country."

"Do we have reason to doubt the merchants? Do you suspect they might be agents of the other side?" Brandt questioned August.

"According to Lev, they are all familiar, well-established merchants who have been in and out of the country since before the war. We can never be certain, but if we suspect everyone, we'll never get anywhere... So far, it doesn't seem like they're distributing information with any sort of agenda in mind. Lev seemed to learn of it by chance, in any case."

"I see." Ginter formed a triangle with his hands and brought it to his mouth, as if in prayer. He did it often while thinking.

"Considering the issue of iron and the nobles liquidating their assets and fleeing the country..."

"Perhaps the situation is dire within Zwelf. Or perhaps they intend to go to war with our country again."

Ginter nodded. "The intelligence we have received is almost identical to what you already know. I can't go into detail, but we have information that high-ranking officials of the collaborationist faction have been ousted and that some personnel changes, especially in the military, have taken place. Whether this is a sign of domestic conflict or all-out war is yet to be seen. What's certain is that something is coming."

August took a deep breath, recalling the events of twelve years prior. The thought of that dark presence casting its shadow over Brungwurt once more was chilling.

"But Zwelf does not currently have the strength to wage war against us— or any other country, for that matter."

After the failed invasion of Zweilink, Zwelf's position had deteriorated dramatically. Fanoren, who until then had taken a defensive stance, made a complete turnaround and launched a fierce counteroffensive after the victory at Zweilink.

When it became clear that the war was lost, Zwelf dispatched a messenger to Fanoren to propose a cease-fire.

The Royal Army initially refused to sign the cease-fire agreement. However, the situation in Fanoren was hardly good, due to the cold wave that had befallen the continent. The royal court managed to persuade the vengeance-driven Royal Army to accept Zwelf's offer on the condition that Zwelf fully accept Fanoren's demands.

Fanoren proposed three conditions for the truce. First, the king, the crown prince, and the military leaders who started the war would be held accountable. Second, in exchange for allowing the then-six-year-old son of the second prince to be installed as king, a moderate civil official who would cooperate with other countries would be appointed acting regent. The last condition was that reparations be paid for twenty years.

In exchange for Zwelf's acceptance of these cease-fire conditions, Fanoren decided to provide aid to Zwelf for the three following years in the form of food, as the cold spell and the war had depleted the nation's treasury. This was a humanitarian decision to help the people of Zwelf, who were starving and exhausted from the war and the cold, while holding the royal family and the military accountable for the war.

"The king who ascended the throne back then will be...coming of age this year, won't he?"

"Yes. And the acting regent will become the chancellor."

"The king has been educated by the moderates, and I hear that he has grown up to be a man of good character, maintaining cooperation with other countries. The regent is still in good health and is in control of the country, is he not?"

"Yes. And the moderate general in the Zwelf army remains the same... except for one of the top officers who passed away suddenly and has been replaced by a man we have, until now, not kept in our sights. I believe his name was Zberav..."

Brandt, who had been silently listening to their conversation until then, opened his mouth. "And how is the disinherited crown prince, Vandarren, faring?"

Ginter shook his head. "I've received reports that he remains imprisoned... What about it?"

"My cousin is married to a member of the family of the crown princess of Zwelf. Remember how that was an issue in court near the end of the war? My cousin got divorced after the war and moved back to Fanoren."

Ginter nodded. "Yes, I remember it well. That's why you were under suspicion, too."

"Right. That's why I thoroughly investigated the crown prince and his surroundings. The crown princess is the daughter of the Duke of Khachanov. And the crown princess's mother, the Duchess of Khachanov, was a member of the Marquis of Sabine's family. But she is not the biological daughter of the marquis—she was adopted by him."

"...What are you implying, Lucas?" August demanded to hear his conclusions.

"The Duchess of Khachanov's surname before she was adopted by the Marquis of Sabine was Zberav. The man is likely related to the crown princess."

The three men looked at one another. There was a suspicious connection between the disinherited crown prince and the man who had newly risen to military prominence.

"...Vandarren wants to stage a coup d'état."

The dignitaries attending the memorial service slowly began to arrive in Brungwurt.

August and his men had made their way into the crown prince's room.

The crown prince, Kyle, was twenty-two years old. He was a young man with curly black hair, blue eyes, a noble face, and a large build. While he may have appeared fierce, he was in fact a calm and intelligent man, and was already recognized as the next king.

"I see. And what of the disinherited prince's supporters? You suspect a possibility that they are secretly plotting a coup d'état through the prince's wife's mother's adoptive family and her family of birth. Hey, Ginter. If they did stage a coup, how does that affect our country?"

"Zwelf does not have the strength to go to war with other countries at the moment. In that respect, even if a coup were to take place, the immediate damage to us would be minimal."

"I wouldn't want the lives of our people to be affected," Kyle muttered in annoyance.

"Since that war, we have stopped relying on trade with Zwelf for vital necessities, so the people should remain undisturbed. Please rest assured."

"I see. In that case, would there be any point to our intervention?" Kyle asked Ginter.

Ginter placed his chin on his fist in contemplation. "I would love to say no...but the crown prince is an extremely greedy man. If he were to usurp the throne, he might go to war for the wealth of the neighboring countries."

"His becoming king is a violation of the cease-fire agreement. You should demand some kind of response immediately, Chancellor," remarked the Marquis of Lagarea who was secretary of the Interior.

Ginter shook his head. "No, nothing has happened yet. We are only speculating. If anything, it would be better to avoid diplomatic channels and inform the moderate chancellor in secret. We can't be sure who's working with the faction of the crown prince."

Brandt nodded. "Ceasing iron trade would be a shortsighted plan. If we follow the line, we might find something at the end of it."

Kyle chuckled. "I suppose the struggle for the throne looks the same everywhere."

The Marquis of Lagarea was about to admonish him, but Kyle laughed him off.

"Ginter, report to my uncle. I must admit that I won't be able to deal with this on my own. Only my uncle will be able to handle this. Marquis of Lagarea, you will report to His Majesty."

They all nodded in approval.

"All right, that's that for the formalities. Things are grim enough before the memorial service as they are." Kyle raised his voice to dispel the heavy air. "I mean, August! Where is he? Why have you kept something like that from us for so long?"

August scowled at that. "What do you mean by 'something *like that*'?"

"Oh, don't play dumb. You know exactly what I mean. Your son with the extraordinary face. I'm starting to doubt he's really human."

August frowned at the way he said it. "What about my son, Your Highness? He may be good-looking, but on the inside, he's just an ordinary child."

"Oh, please. If that were 'ordinary,' then truly ordinary people would vanish off the face of the earth."

August was ready to be done with this conversation.

At first, Maia had been genuinely pleased by the praise for Leorino, but she was now beginning to wonder to what extent she should allow her son to participate in the ceremony, given the many male gazes he was attracting.

His father and three older brothers were also becoming increasingly concerned.

"Unfortunately, I haven't found myself a bride yet. He won't be of age for another six years? I can wait that long."

The overprotective father shot up at that. "I have no intention of marrying him off!"

The crown prince grinned. "If he marries me, he can be queen. I don't think that's a bad deal."

"Your Highness cannot marry someone of the same sex!"

Kyle laughed at that. "Ha-ha-ha...! Forgive me—I was only joking. But I'm certain he will grow up to be even more beautiful in the future. If I were not obligated to produce an heir, I might have seriously considered it. Brungwurt would be a good match for the royal family."

Deputy Commander Kern of the Imperial Guard concurred. "If I may, if Lord Leorino will not be able to inherit your title, then despite being of the Cassieux family, his position as an aristocrat is not the most secure. He may be a boy, but considering his good looks...wouldn't it be wise to place him under someone's protection in the future, instead of granting him independence?"

August released a deep sigh. "That's why I'm so worried. He's just an ordinary boy who wants to be independent. Judging by his appearance, it's hard to imagine him becoming the man he wants to be one day, but...it's about time we thought about his future. I want him to experience the outside world, and yet I can't stand the thought of him leaving the castle."

The father's concerns were more serious than the other men had expected.

"I can protect him for now. But when I think of the future... I'm honestly uncertain if I should respect his wishes and support his efforts to become independent, or if I should leave him under someone's protection."

The men thought of Leorino's dazzling beauty and knew there would be no shortage of volunteers vying for the chance to protect him.

On the day before the memorial service, after the bishop's prayer in the chapel, the attendees had a small dinner and retired to their rooms early. On the eve of the memorial service, it was customary to fast in order to repay the spirits of the soldiers who died hungry.

Leorino had not been allowed to attend the dinner, so he and Gauff ate alone in the family dining room. Gauff, August's third son, was eighteen years old. He had graduated from the academy in the capital and had already decided to join the Imperial Guard. Since they were alone and Gauff was just a few years older than him, Leorino had a lot to say.

Gauff was an aspiring knight of the Imperial Guard and was therefore knowledgeable about the people at the center of the country. He told him about the personal histories and personalities of all the guests he knew about. To Leorino's surprise, Chancellor Marzel Ginter was once a member of the Royal Army and had served in a unit led by His Royal Highness the king's brother, alongside Lieutenant General Lucas Brandt.

Ginter was forced to retire from the army after being severely injured in battle twelve years ago, later becoming a civilian officer and eventually rising to the position of chancellor. Brandt, on the other hand, was said to have been a close confidant of His Royal Highness the king's brother, who was instrumental in the end of the war, and now held the position of lieutenant general.

"His Highness Prince Gravis... So you mean to say that the current general was in command of the recapture force?"

"That's right. His Royal Highness seems to have a very powerful ability, even for a member of the royal family. I don't know the exact nature of his Power, but it takes seven days to reach Zweilink from the capital on horseback traveling at full speed, yet he was able to cover that same distance with the recapture force in one day."

"That's incredible... We're technically nobility, too, but we have no Powers. I wonder what exactly the general is capable of..."

"We're not 'technically' nobility—we *are* nobility. Father may not make that immediately clear, given the way he is, but the Cassieux family is as high-ranking as other dukes of Fanoren."

"No, I know that... But even though Mom and Dad are both of royal blood, they don't have any special abilities."

He did not expect Gauff's next words. "Our mother has Powers."

"What? That's impossible! She does?"

"She is of royal blood, even if she's past her prime. I heard she can accelerate healing from illness and injury."

"Past her prime... And I thought I didn't get along with her. But I really had no idea. Why didn't they tell me?"

"They didn't tell me, either, but I knew. She treated my wounds once. I don't know... It felt like everything healed faster than usual."

Leorino was surprised and a little envious of his brother.

"I wish Mother would treat me, too!"

"No, you fool, I had to get hurt first."

Leorino ducked his head. That had indeed been inappropriate.

"I'm sorry, I shouldn't have said that."

"You look weaker than anyone here, but you hardly ever catch a cold. You've been cruising through life. I bet you've never even gotten properly hurt, have you?"

"Please! I wasn't 'cruising'! I couldn't do anything because of the dresses. Mom would cry if I so much as ripped them."

Leorino wanted to call his parents "Mother" and "Father" the way his brothers did, but when he got distracted, he reverted to calling them "Mom" and "Dad" like a child.

"Well, there you have it. In any case, no one in the royal family would openly say that they possessed such unique abilities. I can't even imagine what kind of Power His Royal Highness the crown prince has."

"The general brought his troops to Zweilink at an unthinkable speed, didn't he? That's an amazing feat."

"It is. If I had the chance, I would love to see him use his Power with my own eyes."

Leorino also wanted to meet the general. He naively wondered if he could ask His Highness Prince Gravis to show him his Power in secret if he ever did meet him.

"Won't the general be attending the memorial service?"

Gauff shook his head at that. "Now that you mention it... I've never seen him in attendance. Which means he's never taken part in the ceremony."

"I wonder why... I'd like to meet him."

*His Royal Highness Prince Gravis... What kind of person is he?*

# Starry-Sky Eyes

On the eve of the memorial service, Leorino dreamed of Ionia again. But not of that tragic battle. He dreamed of Ionia back when he was Leorino's current age.

Ionia was going to start attending the school for commoners next year. Anyone over the age of twelve could attend this school free of charge.

The classes at the elementary school consisted of basic education, such as history and mathematics, as well as an elective vocational training course called "special studies." Before they became half-fledged, the commoner children could consult with their parents on which subjects to take with their future career choice in mind. In most cases, they followed in their parents' footsteps.

Even at a young age, Ionia was blessed with a remarkable physique. While helping his father, a blacksmith, with his work, he became acquainted with the soldiers who came to the workshop, and while they waited for their weapons to be repaired, they taught him swordsmanship, among other skills.

Ionia was as large and agile as an adult and was often praised as being suited for military service. Eventually, the boy himself began to dream of one day joining the Royal Army. After careful discussion with his father, David, he decided not to take over the blacksmith business and chose the specialized courses that would allow him to become a soldier.

One day, a soldier Ionia was well-acquainted with came to his father's workshop. He visited regularly to have his sword maintained and seemed to be a soldier of good standing, judging from his regal bearing. The man's name was Stolf.

On that day, Stolf visited the workshop accompanied by a dark-haired boy. Seeing the boy for the first time, Ionia froze in surprise. He was the most beautiful boy Ionia had ever seen. Stolf did not introduce him to David and his son, nor did David ask for an introduction. The boy looked bored as his eyes wandered around the workshop.

Ionia couldn't help wanting to talk to the boy. He had the good sense to know that it was impolite for a commoner to casually speak to a nobleman, but his amiable nature stirred within him.

He summoned his courage and approached the boy. "Um... Welcome to the workshop. I am Ionia, the son of the blacksmith."

The boy must not have expected a commoner to speak to him. He looked at Ionia, somewhat surprised. Sensing a thin veil of rejection, Ionia began regretting his choices.

But what washed away that regret in an instant was seeing the boy's eyes up close. From a distance, Ionia had assumed they were black, but they were actually the color of dusk, scattered with golden particles.

They looked like the sky on a cloudless night.

*That's incredible...! He has eyes like starry skies.*

From the back of the workshop, he could feel Stolf watching them quietly, alongside his father's concerned gaze.

"Um, could you tell me your name? ...If you don't mind me asking, of course."

"...Why?"

He didn't know how to respond to that.

He had no special reason; he just wanted to get to know him better.

"Uh, because...if you don't tell me your name, I won't know what to call you...?"

The boy's harsh gaze relaxed slightly. "...You're very strange; I hope you know that."

*     *     *

*Oh, I think he just smiled for a split second there!*

"Fine, I'll accept that I'm strange. Just tell me your name... Um, if you will, sir."

The corners of the boy's mouth twitched upward this time. He had a lovely smile for his age.

Ionia was instantly happy. He thought it would be nice if the boy smiled more.

"Don't worry about being polite. I couldn't care less."

"You...don't care? Okay, my bad. In that case, thanks. I'm Ionia."

"Ionia? I'm... Let's go with 'Vis.'"

Ionia figured his real name must have been longer than that. He was a nobleman, after all. And the boy never gave his family name. But his first name was enough. If Vis responded when Ionia called it, that's all he needed.

"Vis, Vis... Has anyone ever called you 'Vi'?"

"...No, no one."

"Great, then it can be our special name. Can I call you 'Vi' from now on? You can call me 'Io,' too."

"Special name?"

"Yeah! Let's be friends, Vi."

The boy stared at Ionia intently and finally nodded slowly.

From that day on, the name "Vi" became special, meant only for Ionia.

Vi and Stolf continued to visit the workshop every now and then. It appeared that Stolf was acting as Vi's chaperone. As usual, Ionia had no idea what Vi's exact status as an aristocrat was or what kind of relationship he had with Stolf. It wasn't like Ionia wasn't curious. But when he was with Vi, he was so absorbed in the boy himself that he didn't stop to think about it.

The boy was reluctant to open up to him at first, but this gradually changed. Ionia's caring, affable nature gradually melted the ice around the stubborn black-haired boy's heart.

Ionia would sneak his father's tools out from the workshop and spend hours talking and playing with him. They even played at dueling with mock swords behind the workshop.

Stolf and David gave them a good scolding only once, when the two of them sneaked out to explore the commoner district by themselves. However, Ionia was happy just to see Vi looking as if he was truly enjoying himself.

Precisely because they only saw each other once in a while, Ionia cherished those moments and eagerly looked forward to them.

Soon, the two boys had become inseparable, transcending their differences in age and status.

Then one day, Vi visited the workshop with Stolf as usual, but for some reason, he stopped at the entrance and refused to enter.

"I won't be able to come here for a while." His expression was gloomy, as if he was holding something back.

That made Ionia sad.

He hated to hear that he would not be able to meet the boy for a while, but beyond that, it hurt to see that Vi had the same sort of darkness in his eyes like on the day Ionia first met him.

Ionia wanted him to keep smiling.

"I'll come back to see you again. I promise."

With these words, the boy with the starry eyes returned to his own world.

# Memorial Service

The attendees left for Zweilink before dawn. Zweilink was a military fortress on the border. It wasn't built to entertain guests, so dignitaries traveled from Brungwurt to Zweilink early in the morning and returned to Brungwurt as soon as the three-hour event was over.

Leorino boarded the carriage with August; his eldest brother, Auriano; and Bruno Henckel, the Marquis of Lagarea. The Marquis of Lagarea was a leading aristocrat and a maternal relative of the current king—an uncle, to be precise. He was also a close friend of August's. The marquis had previously visited Brungwurt on several occasions. Thanks to this, Leorino wasn't too nervous about the trip. The carriage was comfortable and stable, but he had never traveled such long distances before. Leorino sat silently next to his father, praying that he would not get sick and embarrass himself.

Alas, he was bored.

His eldest brother, Auriano, was twelve years older than him. Auriano was like a second father to Leorino, as he had been strictly raised to be an heir and was already involved in managing the province. Leorino loved his eldest brother, who doted on him and loved him dearly, but he was not as easy to talk to as Gauff, who was closer to him in age.

August and the Marquis of Lagarea were talking about recent events at court. Auriano occasionally chimed in, but Leorino couldn't understand what they were talking about, so he spent the entirety of the conversation being bored.

Leorino began to ruminate on his dream from the previous night.

With each dream, Ionia's nebulous life became a little clearer. Before long, Leorino's life and Ionia's memories had become an inseparable part of a larger whole. Leorino was convinced that Ionia was a real person who had died in Zweilink.

Last night, he remembered something very important. The man Ionia was waiting for on the battlefield was likely the same boy who had appeared in his dream that night. A noble boy with extraordinary starry-sky eyes whom Ionia had met at the forge. The boy who had become his best friend, transcending his status and position, and for whom Ionia cared deeply.

The details were already becoming blurry. But that was just the way dreams were; there was nothing he could do about it. And yet he could still clearly remember his eyes and the way they seemed to contain the starry skies within them. It was a shame that the dream had ended without Ionia meeting the boy again. Leorino wished he could meet that boy. He would love to see those starry-sky eyes in real life.

*He called himself "Vis," and he's a nobleman, so I should be able to look into him... I hope I'll get to meet him one day.*

Ionia called the boy "Vi." Vi had later told him that he allowed the special name only because it came from Ionia. Leorino tried to form his lips in the shape of the name without uttering a sound.

*Vi.*

The somehow familiar shape of it made his heart ache.

"Bruno, I was wondering how Prince Kyle's search for a wife is going. Have you decided on a potential bride yet?"

"No, not yet. For two generations now, we have had a queen from outside the country. Now there is conflict between two factions, one insisting that the queen should come from a prominent domestic noble family and the other that she should be a princess from abroad, so we have not made much progress. But why are you so concerned with the marriage of Prince Kyle, August?"

"I have no particular reason. I only want Prince Kyle to settle down as soon as possible."

The Marquis of Lagarea was puzzled by August's words but continued speaking. "Since Queen Dowager Adele and Queen Emilia are both from the Kingdom of Francoure, that country is not on the list of potential marriage partners this time around. However, none of the royal families from the countries we want to establish closer ties with have any eligible daughters around Kyle's age. The bloodline purists are clamoring that if he's ready to marry a foreign nonroyal, a domestic noble should be just as good."

"For royalty, marrying at twenty-two is rather late indeed."

"…Well, we'll have to settle this for good soon enough."

If the Marquis of Lagarea, a relative of the royal family and the secretary of the Interior, made up his mind, Kyle could soon be forced to marry against his will.

Auriano was close to Kyle in age and was on good terms with him. He had heard of Kyle's wishes. He offered helpfully: "Speaking of bachelors, isn't His Royal Highness the king's younger brother still unmarried at the age of thirty-one? Wouldn't it be wise to find him a spouse first?"

"Gravis, he's… His Royal Highness will likely never marry."

The name of the man who had been the topic of his conversation with Gauff the previous night drew Leorino's attention to the adults' conversation.

The general was said to be the most powerful man in the country. Leorino wanted to meet him as much as the boy he had just seen in his dream.

"Excuse me… What kind of a man is His Highness Prince Gravis?"

"Leorino!" his eldest brother chided.

"I apologize for interrupting… I have heard that His Highness was responsible for the recapture of Zweilink. I would love to meet him."

August and the Marquis of Lagarea frowned when Leorino voiced his earnest desire.

"I don't think His Highness will ever come to Zweilink again."

Leorino was disappointed. "Then could you at least tell me what kind of a man he is? I hear he's very powerful."

The adults laughed at the child's curiosity about the hero.

"Yes, he's very powerful. He is in charge of our country's defense. The reason why no country dares to attack Fanoren is because the whole continent knows of his valor in his last battle."

"Really? What does he look like? Is he bigger and more impressive than you, Father?"

The Marquis of Lagarea answered these questions. "Yes, he is a man of great stature, comparable to your father. His appearance and presence are very similar to Kyle's. He has dark hair and...ah, but his eyes are quite different."

"His eyes? What kind of eyes does His Highness have?"

"You will know as soon as you see him," August said. "His Highness Prince Gravis's eyes are like a beautiful starry sky."

# The Stars of the Capital

"Excuse me, Your Excellency. I have some additional documents for your approval."

With a light knock on the door, a young red-haired man with papers under his arm let himself inside the general's office. The man was adjutant Dirk Bergund.

This was the general's office in the Palace of Defense.

"I'll leave them here." Dirk placed a palm-height stack of documents on the large desk in the center of the room.

The man at the desk did not hide his disgust at the fresh pile of paperwork for the afternoon, especially since he had already dealt with a large volume of documents in the morning. The man was General Gravis Adolphe Fanoren, the hero of Zweilink.

"Stop accepting every sheet of paper those fools place in your hands." Gravis offered his second-in-command a cold glare.

Dirk's heart lurched in his chest at the look in Gravis's eyes. He had known Gravis for a long time, and yet every time he saw his eyes, he found himself utterly captivated.

Gravis's most striking feature was his eyes.

Due to their night-sky-blue color scattered with golden light, people called them "starry-sky eyes." It was a unique eye color that appeared only rarely in the Francoure royal family, which his mother hailed from. Depending on the person's mood, the golden flecks of light could shine so brightly that the iris itself appeared golden, or they could disappear completely, like a moonless night. They were so strangely beautiful that they seemed almost divine. Combine them with his perfectly handsome face, and most people would shrivel up after a single glance.

The red-haired adjutant, however, was used to it and did not flinch in the slightest when confronted by his superior. "The documents approved by the secretary of the Treasury have finally come through. What do you want me to do?"

"You can't expect me to deal with this crap anymore."

"Lieutenant General Brandt is in Zweilink for the memorial service. Until his return, they need you to approve his share."

"Let Lucas deal with whatever is meant for the Combat Division when he gets back."

"He's not *you*. It will take him some time to return," the adjutant retorted in exasperation. "I'm sorry, but they really need you to approve this today. Let's just get this over with."

"...Fine. Give me the bare minimum."

The adjutant smiled at his superior's fed-up tone.

Gravis had a habit of intimidating those around him with his strong ambition, but once one got used to it, it made him easy to get along with. He never got particularly angry with anyone, and he never made any unreasonable demands, nor used his status as an excuse. As long as one didn't cross the line, he was the sort of person one could get along with rather comfortably.

"The lieutenant general should be back in five days or so. You'll have to survive until then."

Just as Gravis reluctantly reached for the documents, there came a knock from the office.

"A message for Your Excellency from the lieutenant general."

"Hand it over."

Dirk received the letter and handed it to his superior.

Dirk did not miss the way Gravis's face darkened for the briefest moment as he read the letter.

"What did the lieutenant general say? Is there a problem?"

"No. He says he 'found something interesting for us in Brungwurt.' It's private correspondence."

"Interesting, sir?"

"He says there's something I absolutely must see. He wants me to come 'as soon as *possible*.'"

The adjutant raised an eyebrow. "Well, that's rather extreme. Though I'm certain Your Excellency could get there in no time."

"...Damned Lucas. Why did he go through the trouble of sending me this nonsense by post?"

Gravis tossed the letter away.

Dirk wisely kept silent, watching his superior.

"Come—let's get this over with."

Without another glance at the letter, Gravis turned to the documents.

# Returning Memories

Leorino's carriage finally arrived at Zweilink just as the sun passed overhead and began dipping toward the horizon.

Having skipped three meals since last night, their stomachs were growling at them. Leorino felt dizzy from the long trip and the hunger, and Auriano grabbed him by the shoulders and supported him. Leorino smiled at his eldest brother in gratitude.

He gently pressed on the pit of his stomach, worried about the rumbling. His father and eldest brother watched him with warmth in their eyes.

The attendees slowly disembarked from their carriages. Except for Lieutenant General Brandt and Deputy Commander Kern, who appeared to have traveled by horseback. Leorino was impressed by the stamina of the soldiers, wondering how they could have ridden their horses for such a long time after having skipped three meals. Both the men and the horses must have been incredibly well-trained.

Leorino was overwhelmed by the sheer impact of the stone fortress.

He wondered if such a structure could have really been man-made. The fortress stretched as far up as his eyes could see. He wondered how far the ground would be if he climbed to the top.

"I know, Rino. Now close your mouth and look where you're going."

He had opened his mouth, his eyes darting all over the place, and Auriano pressed into his back and urged him to keep going. He quickly closed his mouth and obediently followed the adults.

From the left and right, the huge stone walls stretched so far it was impossible to see beyond them. Moreover, the central gates were unbelievably huge. After one passed through the gates, the outer fortress could be seen far beyond the lush plains.

Zweilink was a walled fortress made of stone that marked the border with the neighboring country. When their ancestors settled on the land some two hundred years ago, they had spent around ten years building a fort about ten times the height of a person. The fortified wall that extended along the border like a long corridor was commonly known as the outer fort. Across the wide grassy field, an equally long fort was built on the inside. The wall on the side of Fanoren was slightly lower than the outer fort and was known as the inner fort.

This double-walled fortification was given the name of Zweilink.

The only time Zweilink, previously considered impregnable, was invaded by the enemy was during the war twelve years ago.

Leorino, the youngest of this year's attendees, managed to keep up with the series of ceremonies under the watchful eye of his family and the people around him. However, after fasting for three meals, he had soon run out of stamina from the long carriage ride as well as the continuous events without any breaks in between.

Instead of allowing him to grin and bear it until he collapsed, his eldest brother held his hand throughout. The adults took care of Leorino between ceremonies. It would have been easy to pick him up and carry him, but they respected Leorino's dignity and let him walk on his own for as long as he could.

After several ceremonies, the whole group finally arrived at the outer fortress. Here, the guests rested for half an hour while the preparations for the most important event were made.

The guests were divided into several rooms and served tea.

Leorino was relieved that he didn't have to live through the humiliation that would have been being carried around by his father or brothers. Still, he was exhausted and had no energy to explore the fort.

His father, August, approached him with a worried look. "Leorino, are you all right? ...Oh, you look so pale."

"Father. Yes, I'm... No, I am a little tired actually, but I am fine." As soon as he said this, his body staggered. When his father approached him, all tension had escaped his body.

August supported Leorino, who was unsteady on his feet, and turned to Lev, the military commander who was standing behind him. "Lev, is there a place for Leorino to rest in the outer fortress?"

"There should be a settee in the small room on the top floor. I will check with the guards."

The Brungwurt province was adjacent to the border, but it was not responsible for the border defense itself. It was the Royal Army, not the Brungwurt Autonomous Army, that had jurisdiction over Zweilink.

Lev had no issue receiving permission.

August picked up Leorino and carried him to a room on the top floor at the end of a gallery. It was a small room with a settee for resting.

He laid Leorino on the settee. "You can rest here. The next ceremony will begin in another half an hour or so. I will come for you before then."

"...Thank you."

He stroked his son's head as Leorino lay down.

August never lost his worried expression.

He may have been remembering what happened to Leorino when he brought him to the fort when Leorino was a child.

Leorino smiled to reassure his father.

"Are you okay with being here alone? Shall I send Gauff or Johan?"

"I'm fine. I'm certain my brothers would like to get some rest, too. I'll just stay here."

"Lev, can you send someone to check on him?"

"Yes, sir. I will ask the Imperial Guard to keep an eye on him. Lord Leorino, please rest while you can."

Leorino nodded.

He felt sorry for the trouble he had caused his father and Lev.

August cast an affectionate glance at his son, who smiled at him bravely, and patted his head once more.

Leorino was now alone.

At Brungwurt Castle, Leorino was seldom left alone. There had always been someone by his side.

The room was quiet.

He found it a little scary to be left alone in an unknown place, but he could feel the presence of people nearby.

*I wonder if I've actually been here before... I can't remember anything from last time.*

He closed his eyes and was immediately beset by drowsiness.

Even as he thought that he could not allow himself to fall asleep in earnest, before long, Leorino began to drift off.

The dusty smell of the fortress. It was nostalgic, somehow.

*Ah, Zweilink is burning.*

Behind his closed eyelids, he could see the roaring flames.

*It's that dream again. I'm scared. I don't want to see it.*

Leorino struggled desperately to wake up, but his body refused to budge.

*No. Don't show it to me...*

He could see the soldiers Ionia fought alongside. The burning plain.

It was as if Ionia was dragging him into the dream, and he had no choice but to relive *that day* again.

The towering outer fortress was supposed to be impregnable.

It should have been impossible for so many enemy soldiers to enter without being noticed by the guards. Beyond a shadow of a doubt, there was a traitor among them. But there was no time to look for the culprit.

Ionia had given up on recapturing the outer fortress. They would escape in secret. They could fight here and be killed, or they could defend the inner fortress to the death and prevent an invasion from befalling the country.

Protecting their injured soldiers, Ionia and the rest of his men fled toward the inner fort while fighting off the enemy.

After escaping from the outer fortress and standing on the plain, Ionia was shocked to find that Zweilink was on fire. The fire spread quickly in the dry winter air, burning the plains at a breathtaking pace. Ionia and his men fled as fast as they could. Beyond the flames, the central gates of the inner fortress came into view. Ionia could not believe his eyes.

The gates, which should have been closed, were open.

"Close the gates! Why are they open?!" Ionia shouted at the inner fortress.

But as he got closer, he understood why. A huge boulder had been placed in front of the gates. They hadn't closed them because they couldn't. The boulder was taller than a man. It couldn't have been carried here without anyone noticing.

*How did it get here?*

Ionia shuddered with a terrible thought.

Zwelf had an ability user on their side. And possibly—no, in all likelihood, they had the same gift as Gravis.

Someone had warped the boulder here.

Ionia shouted in his mind, praying that it would reach Gravis in the capital. He had never tried it before, but hoping for a miracle, in his heart, he called out to Gravis.

*"Vi! Vi...!"*

*  *  *

Ionia began calling desperately. It was a gamble. He had no idea if the words would reach him.

"Io!"

Suddenly, Gravis's voice appeared in his mind. Thank god. Gravis had heard him. It was a miracle.

"We're under attack. The outer fortress has been taken, and the central gates won't close. At this rate, Zwelf forces will breach the border...!"
"Wait for me! I'll send reinforcements!"

Gravis's words filled Ionia with fear.

"Wait! You'll hurt yourself!"

Using abilities required draining the life of its users. If he overused his Power, Gravis's life would be in danger.

"I'm going to save you! You must survive. Just wait for me!"

There, the conversation was cut short.

The Zwelf soldiers approached from behind. Ionia and his men fought back with all their might. He had to destroy the boulder before reinforcements arrived. Ionia had the unique ability to shatter anything he touched. To close the gates, he had to get close enough to touch the boulder.

But the enemy soldiers were clearly targeting Ionia, launching a fierce attack that would not allow him to approach the stone. They were wary of Ionia's ability.

They know of my Power... They really did have a mole. Who is it? Who's the traitor?!

The Zwelf soldiers continued pouring in from beyond the flames. There was no end in sight. Ionia and his men were outnumbered, and they were being defeated, one by one, their numbers dwindling.

"Captain, the boulder! Destroy the boulder!" the men shouted.

They set up a formation to cover Ionia and attempted to clear a path to the boulder. However, the rapidly burning fire stood in their way.

It was then that Ionia spotted a man beyond the flames. It was his subordinate, a man he thought had died when the enemy attacked. Like Ionia, he was a commoner but possessed a different ability.

The man had the Power to control wind.

He was smiling, stirring up the wind and burning Zweilink.

Ionia caught his gaze.

*So it was you.*

The traitor who hoped to destroy the country from within. *Was it you who turned death's icy blade on us?*

*I will never forget your face. I must tell Vi of this traitor.*

# Betrayal Revealed

"Can you stand up, my lord?"

Leorino jerked awake from his dreamy state. He could hear his heart pounding deep in his ears.

*Who am I? I'm...*

When he opened his eyes, he saw a middle-aged soldier peering at him with a concerned look on his face. He wore the uniform of the Royal Army. He must have been instructed by Lev to come and check on Leorino.

However, Leorino found himself unable to answer his question.

"...Sir?"

Because now, after twelve long years, the traitor who had led the enemy into Zweilink that day—the man who had caused the deaths of so many of his friends and forever separated him from Vi—stood before him.

The traitor's name was...

"Edgar Yorke."

"...? How do you know my name?"

Twelve years had passed, but his ordinary face was still the same as it had been back then. He was a man of no particular distinction, but he'd had a gentle disposition that had lightened the bleak atmosphere of their unit. He may have been an ordinary soldier, but to Ionia, he was a cherished subordinate and comrade with whom he had shared many joys and hardships alike...

...At least, until his betrayal was discovered.

"Why, Edgar...? They told me you had died when Zwelf attacked. But you were there, back then, by that boulder."

"...No... No, that's not possible."

"Why? Why did you betray us that day?"

"Your eyes... Captain Ionia...?!"

There was venom in Leorino's grin as he sat up from the settee. His body looked so thin, as if it could break at any moment. His face was beautiful and lovely, like a young lady's. But his expression was not that of a boy. A presence rose from his small body. The worst thing by far were those rare violet eyes, which felt so disgustingly familiar to Edgar.

"...You can't be... You're dead! Y-you died here!"

"Oh yes, I did. I *died* here. By *your* betrayal. In the flames *you* spread. I burned to death, alongside many others."

Edgar let out an inarticulate yelp and backed away to escape Leorino's gaze.

"Do you remember, Edgar? Do you remember the excitable Tobias, with his sharp hearing? Remember Ebbo, the supremely powerful archer? Remember Xavier, who was soon to marry his fiancée? Or have you forgotten them already? They were our friends, Edgar, and they all died because of *you*."

"H-how...?"

"And you ran away once. You disappeared while I destroyed the boulder. And when you came back, you ran your sword right through me... I remember it all now. You were the traitor, and I died before I could tell anyone, and it's been haunting me ever since."

Edgar trembled with fear at his words.

He did not know what was happening. The ghost of twelve years' past had suddenly appeared. And it took the form of a young, innocent boy.

"P-please forgive me! Forgive me, Captain Ionia...!"

Edgar stumbled out into the gallery, screaming. He wanted to escape the violet eyes that were etched into his memory.

A cold wind blew across the rooftop. The forested area on the Zwelf side of the fortress spread before violet eyes.

*Oh, how I've missed this place. I used to gaze at the stars here every night.*

The night sky seen from the walls of Zweilink was clear and beautiful.

Edgar was cornered on the stairs to the outer wall. Behind him, there was nothing but air.

Leorino tilted his head and looked at Edgar in silence. Unable to bear the icy stare that exposed and condemned his sins, Edgar begged for forgiveness.

"Please forgive me. I was given no choice...!"

"...No choice? Did you have no choice but to invite the enemy soldiers inside and set Zweilink ablaze?"

"I was just following orders..."

Leorino's eyes flashed darkly.

"Orders? ...Someone *made* you do it? Who was it? Who gave the order?"

"...I-if I tell you, th-they... They'll kill me!"

"Kill you? They're still alive? Who is it, Edgar? Tell me! Who gave you the order?!"

"It was... It was..."

But their conversation was cut short.

"Leorino? What are you doing here...?"

A sharp voice echoed through the gallery of the fort.

The boy's body shuddered.

When he turned around, he saw his father, August, and Lev at the bottom of the stairs. The moment he recognized his father, the air around him changed completely. Leorino awoke from his dream.

"Father... Lev."

That's right. This was Zweilink.

It was then that Leorino was struck with an epiphany. The dreams he had been having of the boy were not dreams at all. They were all real events from the past. He had inherited Ionia's memories following his death. The horror of what had taken place made Leorino want to cry.

"…Father, help me… I'm scared."

August and Lev could not believe their eyes.

Leorino, who was supposed to be resting in the small room, stood with his thin body exposed to the wind on the unfenced stairs climbing up to the stone wall.

"…Leorino, stay where you are."

At his father's words, Leorino nodded, trembling. He was frightened to his very core.

"Father, Lev… I'm… Ah!"

Suddenly, the man picked up Leorino from behind.

"Leorino!"

August tried to run up to him.

"Don't come any closer! I'm done for! I'm done!" The man's screams echoed through the fortress.

"Have you gone mad?!"

The soldier restraining Leorino rambled with bloodshot eyes, frothing at the corners of his mouth.

The man ran to the top of the stone wall with Leorino in his arms. He stood at the very edge of the wall, where he could easily fall if he lost his balance even slightly.

August had never been so terrified in his life.

The fortress wall was ten times the height of a person. If Leorino fell, he would surely lose his life.

"Leorino… You're okay. Just stay still. I'm coming for you… Just don't move."

Mere feet away, the life of his beloved son hung in the balance. Caught in the man's arms, Leorino looked so thin, so small, and so very fragile. If August made the wrong decision, his precious son's life, however brief, would come to an abrupt end.

"What is it that you want? Speak."

Edgar's body trembled at these words.

"I'll do whatever you want, but please let my son go... Let Leorino go. Please."

Tears welled in Leorino's eyes as his father's lips trembled with despair.

He may not have been himself, but he remembered what he had said to Edgar. Taken over by Ionia's memories, he had inadvertently driven the man to the edge. Because of that, he had put himself and his father in this horrible situation.

"Father... Father, I'm sorry..."

His body wasn't strong enough to fight off the attacker like Ionia's was.

*If only I had a Power like Ionia's...*

Leorino didn't have the strength to escape the man's restraints. For all his wishing, he didn't have a special ability like Ionia, either. In this life, Leorino was a helpless young boy.

When August called out to him, Edgar only rambled incomprehensibly.

"I'm finished... If they find out, it's all over for me! If I'm going to be killed anyway...I'll just die here and kill the captain *again*...!"

With that, he shifted his heel backward.

It quickly became clear that Edgar was going to kill himself and take Leorino with him.

Leorino did not want to die.

Now that he had remembered everything, he had to expose Edgar Yorke's betrayal. He had to find the real traitor who had been manipulating Edgar behind the scenes.

At that moment, Leorino made sense of his destiny.

*I am the bearer of Ionia's memories.*

Everything had been fated. Leorino had been born in Brungwurt to inherit Ionia's memories.

"*Vi! Vi! ...Help!*"

Leorino cried out in his mind to the royal capital, overcome by his fear of death.

He was not Ionia. There was no way Vi could hear him. And still, Leorino prayed.

Even if he was destined to die here, if there was even the slightest chance Gravis might hear, he wanted to see him one last time. He wanted one last glance. He wanted to tell him everything he had remembered.

A strong wind blew up the stone walls. The staggering soldier and the restrained boy swayed precariously on the edge.

"Leorino!" August and Lev screamed in horror.

The sound of quietly flipped pages echoed in an office of the Palace of Defense.

The general was checking the last of the documents.

Dirk suddenly had the useless realization that Zweilink must have been in the middle of the memorial service.

"I'm done."

"Thank you."

Dirk picked up the documents and was about to leave when his superior stood up so suddenly that he knocked over his chair.

He seemed dazed, his eyes darting around but looking at nothing in particular. His face was pale.

Dirk was startled by his superior's unusual behavior.

"Your Excellency! What's wrong?!"

Gravis suddenly heard someone's voice echoing in his head.

"*Vi!*"

It was a special name that only one person was allowed to use. Whom could the voice calling him by that name belong to?

*"Vi! ...Help!"*

"No... It can't be."

The voice came from Zweilink, just as it had that day.

"Is that you...Io?"

The general's hand reached into the air as if grasping at something. The adjutant stared wordlessly at the man's strange behavior. Then the very space in front of him seemed to *bend*.

"...! Sir!"

In the next instant, Gravis was leaping from the royal capital to the far border, to Zweilink.

August was stunned.

The space in front of him seemed to distort, and before he knew it, a man appeared out of thin air.

He was a soldier. And he was wearing a military uniform of the highest rank.

"No..."

August was dumbfounded, forgetting the situation for the briefest moment.

The soldier who was holding Leorino also stared at the man in disbelief.

Gravis did not immediately understand the situation, either. He knew that this was Zweilink, the place where he had traveled when the voice called him.

He quickly surveyed his surroundings. They were on the roof of the outer fortress. A soldier of the Royal Army was standing on the stone wall. In the man's arms was a slender, well-dressed boy.

He had thought he had been called by the voice of his late best friend. But, of course, Ionia wasn't there.

Before Gravis stood a boy he had never seen before.

*What is this? What's going on...?*

He glanced behind him. Two older men stood there. It appeared the soldier was holding the boy hostage.

But they were standing on the very edge, ready to fall at any moment. The man's eyes were bloodshot. If he was delirious, there was no telling what he would do.

*Did he take a guest's child hostage...?!*

Gravis immediately measured the distance between jumps necessary to at least save the boy.

He looked at the boy to reassure him. However, when the boy met his gaze, an intense current shot through Gravis's entire body.

*Those eyes...!*

For a moment, Gravis forgot what was going on and just stared.
"You're..."
Before he knew it, he had reached out his hand.
The soldier restraining the boy began raving again. "It's over...! If the general learns the truth, everything ends here!"
Gravis remembered himself at the man's outburst.

"You! Did you call for me?"
The soldier holding the boy cried out in agitation. Foaming at the mouth, he shook the boy's body.
"Look out! Stop!"
The boy's expression of anguish made Gravis's face turn pale. The men behind him were also shouting.

*I must save that child.*

"...Let the boy go!"
"No! If I let him go, my crimes will be exposed, and my life will be over! Everything will be over...!"

The soldier inched farther back. His heels were half in the air. There was nothing behind him, only the vast forested expanse of the neighboring country below.

The boy did not flail. He only stared at Gravis, tears spilling from his violet eyes.

He was about to say something with trembling lips, when the soldier announced: "...If I'm to be sentenced to death, I'd rather take you down with me here and now... How does that sound, *ghost*?!"

The next moment, the soldier fell backward.
"Dammit...! Stop...!"
The boy was dragged through the air behind him.
Gravis instantly leaped onto the wall and reached for the boy.

*Please let me catch him...!*
The boy reached out a hand to Gravis. He wouldn't make it. Gravis leaped once more and extended his hand toward the boy.
Violet and starry gazes met, and each saw deep into the other's soul.
But Gravis's hand grasped at air.
The boy fell over the wall with the soldier.

Gravis stood there in the wind, frozen in horror.
"Leorino!"
A cry of grief tore through Gravis's consciousness.
"Lord Leorino! ...Oh my god! Oh my god!"
Behind him, August, the Margrave of Brungwurt, and another man were screaming.

*Was that August Cassieux's son?!*
"Lord August! Let's go!"
Gravis leaped in front of August, grabbed him by the shoulders, and leaped again toward the ground where the boy had fallen.

Beyond the border was a forest. He had not seen it in twelve years.
In front of the forest, just below the fortress, the soldier and the boy were

lying in a heap. The man lying underneath was clearly dead. The back of his skull had been crushed by the impact of the fall, and a dark stain was spreading on the ground.

The boy was lying on top of the man.

His small face was pale, bloodless. Below the knee, his left leg was bent at an impossible angle. The boy looked like a doll that had been swung around by an infant and thrown aside carelessly.

The margrave staggered closer to the boy. Kneeling on the ground, he traced the boy's cheeks with trembling fingertips. "Rino...open your eyes... Leorino."

August gently embraced the small body.

The gates of the outer fortress opened, and the crown prince, Lev, and other attendees rushed forth.

"Lord August! What happened?! What—?"

They saw the margrave, his whole body trembling silently, embracing the small body of his son.

The people who rushed to the scene immediately realized what had transpired when they saw the corpse of a soldier of the Royal Army with his head crushed.

Leorino and the man had fallen from the fortress walls.

"Oh my god..."

No one knew if Leorino, motionless in his father's arms, was dead or alive.

Among the dumbfounded crowd, Ginter and Brandt noticed Gravis's presence.

"Your Highness Prince Gravis!"

"General, why are you here...?"

Gravis, who had so stubbornly refused to come to Zweilink since the tragedy, now stood there with a somewhat dazed expression on his face.

"Your Highness... What in the world happened?"

The usually calm and collected man was clearly shaken.

"I thought I heard Ionia's voice calling me. I didn't think it was possible, so I leaped, and there in front of me was...the boy who had been captured on the roof by the dead soldier there."

Brandt and Ginter gasped at his words.

"No...!"

"Did the spirit of Ionia tell His Highness of the danger to the boy with the same eyes as him...? No, that's ridiculous."

Brandt doubted his own words, knowing that such an impossible thing could not be.

"The man threw himself off the walls, taking the boy with him."

Hearing that, the two men looked to the soldier who now was a mangled, voiceless corpse.

When Gravis had heard the voice that he should have never again been able to hear, he leaped from his office in the royal capital to Zweilink on impulse. It had been the same voice as on that day, the unmistakable voice of his best friend calling for help.

But his best friend was not at Zweilink.

Of course he wasn't. Ionia was dead.

But there was a boy held captive by a soldier.

The boy did nothing but stare at Gravis, his eyes wet with tears. Those eyes were filled with a painful longing, as if he had known that Gravis was coming.

Then it took only the briefest moment for the boy to slip out of Gravis's outstretched hand and fall from the walls of the fortress.

"I reached for him, but...I didn't make it in time."

Lucas and Ginter gasped at the words.

"...Rino? Leorino...?"

The margrave called the boy's name in a hoarse voice. Everyone turned to them. Then they saw the boy's eyelids quiver slightly.

"He's alive!"

"He survived!"

Suddenly, the scene became frantic. The fire of the boy's life had not yet been extinguished.

"Rino! Rino, wake up...!"

"Get him a doctor!"

"Lord August! Don't move him!"

Suddenly, the margrave shouted with bloodshot eyes.

"Maia...! Call Maia! We need her Power!"

With this heartbreaking scream, the people thought that the margrave had finally lost his mind.

However, a few, including Gravis and Kyle, understood the meaning of his words.

Gravis immediately exchanged glances with his nephew, the crown prince. The margravine was the cousin of the former king.

"Kyle, what is the margravine's gift?"

The crown prince was blindsided by the sudden appearance of his uncle.

"Uncle... What are you doing here? No, I'm sorry. I don't know."

Then the eldest son of the margrave exclaimed with a pale face: "My mother has the gift of healing!"

Gravis nodded.

Brungwurt, where the margravine resided, was far away. The boy would likely not make it if carried by traditional means.

Gravis tapped August on the shoulder.

"August, move. I'll carry him. You put your hand on my shoulder."

August pleaded with Gravis, his eyes stained with despair. "Please, Your Highness... Lend us your Power."

"I will."

Gravis, on behalf of the agitated margrave, lifted the boy's body with the utmost care.

"Brungwurt Castle?"

"Yes."

Gravis turned around.

"Marzel, Lucas, take care of the rest."

The two men nodded, their faces pale.

"August, let's go."

The margrave and Leorino disappeared as suddenly as the general had initially appeared.

Those who remained behind all looked equally heartbroken.

Leorino's brothers were frozen in place, their faces pale. Gauff was weeping, unconcerned with the gazes of the other attendees.

Ginter gave instructions to the soldiers, wondering whether they should continue with the rest of the festivities. He had much to think about. He looked at Brandt and nodded with a stern expression.

They couldn't treat this as an accident. A soldier from the Royal Army had jumped from the fortress wall, taking the youngest son of the margrave with him. During the memorial service, of all times. Considering the position of the Margrave of Brungwurt in the country, it was a major incident for which the Royal Army could be held responsible, even if it was the work of a single soldier.

"Excuse me… Are you Lev?" Ginter approached the man who was talking to August earlier. He was the military commander of the Brungwurt Autonomous Army. "I am Chancellor Marzel Ginter. Did you witness the moment Leorino fell with that soldier from the rooftop gallery?"

Lev nodded regretfully.

The Marquis of Lagarea approached.

He was a sworn friend of August and must have already been familiar with Lev as well. He patted the military commander on the shoulder with concern.

"Lev, tell us what happened."

"…That soldier took Lord Leorino hostage and jumped from the rooftop in hysteria."

"…But why?"

"I don't know…but when I went to pick up Lord Leorino, who had been resting, the room was empty. The master and I searched for him, and when we got to the rooftop, Lord Leorino was already restrained by the man, and…he climbed the wall…rambling on about something, and then he just…"

Ginter frowned.

Was it an accident caused by delirium or suicidal ideation? Why did that man, who couldn't speak for himself now, jump down with Leorino in tow? What happened between Leorino and that man in the space of that brief moment?

"What did the man say?" the Marquis of Lagarea asked with an equally pained expression on his face.

"Lev, Chancellor, let's talk about what we must do."

Ginter and Lev nodded.

The whole group, with heavy hearts, set to work to resolve the situation.

A fragile life had nearly been snuffed out in front of their eyes. And they still did not know if he would live to see another day.

Everyone there prayed to God that the fire of the boy's life would not be extinguished.

# To Take His Hand

The memorial service at Zweilink ended with the third event abruptly canceled and the last event, the prayer before the cenotaph, moved up at Ginter's suggestion and with the crown prince's approval.

As soon as the memorial service was over, the attendees returned to Brungwurt.

When they arrived, night had already fallen.

A heavy atmosphere had fell over Brungwurt Castle. The margrave and his wife did not stand in line to welcome the returning guests.

A somber butler stepped forward to greet the guests on behalf of the head of the family. He apologized for the rudeness of his master's absence.

August's second son, Johan, and the third son, Gauff, jumped out of the carriage as soon as they arrived, and without so much as a word of greeting, they ran off to the family wing with grief-stricken expressions.

But who could blame them?

Only the eldest brother, Auriano, remained in place to act on his father's behalf, and he thanked the guests for their presence. He, too, must have wanted to rush to his youngest brother's side immediately, but his resolute attitude was to be expected as the heir to the Brungwurt frontier.

Auriano apologized to the guests and asked them to have dinner in their rooms tonight, as he was unable to provide them with satisfactory hospitality, and they agreed. They had all witnessed the tragic incident. Considering the feelings of the family and the young boy whose survival was still uncertain, the guests couldn't imagine being upset with the way their hosts handled the situation.

Auriano expressed his gratitude for the silent support of the guests. After instructing the butler on how to see the guests off the following day, he, too, quickly headed off to Leorino's side.

The guests returned to their respective rooms in silence, with melancholy expressions on their faces. There, they wiped off the dirt and exhaustion from the trip and took a light meal that already waited for them in their rooms. It was the end of the fast anyway. They wouldn't be able to handle a hearty meal even if they received one.

After finishing his meal, which felt like chewing sand, Brandt went to Ginter's room. They decided to look for Gravis, who must have still been at Brungwurt. They asked a servant, who told them that the general was in the study. They asked him to show them the way.

Gravis was alone in the margrave's study, sinking into a chair with a somber expression on his face. He glanced at the two men entering the room, but then quickly averted his gaze and stared at the fireplace. It was very dark in the study late at night, with only a small light on. The men remained silent for a while.

Eventually, Ginter quietly spoke up. "I heard that a Royal Army doctor is taking care of him. Dr. Sasha? You brought him over from the royal capital, General?"

"Yes, he's the greatest doctor in Fanoren... That's the best apology I can offer at present, seeing as our soldier was the cause of so much pain."

"You used your Power, didn't you? How are you feeling?"

"This much won't faze me... What happened with the memorial service at Zweilink after that?"

"After that, we only held the prayer in front of the cenotaph and ended the memorial service. The proclamation of the Atonement for the Flame was to be held in the rooftop gallery, where Leorino fell, so the crown prince himself decided to cancel the ceremony."

"How is Leorino?" Brandt asked Gravis.

Gravis shook his head. "We don't know yet. The dead soldier's body cushioned his fall, and although that saved him from head trauma and internal injuries, he still felt that impact throughout his entire body. They say his heart stopped several times."

"No..."

"He was in critical condition for a while after the resuscitation procedure, but he seems to have improved. Sasha came out of his bedroom a few minutes ago, but he has not yet regained consciousness. Tonight is the night they find out if his heart will hold."

The two men wore grave expressions.

"The margrave and his wife are attending to him. She is stouthearted and shows no tears, using her Power to heal him, but...according to Sasha, both of his legs are badly damaged. The right leg has a broken thigh bone. The bones in the left leg are shattered below the knee and the muscles are torn. Even if he survives, they don't know if he'll ever be able to walk normally again."

Brandt swore fiercely.

Ginter released a deep sigh.

"...I have no words. What a terrible ordeal for that angelic child..."

The fact that such an innocent person was gravely injured left a terrible aftertaste—an unbearable one—even for men who had seen many deaths in countless battles.

In the somber air, Gravis murmured, "...Lucas, was the boy the 'something I absolutely must see' from your letter?"

Brandt nodded. "Yes... Your Highness, I wish you could have seen the boy's eyes."

"I heard a call for help, and when I leaped to Zweilink, he was right in front of me."

"Did you see those eyes...? They're identical."

"Yes... Ionia's eyes." Gravis laughed at himself. "I reached out to him, but he slipped away...just like Ionia did twelve years ago. I suppose I really can't save anyone in that fortress."

The men hung their heads at Gravis's regret. And it wasn't just Gravis. Everyone had been helpless that day.

"...The boy was born the morning after Ionia's death," Brandt murmured.

"...What?"

Brandt nodded at the stunned Gravis. "Your Highness...could this really be a mere coincidence?"

"Lucas, don't bring that up at a time like this!" Ginter snapped at him.

But Brandt kept going. "His appearance is certainly different, but those violet eyes. And the circumstances of his birth... Can that be a coincidence? Today's incident was the pièce de résistance. He almost disappeared from our lives again at Zweilink."

Gravis furrowed his brow.

"...Lucas, what are you implying?"

Brandt's eyes lit up. "Please, Your Highness. What if our treasure has been reborn? What if the man who died twelve years ago, your irreplaceable best friend and...my *significant other*, Ionia, lives again?"

"What are you trying to say?"

"He's still young. But if he really is Ionia's reincarnation... Your Highness, I wonder what choices you and I could make this time."

The two men glared at each other.

"...I didn't have a choice back then. And you know that."

Brandt nodded.

"Perhaps you didn't. I can only imagine how difficult a position you were in."

"Then what's the point of digging up all of that right now?"

"Because you had a choice. A choice that would have made you happy."

Gravis shook his head. "We... Io and I, we didn't have a choice."

Brandt glared at him sternly. "No, you did. Ionia had made up his mind. It was your choice not to take his hand back then."

Gravis's eyes flashed darkly. His anger at Brandt was clearly smoldering. "Lucas, you're overstepping."

But it was Gravis who looked away first. It wasn't a sign of weakness. He was trying not to take his anger out on Brandt.

Brandt remembered.

The man had been that way since he was a boy.

Deep down, he must have held a burning rage against fate but kept it locked away so that no one would get hurt, not then and not now.

A prince blessed with a brilliant mind and perfect appearance, he was the most powerful man in Fanoren, praised as a hero and renowned throughout the continent for his valor. However, Brandt knew that the life of this man, whom everyone revered, had been a path of trials and tribulations orchestrated by fate.

For Brandt, Gravis was not only a master to serve but also a junior colleague and a love rival for Ionia's favor. Brandt and Gravis's relationship had already been a complicated one for over twenty years. They were, for all intents and purposes, sharing the same destiny. Brandt had no hesitation about opening Pandora's box.

"...I suppose this is what I get for not properly discussing this with you twelve years ago."

"What do you mean by that?"

"I'll be honest with you, Lucas. I have always envied you."

Brandt felt blindsided by his words.

Gravis laughed at himself. "I've always envied you for being able to stand next to him in a fair and honest manner, for being the same age as him, for being able to hold him in your arms without fear."

"Your Highness..."

"If I made a mistake, it was not telling you how I felt."

Brandt's face contorted. "...I haven't been honest, either, Your Highness. I've always been jealous of you. His heart was yours. Ionia died without ever truly being mine."

The two men watched each other in silence for a long moment.

Gravis's expression tightened as he put on his usual air of coldness.

"...That's right. Ionia is dead. My best friend, your significant other, is no more. The boy being Io's reincarnation is a fool's wish, Lucas."

"But what if he really is?"

Gravis shook his head. "Be reasonable. I can understand your obsession with his eyes. I was shocked, too."

"Then you see—!"

"...Even if you can find a glimpse of Ionia in his eyes, he is not *Ionia* himself."

Brandt's shoulders slumped at these words.

"I know...but I can't simply dismiss this as coincidence."

When he looked into the boy's eyes, Brandt was shocked.

It was as if he had found again in Brungwurt the light of the man he had mourned twelve years earlier—the man who had disappeared, leaving a festering wound in both Gravis and Brandt.

For Brandt, it was a ray of hope.

"Let's not do this, Lucas. We are both in our thirties, and there is no point in reminiscing about a past we can never return to. And it doesn't change the choices we made that day."

"Your Highness..."

"Ionia is dead. Now we can only hope that the poor boy's life will be spared."

Gravis finished the conversation and motioned to Ginter, who was quietly watching them.

Ginter had also known Ionia well. They had nothing to hide.

"I'm going back to the royal capital tomorrow. I'll take you with me."

"Yes, sir. Thank you."

"That man committed suicide. He was delirious, but it was no accident. Find out what you can about him."

Ginter nodded.

"The secretary of the Interior has agreed to look into the man's origins."

"Good. Find out what happened to him after he joined the Royal Army."

"I've instructed the secretary of the Interior to report on the man's military history and personal relationships. The head of Brungwurt's Autonomous Army, Commander Lev, is still on the scene."

"I will speak with the Marquis of Lagarea later. A son of Brungwurt was injured by one of our soldiers. The Royal Army must take responsibility."

The men nodded.

The next morning, Sasha, the military doctor, came to report on Leorino's condition.

In addition to Gravis, the crown prince, Kyle; Chancellor Ginter; Lieutenant General Brandt; and the Marquis of Lagarea were all present in the parlor to hear the news before they left.

"I'm sorry for the sudden call yesterday, Sasha."

The first thing that Gravis did the previous night, immediately after carrying Leorino and his father, was return to the royal capital and bring Sasha, the Royal Army's military doctor, who was in the Palace of Defense, to treat the boy.

"You should be, Your Excellency. You suddenly grabbed me by the neck, and the next thing I knew, I was in Brungwurt. You could have at least let me prepare my tools. If they didn't have the proper medical equipment here, I wouldn't have been able to help him in time."

Despite his dour manner, Sasha was the best military doctor in the country. With his light-brown hair, eyes of the same color, and a baby face, he didn't look it at all, but he was a veteran military doctor in his midforties who possessed a wealth of experience.

"I'll hear your complaints in the royal capital. For now, report on the condition of the boy."

Sasha nodded. The doctor had been treating Leorino all night and had bloodshot eyes like a rabbit's. "I think Leorino's life is not in danger for the time being."

At this report, everyone's shoulders relaxed with relief. Brandt looked particularly pleased. "Really? ...Thank god."

Gravis let out a deep, quiet sigh, making sure no one noticed.

"Although it's still too early to relax. For now, his heart has not suddenly stopped beating, but his condition is still very bad and could quickly change for the worse again."

Sasha's words turned everyone's faces somber.

"That's all I can say at the moment... Nevertheless, he was very fortunate that the general was at Zweilink. If the boy had been sent on a horse-drawn carriage, he certainly would not have made it in time. Well, bringing me along was the wisest choice you could have made."

"Yes, His Highness Prince Gravis's presence was a godsend."

The men nodded at the Marquis of Lagarea's words.

"The rest was Madame Maia's feat. Without her Power, he would not have survived."

"Is Madame Maia's gift really that powerful?" the crown prince asked in surprise.

"It's not magic that can instantly heal any wound, but it does boost the human body's ability to heal itself. I believe that Madame Maia's continued application of her Power boosted Leorino's life force and allowed him to escape from the brink of death."

The Marquis of Lagarea must have had his good friend August on his mind. "So has Leorino regained consciousness yet? Has he been able to talk to August?"

Sasha shook his head.

"No, not yet. That's why I'll be staying here for a while," Sasha told his superior with a resolute look on his face. "That won't be an issue, will it, Your Excellency? I cannot abandon a patient in this condition. I heard that he was taken prisoner by a deranged soldier of our army who jumped to his death. A beautiful child like that has been injured so badly by something so senseless... I want to do everything within my power to help him."

Gravis agreed.

If Sasha stayed, Gravis would receive regular updates on Leorino's condition. In any case, it was the best apology the Royal Army could offer right now. If Sasha was needed in the royal capital, Gravis would leap here himself and take him back and forth between the capital.

Then Brandt asked Sasha: "Even if Lord Leorino gets better, will he still suffer from any...ailments?"

"I suspect so. His legs will likely remain damaged in some capacity."

The whole group gasped.

"I can't say for certain until he wakes up, but he suffered horrible damage to his left leg. I reconnected the broken bones, but the tendons that allow him to move his leg are badly damaged. He will be lucky if he can walk again, but he will likely never run around like a boy again."

"...My god." Brandt covered his mouth.

"If Madame Maia is with him, he may... No, I do think that if he is to walk again, the road to that point will be long and hard."

"Have you told the margrave yet?"

"Yes, just now. I informed the margrave and his eldest son. They were shocked, but they were more concerned that he has not regained consciousness yet. They are probably too busy praying for him to survive to think about what might be when he recovers."

"And what about Madame Maia?"

"Madame Maia has been overusing her Powers, and she herself is in poor condition, so she is taking medicine and resting. She is very tired, and I have not yet told her, as the margrave has instructed me not to burden her with any more sad news."

The men looked heartbroken.

"Still...that woman has the Power to heal. She must have some deeper understanding of Leorino's condition. She told me many times that her Power cannot save his legs."

Sasha bowed his head.

"I apologize for my inability to help any further, but...from here on out, this is God's domain."

There was no need for the doctor to apologize.

"The margrave said only, 'His potential disability is not my immediate concern. I only wish for him to survive... I refuse to give up on him.' Even if I can't restore the life he used to have, I'll beg God for mercy that he may yet walk."

Gravis clenched teeth in regret.

He felt so utterly helpless.

The violet eyes had stared single-mindedly at Gravis through a thin veil of tears as if they had wanted to say something.

The small body tumbled without so much as a noise.

*Why am I always too late...? I had almost reached him...*

Twelve years ago, a life disappeared behind the closing gates. The image of the man he couldn't save flashed through his mind.

At that moment, Brandt's words came to mind.

*What if he really is him?*

Gravis wanted to think that the feelings stirring within him were simply guilt for not being able to save the child.

He didn't care what he looked like; he just wanted the child to live.

He wanted to see his violet eyes full of life and light once more.


Sasha decided on a means of communication with Gravis and Brandt and returned to Leorino.

The guests from the capital decided to leave Brungwurt at the same time to spare the family the burden of seeing them off. Everyone there, including Gravis, had urgent work to return to at the heart of the kingdom. They could not afford to remain in Brungwurt any longer.

Only the Marquis of Lagarea, who was, of course, busy as secretary of the Interior, decided to postpone his return to Brungwurt for a few more days for the sake of his good friend August.

The men were shocked to see August appear in the parlor.

They had just told the steward that they did not need to see the head of the family off and that they would quietly take their leave instead.

August, the Margrave of Brungwurt, was usually a very gallant man and a lord of venerable origins who protected a vast territory near the border. However, now he was a shadow of his former self, looking as gaunt and tired as if he had aged ten or twenty years overnight.

Considering August's mental state was so painful, no one dared to speak up.

"...Dear guests, I can't even begin to apologize for the trouble I have caused you with my son." August bowed deeply.

He apologized for the fact that the memorial service had not gone as originally planned and, as a result, had inconvenienced the attendees who came all the way from the royal capital.

Ginter looked at August with a pained look in his eyes and responded to his apology on behalf of the entire group.

"August, it was our decision to alter the memorial service. The Cassieux family is the victim of this accident. I beg you to raise your head."

The Marquis of Lagarea placed his hand on his friend's shoulder. "Yes, August, you are not at fault for any of this."

August shook his head and clenched his fists with a weary look on his face. "No, it was my fault for leaving my son all alone. It is all my fault. I heard that they omitted the oath in the gallery at the memorial service. Please forgive me, Your Royal Highness, for wasting your time."

Kyle waved a black-gloved hand. "Don't mention it. Lagarea is right. There's no reason for you to feel responsible. The military doctor told me about Leorino's condition. I wish him a speedy recovery."

August nodded in gratitude. Next, he turned to Gravis. His blue-green eyes were slightly wet.

"...Your Highness Prince Gravis, I cannot thank you enough for bringing my son to Brungwurt and for bringing Dr. Sasha with you. Sasha will stay here for the time being and take care of Leorino... I owe you a debt of gratitude that I will never be able to repay."

Gravis nodded reassuringly, without uttering a word.

August looked around at everyone.

"I want you to know... Today is actually Leorino's birthday. He is now half-fledged."

The men gasped. What a tragic birthday.

"I've been thinking about it. Twelve years ago this morning, Leorino came into the world. My wife went into labor on the night of the Zweilink tragedy, and he was born at dawn. And now after suffering such misfortune on that very land, he is fighting to stay in this world. Is this coincidence, or is it fate?"

Gravis and Brandt silently exchanged glances.

"I prayed all night. I watched and prayed for him and for Maia, who was doing everything in her power to keep him alive... I prayed that he would come back to us, no matter the cost."

August looked around at the speechless group and, with silent strength in his eyes, said, "And he survived. We believe that today marks another birthday, the day he came back into the world. If this is not good fortune, what is?"

"Lord August..."

"We will continue to protect him at all costs, no matter what happens. He is the hope of Brungwurt...and of all of Fanoren."

The Marquis of Lagarea extended his stay for another week, during which he remained close to his best friend and comforted him.

Lev returned from Zweilink. However, he had no information that would help discover the truth. August and the others were terribly disappointed.

According to Lev's report, there was no evidence that the soldier who had committed suicide had been in poor mental health, and no suspicious associations were discovered.

However, the man's background was known. He was a member of the fortress guard twelve years ago and a survivor of the Zweilink tragedy. They also learned that he was from the royal capital and that his brother and sister-in-law lived there at present.

The Marquis of Lagarea returned to the royal capital, promising August that he would look into the man and that he would visit Brungwurt regularly.

What really happened during that span of time when the soldier was alone with Leorino? There had been no one to witness it. Only Leorino knew the truth.

However, Leorino remained comatose and had not yet regained consciousness.

What awaited Gravis and the other men upon their return to the capital was the problem of the neighboring country of Zwelf. The men at the center of national politics had little time for personal matters. Since the incident, the men had left no small space in their hearts for Brungwurt, but they could not make time to visit the boy.

They were told that the Marquis of Lagarea, the secretary of the Interior, would continue to investigate the matter, and they instructed him to regularly report his findings to them.

After hearing several reports from the Marquis of Lagarea on the lack of progress, Gravis and the others were soon busy with their daily responsibilities and gradually drifted away from the incident.

In the capital, daily discussions were being held and countermeasures taken in the Palace of Defense to address the signs of a coup d'état in the neighboring country of Zwelf. The scenario that Chancellor Ginter had envisioned did not go as expected. According to the reports of the intelligence officers who had been sent to Zwelf, the man who had been newly appointed to a key military position, Zberav, was indeed a relative of the mother of the former crown prince, Vandarren, who had been disinherited after the war. However, the connection between the imprisoned former crown prince, Vandarren, and Zberav was cleverly concealed, and no hard evidence could be found.

Zwelf, which had surrendered in the previous war, was a defeated nation, but it was not a vassal state, although it continued to pay reparations. As a nation, it was on equal footing with Fanoren, so to accuse the former crown prince on mere suspicion would be considered interfering in their internal affairs, even if he was no longer in line for the throne.

For that reason, Ginter intended to use the pause on iron exports, an event related to the interests of Fanoren, as an excuse to inform the Zwelf collaborators of the danger.

It had been about a month since Gravis had returned to the royal capital from Brungwurt, when the agents who had been sent to investigate the mines disappeared, and the royal court was suddenly thrown into disarray.

On that same day, a message arrived from Dr. Sasha in Brungwurt, saying that Leorino had awakened.

# The Awakening

Like bubbles floating up from the bottom of a deep lake, he slowly ascended from the dark depths of life into the light. It felt so good to float softly, gently to the surface.

*Ah... It's so bright I can't see anything.*

When the white in his vision cleared, he could vaguely see the familiar ceiling of his bedroom. At the edge of his hazy vision, he saw a slender man he didn't recognize. Then he saw Maia, his mother, who was speaking to him with a serious look on her face.

*...I was at Zweilink, and I... Uh...?*

The next moment, Maia turned to him and put her hand over her mouth, a look of shock on her face.

"Doctor! Rino is...! My little angel! You're awake...!!"

Maia held Leorino's hand resting on top of the sheets. Tears welled in her eyes before finally spilling down her cheeks. His mother had lost a lot of weight since the last time he had seen her. Leorino wanted to squeeze her hand back to reassure her, but he wasn't sure if he was putting any pressure into his fingertips at all.

A strange brown-haired man approached the bedside. His big, round eyes were full of tenderness and sympathy.

*　*　*

*Who is he...? Some older man I've never met...*

"I'm so glad you're awake, Leorino. My name is Sasha. I am a doctor from the royal capital."

"...Ah."

"...Oh, you don't need to force yourself to speak. Can you stay awake a little longer?"

Leorino thought he nodded in affirmation, but he wasn't sure if he had actually moved.

Still, Leorino's feelings seemed to be properly conveyed to Sasha. He nodded with a smile and instructed the lady's maid in the room to send for August and Leorino's brothers.

Maia shed tears of joy.

"Rino, my angel... I'm so glad. Mother has been waiting for you to wake up for a long, long time."

*Oh no, Mother is calling me "Rino" and "angel" again...*

Silly, meaningless thoughts floated in and out of Leorino's mind.

Chuckling at Maia, who was clearly agitated from both joy and exhaustion, Sasha kindly addressed her.

"Madame, if you're tired, you can go straight to sleep. Now, Leorino, let's talk a little."

Maia immediately interrupted. "Doctor, isn't it too early? Leorino just awoke. Do you want to remind him of everything he has been through?"

Leorino wanted to know what was going on.

*Please.* He nodded toward the doctor. This time he could move his head, albeit only a little.

"Then a few words. Leorino, you fell from the gallery of the outer fortress at Zweilink with a Royal Army soldier. Do you remember that? There, you suffered a serious injury that has kept you unconscious to this day."

"—ow...long...?"

"Oh, you've found your voice a little, have you? That's a good sign. You were asleep for a long time. It's been exactly thirty days. Everyone has been waiting for you to wake up."

*...Thirty days. At Zweilink... Oh, I was there. I remembered something important...*

At that moment, August, Auriano, Johan, and Gauff came running into the room. Leorino's thoughts fizzled out as soon as he was about to focus on something.

"Leorino!"

"Rino!"

"Rinoooo! Thank god!"

Maia, her eyes widening upon seeing her husband and children rushing to Leorino's bedside with shouts of joy, reprimanded them.

"August, Auriano! And, Johan and Gauff! Can't you be quieter?! Leorino just woke up!"

"Well, gentlemen of the Cassieux family. Let's calm down first. You mustn't overstimulate Lord Leorino."

The family became flustered at the doctor's warning.

*Ah, that's how it's always been... Mother is still the loudest...*

Leorino's consciousness was slowly fading out again.

"You're sleepy again, aren't you? Get some more rest... You're all right now."

Beyond his fading consciousness, he vaguely saw his father's face as he came to his bedside. He felt his large hand stroking his head. "...Thank you, thank you for coming back to us, Leorino."

For the first time in his life, he saw his father cry. Leorino thought he smiled at his father's words. He wasn't sure if he actually did or not.

*...Father, I'm sorry for worrying you so much... I'm fine now. I'll be fine...*

Leorino once again fell into a healing sleep, the lively voices dancing on the edge of his consciousness.

Leorino slept and woke up, woke up and slept again, and slowly recovered. For a while, the boundary between reality and sleep was blurred. However, slowly but surely he began to spend more and more time awake.

Each time he woke up, little by little, his body and mind became more in tune with each other. Gradually, he began to understand his condition.

His broken bones were immobilized, so he could hardly move the lower half of his body. Moreover, he was bedridden for so long that his muscles had weakened, and he was surprised to find that he could not move his body at all. He was being cared for as if he were a baby in every aspect of his life. When he tried to sense his limbs, he felt as if his whole body was trapped beneath a rock.

As Leorino stayed conscious for longer periods of time, he became more and more anxious about the state of his body.

After ten days, he was able to listen and respond clearly, much to the relief of his family.

With the family's approval, Sasha agreed to explain the state of his injuries.

Leorino started with what he wanted to know most. "...Doctor, will I be able to walk again?"

"Let's see. The first thing we need to do is get you out of bed and get some strength back into those muscles. Rino, you've been asleep for a very long time. Your body has forgotten how to move."

He was surprised to realize it didn't upset him when Sasha called him "Rino."

"So if I can get up and start moving my body...will I be able to walk?"

Sasha didn't answer immediately.

"I've repaired the broken bones nicely. I am a very skilled doctor after all," Sasha joked, and Leorino smiled softly with that adorable face of his. His small face had become even smaller and thinner, but his smile was so beautiful that it made the doctor's heart ache.

Sasha was so glad they were able to save him.

The fact that this beautiful child's life had been saved was the result of a miraculous chain of coincidence:

The fact that Gravis, for whom distance was no obstacle, had been there. That Leorino's mother, Maia, had the Power to heal. And that Gravis had immediately brought Sasha, the best doctor in the kingdom, from the royal capital.

Sasha was an atheist. As a military doctor, he knew death better than most. He was able to save some lives but lost many more. For him, human life and death was a matter of two options: Either he had the skill to save them or he did not. However, he felt that the fact that the boy was alive today was brought about by some fateful series of coincidence.

For the first time in his life, Sasha could understand why people thanked God.

"You are a very bright boy, Rino, so I'm going to be honest with you. I have reconnected the bones properly. However, in the human body, there are tendons that connect the bones to the muscles that move the body. There are also strings that run throughout the body, which are like a circuit that conveys a person's commands, such as 'I want to move this way.' In your legs, the broken bones damaged those tendons and circuits."

"Tendons and circuits that convey my commands..."

Sasha nodded. "At this point, only God knows how much of that damaged tendon and circuitry will heal in order to allow you to walk and run."

"I see."

Sasha softly stroked Leorino's shoulder with his gentle hand.

"Once you're able to get up, you will have a very hard time, Rino. If it was just one of your legs, it wouldn't be nearly as bad, but alas. Learning to walk again will probably be very painful."

"But...if I keep trying, without giving up, will I be able to walk eventually? Even if only a little?"

"There is hope. But first you have to build up enough strength to be able to sit up in bed."

"All right."

Leorino did not despair.

He didn't know how far he would be able to recover. He mentally prepared himself for the difficult training the doctor mentioned. But for the sake of his loving and supportive family, he wanted to be able to proudly say that he had done everything in his ability. Leorino promised himself that he would work as hard as he could.

Although he could not tell anyone, there was one more thing he wanted to do after he recovered. He wanted to find out the truth about the betrayal, about what Ionia had learned just before his death.

"...Dr. Sasha, I'm going to get well. There is something I want to do."

Leorino looked at him with strength in his eyes, and Sasha nodded in satisfaction at his spirit. Then, at the end of the long conversation, Sasha said good-bye to Leorino.

"I'm leaving the day after tomorrow, Rino. I really want to keep an eye on your recovery, but my work is in the royal capital, and I must return soon. I have handed over the rest of the work to Dr. Willy here. He is also an excellent doctor who used to work in the capital. I am certain he will do a fine job supporting your physical therapy."

Leorino looked sad for a moment, but he quickly donned a brave smile. Then he held out his hand toward Sasha.

Sasha gently shook it.

"Sasha, thank you so much for your help. I'll do my best."

"I will come back to see you regularly."

"Thank you. I'll be happy to see you again."

"Well, it'll depend on my superior, so I can't promise when exactly I'll be back, unfortunately."

"...? Who is your superior?"

"I am a doctor in the Royal Army. Do you remember, Rino? It was His Excellency the general who brought you here from Zweilink."

Of course, he remembered.

That day in Zweilink, their eyes met for the briefest moment. Gravis had really come to his aid.

*Vi…*

"He's a real coldhearted man who works me to the bone, cramming in one job after another." Sasha shrugged and swore in jest. Leorino smiled. "He will be here the day after tomorrow to pick me up. His Excellency appears to be coldhearted… Well, no, he *is* coldhearted, but he was sincerely worried about you. Would you like to see him?"

Leorino took a moment to think and finally shook his head slowly. His platinum hair rubbed against the sheets with a small sound.

"I'm sorry, Doctor. I still don't want to see anyone other than my family… Could you please tell His Excellency…how grateful I am for his help?"

"I understand. I will let him know. Now, take your medicine and rest for the day."

Leorino nodded and obediently followed the doctor's instructions.

He wanted to see Gravis again.

But that wish could never come true.

Ionia and Leorino, who didn't even know if he would ever walk again, were too different in every way.

*I am far too weak for you to entrust your back to me.*

The thought broke his heart.

Two days later, Gravis came to pick up Sasha. Ginter and the Marquis of Lagarea were also there.

Sasha, who had been brought with only the clothes on his back, had nothing to pack and was waiting for Gravis empty-handed.

"Thank you, Your Excellency, for going out of your way to take me back with you."

Sasha had never cared much about status or decorum and was quite at ease with Gravis, a member of the royal family and the highest-ranking member of the Royal Army, to which they both belonged. Gravis was used to it, too.

"Well done. Your second-in-command in the royal capital has been frantic in your absence."

Sasha smiled and nodded toward Gravis. "I'm just glad Leorino has awoken. He seems to be fully conscious now, too. It's a shame I won't be able to help in his recovery, but...well, I hope I can ask Your Excellency to bring me back here every now and then."

August and Maia, who were standing behind Sasha, bowed deeply to Gravis.

August looked much calmer than when they had parted. Maia, too, had lost weight, but she welcomed everyone with a pleased expression on her face. The recovery of their youngest son must have breathed new life into them.

The Marquis of Lagarea patted August on the shoulder. "August, I am so happy for you."

"Bruno, I wouldn't have made it without your support. I really appreciate it."

Everyone was excited for Leorino's recovery.

"We don't have much time, Your Royal Highness."

At Ginter's words, Gravis nodded.

"Right. I need to speak with you, August."

Ginter took over. "I would like to share some information with you. Lord August, may we have a moment of your time?"

After leading the men into the parlor, August bowed deeply to Gravis and the others once again.

"Your Highness Prince Gravis, Dr. Sasha, Chancellor, and Bruno. I would like to thank you again for what you have done. Leorino lives thanks to all of you."

"I'm glad to hear that his condition has stabilized. How is he? Sasha reports that he is recovering well," said Gravis.

"He can't quite get up yet, but he is indeed recovering. My wife is very happy."

"Madame Maia must have worked very hard. I wish I could leave Sasha with you, but unfortunately that is not an option. I apologize for retrieving him before he's finished his work."

August immediately shook his head.

"I am very grateful to you, Sasha. We can't hold up a man who has such an important role to play in the capital any longer."

It was a Royal Army soldier who had, after all, injured the son of the Margrave of Brungwurt. It couldn't compensate for Leorino's long-term injuries, but Sasha still saved his life and helped him recover, so he made up for the horrible crime at least a little.

"Sasha, you did very well."

Sasha smiled at his superior's praise.

"Lord August, I would like to continue to help Lord Leorino however I can. I'm studying how wounded soldiers train to recover from their injuries. I have handed over the basics to Dr. Willy, and I will continue to support Lord Leorino's recovery by exchanging information with him."

"We would be happy to repay you for everything you have done for us."

"I hate to bring this up at a time like this, but we must inform you of something... Please, Marquis of Lagarea."

The Marquis of Lagarea nodded at Ginter's words.

"We have made progress on the Zweilink incident. Edgar Yorke, who jumped with Leorino in tow, was from the royal capital. At the age of eighteen, he enlisted in the Royal Army as a general recruit, and during the war twelve years ago, he was sent to Zweilink from the mountain troops and suffered serious damage to his internal organs, but he lived. He, too, was a survivor of that tragic night."

August frowned.

"He was also a survivor of that tragic night, but committed suicide on the day commemorating it, attempting to take my son with him."

The Marquis of Lagarea's expression turned somber.

"...August."

"No, I'm sorry. Please continue."

The Marquis of Lagarea looked at his best friend with a frown.

"I hate to say it, but there's more. Edgar Yorke's brother and his wife were horrified that his brother had wounded the son of a nobleman...but the other day, they were unfortunately killed in a carriage accident in the royal capital. Both husband and wife."

"What...?"

This was news to both Gravis and Ginter.

"...What kind of a coincidence is that?"

The Marquis of Lagarea nodded with a morbid expression at Gravis's words.

"I also looked into it to see if there was any foul play involved. But it wasn't only Yorke's brother and his wife who died in the accident. They simply happened to be there and got caught up under a runaway carriage. The timing was poor, but it seems to me to have truly been an accident."

The men were silent.

August's face contorted in exasperation as he stared at his best friend.

"I suppose that means we're out of options."

"...August, I'm sorry I can't help you."

August rejected the Marquis of Lagarea's words with a hint of anger.

"That day...that man said to Leorino as he held him: 'If they find out, it's all over for me! If I'm going to be killed anyway...I'll just die here.' The man had committed a crime, and Leorino had found out about it. He must have committed suicide out of despair and delirium."

The Marquis of Lagarea nodded vigorously.

"That is why I want Leorino to tell me what that man said and what he heard from Yorke at the time. And in order to get to the bottom of the matter, I need him to tell me as soon as possible. Would that be all right with you?"

August nodded at the Marquis of Lagarea's request.

"I understand. I will arrange a meeting with Leorino."


Before leaving, Sasha visited Leorino in his bedroom. Maia, the margravine, who was accompanying him, gasped when she noticed the man behind Sasha.

"Your Highness Prince Gravis! There was no need..."

Sasha beamed at her.

"We are heading back to the royal capital. We wanted to say good-bye to Lord Leorino."

"He was awake until a few minutes ago, but he just fell asleep. I'm sorry."
Sasha shook his head at Maia's apologetic tone.

"Please don't wake him up. I'll just have one last look... If I may, sir?"
Gravis nodded quietly.

"I don't mind just seeing his face. Please remain as you are."
Maia nodded and invited them in.

They approached the bedside, breathless.

The boy was sleeping peacefully.

He was so beautiful that just looking at him made their hearts ache.

"He's sleeping soundly... Sir, isn't he a beautiful child? He's wonderful...
He said he has something he wants to do when he gets well," Sasha said.

He pictured Leorino's violet eyes, hidden behind closed eyelids.

"Your Excellency, please don't wake him up. He said he doesn't wish to see
anyone but his family, and if he finds out I brought Your Excellency here in
secret, Lord Leorino will be furious with me."

"...Right."

At that moment, Gravis realized that he had unconsciously extended his
hand toward the boy.

"Shall we get going?"

Gravis nodded silently. He reached out and touched a lock of platinum-
colored hair. The soft hair tangled in his hand. He gently stroked it with the
underside of his fingers.

Leorino's thin chest rose and fell slowly, the ultimate proof that he lived
and breathed.

Brandt said that this boy was the reincarnation of Ionia. Indeed, back then,
Gravis felt as if Ionia's voice had called out to him. But it was without a doubt
this boy who had called out to Gravis.

Staring at the boy's sleeping face, Gravis stopped thinking. What mattered
most was that the boy's life was saved. Whether or not the boy was a reincarnation of Ionia, he should simply be thanking God for preserving this life.

The life that slipped through his hands that day and was saved by some
miracle.

"Get well soon… I'll be back before long to see you," Gravis whispered to the boy.

But the man never fulfilled his promise.
It would be six years before their paths would cross again.

Immediately after Gravis and the men returned to the capital, the political situation in Zwelf deteriorated rapidly.

Three months later, news of the sudden death of the recently turned adult king of Zwelf came as a shock to Fanoren. The cause of the young king's death was reported as illness, but this claim could not be confirmed. He had never married and sired no heir.

The bloodline purist nobles and some soldiers strongly appealed for the restoration of the disinherited crown prince, Vandarren. The collaborationist faction wanted to maintain the truce with Fanoren, and the faction that demanded the restoration of the former crown prince went to a head, and the absence of the king left Zwelf spiraling out of control.

Key figures of the collaborationist faction began dying in mysterious accidents, and the former crown prince's faction was quickly gaining momentum.

Gradually, the power of the military forces that supported the former crown prince increased, and three years passed. After the purge of the chancellor, who had been the last stronghold of the collaborationist faction, the former crown prince's faction came to power. The once-disinherited Vandarren was restored to power and finally acceded to the throne. With that, the cease-fire treaty between Fanoren and Zwelf was broken. The two states broke off diplomatic relations.

Gravis and his men continued to be vigilant of the situation in Zwelf.
Vandarren held a grudge against Fanoren and would surely attempt something in the future. Zwelf had been ravaged by civil war, but they could eventually accumulate enough strength to go to war again.
A threat hung over Fanoren once more.

About two months had passed since the Zweilink incident, and Leorino was still bedridden.

In August's presence, he was visited by the Marquis of Lagarea, if only for a short time.

Bruno Henckel, the Marquis of Lagarea, was a leading nobleman approaching old age, about eight years older than August. He was the brother-in-law of the former king's concubine, Brigitte, and a relative of the current king, Joachim. He had long served as secretary of the Interior and was trusted by the royal family and the nobility for his intelligence and moderate beliefs.

"Bruno... Leorino is still easily fatigued. I don't want to distress him by talking about what happened that day."

"I know, August. I will be brief."

The Marquis of Lagarea nodded toward his best friend.

Smiling, he approached the bedside and gave a small tap on the covers. "Leorino, how are you feeling? You've been through a lot. I'm glad you're still with us."

"...Thank you, Uncle Bruno."

"I want to talk a little about that day. May I?"

Leorino nodded.

"Do you remember falling from the gallery? ...I see. What about the man who fell with you? Do you remember anything about him?"

"...Oh, not much... My head is still a bit fuzzy. I..."

"I understand... Then tell me just one more thing. Do you remember what that man, Edgar Yorke, told you back then?"

Leorino shook his head.

*...I remember. But I'm sorry, there's nothing I can tell you* now.

Leorino was a child—they would never believe his word that the Zweilink tragedy was brought about by Edgar's betrayal, much less that there could have been a mastermind behind Edgar's betrayal of Fanoren who was in cahoots with the enemy.

He had no way to prove any of it.

The proof was Ionia's memories in his dreams. The truth could be found only in those memories.

Leorino decided to remain silent.

"I'm sorry, Uncle... When I try to remember...I get a headache..."

August rushed to stop the Marquis of Lagarea.

"I'm sorry, Bruno, but he's not ready for this. I apologize, but we should end this here."

The Marquis of Lagarea released a deep sigh and nodded to August. He watched Leorino with concern in his light-brown eyes.

"I'm sorry, Leorino... You don't have to force yourself to remember that incident. Forget about Edgar Yorke... You don't have to suffer any more than you already have."

The Marquis of Lagarea's kind voice echoed through the room. Leorino nodded absentmindedly.

"Forget about the pain and focus only on letting your body heal."

August nodded.

"Yes. Leorino...you don't need to think about anything right now... You can go back to sleep."

Leorino nodded again and closed his eyes. They were right; he needed rest.

August softly stroked his little head. The Marquis of Lagarea also gently patted him on the shoulder in reassurance.

After another two weeks, Leorino was finally able to sit up in bed.

Gradually, he returned to eating solid food, and under the guidance of the doctor and assisted by his attendants, he began functional recovery exercises, moving his weakened and stiffened muscles, mostly in his upper body.

The Cassieux family's doctor was a physician named Willy. He had served as deputy chief of medicine at the royal court, but some twenty years prior, he had left his post and returned to Brungwurt, explaining that he wanted to *give back to my birthplace while I'm still in active service.*

His son, known as Willy Jr., returned to Brungwurt after completing his medical training in the royal capital.

About three months had passed since the accident, and Leorino finally began physical therapy on both his legs in earnest. The therapy was carried out by Dr. Willy Jr., who had received Sasha's guidance.

With tears in her eyes, Maia insisted that she would like to accompany him during physical therapy. However, Dr. Willy Jr. recommended that Maia leave, as the exercise would be extremely painful for both Leorino and those watching over him.

Even so, Maia did not want to leave her youngest son's side.

Maia treated Leorino every day and continued to channel her healing Power into his body. Considering her feelings, Dr. Willy Jr. could not refuse his mistress.

It was Leorino who persuaded his mother.

"If you stay, Mother, you will see me in pain, and you will tell the doctor to stop. But that would only leave me unable to walk forever."

"Rino... I hate to think that you might suffer..."

Leorino smiled at Maia. Maia's eyes filled with tears of joy at the sight of her child's bright smile, which she worried she might never see again.

"I didn't know of your Power, Mother. When Gauff told me about it, I was so envious that you had treated him."

"Yes, you've always been a very strong child, haven't you?"

"Yes. And now these injuries have ruined my legs. I am grateful to you, Mother, for saving my life and for helping me recover. But from this point on, it is up to me to do my best."

Maia burst into tears.

"Rino... You're so brave... Doctor, did you hear that? Rino says such admirable things...!"

"That's a fantastic attitude."

Dr. Willy Jr. agreed with Maia.

Leorino found his moment and looked pointedly at Hundert. The attendant knew exactly what his master meant.

"Well, Madame, you heard Lord Leorino. Let us leave this to Dr. Willy Jr. and report to Lord August."

Maia was wringing her handkerchief, clearly conflicted, as Hundert escorted her to the other side of the door. She kept saying "Of course, you're right" until the door closed behind them.

"Hah... Mother is too much."

Dr. Willy Jr. chuckled and secretly marveled at Leorino's ability to handle the situation so calmly.

"Lord Leorino, you're so positive, really admirable. Now, are you ready?"

"Yes, Doctor. I appreciate it."

For the foreseeable future, he would lie on his side and have a caregiver move his legs to gradually increase the load and stretch the stiffened muscles.

He was later informed that they had been massaging and moving the uninjured part of his legs while he was unconscious. However, both legs had to be immobilized until the broken bones healed. The muscles had therefore atrophied quite significantly.

Dr. Willy Jr. flipped up his jacket.

Now the painful physical therapy would begin.

Leorino was shocked to see his bare legs free of the splints for the first time. His muscles had completely wasted away, and his legs looked like twigs.

"Doctor...my legs...look like sticks."

"It's all right, Lord Leorino. You've been bedridden for three months, so it's only natural that your muscles have partially atrophied."

"...I wonder if I'll ever really be able to move them."

"We recently checked to see if you had feeling from your toes to your thighs, remember? You were able to wiggle the toes of both feet. They may be damaged, but your tendons are connected as they should be. The rest is up to you, Lord Leorino."

Leorino nodded to the young doctor.

"Please begin."

The young doctor lifted Leorino's left leg and placed his hand on the sole of Leorino's foot, holding it so that his hand encircled the heel. With his other hand, he held Leorino's ankle and tipped his toes toward his upper body, stretching his atrophied calf muscles.

Leorino's upper body buckled as he writhed in pain. It was excruciating. It hurt. It felt like he was going to die.

When the doctor turned his heel just a little, the pain was so intense that it brought tears to his eyes. But Leorino bit his lip and stifled a groan.

He was still alive. And as long as he was alive, he had a future. Ionia, whose future had been cut short at Zweilink, had been in more pain, had suffered much worse than this.

*I will endure this pain.*

Leorino swore to himself and gritted his teeth.

# Romantic Partner in Crime

Leorino's wish to attend the academy in the royal capital was not granted.

He gritted his teeth and endured the daily physical therapy without complaint, but the whole affair made him appear very depressed. In any case, his body was still so weak that he could barely stand up even with assistance. It would have been impossible for him to attend school in the royal capital.

August and Maia consoled Leorino, which helped him recover his spirits. He was to receive as much education as possible in the province of Brungwurt with a private tutor as originally planned.

The Marquis of Lagarea, despite his busy position, visited him frequently, but Sasha, who had promised to come regularly, only sent messages and came hardly at all.

Leorino did not want his friends from his past life, such as Gravis or Brandt, to see him in his current pitiful state.

But Sasha was different. He wanted Sasha to see him recovering, however slowly.

Sasha finally came to visit from the royal capital just as he began practicing standing up. Leorino wanted to show Sasha how much progress he had made, so he sat in a chair to greet him.

"Dr. Sasha! It's so good to see you again."

"Awww, Rino! You look so much better! Oh, what rosy cheeks you have! You're so cute, I could eat you up. Just look at you!"

Leorino rolled his eyes at Sasha's words, but he was delighted to be praised for getting better.

"I've received regular reports from Dr. Willy. I was very proud to hear of your hard work."

Leorino offered him a wide smile. Sasha held his chest and swooned.

"My... It's such a joy to see your true nature. Your smile is so bright, it hurts my eyes... Wouldn't you agree, Lieutenant General?"

With those words, Leorino turned around.

"Oh yes, indeed. You have such a radiant smile."

Leorino gasped.

Behind Sasha stood a man, his presence near imperceptible despite his large body.

Lucas Brandt.

The man who had been Ionia's significant other and accomplice stood right there.

Brandt knelt in front of Leorino and held out his large hand. The familiar man smiled at him softly, his gaze fond. "You introduced yourself to me the night before the memorial service. Do you remember?"

"Yes... Lieutenant General Brandt. Um, welcome to Brungwurt. It is a pleasure to see you again."

Leorino rushed to take the proffered hand.

Brandt took his slender hand gently, as if he were handling a delicate object, squeezed it lightly, and released it.

But even after the handshake was over, Brandt remained on his knees, staring intently at Leorino.

Leorino could not avert his gaze from those inquiring eyes.

"...Ah, I've missed those eyes so."

Leorino shuddered. He may have had Ionia's memories, but the man was still a stranger. He hadn't realized how much Brandt's presence intimidated him.

The man forced a smile at his wide violet eyes.

"No need to be so nervous. Besides, 'Lieutenant General' is so formal. Please call me 'Lucas.'"

"Huh? No, I think that's a little… What brings you to Brungwurt?"

"I came to see you, of course, Leorino."

Leorino tilted his head in confusion. He wasn't nearly young enough to believe that at face value. A busy man with major responsibilities such as the lieutenant general would not come all the way to such a remote area to visit a boy he had seen once or twice in his entire life.

If there was a reason, it must have had to do with national defense.

"I may look like a child to Your Excellency, but I am not so naive as to believe that a man as busy as yourself would come to the frontier simply to see me."

"I told you to call me 'Lucas.'"

"…Lord Lucas."

When Leorino called his name, Brandt smiled, the corners of his eyes wrinkling.

He had always been cheerful and bighearted, like the sun. When he smiled, his natural charm immediately broke through his gruff facade.

"I came to discuss something with your father. I decided to see you while I was here… That's the official story, at least. I'm mainly here to see you; my business with your father is secondary."

"Is this business with my father about Zwelf? Is there something wrong with the country?"

"It's nothing you need to concern yourself with."

Leorino was disappointed.

They really wouldn't tell him anything. August must have insisted on that. But judging from Brandt's attitude, he must have meant it when he said he came to see Leorino himself.

"…Why do you care about me so much?"

"I'm not entirely certain how to explain it. Because of your violet eyes, I suppose."

Leorino felt flustered by that.

Ionia and Leorino looked nothing alike. Except, of course, for their violet eyes.

"Leorino."

"Yes, Lord Lucas?"

Brandt's bright eyes were fixed on Leorino.

"Do you feel anything when you look at me? Or when I call you 'Ionia'?"

"I..."

He was half expecting it.

Brandt had seen a trace of Ionia in those eyes. And with his wild intuition, Brandt was about to arrive at the truth. Leorino would keep the fact that he was Ionia's reincarnation a secret forever. No one could ever find out. He had already made up his mind. He felt so useless, not knowing if he would ever be able to walk again, and he would be nothing but a burden to those who risked their life in the battle.

Leorino tried his best to put on the right expression.

He tried to look as innocent as possible, to make sure his voice would not tremble.

"Who is 'Ionia'...?"

The man looked back at the violet eyes that stared at him pointedly, somewhat melancholic.

Sasha interrupted the conversation.

"What's the matter with you, Lieutenant General?! It's true that Major Bergund had violet eyes, but...he was a commoner, and this is a child of the Cassieux family! How could they be related at all?"

Sasha had once treated Ionia after an incident that left him badly injured. That's where he must have remembered him from.

"I know. I know it sounds strange, but this defies logic, Dr. Sasha."

*...Oh, Lucas. Luca, I'm so sorry.*

"I'm sorry. I don't understand what you're saying, Lord Lucas... I don't know what to tell you."

It wasn't a lie.

Even though he inherited Ionia's memories, Leorino had his own identity as Leorino Cassieux.

Leorino was *not* Ionia.

Leorino had no experience with this and truly did not know how to answer the man's questions.

"But those eyes of yours…"

Sasha glared at Brandt in reproach. "…Lieutenant General! That's quite enough."

Brandt was about to say something when Sasha stopped him sternly. The doctor had spoken.

"Lord Leorino is tired. I, too, am somewhat confused by your words. Let's stop here."

Brandt let out a deep sigh.

The boy was indeed looking very pale.

"…I apologize. That must have been a lot to take in."

"It's fine."

"I'm sorry for confusing and tiring you when you're still recuperating. It's just that for me, those eyes are… No, I'm sorry."

"No, I should be the one apologizing…"

Leorino's heart hurt.

The man who had once been closer to him than anyone else, who had always supported him, was right in front of him now.

He was the man who embraced Ionia without question; who kept him warm, even on the nights he wept, exhausted by his love for Gravis; and who accepted the wounds he received on the day of their parting.

"I'm sorry…"

Both in the past and now, Leorino took advantage of Brandt's kindness, and in the end, he couldn't give anything in return.

*I'm sorry I can't tell you the truth…Luca.*

Leorino struggled under the weight of his sins.

Sasha agreed to stay at the castle for a few days to examine Leorino.

First, he praised Leorino for his diligence in his daily physical therapy. He also said that Maia's Power had helped immensely. Maia continued to heal him every day. It had become a time for mother and son to hold hands and talk in peace. It appeared that his mother's daily care had contributed greatly to Leorino's recovery.

After examining Leorino, Sasha instructed Dr. Willy Jr. to provide him with additional exercise. He also advised Hundert, his full-time attendant, to massage Leorino's lower body daily. He taught Leorino exercises to increase the range of motion in his joints.

The day came for Brandt and Sasha to return to the royal capital.

Leorino could not see them off to the gates, so he decided to say good-bye to them in his room. After they parted, Brandt, perhaps reflecting on his behavior, remained composed throughout his stay. The man knelt in front of Leorino.

Leorino couldn't help the feeling stirring in his chest in Brandt's presence. He felt a strange lingering attachment to him.

"Leorino, I wish you a speedy recovery. Sasha tells me that you're training very hard, but don't overwork yourself."

"Thank you, Lord Lucas."

When Leorino called his name, Brandt smiled faintly. The rugged man immediately appeared charming.

The mix of sorrow and anticipation in his eyes made Leorino's heart ache. It was impossible for Brandt to know that he had Ionia's memories. Yet the man's gaze held too much sentiment to be directed at a twelve-year-old boy. It was a sweet, piercing look, as if he was trying to reveal the person hidden inside Leorino.

Leorino couldn't take it anymore and looked away.

The moment the man stood up, a strange, familiar scent wafted through the air, and Leorino's heart fluttered once more. He remembered, albeit vaguely, the sensual moment between Ionia and this man he had seen in his dreams. Brandt was an important man to Ionia in a different way from Gravis. In the physical sense, they had been even closer.

"Can I come see you again?"

"…I wouldn't dare ask," Leorino responded simply.

He didn't want to see him.

Meeting him hurt. He knew that it would make him doubt his decision not to tell him anything.


That evening, Leorino asked his attendant to send word to his father, August, to come to his room.

August soon appeared and softly stroked Leorino's small head. "What's wrong? What is it that you want to talk about?"

"…Father, I… If anyone other than Dr. Sasha comes to see me, could you deny them entry in the future?"

"Why? Did Brandt say something hurtful to you?"

"Not at all… It's just…"

Leorino hesitated. He thought for a while about what he should say and finally revealed only half of his true feelings. "It's painful for me when anyone outside of the doctors and my family sees my useless body, which I can't even move anymore."

"Leorino, what are you saying? Nothing about you is useless!" retorted his father in a voice full of indignation.

Leorino shook his head. "No, I'm causing you nothing but trouble, living only protected by you, Father, and Mother and everyone else. I can't do anything… And for the rest of my life, I may not be able to move properly, and I may be of no use at all."

August was shocked by his son's plaintive words.

"Leorino… Rino, listen to me. That's not true at all. What do you mean by 'of use'? Are you saying that people with disabilities are useless? That they shouldn't exist? That they have no reason to live?"

"I'm not! I'm not saying that, but… I am a son of the Cassieux family…! I should be strong…"

August hugged his son's frail body. He made Leorino raise his head and look at him. "Leorino...listen, people have value, no matter what they can or cannot do."

Leorino shook his head emphatically. "I don't think so... I can't even fight in this body."

August was saddened by his son's complete lack of confidence.

"Leorino...are you saying people who can't fight don't have the right to live? ...How could that ever be true?"

"...Is it not?"

August shook his head vigorously.

"What about children? What about the elderly? Is being able to fight what makes a man valuable? I will be too old to fight one day. Will I be worthless then?"

"Of course not...! You're different, Father! But me. I'm..."

Leorino buried his face in his father's chest and choked back a sob. August hugged him tightly. Leorino's tears spilled onto his father's chest.

"Leorino...you are our hope. You were born as the hope of Brungwurt, and you have always made everyone smile. You make us happy with your presence alone. Please don't put yourself down like that... That's the one thing I don't want you to do."

August's voice was trembling as well.

"Father... I'm sorry."

"Remember, you must never doubt your own self-worth, not even out of desperation."

His little head nodded slightly.

"You have value. That will be proven in time. But for now...we are happy just to have you alive and smiling."

Quietly, his father's words sank deep into Leorino's heart.

Leorino stared blankly at the ceiling, remembering the day's events.

The longing in Brandt's eyes as they parted. The meaning of his father's words.

If there must be meaning to this life...

Was there anything he could do, flaws and all? Would he eventually find the meaning of life?

The medication he took every night put him to sleep.

Since the accident, Leorino dreamed about Ionia every night. More vividly than ever, he fell into the dream.

He felt a tremendous heat and pain in his back. The flames were relentless against his wounded body.

Every time he woke up, the dream brought Leorino intense suffering.

But he was not allowed to look away.

*I have to tell Vi about...*

In the depths of his fading consciousness, Leorino shuddered.

Just before his death, Ionia had learned a secret that he could never forget. And Leorino should have remembered what it was while in Zweilink.

*Why...?* Who *stole the memories of the traitor?*

He had to find them again. For in Ionia's memories lay the answer.

And tonight, Leorino continued to dive into those memories. Deep, deeper, endlessly deep.

# Ionia: Beasts Roaring in the Night 1

When the young man's warmth erupted inside him, Ionia devoured the intense pleasure running up his spine and flooding his brain. His vision behind his eyelids turned white with rapture. The man's breath was hot and heavy on his back. On top of Ionia, the man thrust into him over and over, emptying himself inside him.

Ionia collapsed onto the bed and exhaled heavily. The man coiled himself around him. His breathing was equally erratic.

Sex with men usually left Ionia feeling empty. After an outpouring of passion, there was always a moment of sober contemplation. But what Ionia was feeling in this moment was the never-ending pleasure of unbridled passion. Ionia looked back at the man who had driven him to climax so many times he'd lost count and stared at him through hazy eyes.

Ionia's insides had been rubbed raw, so racked with ecstasy, and he continued to squirm as if reluctant to part with the flesh of the man who was still inside him. The man had stiffened, fueled by the desperate bucking, and began to move once more.

"Why are you...hard again...? Hng... We *just* finished..."

"You agreed to it. You said you'd let me do anything tonight."

The man wrapped himself around Ionia's back and put a hand on each hip to steady himself.

"Ah...you're so good... I'm going to melt. Io..."

"I... Vi... Ah, me too..."

Ionia reached new heights of pleasure with each thrust of the other man's hips. Climax came in rippling waves.

The bed creaked loudly with the intense movements of their well-honed bodies. The moonlight cast fresh shadows on their glistening skin.

Fresh beads of sweat dotted Ionia's neck as their breathing grew ragged. The man lapped up the droplets that trickled down his neck. Ionia's whole body was so sensitive that every time he felt the tongue on his neck, he nearly lost himself.

A wordless cry spilled from his lips.

In the past, he had given, and he had received.

But had there ever been a time when he felt as good as he did now that *he* was taking him, roughly grinding his hips against his own?

Pulling out, the man flipped Ionia onto his back and leaned in again. Without hesitation, he thrust himself deep inside once more.

"...Hnah...! Ahhh!"

He just barely fit. Pleasure and pain danced at the forefront of Ionia's mind.

Their gazes met.

The starry-sky eyes shone with a golden glint and stole Ionia's gaze.

Ionia's mind was melting.

At that moment, he couldn't help the words that formed on his lips.

"...Vi, I..."

"Io... Io..."

"Vi... I'm... You and I should..."

At that moment, the face of the girl who was to be Gravis's wife appeared in Ionia's mind.

*"You will stand in front of His Highness as his shield and protect him. As a commoner, you do not have the right to stand by his side."*

In an instant, his heart went cold.

Ionia gritted his teeth and bit back the emotion threatening to spill out of him. He tried to distract the voice in his mind, turning it into a plea of physical desire.

"Go harder... Keep going... Deeper..."

"Io..."

The man used his muscular hips to thrust into Ionia even harder. Ionia was delighted by the pain.

But Gravis sensed the sadness in Ionia's eyes.

"Io... I want you to choose me... Be mine—"

Ionia quickly covered the man's lips.

"...Io..."

Ionia let go of his lips and smiled softly.

"...No. Say no more, Vi."

That's right. He couldn't say it.

No matter what lay just beneath the surface... No matter what was gleaned from their enraptured expressions, they could not speak their true desires aloud.

"This is just sex."

"Io, no...!"

"It is. Our relationship will never change...will it?"

"Io, it can. Please just choose me..."

The young man nuzzled his forehead against Ionia's neck as if pleading with him.

In that moment, it wasn't just sweat that dripped from Ionia's neck. The man's anguish manifested in the corners of his eyes. Ionia buried his face in the sheets as if overcome by his pursuit of pleasure and wiped away tears in secret.

"I can't, Vi. I have a significant other, and you have a fiancée. So this...will be our secret...just for tonight."

This night was a mistake... A mistake caused by the men's heightened sexual desires. It had to be.

It could be nothing more than a tryst; an illicit favor; an act of service to royalty.

They would embrace for the first and last time that night.

"Keep going... Harder."

*So please make the most of my body until the end. Remember me, so no matter who else you hold in your arms, you will never forget this night.*

*Tomorrow, I will return to my place as your shield, and I will protect you.*

*If I say even one more word, I won't know how to keep living tomorrow.*

Ionia first met Vi the year before Ionia became half-fledged.

Their meeting had been a miracle, something he treasured. His separation from the boy came just as suddenly.

At the end of the year in which they stopped seeing each other, the Kingdom of Fanoren was struck by a tragedy.

The king's concubine, Brigitte, died at the young age of thirty-seven. She had been ill for six months and passed away just after getting to witness the betrothal of Crown Prince Joachim to Princess Emilia of Francoure.

The year ended without another visit from Vi.

The mourning of Lady Brigitte concluded with the end of the year, and Ionia was finally about to enter school.

One day, he went to the prep school attached to the local church and received a sealed letter from the bishop. When he tried to open it on the spot, the bishop shook his head and told him to open it at home with his parents.

He returned home and presented the sealed letter to his father, who was at work in his workshop at the back of the store. The letter was an unexpected letter of admission.

IONIA BERGUND, YOU HAVE BEEN GRANTED ADMISSION TO THE ACADEMY OF HIGHER LEARNING.

Ionia and his parents consulted the bishop on how they should proceed. The bishop did not know why Ionia had been selected but assured them that it was a great honor for a commoner to attend the academy of higher learning and that refusal was not an option.

None of them had a clue what was the cause for the admission.

One day, Ionia received a letter from the head of the academy asking for a meeting with him and his father, David, at the school. It also said he would be able to tell them why Ionia had been admitted.

Ionia and his family felt this was all too good to be true and had no choice but to agree.

The day came, and Ionia and his father entered through the large front gate of the academy of higher learning.

A man who looked like a teacher was already waiting for them at the gate. They immediately felt overwhelmed by the opulent building, so far removed from the world of commoners, and walked down a long corridor to the head-master's office.

There, a man in his sixties, with gray hair and an agreeable air about him, was waiting for them.

"Ionia Bergund, Mr. David Bergund, welcome to our academy."

The headmaster smiled softly.

Ionia saw his father bow awkwardly and hurried to do the same. The headmaster responded with a sympathetic smile.

"Now...I will be brief. You must be wondering why Ionia was allowed to attend this academy."

Ionia had a faint hunch that it might have had something to do with Vi. He hadn't expected the reason he received.

"The reason is your unusual ability. Ionia, you have a special Power. Isn't that right?"

Ionia and his father gasped and looked at each other before they could help it.

The headmaster was right. Ionia was born with a Power.

It just so happened that the bishop who was sent to the diocese where Ionia lived was from a family related to a high-ranking nobleman.

According to the bishop, Powers were unique abilities that were originally manifested only by royalty and nobles of royal blood, and it was extremely rare for a commoner to possess such a Power. Therefore, commoners were unaware of their existence.

Ionia's Power was the ability to shatter any object he touched into small pieces.

According to his parents, he had been using it unconsciously since he was little. He would, for instance, shatter a piece of wood he was playing with, but he never posed any danger to himself or his family.

Once they became aware of the existence of the Power, they used it for trivial things, such as his mother asking him to crush rock salt or his father requesting him to crush iron ore into finer chunks, to solve everyday inconveniences.

Until the bishop's explanation, Ionia's ability was regarded in the Bergund family as a useful skill of an exceptionally strong child.

Ionia's Power had become known to the clergyman during the renovation of the church. When a load of stones leaving the building site fell off the cart, the workers went to call for reinforcements. Ionia, seeing the bishop in distress, approached him and used the palm of his hand to crush the fallen stones into pieces that were easy to carry.

The bishop, seeing him use his Power, turned pale with fright. When he came to his senses, he rushed to call Ionia into the pulpit room and told him that the Power was something very special in Fanoren.

Ionia was dumbfounded at the thought that this Power had led him to a life so completely opposite to what he considered ordinary.

Seeing the expressions of surprise on the faces of the father and son, speechless at the unexpected reason, the headmaster forced a smile. Then he revealed the secret.

"The church had reported to the government that there was a boy who possessed a rare gift among the commoners." The headmaster continued matter-of-factly. "I hear that your Power can shatter anything you touch. That's very valuable. I also heard that you are interested in joining the Royal Army in the future. As a future cadet, we want you to study at this academy and become an asset to your country. That is why you are here now."

It was an incredible offer.

However, Ionia didn't know the true extent of his ability. He didn't want them to get their hopes up.

So Ionia answered honestly. "I have no idea how useful this Power may be to you... Sir, I may only be able to smash stones or break wood..."

"Feel free to speak as you usually do, Ionia. We will confirm the extent of your Power in due course. But I heard from the bishop that you crushed a cart-worth of stone in an instant. That's a fine Power indeed."

The headmaster then motioned to the teacher who stood behind them to leave the room. After the door closed, he turned to them again.

"There is one more reason for your admission."

Ionia's heart was loud in his chest.

"Next year, a nobleman will skip a grade and enter this academy. We reached out to you at his request."

Could it be Vi?

Could it be that the boy who had promised to meet him again had invited Ionia to this academy?

Ionia could not keep himself from hoping.

He was about to ask who it was, when the headmaster smiled softly and said: "It is the academy's intention that you will be both a student and his guard during your time here."

"...Guard? Me...?"

"Yes, you. With your Power, you would almost certainly make for a fine *human shield* against anyone who may approach him with ill intent."

He wasn't sure he'd heard that right.

"...What is a 'human shield'?"

"Exactly what it sounds like. It means that you will use your body and your Power to shield that nobleman."

Ionia and David understood the implication behind the headmaster's words and shuddered.

"Sir...but if my son uses his Power against a person...that person will..."

"Of course, his Power can shatter stone in an instant. The fragile human body wouldn't stand a chance. That's what makes Ionia the perfect candidate for a guard, Mr. David."

Suddenly they felt like the man sitting in front of them with a kindly smile on his face had been replaced by a hideous monster.

"...A-are you telling my son to become a murderer?"

The headmaster forced a laugh, then replied, as if talking to a stubborn child: "What seems to be the issue? If he's going to become a soldier, Ionia will sooner or later commit 'murder' anyway."

"That's...different."

"If you do it for a good cause, you are a hero, and if you do it for a lawless cause, you are a criminal. All that matters is intent. Regardless of whether the experience comes sooner or later... That's the only difference."

Next to his father, stunned by the man's heartless words, Ionia stared at the headmaster with violet eyes.

"...The nobleman you mentioned... Is he Vi?"

The corners of the headmaster's mouth raised.

"...He is. No point in hiding it. Everyone will know once he's here anyway. The noble gentleman who accompanied General Stolf to your workshop... whom you dare to call by the profane nickname of 'Vi,' is His Highness Prince Gravis Adolphe Fanoren. He is the second prince of this country. When he reaches the age of ten next year, he will skip a grade and enter this academy."

David and Ionia turned pale.

The way Vi dressed and behaved made Ionia think that he was a high-ranking nobleman, but he had no idea that Vi was a member of the royal family—and a second prince at that.

"...Vi is the second prince..."

"Indeed. The only child born to Queen Adele, he is of the noblest bloodline in the country. But for some reason, he has recently requested that a lowly commoner boy whom he met while concealing his identity be placed at his side as a schoolmate—something previously unheard-of, something we could never accept. But then we found out you have a Power. That was good news for us."

This seemingly gentle and kind educator turned out to be a firm believer in the superiority of certain bloodlines. Behind his soft smile, it was clear that he thought of Ionia as an easily replaceable pawn, an insect that could be crushed at will.

Ionia was gripped by doubt. Did Gravis get close to him so he could make him into his shield?

No, he recalled, they became friends because Ionia had approached him in the first place.

"...His Highness Prince Gravis doesn't know about my Power."

"Indeed, he is not yet aware of your Power. He asked me to enroll you purely because he wants to be your friend."

Ionia exhaled in relief. He regretted that he had doubted his dear friend even for a moment.

"If you didn't have an ability, of course we wouldn't have considered it, but...the truth is, His Highness has one of his own. A very special, seldom seen ability. Therefore, he can avoid most dangers by himself."

Ionia was surprised to hear that Vi also had a Power.

"But his ability becomes meaningless if his body is touched. That is where your Power comes in."

"What do you mean by that?"

The headmaster did not give a clear answer, saying only that Ionia would learn once he became his shield.

"His Highness's position is in great danger. But at the academy, security is not nearly as tight as at the royal court. The decision to make you his schoolmate and his guard was a security measure decided upon by the royal court and ourselves. Although your bloodline is not suitable for having you by His Highness's side...it is a good idea that will please His Highness, who is hoping to have you as his schoolmate."

Ionia bit his lip, thinking how stupidly arbitrary it all was.

"What do you mean Vi's—His Highness's position being in danger?"

"You will understand that when you come to be at His Highness's side. Let's just say that His Highness is facing some difficulties because of his noble bloodline."

The headmaster leaned forward.

"With your Power, you will be His Highness's human shield and destroy those who would harm him. How would you like that? Wouldn't that be an honor?"

But David was not convinced.

His son's life was being made light of. How could he not protest?

"How dare you... You want to turn my son into a human shield...?"

"I think you'll find protecting royalty a very common practice."

"You... Maybe so, but to demand such a horrible thing of a child who has just become half-fledged?!"

Ignoring David's protests, the headmaster stared into Ionia's violet eyes and continued the conversation.

"Ionia, you have been given a wonderful opportunity. You, a commoner, will be able to stay by His Highness's side from now on. I hear that His Highness is very fond of you. I am certain His Highness will come to rely on you greatly."

"...I'll be...by his side."

"Yes. It is a great honor for a commoner to be entrusted with his back."

*To be entrusted...with Vi's back...*

"To protect His Highness's life means to protect this country. It is a noble duty. That honor will last even after you graduate from this academy. Perhaps you may be allowed to serve His Highness even after graduation."

"Even after graduation?"

"That's right. It's true—you may also face some dangers. In return, you will be exempt from all tuition fees, and we can promise to compensate your family in case anything happens to you."

David was trembling at the headmaster's attitude, speaking as if he were doing him a favor, and finally stood up and shouted: "I don't know how special you nobles think you are, but...you will not speak about my child's life this way!"

"Father!"

"Ionia! We're not doing this! You're not becoming a soldier! You'll take over the blacksmith shop!"

"Father... Father, please..."

"Come on! Get up! We're going home...! I can't just send you off to a place like this, knowing you might suffer or worse!"

"...Father, please, I'm..."

"…Io? Ionia, what's wrong?! Get up! We're going home! We're going home now."

Ionia held back the tears that threatened to spill onto his cheeks and shook his head.

David's expression was full of despair.

"…Father, I'm going to enter this academy. And I will become Vi's shield. And if anything happens to Vi, I'll use this Power… With my own hands, I'll—"

"Ionia…!"

The heartbreak was plain in David's voice.

Ionia still didn't know what to call this feeling.

But what he did know at that moment was that if he missed this opportunity, he would probably never see Vi again.

"If this is the only way I can be by Vi's side…then I choose to be his shield."

Ionia was admitted to the academy of higher learning, despite his status as a commoner. In that school year, he was the only student from a commoner background, which attracted a great deal of attention when he first entered the academy.

However, that wasn't the only way in which Ionia stood out from the crowd. The rare hue of his flame-red hair and mysterious violet eyes caught people's attention without fail. He stood a head taller than his peers, with an impressively muscular upper body. His arms and legs were long and graceful. His body, slowly growing into adolescence, had an air of sensuality about it despite his age.

There was nothing particularly remarkable about his appearance. However, the contours of his waist, stretching from his beautiful back to the tightness of his hips, revealed a hint of sensuality that made the heart of anyone who saw him throb. He had a unique presence that attracted the gazes of everyone around. Ionia was that sort of boy.

The academy curriculum was divided into basic courses and specialized courses. As an officer cadet, Ionia took mainly the required specialized subjects, such as tactics and foreign languages, as well as practical skills like martial arts and swordsmanship.

The classes were so advanced that, at first, he was astounded by the difference in level from the preparatory school and struggled to keep up. But Ionia had faith. There was only one year until Gravis entered the academy. He wanted to learn as much as possible and become stronger before then. He worked himself to the bone in every subject, trained until he collapsed in martial arts and swordsmanship, and held on for dear life even when he got injured.

Ionia was determined to become strong enough to protect Gravis.
With this singular thought in mind, Ionia pressed on.

Eventually, Ionia came to be regarded by those around him as a member of the most talented group in the academy.

One of the people he befriended in that group was Lucas Brandt, who was the same age as him. Ionia had always had a friendly, cheerful personality, but since entering the academy, that cheer had faded. Lucas was the one who came to close the distance between them.

Lucas was the second son of Count Hexter, the head of a family known for its bravery that had produced major figures in the royal army for generations, and he aspired to join the army himself. He was even larger in stature than Ionia, with unruly blond hair like a lion's mane and eyes the color of amber. For some reason, he had taken a liking to Ionia early on and spoke with him often.

One day, Ionia asked Lucas why he had approached him, a commoner. Ridiculously enough, Lucas replied that he liked Ionia's personality *and* his body.

Lucas laughed at Ionia's astonishment and said that he was joking.

He said that since both he and Ionia were bigger than other boys their age, it was easier for them to fight each other in martial arts classes without having to hold back their full strength.

Ionia had one more person he could call a friend.

Marzel Ginter was a year older than Ionia and Lucas. He was a tall, slender boy with ashen hair and blue-gray eyes. Ionia became friends with Marzel through Lucas. As it turned out, the two had been childhood friends. Marzel was from a prestigious family that had produced chancellors for generations, and in defiance of his father's expectations for his future as chancellor, he was a strange boy who took specialized courses for military officers.

When Ionia first entered the academy, he learned of the radical bloodline purists who discriminated against commoners and were obsessed with bloodlines among the nobility. The headmaster was a prime example.

Marzel's own family was also rather adamant about bloodline purity. Marzel himself, however, was different. Despite both being the children of high-ranking aristocrats, he and Lucas were open and friendly with Ionia. A year after enrollment, they had become such close friends that they were comfortable sharing nearly everything with one another.

One day after training, Ionia stayed in the training grounds to show them his Power for the first time.

They gasped at its might.

"Is this why you were admitted into the academy?"

"That's incredible... Ionia, what could you do with it if you really tried?" Lucas asked with a twinkle in his eye.

Ionia opened his palm, dropped the shattered rock, and spread his arms shoulder-width apart. "I think I could probably break a stone this big."

The boys were terribly impressed.

Ionia had not told them the truth.

The truth was that he could crush a rock three times his size. Although it took all his Power to do so and left him feeling faint afterward.

Immediately after entering the academy, Ionia was taken to a quarry where he was tested by soldiers dispatched from the Royal Army to understand the full extent of his ability.

When he pulverized the bedrock that had collapsed from a corner of the quarry just by touching it, his sheer strength made the soldiers wince. Watching them with his vision blurred by the excessive use of his Power, he intuitively understood that his ability was a fearsome one.

That was why he was afraid to tell his best friends about the true potential of his Power.

"It is a truly rare gift. I can see why you were allowed to enter the academy despite being a commoner. As a soldier, you will be a great asset."

"But if I ever have to use it... I'm sure you'll end up despising me."

Their faces stiffened. They were the only people he'd told the reason behind his admission.

Vi would be there soon.

Then Ionia could be by his side again. But protecting Vi with his Power likely meant one day shattering human beings.

Since that day, Ionia had loathed his Power. Even more so when he thought that he was expected to use it to destroy people.

With a pained expression on his face, Lucas hugged Ionia's shoulder tightly in an attempt at comfort. "Even if one day you may end up killing someone in defense of His Highness...I will never despise you."

"Luca..."

Marzel nodded with his hand on Ionia's opposite shoulder.

"That's right, Ionia. Whatever you do, it is an order, not your responsibility."

Their kindness flowed into him from the hands placed on his shoulders. Meeting them had been one of the few joys the academy had granted him.

Lucas took Ionia's sand-covered hand and squeezed it.

"I'll protect His Highness alongside you."

"Lucas..."

"If these hands destroy the bodies of our enemies to protect His Highness... we will... protect you so that your heart may remain in one piece," Lucas vowed.

Marzel squeezed his shoulder. "I will provide all the help I can so that such a necessity never arises. We will always be friends, Ionia, no matter what."

Tears welled in Ionia's violet eyes, and he hugged them tightly.

"Thank you..."

These boys had become important to him in a different way from Gravis.

They would continue to be there for him. No matter what happened, no matter what he did, they would never hate him.

This realization made him feel a little less anxious about the future.

His reunion with Gravis in a year's time was fast approaching.

# Leorino: A Changed Angel

Despite the best efforts of the Marquis of Lagarea, the truth of the Zweilink incident was never discovered.

Tired of being stuck in the past, the Cassieux family decided to move on and put all their efforts into Leorino's recovery.

Leorino's days consisted of a set timetable. He engaged in physical therapy twice a day, once in the morning and once in the afternoon. In between, he received lessons from his tutor and then took a break, during which Maia tended to him for a brief moment. Before bedtime, he had his body massaged by his attendant to relax his stiff muscles and prepare for the following day's exercise.

This monotony continued every day.

Sometimes he felt incredibly helpless, but his family encouraged him every time, occasionally scolding him, as Leorino silently worked on his recovery and studies.

*I must do all I can now.* He told himself this over and over and spent his days enduring the pain and striving to recover.

It took about two years for Leorino's legs to recover to the point where they no longer interfered with his daily life. Little by little, he became able to walk greater distances, and his gait gradually became smoother.

However, the damaged tendons and nerves never fully recovered. Walking long distances was difficult and running practically impossible. After prolonged overuse, the tendons became painful and numb. He would trip over his legs, requiring him to take regular breaks. In addition, he had developed a weak constitution that confined him to his bed if he ever overexerted himself.

Sasha, who came to see him every six months from the royal capital, told him that his leg function had recovered as much as he could hope for and that any further recovery was unlikely.

In the end, Leorino never quite returned to his pre-injury condition. Nevertheless, he was finally able to walk by himself without the aid of a cane.

It had truly been a miracle.

The family wept with pride in their beloved youngest son's accomplishments.

Peaceful days continued in Brungwurt.

However, in the midst of such an uneventful life, Leorino gradually lost his childishness, as if shedding a thin layer of skin. The change was quiet, unnoticed by anyone but his family and servants, who kept him hidden away like a jewel in Brungwurt Castle.

Leorino was no longer a boy, but a young man, and his beauty, which transcended gender and earned him the nickname of "angel," only grew more prominent.

Platinum hair falling just above his shoulders. His rare violet eye color. The smooth curve of his cheeks, which had lost their juvenile roundness. The graceful limbs stretching out from his slender frame and beautifully taut shoulders, combined with his slow movements, created an otherworldly air around him.

At the age of fifteen, Leorino's innocent and sensitive nature remained intact, but he had transformed into an enchanting presence that took away the breath of anyone who saw him.

The change was such that his second and third brothers, who worked in the royal capital, couldn't help gazing at him, captivated for a while whenever they returned home.

One day, as soon as Johan arrived home from the capital, he hugged Leorino, who had come out to greet him. Johan let out a sigh of admiration and nuzzled his cheek against Leorino's soft platinum hair.

"J-Johan, Brother, that hurts..."

"Leorino, I'm so worried about your future. Every time I see you, you become more beautiful."

Leorino laughed at his brother's antics. This always happened whenever his brothers saw him for the first time in a while.

"...If you are this beautiful at fifteen, how beautiful will you be by the time you reach adulthood? Goodness, I'm so, so, *so* worried about you."

"...You don't need to worry about me *that* much. I'd appreciate if you calmed down and let go of me right about now. I'd like to say hello to Gauff as well, all right?"

Leorino's personality had also undergone a change. Perhaps it was the years of enduring pain that were to blame, but he was no longer eager to voice his complaints or concerns.

When Johan reluctantly released Leorino, his third brother, Gauff, immediately embraced him instead. "It's so good to see you, Leorino. I know I say this every time, but you look more beautiful every time I see you."

"Welcome back, Gauff. I don't want to hear any more jokes like Johan's. How's your service in the Imperial Guard?"

"I wasn't joking, but...it's been three years and I've gotten used to it. They decided to appoint me to the Inner Palace Guard soon. I've already reported it to Father."

"That's incredible! Congratulations, Gauff!"

Leorino celebrated his brother's success by giving him a kiss on the cheek. Gauff was ticklish.

"Speaking of congratulations..."

"I know! Auriano," said Leorino with a grin.

"Congratulations, Brother."

"Congratulations!"

Auriano nodded at his brothers' blessings with an unusually bashful look on his face.

Leorino's condition had stabilized, and now Auriano, the eldest son, was to be married.

Brungwurt Castle was filled with excitement for the first happy event in a long time.

# Ionia: Beasts Roaring in the Night 2

The second prince entered the academy of higher learning. The whole academy was buzzing with excitement.

Alongside the other students, Ionia watched from afar as Gravis walked down the hallway to his classroom. Seeing Gravis for the first time in a year, he noticed Gravis had grown a little taller and his face was a little more mature. The headmaster, the same one who had called Ionia a "human shield," was leading the way with a flushed face, talking to Gravis about something. The prince, seemingly uninterested in the headmaster's explanation, simply kept walking.

He had a beautiful, graceful gait; a noble beauty with a hint of immaturity; and a cold look in his eyes that did not match his age. With Gravis next to other children of noble families, it quickly became clear that he was a very special boy. He wore his ambition on his sleeve.

Was the special aura that made people want to bow down to him a product of his royal blood?

*I really didn't see anything back then, did I?*

Now that Ionia thought about it, he had heard rumors in the city of the second prince's starry-sky eyes. Why hadn't he guessed the identity of the boy with such special eyes? He was ashamed of his foolishness at the time.

He had asked himself many times since then what he would have done if he had known Gravis's identity back then. Would he have kept his distance? Or would he have chosen the same path?

They had already made their choices. The small, secret world they had enjoyed together no longer existed.

Still, Ionia couldn't help but wonder.

Ionia could not see the color of the prince's eyes from where he stood. He used to gaze into those starry-sky eyes from so close back then that their foreheads nearly bumped into each other. Now all he saw in them was darkness.

This current distance between them must have been the distance that should have always been there.

He had no intention of approaching him. He knew they would be brought together sooner or later anyway.

Ionia moved out of his parents' house that year and entered a dormitory attached to the academy. Few students used the dormitories, and the twenty or so who did were the children of middle-class nobles from the countryside who did not have residences in the royal capital.

The headmaster had demanded he move into the dorms. From now on, Ionia would spend most of his school life with the second prince as his schoolmate—or rather, serving as his guard.

"Io. We should head to the training grounds."

Standing next to him, Lucas tapped him on the shoulder.

Ionia nodded silently. Noticing Lucas's concerned look, Ionia laughed and insisted he was fine.

At first, Ionia was puzzled by the distance between himself and Lucas, but he had noticed the delicate kindness that was hidden in his seemingly rough, unreserved behavior.

For the past year, Lucas had not asked any questions.

Why was Ionia so desperate to acquire knowledge and skills? Why was he so bruised and battered? And why did he push himself to his limits as if in an act of self-flagellation?

Lucas never asked any of these questions. He was always there for him. He trained as hard as Ionia, until they were both covered in wounds.

This continued even now. Just as Ionia moved into the dorms, so did Lucas. His family had a splendid mansion in the noble district of the royal capital, but Lucas insisted on it, explaining it was easier for him to commute to the academy and the training grounds this way.

Ionia had his mind firmly set on his own problems, but even he was aware of the favor that Lucas had shown him.

Still, Ionia would likely never return his feelings.

The only person Ionia's heart would ever pursue was that noble boy with dark hair.

"Can we go?" Lucas asked.

"Yes… Let's go," Ionia answered.

*…I should be ashamed of myself,* Ionia thought.

He had given his heart to Gravis, and yet somehow he was finding comfort and solace in Lucas. He knew he was taking advantage of his best friend's kindness.

Little by little, the real world diverged from the truth he had held in his heart.

It happened just as Ionia turned on his heel.

"Io!"

When he turned around, the noble boy was standing before him.

"Ionia… I missed you."

Gravis's starry-sky eyes spoke volumes. Their twinkling alone was proof enough of his excitement for their long-awaited reunion.

"It's a pleasure to see you again, Your Highness Prince Gravis."

As soon as he heard Ionia's reply, Gravis's eyes grew dark.

He realized that Ionia had drawn the line between them at that very moment.

"You heard I was coming?"

"Yes. I have been looking forward to meeting you."

That wasn't a lie.

Ionia still remembered the promise. He had been dying to see Gravis again. He just hadn't intended for it to be like this.

"Ionia, I need to talk to you. I'm—"

"Congratulations on your enrollment, Your Highness Prince Gravis."

Lucas stepped in front of Ionia.

Gravis looked up at the boy who had suddenly interrupted him. His face was familiar.

"...I believe you are the second son of Count Hexter."

"I am honored that you remember me. I am Lucas Brandt, second son of Nicolas Brandt, the Count of Hexter."

Gravis did not hide his irritation at the boy who had interrupted his reunion with Ionia.

"...I'm speaking to Ionia right now."

"Oh, my apologies. But it's almost time for class to start."

Ionia looked up at his friend in shock.

"Mr. Brandt, is that any way to speak to His Highness?" said an approaching gentleman.

Lucas, in his indignation, offered the headmaster a stern rebuttal.

"You have always said it yourself, sir. Learning should be everyone's priority here. Why single us out? Isn't it time for all the students who have been watching His Highness from afar to focus on their student duties?"

"What? No, that's..."

"As you can see, Your Highness, I hate to interrupt, but Mr. Bergund and I are on our way to the training grounds now, so please excuse us."

Ionia was on edge as he watched the scene play out.

Why was Lucas, supposedly trained in strict etiquette as the son of a noble, being so belligerent toward Gravis, a member of the royal family?

Lucas placed his hand on Ionia's shoulder and looked back at the younger prince as if to provoke him further.

"...Get your hands off him."

Ionia stared wordlessly at the two as they glared at each other.

Then a slender boy quickly approached Gravis from behind.

Gravis was sensitive to the presence of others, and yet he allowed the boy to come up from behind him. Who was he?

"Your Highness, Lucas is right. We should be moving on."

The boy chided him, and Gravis released a small sigh. He nodded toward the boy. His face had returned to his usual cold, haughty expression.

"I understand. Let's go, Theodor... Ionia, I want to have a proper talk with you at some point."

"...Yes, sir."

Gravis nodded toward Ionia, then quickly turned on his heel and left.

Ionia was finally reunited with the boy he had missed so fiercely for so long.

He had dreamed many times about how Gravis would react when the time finally came and how he would respond in turn.

However, he would have never imagined their reunion would end with the intervention of his best friend.

Ionia could not help but question his friend. "...Luca, why did you do that?"

"Do what?"

"You know what you did. Your attitude toward His Highness... You have to know how insolent that was."

Lucas put on his usual facade of fierceness.

"Oh, are you concerned for me? Or perhaps..."

Ionia was offended.

"Of course I'm concerned for you!"

Hearing this, Lucas smiled, clearly pleased.

When Ionia glared at him as if to ask what he was smiling at, Lucas held up his hands in a playful manner.

"That was my best attempt at diversion... But of course, he's royalty. If looks could kill, I'd be dead the moment I put my hand on your shoulder."

"Diversion…? Why the hell would I need you to stage a diversion against Vi?"

When he realized he'd called Gravis by his nickname in his excitement, Ionia clamped his mouth shut.

"'Vi'…? So you did know His Highness? Where on earth did you meet?"

Ionia remained silent, and Lucas scoffed. "Huh, I see how it is. I guess I'll learn soon enough. I'm not going to ask you anything until you're ready to tell me. How's that sound?"

Lucas had provided him yet another escape route from the conversation. Ionia looked at his best friend with mixed feelings.

"…Lucas."

"Let's go, Io. They'll give us extra practice for being late. Let's run."

With a push on his back, Ionia ran toward the training grounds.

Ionia returned to his room after class and training and immediately collapsed onto his bed. With a sleepy, foggy mind, he ruminated on the day's events.

Back then, Ionia could only watch as his friends stared each other down with him in between them.

"…Why would Luca…?"

He remembered his best friend's inexplicable behavior. He mumbled his name without much thought.

"Won't you call my name, too? Io."

He jerked up at the voice.

"…What?"

Someone was standing by the window, blocking the moonlight.

"…Vi? How did you get here?"

Hadn't he returned to the royal palace? How had he appeared in his room? Ionia was confused. Gravis approached the bed and smoothly sat down next to him. Ionia rushed to fix up his room.

"…You didn't come here alone, did you? Where's your guard?"

"I'm fine."

"How are you fine…? Oh, I'm sorry."

He had forgotten about being polite. The prince looked disappointed at seeing Ionia rushing to apologize to him.

Now that he knew that Gravis was royalty, Ionia wasn't sure how to behave.

Ionia was about to get up, thinking that sitting next to him on the bed was inappropriate, when the prince said: "Ionia, I missed you…"

Gravis extended his fingers to Ionia's cheek. His slightly trembling fingers touched the hairs on his cheek. Ionia's heart, which had been stiffened by confusion and anxiety, finally relaxed.

"Your Highness…"

"Call me 'Vi,' like you did back then."

"B-but…"

"Why not? We're alone now."

There was no one here to accuse him of disrespect.

Ionia listened to his heart and gently placed his own hand in Gravis's palm. It was warm.

*Ah, it's Vi. It's really him…!*

Ionia squeezed his hand tightly.

Gravis squeezed back with the same force. The warmth of their bodies made them realize that they were reunited at the same time. They shivered with joy.

"Vi… I missed you, too. I was lonely without you."

"I'm sorry about today. I shouldn't have approached you back there, but I found you and…forgot myself."

Ionia was so happy to hear those words.

"Ha-ha… I know you said you wanted to talk, but I didn't expect it to be tonight."

"The headmaster told you I have a gift… This is my Power."

Ionia tilted his head, not understanding what Gravis meant. The next moment, Ionia's body on the bed seemed to sway limply, and the prince who was sitting next to him disappeared.

"…What?"

"I'm right here."

Gravis was standing by the window.

"I can instantly leap wherever I want. That's my gift. Not only myself, I can also take people and objects with me, as long as I'm touching them."

Ionia was truly surprised.

He thought his own abilities were unusual, but Gravis's abilities were truly extraordinary.

"Does all royalty have such gifts?"

"So you've heard. Many members of the royal family have Powers. But the abilities they possess vary widely."

With this Power, Gravis would hardly ever feel his life was in danger.

Ionia came up with an idea.

"If I touch you, will I leap with you?"

"Yes."

Ionia finally understood.

So that was why the headmaster had said "*his ability becomes meaningless if his body is touched.*"

Ionia looked at Gravis, who sat down next to him once more.

He looked a little more mature than he did a year ago. And his eyes were even darker and sadder than they had been back then.

Ionia reached out and squeezed his hand with both of his, just as he had done in the past.

"Vi...you're making that face again. What's wrong? What happened to you over the past year?"

Gravis's face scrunched up.

His expression looked so different from the princely, emotionally stifled one he wore during the day.

Ionia brushed his fingers across the boy's cheek.

Gravis reacted with a twitch, and the corners of his eyes softened a little as he smiled.

That smile. That's what Ionia had wanted to see this entire time.

He felt as if Gravis was giving him and only him a glimpse into the folds of his heart, and it made Ionia's chest feel full, heartrending, and ticklish all the same.

"Thank you for inviting me to the academy, Vi. I never thought I'd be able to attend a school like this... Thanks to you, I'll be by your side for a long time to come."

Ionia smiled sincerely for the first time in a long time.

"Ionia... I just wanted to be with you."

"I know."

"I heard of the terrible things the headmaster told you, of how much pressure he put you under... I didn't mean that for you. I just wanted to learn here with you... I didn't know about your Power."

"I know, Vi. I know."

"You don't need to protect me."

Ionia no longer hesitated and pulled Gravis to him as he had done in the past. He patted Gravis on the back in hopes of soothing him. *Oh, the size difference between us has mostly disappeared*, he distantly thought.

The black hair brushed against Ionia's shoulder.

"I want to be with you always. You're the first person I've ever felt that way about... That's all there was to it. I didn't realize what having you by my side would mean for you. I didn't understand anything at all."

So Gravis really had called him here because he genuinely wanted him by his side. Just knowing that was enough for Ionia.

"I know your position is difficult; the headmaster told me. This is the path I've chosen, so don't worry about me, Vi."

"I can't bear the thought that you might get hurt if you stay with me. But if this is my only chance to spend time with you, I don't want to give it up, either."

Ionia was glad to hear Gravis say that.

"...Do you hate me now?"

"No, silly... Of course not. You promised me. I'm happy to see you again... I'm so happy."

There was Ionia's answer to the question he asked himself earlier in the day.

Just being so close that he could feel the warmth of his body made Ionia feel like a fool for worrying so much for the past year. Even if he had to be Gravis's human shield for them to be together, he was certain that always and forever he would make the same choice again, as many times as it took.

Once he realized this, Ionia's doubts vanished.

"Io... I can't bear to see you get hurt because of me."

He hugged Gravis's shoulder.

"I'll be fine. Nothing will happen to me."

"Io..."

"We'll be together from now on. So it's going to be all right... We'll be all right."

Ionia would say it as many times as it took.


For a while after that, peaceful school life continued, just as Ionia had predicted.

The academy was initially astir due to the appearance of a member of the royal family, but it gradually calmed down, and Gravis's school life began in earnest. Although he did not flaunt his status and tried to blend in with his surroundings, in reality it was difficult for him to be treated as a normal student.

The second prince was rumored to have surpassed the first prince in genius from an early age. The prince had already mastered not only the Frankish language of his mother's country of origin but also the languages of the neighboring great nations. He also had a complete knowledge of the history, politics, and economics of each country.

His vast knowledge was due to the fact that his family had invited people who had held important offices in various countries as his teachers, and he had been taught in the languages of each country from his childhood to the present. In other words, he had received the same education as the royalty from five different countries on a daily basis for as long as he could remember.

When Ionia learned of this, he should have admired him, but he felt sorry for Gravis, wondering what a hard and limited life he had led. As a boy, he had been denied children's games and laughter and was expected to be perfect as a member of royalty. He may have been a prince, but he would have been an ordinary child at heart.

Where was the love of his father, the king, and his mother, the queen, for Gravis?

His life seemed unimaginably lonely to Ionia, having been raised by loving parents.

Gravis and Ionia were once again sitting next to each other on the bed in Ionia's dorm room. Gravis would return to the palace and later secretly visit Ionia's room before bedtime. Their secret encounters had become a part of their daily routine.

"Why did you decide to go to school after all this time? Isn't it too boring for you?"

There was no point for Gravis to attend school in terms of acquiring knowledge. He had been under the tutelage of his personal adviser, General Stolf, for the past few years and was already informally attending meetings discussing the defense of the country. His knowledge far surpassed that of his teachers, and all that he was missing was experience and practical combat. Few teachers could satisfy Gravis's appetite for learning.

Under such circumstances, Ionia didn't understand the point of this genius attending school for six years, mixing with ordinary people.

Wasn't it a waste of time? When Ionia asked this question, Gravis immediately showed his displeasure.

"There's a point to this. For me, this is a very meaningful time."

"Really? All you need are lessons in martial arts and practical science."

"No, that's not... You know what I mean."

Ionia brought his face closer.

Gravis didn't want him to see the expression on his face, so he turned his head away.

"Spending time with you like this...means a lot to me."

"...Oh."

Gravis sulkily cast his eyes down.

"Unless you go to school, there's no way you and I can spend time together when I live in the royal palace."

The prince's passionate confession made Ionia's heart flutter. Why did he feel happy but also a little tickled and embarrassed?

"I was going through a lot back then... I was fed up with the palace, and Stolf took me away from it as a distraction. He took me to your father's workshop. And there you were, and you—you..."

"I didn't realize you were a prince and badgered you to be friends with me."
Gravis smiled.

"I was surprised at the time, and at first I thought how incredibly rude that was of you. No one had ever asked me that before. To be friends, I mean."

"...I mean, your eyes were so sparkly, I just couldn't help myself..."

"It made me happy to know that you wanted to be my friend, even though you didn't know me."

"You're making me sound like a complete airhead."

Seeing Ionia's frown, Gravis smiled again.

"I was happy. You were the first person to treat me like a normal human being. So...that made me happy."

"Vi... I didn't mean it that way."

"I know. That's just the impression I got. That's why I wanted to be with you. For the first time ever, I decided to be selfish and say that if I had to go to school, I really wanted it to be with you."

Ionia's chest felt so tight that he could not speak. He wondered if Gravis's life had been so lonely that an encounter with a commoner child was the only solace he could find.

"Our six-year stay here is the only time I'll be able to spend with you without needing to worry about anything else."

Gravis's starry-sky eyes shone brightly.

"And in those six years, I'm going to do something to put out the sparks of mayhem."

"...'Sparks of mayhem'?"

"I'm talking about myself."

"Vi...what does that mean?"

Gravis didn't answer, only shook his head,

"My presence will bring chaos to this country. These six years...will buy me time to fix it without hurting anyone."

Gravis and Ionia always moved together. Then Lucas, Marzel, and Gravis's valet joined them, and before they knew it, the five of them were spending time together more often than not. Surprisingly, Gravis and Lucas somehow came to seem to be on the same page. Sometimes they were like children competing for a best friend, with Ionia stuck in between, and at other times they fought with a strange hostility toward each other.

They were perfect opposites in both appearance and the impression they gave off. Gravis, with his black hair and starry-sky eyes, was reminiscent of the deepest night. Lucas, on the other hand, had blond hair and amber eyes like the sun. Similar to their appearances, their personalities were also polar opposites. Gravis was ascetic and calm, while Lucas was bold and bighearted.

Ionia thought they would get along well, but when he told them as much, they both frowned at him, which never failed to make him laugh.

Gravis's valet, whose name was Theodor Anhalt, was the second son of Count Moreau.

He was two years older than Gravis, and since Theodor's mother was a former lady-in-waiting of the queen, he was selected as a candidate for the position of valet after he was seen getting along well with Gravis at a young age.

All this information was obtained and shared with Ionia by Marzel. Marzel was the grandson of the former chancellor and had such a brilliant mind that it was a shame that he was aiming to become a military officer. Ionia was always grateful to have a good friend who was familiar with the affairs of the royal court.

At first, Theodor tried to exclude Ionia because of his being a commoner, but when he eventually learned that Ionia possessed an ability capable of protecting Gravis, he reluctantly allowed him to stay by his master's side. Compared to the school headmaster, who was a radical bloodline purist, Theodor's brusque attitude seemed cute at best. Ionia himself could not be bothered by the fact that a boy thinner than him held some ignorant opinions on the status of his birth.

School life had mostly been peaceful. However, one phrase remained in the back of Ionia's mind the entire time. Gravis had called himself a "spark of mayhem" that one night. Ionia was a commoner. He knew little of the royal family's affairs. He felt there was a major problem lurking behind the apparent peace and quiet, so he decided to voice his concerns to Marzel.

He invited Marzel to his dormitory and took him to his room after having dinner together. For some reason, Lucas invited himself over, which made the small room even more cramped. Lucas and Ionia sat on the bed, while Marzel sat in the chair by the desk.

"I see... His Highness has referred to himself in that way... That's a shame."

"I'm sorry, Marzel. I don't know why Vi said that."

Marzel sighed. "I'm not entirely certain I understand the full picture, either... But perhaps that statement of His Highness Prince Gravis concerns the issue of the succession to the throne."

"Succession to the throne...? But the crown prince is first in line for the throne, isn't he?"

"He is. His Royal Highness Crown Prince Joachim is ten years older than Gravis. The year before last, he married Princess Emilia from Francoure, and last year Prince Kyle was born."

"I know that much..."

"According to the royal law of Fanoren, concubines also count as official wives. The first prince, His Highness Prince Joachim, is the crown prince, according to the custom of firstborn inheritance, but...the issue is that His Highness Prince Gravis is a far better choice. Apart from that, there is the difference in status between the mothers of the two princes."

"Large enough to make the bloodline purists squawk."

Lucas was the son of a nobleman, and he quickly understood what Marzel was implying. But Ionia, a commoner, still did not see the problem.

"Crown Prince Joachim is the child of Lady Brigitte... Ionia, you know this much, correct? She is the concubine who died the year before last."

Ionia nodded. He remembered well that the news of the concubine's death came just around the time when Gravis could no longer visit the blacksmith shop.

"Lady Brigitte married into the royal family as a concubine under the Lagarea name, but she was originally a distant relative of the marquis. Since she was too lowborn to marry into the king's family, she was adopted by her relatives in the marquis's family and became a concubine from there."

Ionia was surprised. The idea that one could resort to adoption in order to match one's status with that of royalty would have never occurred to a commoner like him.

"On the other hand, Queen Adele is the mother of Prince Gravis, the first princess of the Kingdom of Francoure, and a full-fledged queen. Queen Adele's grandmother was a princess, the sister of the king of our country two generations back. In terms of maternal lineage, His Highness Prince Gravis has by far the highest status in the country."

Ionia fell silent. Now that he was surrounded by nobles, he could imagine how the differences in the status of the mothers of the two princes had caused friction in the royal court.

Marzel continued with a frown.

"It all took place before I was born, so I don't know the whole story, but... I'll stick to the facts: Queen Adele and Lady Brigitte were introduced to King George as his wife and concubine only half a year apart from each other. Apparently, the Kingdom of Francoure, where Queen Adele came from, was outraged that the princess was being neglected... What's worse, Lady Brigitte became pregnant soon after she was brought into the palace and gave birth to the crown prince. On the other hand, Queen Adele finally gave birth to Gravis eleven years after she had married into the family... That alone should tell you which of the two was favored by His Majesty the king. In other words, that long-standing friction finally came to a head because of His Highness's brilliance."

Ionia did not understand.

"Ionia, what do you know of the crown prince, Joachim?" Lucas asked Ionia in a bitter tone.

Come to think of it, even back in the city, Ionia had hardly heard of the crown prince, Joachim. That hadn't changed in the academy.

"What does it matter?"

"...Marzel, you get it, don't you?"

Marzel seemed to know what Lucas meant. He nodded grimly.

"The crown prince, Joachim, is a mild-mannered man with a gentle disposition. Under normal circumstances, he might have been a suitable choice for king."

"So what's wrong with the crown prince?"

"Can't you tell? ...You've been watching His Highness Prince Gravis's fearsome brilliance up close and personal."

The crown prince had no reputation worth mentioning. The second prince was too conspicuous in comparison.

"The issue is that His Highness Prince Gravis is a natural fit to be a king."

Was it that Gravis's brilliance overshadowed the crown prince, Joachim?

"There is a ten-year age difference between them..."

Marzel shook his head. "Do you think age has anything to do with the qualities of a king?"

"I..."

Marzel sighed. "Frankly, His Highness is *too* exceptional, to the point that the virtuous crown prince, Joachim, who's no fool, either, appears mediocre. Those who have seen the two up close at the royal palace would feel that way all the more. Some of them are all too happy to fuss over the difference in their mothers' statuses to boot."

Ionia recalled the headmaster. Suddenly everything made sense.

"There are many who want His Highness Prince Gravis to be king, even if it means rejecting the tradition of firstborn inheritance. Especially among the high nobility in our country, there are many bloodline purists... Incidentally, my grandfather, the former chancellor, is one of them."

Wearing a sad expression, Lucas nodded in agreement with Marzel's words.

"As a person who could threaten the position of the crown prince, His Royal Highness Prince Gravis considers himself a 'spark of mayhem'? That's a shame... His Highness probably doesn't even want the throne for himself."

Gravis was saying that he should have never been born.

A spark of mayhem—Ionia's chest felt tight at the immense sadness hidden beneath those words.

# Leorino: Eldest Brother's Betrothal

Auriano's fiancée was Erina Munster, the eldest daughter of the Duke of Leben. Auriano had been putting off the question of his own marriage for some time, partly because of Leorino's injury. But now that his youngest brother's health had improved, the time had come to seriously consider marriage. At a soiree in the royal capital, which he attended in the name of his father, August, he was introduced to Erina by the Marquis of Lagarea.

That was where they first met.

The Duke of Leben had also been searching for a marriage partner for his eldest daughter, who had just reached the appropriate age. The duchess asked her brother, the Marquis of Lagarea, for advice, hoping that he, as secretary of the Interior, would be able to introduce her to someone suitable. As a result, Auriano, the heir to the Margrave of Brungwurt, was selected as the most suitable partner from a status standpoint, despite being slightly older.

Both Auriano and Erina were children of the highest-ranking noble families in Fanoren, and matching family status was seen as an important aspect of marriage. If no suitable partner could be found within the country, they would have to look for one among the leading aristocrats abroad. However, the Cassieux family, which ruled over Brungwurt, would inevitably struggle to establish relationships with foreign nobles due to Brungwurt's geographical location.

The two were brought together for political reasons, but they slowly developed a liking for each other as they met a fair number of times and confirmed their compatibility. Six months after their meeting, Auriano formally asked Erina to marry him.

The procedure for a nobleman's engagement began with the king's approval. The betrothal ceremony usually took place at the groom's estate. However, since Erina was a princess of the highest-ranking ducal family, the engagement ceremony was to take place first at the groom's estate in Brungwurt and then a second time at the estate of the Duke of Leben.

Auriano's fiancée came to Brungwurt the month after the annual memorial service, accompanied by her mother, the duchess, and her brother, who was serving as the duke's representative.

"Lady Erina, welcome to Brungwurt. We have been expecting you."

Auriano stepped forward to greet his fiancée and pressed his lips to her hand.

Erina was a dignified woman with flaxen hair and gorgeous hazel eyes. She may not have been the most beautiful woman in the land, but her intelligence was plain on her face, and she and Auriano appeared to be a perfect match. Although she was eight years younger than Auriano, she was the eldest daughter of a duke and had a calmness about her that one would not expect from a nineteen-year-old woman.

Erina may have been nervous, but she seemed relieved to see her fiancé's gentle smile, which belied his rugged appearance.

"Thank you, Lord Auriano. It is my first time visiting Brungwurt, and I am very pleased to behold such a beautiful place."

Maia welcomed the bride and her family, her cheeks flushed with the excitement of her eldest son's engagement. "You've come a very long way to meet us. Lady Erina, Madame Hannah, Lord Julian, welcome to Brungwurt."

Erina looked nervous in front of her future mother-in-law, but Maia seemed pleased with her perfectly disciplined curtsy, fitting for a lady of her standing. Maia welcomed the addition of another woman to the family.

Erina's brother, Julian, who accompanied her this time as the representative of the Duke of Leben, also returned Maia's courtesy with a graceful bow.

His hair and eye color were similar to that of his sister, but she had a more subdued atmosphere, while he was a surprisingly gorgeous young man.

Hannah, the Duchess of Leben, who had also been there for Maia, was beaming with joy at the news of her eldest daughter's betrothal. She hurriedly approached Maia and took her hand in hers.

"Maia, my daughter and your eldest son are a truly delightful match!"

Maia, the daughter of the Duke of Wiesen, and Hannah, the daughter of the Marquis of Lagarea, were close friends when they were girls. Maia, the noblest of the noble children at the time, was the object of Hannah's admiration. Even now, standing in front of Maia, Hannah was filled with a sense of excitement, remembering the longing she felt when she was a girl.

"I really have to thank Bruno. I never thought Auriano would find himself such a lovely princess," August joked, and Erina's cheeks flushed with embarrassment.

Auriano gazed at her with kind eyes.

The Duchess of Leben smiled at the intimate moment between the couple.

"Erina was very lucky that such a wonderful man like Lord Auriano was still unmarried at his age."

"Mother, you are being rude." Julian forced a smile, chiding his mother. The duchess, realizing her gaffe, put her fan to her mouth.

Auriano nodded with understanding.

For the sake of his eldest son's honor, it was August who responded. "As you must have already heard, my youngest son was seriously injured in an accident four years ago. Auriano had refrained from discussing marriage until his brother had regained his health."

Julian nodded. He seemed to already know the details.

"My uncle told us that Lord Leorino was very badly wounded."

"He is now mostly in good health. He will greet you later."

"I am glad to hear that he is doing better. How old is your brother now?"

August answered Julian's question with a sour expression on his face. "He recently turned sixteen. Since the Munster family will be joining ours, I will not conceal the fact that...my youngest son is a bit out of the ordinary. I hope you can rein in your surprise when you meet him."

The three members of the Munster family looked at one another.

Most of the nobles had never met or even seen the youngest son of the Cassieux family. All they knew was that he had been unable to attend higher education because of a serious injury and had lived in the castle all his life. They wondered if he had withdrawn from the public eye due to the severity of his injuries—or if his mental health had taken a steep decline.

When Erina somewhat anxiously questioned her fiancé with her eyes, her future husband responded with a solemn nod. She did not know how to interpret that nod.

Just as the guests' dread grew even greater, a knock sounded in the room.

"Ah, our youngest son has arrived!" Maia sounded cheerful. Erina and her family were nervous, wondering what sort of person they were about to meet.

The next moment, the three of them froze with their mouths open.

Standing there was a beautiful boy who seemed to emit a soft, faint glow.

"I apologize for the delay."

Auriano quickly approached his brother.

"Are you all right?"

"I'm fine, thank you."

Erina and the others stood dumbfounded at the sight of the boy smiling at his brother.

The word *beautiful* could not accurately describe the boy's features, and *angelic* seemed far closer to the truth. As he approached with slow steps, the boy greeted them in a low, sweet, husky voice. "It is a pleasure to finally make your acquaintance. I am Leorino, the fourth son of August Cassieux. I bid you welcome to Brungwurt, Lady Erina, Madame Hannah, Lord Julian."

The three of them were frozen stiff, unable to reply.

"...I knew it would come to this... Auriano." August sighed and waved his hand toward his son. Auriano also heaved a breath.

First, he gently tapped his fiancée on the shoulder, urging her to remember herself. "Lady Erina, this is my youngest brother, Leorino. He has just introduced himself, my lady."

Her fiancée's words jolted Erina back to her senses. "I-I'm so sorry..."

She knew she must greet him, but as soon as her eyes met those of the young man who stood there quietly with that beautiful smile of his, Erina was rendered speechless once more.

August had been right. His son was many things, but ordinary was...certainly not one of them.

The angel tilted his head uneasily.

Seeing this, Erina, with the dignity of a daughter of a duchess, took a deep bow toward her future brother-in-law.

"I—I am Erina Munster. Lord Leorino, i-it's a pleasure to meet you."

Her voice trembled, even though there should have been nothing nerve-racking about the encounter.

"Lady Erina—no, may I call you 'Sister'? Please think of me as your brother and simply call me 'Leorino.'"

"M-my brother..."

When he replied with a sincere smile, Erina nearly collapsed.

Auriano rushed to support his fiancée.

Leorino looked up at his brother as if to ask if there was anything rude in his greeting. Auriano looked at Leorino with a strangely disappointed look on his face.

Later, the Duchess of Leben staggered so hard they thought she might faint, and Julian looked feverish the entire time, gazing at Leorino's beauty in a state of euphoria.

# Ionia: Beasts Roaring in the Night 3

"Ionia."

He was about to return to his room when he heard his name, and he turned around to see Lucas sticking his head out of his room and beckoning Ionia to him.

"Come here for a moment."

Ionia inclined his head and headed into Lucas's room.

"What? What's wrong...? Whoa."

As soon as he entered the room, Lucas tossed him the package he had been holding. Ionia caught it with both hands and blinked.

"...What's this?"

"A present. Isn't it your birthday today?"

Ionia's eyes widened in surprise. It was true; he had turned sixteen that day.

It had been five years since he entered the academy of higher learning. His best friend had grown ever stronger since they first met, achieving the physique of a grown man. Lucas had the muscular body of a warrior, which no ordinary adult male could compete with.

Ionia was no different.

Over the past four years, he had shed the shell of a boy, both physically and mentally. He was half a head shorter than Lucas, but still plenty tall. His well-trained limbs were firm, supple, and toned with utilitarian muscle. The innocent light in his violet eyes had disappeared, and instead he had become a young man with a secretive, watchful look in his eyes.

Now, however, Ionia tilted his head at his best friend's sudden gift. Lucas laughed at the unexpectedly endearing expression on Ionia's face.

"...Thank you. What is it?"

"A pair of gloves. I saw your gloves during swordsmanship training, and they were frayed and almost torn at the thumb."

"Thank you... But until last year, you always took me out on the town and bought me drinks and...all that stuff. What changed this year?"

"You didn't like last year's present, so I decided to give you something tangible this time."

Lucas smiled wickedly as he recalled the incident on Ionia's birthday last year. Ionia prickled at the memory.

Last year, Lucas took him out on the town to celebrate his birthday. But after a night of fun, he took him to a brothel to unburden him of his virginity. When they stepped into the red-light district, Lucas did not look fifteen years old but rather like a man who was used to the company of women.

Ionia desperately resisted the invitation.

He was far from pleased, instead stubbornly shaking his head in discomfort. Understanding that Ionia was firmly against it, Lucas let him go and apologized.

"I'm sorry I forced you to go with me. You didn't seem to be expelling your demons at all, so I thought you'd enjoy it."

Ionia was indignant at Lucas's shameless words.

"That's none of your business! Besides...I don't need that kind of thing, not yet."

"Why? Aren't you interested in sex? You must be really pent up."

It was true that these days, he felt a heavy pent-up sensation in his abdomen, and he took himself in hand to release it. But he had never felt the urge to experience that sort of release with anyone else. His body had grown, but his interest in love and sex was something Ionia had stored away and left behind entirely at some point.

Since the age of eleven, there was only enough space for one person in his heart.

\* \* \*

Was there something wrong with him? As Ionia pondered this, Lucas said something he hadn't even considered.

"Even your beloved Prince Gravis is doing it. Surely he must be."

Ionia was blindsided.

"H-how could he?! Vi is only thirteen years old."

"What do you mean, 'how'? You know exactly how. Royalty marries young. And you've seen his body. He has to deal with his urges somehow. He must have begun his bedchamber education by now."

Ionia felt as if he had been hit over the head.

Marriage. The bedchamber education for marriage.

He had never truly thought about it, but it was true that members of the royal family married early. Prince Joachim, Gravis's elder brother, was betrothed to a princess from a neighboring country at the age of seventeen, married at eighteen, and became the father of Prince Kyle the following year.

But it never occurred to him that the same could be true for Gravis.

Gravis was still slimmer than both Ionia and Lucas, partly because of the three-year age difference, but he was still far better built than the average boy of his age. He would likely soon develop a thicker torso and become as physically fit as Lucas. Combined with his dignity and composure, he appeared at first glance to be about sixteen or seventeen years old.

But this was Gravis, who had always erected a transparent wall around him. It was hard to believe that he would be doing such things for the sake of physical gratification. Even when they were alone, they never talked about anything even vaguely sexual.

"But...he comes to me almost every night. He couldn't possibly be doing that..."

Lucas's eyes flashed darkly.

"Every night? He comes to you every night...? Oh, of course. He uses his Power... So *you're* helping His Highness in that area?"

"N-no, you idiot...! I would never do such a thing! Vi and I, we're...we're not like that!"

"What, then, is His Highness, who must be extremely busy with his studies and official duties, coming to your room every night for?"

"What for...? He just comes to see me, we talk, and then he goes home!"

Lucas snorted in exasperation.

"Oh, so you're just playing house, then? You meet, you talk, he leaves... and you expect me to believe that?"

"What? It's not like I can just go and see him myself..."

Ionia couldn't understand why Lucas was so upset.

Now that he thought about it, students their age would talk about losing their virginity and finding partners, which was certainly a risqué topic of conversation. However, he had never imagined that he himself would one day have a partner or that Gravis would get married.

Why had he never thought about it before?

The only time Gravis and Ionia could be on equal footing was during the brief moments when they were alone together in Ionia's dorm room.

But how long could that last?

In the real world, he had been spending time with Gravis as his guard and schoolmate for three years now. Outside of their safe haven, time had been passing, and both Ionia and Gravis had begun climbing the ladder to adulthood. So why did they think that the pure, childlike friendship they had when they first met would last forever?

In truth, perhaps they were afraid of revealing the feelings that lay deep in each other's hearts. Perhaps they had both unconsciously swept these feelings under the rug, afraid of the future they might lead to.

"...Lucas?"

Ionia noticed that Lucas had gotten closer while he was lost in his train of thought.

"Ionia..."

Lucas's large frame blocked the light and darkened his vision. Ionia's heart was beating faster now.

He backed away, frightened by the look on Lucas's face as Lucas stared at him from up close, as if he were holding himself back.

Ionia's back hit the door, making it impossible for him to retreat any farther.

He couldn't allow Lucas to close the remaining distance between them.

Ionia forced himself to look away. Shifting his body, he turned his back to Lucas.

"...I'm going back to my room now. Thank you for the gift."

He thanked him and placed his hand on the door. A large palm covered his hand.

As Ionia shivered at the hot touch, Lucas put his lips to his ear.

Ionia shuddered.

"Ionia...you need to accept reality. You have to grow up."

"...Wh-what are you talking about?"

"I've been watching you for a long time. I know... I know that you want to be the same person you were when you first met His Highness. So that your relationship may continue... You wish that you could freeze time to keep things as they were..."

Ionia began to tremble, and Lucas gently placed his lips on his neck.

"...No matter how childish your mind may be, no matter how much you ignore your physical desires, you've already changed. See..."

Ionia was stunned by the hot sensation spreading across his neck.

"Ah... Luca, stop!"

He reflexively bent his spine as hard as he could, resisting the initial urge. Ionia was caught by Lucas's left hand, which held his own, and his right hand, which Lucas had placed on the door next to Ionia's head. Lucas's lips gently caressed the exposed, defenseless nape of his neck.

He didn't know how they'd ended up in this situation, but Ionia was at the mercy of his own desire and could not escape Lucas's passion.

"It's not only you. His Highness is changing, too. We're growing up, all of us."

With that, Lucas's large palm squeezed Ionia's groin, which was giving off a faint heat.

Burning arousal surged up from Ionia's abdomen.

"No... Stop... Ah!"

Ionia let out a small cry. Lucas rubbed him as if he hadn't heard him.

"I love you...Ionia. I love you."

"...Ah... Ah... Ungh!"

Lucas only made the heat worse.

Ionia's flesh, caressed by someone else's hand for the first time, abandoned his mind in its arousal.

"...Ah... Ahn!"

He let out a cry of ecstasy.


Lucas undid the front of Ionia's pants, pushed aside his underwear, and took the length of him in hand. Ionia was already hard.

Lewd sounds filled his ears.

"Stop... Please... Luca, stop!"

"This is what you want..."

"Ah... I don't... Ugh."

He collapsed against the door, and Lucas followed. Ionia's supple hips were moving involuntarily, relishing the pleasure. Lucas was further tantalized by the crevice of Ionia's behind peeking out from his lowered underwear.


"Ahhh... En...ough..."

"Io, Ionia... Choose me, Ionia...! I don't want to see you get hurt."

Ionia was nearing his limit.

Lurid sounds and ragged breathing echoed around the room.


"The feelings that you and His Highness have for each other shouldn't be nurtured any further... You know that. That's why you desperately cling to your innocent childhood friendship."

"Shut up...! I don't want to hear it..."


Dropping his gaze, Ionia could see his slick, swollen manhood delighting in the man's caresses.

"Choose me, Ionia...! I can always be by your side... Just—"

Ionia arched his back as he climaxed.

He saw a flash behind his eyes.

White spilled from between Lucas's fingertips as Lucas gave him one last tight squeeze.

The passion left like a receding wave.

Ionia's forehead hit the door, his breathing shallow. The sound echoed loudly in the otherwise quiet room. He slammed his forehead against the door again and again. If he hadn't, he would have screamed instead. How could he have let this happen? Was this who he really was? Was he really just a wretched slave to pleasure?

He could hardly believe how good it had felt.

Lucas, suddenly filled with regret, let go of his body.

"I'm sorry… I know it's too late for excuses, but I didn't mean for things to go this far."

Ionia's stiff body relaxed. He turned around, leaned his back against the door, and held his head in his hands. Hanging his head, he choked back tears at his own loathsome weakness.

He had no right to cry.

How could he when Lucas's hand had felt so good?

Ionia's answer to Lucas's feelings was thick, white desire. His lust had tainted the love that Lucas had always hidden behind jokes.

Lucas pulled out a handkerchief and wiped his soiled hands. He approached Ionia with a fresh piece of cloth. Ionia gazed at him with stunned, somewhat vacant eyes. With a gentle hand, Lucas quickly wiped the filth from Ionia's abdomen and clothes. He even went out of his way to fix the disheveled garments on his legs.

Ionia silently accepted the act as a sort of apology. He had also run out of energy to resist.

All traces of desire had been wiped away. But he would never be innocent again.

"…Lucas. It's my fault."

Lucas looked hurt by these words.

How much had he inadvertently toyed with his best friend's feelings until now, even though Lucas had always been there for him and never asked anything of him?

*"If these hands destroy the bodies of our enemies to protect His Highness... we will...protect you so that your heart may remain in one piece."*

Lucas had vowed that to him. He had always been there for him. Ionia was the one who had unwittingly exploited that pure love, which asked for nothing in return. He could never give his heart to Lucas, but he always used Lucas's kindness as an escape, a comfort to help him forget the painful reality.

"...I didn't want to do this with you."

Lucas shuddered at the words, his lips quivering with pain.

"I love you, Ionia. I've always loved you, even though I knew your heart belongs to His Highness."

"...I've known for a while now... I'm sorry, Luca."

Lucas hung his head at Ionia's answer.

"I wanted to treat you right... I know I don't have the right to say that now, but... I still love you."

"Thanks to you, I've finally realized..."

"Ionia..."

"You were right. I've been unconsciously nurturing feelings that I shouldn't have had in the first place." Ionia's face crumpled, and he placed a hand where Lucas had stroked him. "...He may be three years younger than me, and the difference in status between him, a member of royalty, and me, a commoner, may be like heaven and earth, but I've loved Vi in *this* sense."

The proof of his carnal desires lay right there.

"Io, don't reject me like this," Lucas pleaded, pressing his forehead to Ionia's chest.

"Luca... I do like you. You're my best friend, and in that sense, I love you."

Lucas said nothing.

"But I'll probably always, always want Vi."

*Do you still want to be my best friend now...?*

"I'm such a fool. Maybe it's because I'm a commoner... I really didn't see anything but Vi. Why...? How could this happen?"

Tears spilled from Ionia's eyes.

"Now you know who I really am, Luca... You'll regret falling in love with me."

"It's too late. I'm long past the point of no return."

"My entire heart belongs to Vi...and you're okay with that?"

"I don't care. I've noticed a long time ago that all you see is His Highness. I've been watching you for years. But I don't care. Just let me stay by your side."

Ionia weakly put his arm around Lucas's shoulder as Lucas clung to his chest, begging for his love. He realized he would likely take advantage of his best friend's affection many times in the future. With Lucas's love as a suit of armor around his heart, Ionia would forever devote his blood and loyalty to the boy with the starry-sky eyes.

"Luca, I love Vi. I may be nothing more than his shield, but I *want* Vi."

Lucas's tears stained the front of his shirt as he sobbed.

Ionia shut his eyes tightly.

He had no right to cry.


When Ionia returned to his room, Gravis was sitting on his bed as usual, waiting for him.

"...You're late."

The boy who filled the small room to the brim with his ambition now seemed upset.

Normally, Ionia would be elated. But now, for once, he didn't want to see him.

"Vi, I'm sorry. I'm tired today..."

He felt so guilty that he could not look Gravis in the eye.

Gravis grew suspicious of Ionia's attitude, and he irritably cornered him in front of the door.

Ionia's eyes were still higher than his.

"Ionia, look at me."

"Vi…"

"Are you avoiding me?"

"No! But I'm sorry. I just can't do it today. I need you to leave."

"Why? I can't leave until I hear a reason."

That dazzling shimmering darkness. Ionia didn't want those eyes, which saw right through him, to expose his filthy carnal desires.

Gravis was upset that Ionia hadn't been waiting for him.

There was an unacknowledged desire for exclusivity hidden in his eyes. Some ugly part of him delighted in it. Gravis was seeking Ionia without knowing the difference between friendship and love that came with lust. Until a few moments ago, the same could have been said for Ionia. Lucas must have realized long ago that the older Ionia would eventually suffer more from their mutually blind, cruel possessiveness.

Ionia had never realized that a three-year age difference could be so cruel. Even though he had grown taller than boys his age and possessed a prodigious mind that put most adults to shame, Gravis was only thirteen years old. There was no way he could ask a boy three years younger than him—and a prince, at that—to accept his feelings and the entirety of his lust-ridden body.

It hurt him to think about the sensation between his legs; the result of his unexpected encounter with Lucas. But what if the fingers that had trailed his arousal at that moment had belonged to Gravis? The thought that he wanted to connect with the prince on that level, even though he was three years younger than him and so far removed from him in status, embarrassed and pained Ionia all the same.

Gravis drew his fingers down his neck.

"…Io. What are these marks?"

His fingers ran across the exact spot Lucas had traced with his lips, and his gaze looked ready to kill. Ionia was horrified.

"Ionia…! Explain… Who gave you these marks?!"

Ionia brushed his fingers away before he could think better of it.

"…Io… You—"

Gravis's face contorted in frustration at the rejection.

The flicker of stars had disappeared from his eyes, and they now seemed like a perfectly moonless night.

"…Am I not allowed to come to you anymore?"

"…No, of course you are."

His voice sounded like a plea.

"But if you have a certain someone, I can no longer visit you."

"*A certain someone.*" That's what Gravis had just said.

Oh, he already knew. He knew exactly what a mark from a love bite looked like.

Lucas had been right. The prince, who Ionia believed to be as innocent as he was, already knew what carnal desire led to. And yet, within Gravis, only his feelings for Ionia did not take a clear form. Or perhaps he didn't even feel the need to give them a form.

*How could I have thought that we could remain children forever?*

Gravis was at a loss for words. Ionia leaned back against the door and watched in silence. The situation, so similar to the one in Lucas's room, was so terribly absurd that he couldn't help but laugh dryly.

Gravis's face twisted in pain. "You don't care about me anymore, do you?"

"No, you're the only thing I've ever cared about," Ionia assured. That would always remain true. "Listen to me, Vi. No matter what happens, my heart will never change. You will always be my first priority."

Gravis's starry-sky eyes shook at his words.

"I want you to entrust your back to me forever. I want to always be by your side… Please believe me."

"Is the person who left those marks your significant other?" Gravis pressed. "Tell me... Is it Lucas Brandt?"

"...Vi. I don't want to talk about this anymore."

"Answer me, Ionia!"

Seeing Gravis's indignation, Ionia felt both joy and sorrow.

Gravis was jealous. He was jealous because he knew that someone had touched Ionia sexually.

So Ionia lied.

"Yes... Lucas is my significant other."

He did not hesitate to use Lucas.

Gravis bit his lip, his face pale, and disappeared from the room immediately.

Consumed by a storm of violent emotion, Gravis never noticed the traces of tears on Ionia's cheeks.

Gravis stormed into his room at the palace and angrily swiped the jug and glasses off the side table.

Someone impatiently knocked on the door at the horrible noise.

"Your Highness! What's wrong?!"

"Don't come in!"

The other side of the door instantly fell silent at Gravis's agitated voice.

"Are you hurt? ...May I enter the room?"

"I'm fine. Nothing happened. I just dropped the jug. Leave me be until tomorrow."

The person outside the door fell silent once more.

Gravis clenched his fists tightly, trying to collect himself. But then he remembered the red marks on Ionia's neck, and his anger welled up within him again.

Ionia had said that his significant other had given him those marks.

What of it? Gravis had already had his bedchamber education. He would feel pent up, too, and he knew that he needed to deal with it regularly.

Ionia was sixteen years old. Gravis shouldn't have been surprised that he would have someone to handle those physical urges.

To Gravis, Ionia was unique and irreplaceable. Ionia even told him that he was the most important person in his life and that he would be by his side forever.

Gravis was partly responsible for changing the course of Ionia's life by force—those were the best words he could have ever hoped for. Whether he had a significant other or not, Ionia would always belong to Gravis.

So why did his chest hurt so much?

*Why? Am I not your first priority after all...? His significant other would know everything about Ionia, even things that I don't know... How dare he?!*

The thought of Lucas touching that toned, beautiful body, the skin hidden by his clothes, made his thoughts turn dark with anger. Gravis finally understood. This was jealousy. Unmistakable possessiveness and jealousy.

*I want all of Ionia to be mine...*

Lucas was already becoming a grown man. In terms of height and girth, Gravis was still no match for Lucas. He hadn't even outgrown Ionia's height yet. The three-year age difference was insurmountable during that period when boys turned into young men.

Above all, Gravis did not have the luxury of indulging in love. The king had fallen ill. It was not a serious illness that would kill him immediately, but if it came to light, the issue of succession would flare up once more. This time, Gravis could find himself at odds with his brother for the throne, whether or not he wanted it. Which meant Ionia's life could be in danger.

*I don't have the right to beg for Ionia's affection. I'm still a child, immature in every sense.*
Gravis bit his lip.

Five years ago, when he first met Ionia, Gravis was going through a difficult time. It was around the time of the death of the crown prince's mother,

Lady Brigitte. Gravis was eight years old. The death of the concubine triggered a conflict between the crown prince's faction and the faction that wanted the second prince to be the next king.

Gravis adored his half brother, who was ten years older than him. Compared to his adorable little brother, the crown prince had rather ordinary-looking light-brown hair and eyes and a gentle demeanor to go with them. Despite the age gap, he was a kind older brother, and he would always stroke Gravis's head and offer a few kind words to him whenever they met.

He was also the only person who showed him such familial affection through his actions. Adele was a respectable woman, and Gravis did feel her affection for him at times, but she was a queen before she was a mother, and she never hugged or doted on him.

As Gravis began to show his superior qualities, unbeknownst to him, a wall was slowly erected between him and his brother. Gravis could not understand why his brother had become so distant, and it saddened him. By the time he was six years old, Gravis already understood the complicated situation he and his brother were in.

The crown prince, Joachim, had a mild disposition. Under normal circumstances, this gentle nature would have been a virtue. Unfortunately for him, however, he was born the heir to a great monarch and had a younger brother who radiated overwhelming brilliance and charisma. Gravis's presence made his gentle demeanor appear banal—some might even say *feeble*—in the eyes of the people.

When they met after a longer period of separation, the crown prince stroked his brother's head and murmured: "You are more worthy to be king, both in blood and in intellect."

Gravis knew that his presence was driving his brother up the wall, but he did not know what to do. Gravis could not disappoint his mother. He understood Adele's difficult life and the suffering it brought her.

Adele was born as the first princess of the Kingdom of Francoure, a country as powerful as Fanoren, and married George at the age of eighteen. Adele's grandmother was a member of the Fanoren royal family who had married into Francoure, and so Adele was welcomed with open arms by the people of the kingdom due to her bloodline, her beauty, and her exceptional eyes. However, despite her blood, intelligence, beauty, and position as queen of a great power, the only thing Adele could not have was the love of her husband, King George.

Only six months after Adele's marriage, King George brought Brigitte, then eighteen years old, into his palace as his concubine.

Under normal circumstances, it would have been scandalous for a king to take in a concubine immediately after marrying a princess of a country as powerful as Francoure. However, George was an impulsive man, and the more the people around him opposed him, the more he became abnormally attached to Brigitte.

Brigitte was the daughter of a low-ranking nobleman, too lowborn to be a concubine. But once Brigitte was adopted by a distant relative, the marquis, to keep up appearances, the king high-handedly decided to make her his concubine, ignoring the opposition of his closest advisers and the vehement protests of Francoure.

To add insult to injury, Brigitte became pregnant soon after her arrival and gave birth to Joachim, the crown prince, a year later. By then it was clear to all within the country and abroad that the king's favor lay with his concubine, and Adele was doubly humiliated, both as a woman and the rightful queen.

However, Adele's innate pride and good sense did not allow her to sully relations between the two kingdoms, and so she carried out her official duties as queen. Brigitte, on the other hand, was a weak woman who had no will of her own and was easily manipulated. It was due to her fragility that George became fixated on her and favored her. However, Brigitte was not educated to be a queen. She did not have the backbone or the wisdom to advise George to give her Adele's position as rightful queen.

It was eleven years after marrying into Fanoren that Adele conceived a child in the arms of her husband, who had no love for her and went to her bedchamber obligingly only to keep up appearances.

She gave birth to a beautiful boy with black hair, inherited from King George, and eyes of an extraordinary color rarely seen in the Francoure royal family: indigo flecked with gold, known as starry-sky eyes.

*　*　*

Adele was delighted.

The period of longing for her husband's affection had long passed. Instead, she devoted herself to Gravis. When her beautiful son, who resembled her so much, began to show his aptitude as a potential monarch, wise Queen Adele's pure heart, concerned for her country, gradually turned to other desires. Some of Adele's admirers also began to call for the second prince to become the heir, given his brilliance and his superior blood.

The death of Lady Brigitte, the concubine, brought this conflict to the forefront. Joachim, who had lost the backing of his mother, the king's favorite mistress, was stripped of the title of crown prince, and a movement to endorse Gravis as the new crown prince had surfaced. Although his mother, the rightful queen, was ostensibly not involved in the battle for succession, Gravis was aware that her wishes played a major role behind the scenes.

Gravis was torn between his love for his brother and his love for his mother. Above all, he despaired that his existence would be the fuse leading the country into conflict. He wanted his brother to ascend the throne without disappointing his mother at the same time.

It was then that Stolf took the young prince, struggling with the position he was stuck in, out to get his mind off things. Stolf also recognized the second prince's qualities and thought he was more suited to be the next king. However, he also understood Gravis's desire to avoid creating unnecessary conflicts that would weaken the country. If they bent the laws of the land in the battle for succession, Francoure would be involved, and the country would be irreparably divided.

Then Gravis met a boy with violet eyes at a blacksmith's shop in the commoner district. Like a ray of morning sun, the boy plunged straight into Gravis's darkness. Even though he knew how perilous the future he was leading him down was, Gravis desperately wanted to keep Ionia by his side.

He had no idea that the consequences of that choice would be so painful.

One day, Ionia was summoned by the headmaster after training.

The gray-haired old man smiled softly as usual and welcomed Ionia into his office.

"Ah, there you are, Ionia. I am pleased to see that His Highness Prince Gravis trusts you so much. It has been five years since you came here, hasn't it?"

Ionia nodded silently.

The headmaster did not seem bothered by this response. He did not recognize non-nobles as equals, so he couldn't care less about Ionia's attitude.

Ionia hated the headmaster and his bloodline purism. Talking with this man, he quickly realized that the idea of Fanoren as a country where commoners were given opportunities was a total illusion. It didn't take a genius to figure out why such a man was the head of the academy of higher learning.

"I am glad to see that His Highness has so far been at peace, at least on campus... And of course, your family must be relieved that you are not in any danger."

"...Why have you summoned me, sir?"

"Right. I suppose that'll do for small talk. I have a word of advice for you today."

Ionia inclined his head slightly. The headmaster turned his gaze to Ionia for the first time. "Am I correct in assuming that you are on His Highness's side?"

He didn't know what the headmaster was trying to say. However, there was absolutely no world in which Ionia would betray Gravis. So he nodded silently.

"Very well. In that case, please keep what you hear here confidential. His Majesty the king has fallen ill. Only the people in his immediate vicinity know about it, but he has been diagnosed with an illness of unknown cause."

"...What?"

He did not expect to be told of such an important matter for the country.

"Are you allowed to share such important state secrets with me?"

"You are special. I'm sure you'll understand. If something should happen to His Majesty...that would mean *the time* has finally come. You know what this means, don't you?"

Some nobles, worried about the future of Fanoren, were concerned about who the next king should be, the headmaster continued in an impassioned tone.

Ionia, angered by the selfish desires of those around Gravis who insisted on ignoring his wishes, asked: "…What about the wishes of Gravis himself? Everyone, even you or the queen, must already be aware. You want to depose the crown prince and make Gravis king, but…Gravis doesn't want that."

The headmaster shook his head.

"The queen understands that His Highness is refraining from pursuing the position out of consideration for the crown prince. But you can see it as well as I can. His Highness Prince Gravis is the most suitable person to be king."

In the end, it all came back to the same question.

Even Ionia knew that Gravis had the qualities of a king.

For the past four years, Ionia had been watching the prince's natural talent closer than anyone. But Gravis himself did not want to be king. He did not want to become the spark that destroyed the country. He wanted to let his brother, whom he loved and respected and considered a kind and gentle man, succeed the throne, and to remain in the shadows and use his military prowess to support his reign.

"Some are concerned about the fact that his mother is of foreign blood. However, Queen Adele is also the granddaughter of the former king's sister. As a member of the Fanoren royal bloodline, Queen Adele is of a far nobler, more precious bloodline."

*Damn bloodline purists*, Ionia thought in anger.

"Besides, that concubine was in league with Lagarea's son. She seduced the king and gave birth to his firstborn son. We can't even be certain that the crown prince truly carries the king's blood."

Ionia could not believe his ears.

They may have been alone, but the man's statement bordered on blasphemy. Such a reckless remark could get them both punished—what could the headmaster have to say for himself?

"Crown Prince Joachim's mother, Lady Brigitte, was from the family of a viscount related to the Marquis of Lagarea. She was too lowborn to become a concubine, so she was adopted by a relative before getting married. She and Bruno, son of the Marquis of Lagarea, were adoptive brother and sister… But I know the truth. Bruno and Lady Brigitte must have been lovers. I don't doubt that it was King George who got between them, when he fell in love with Lady Brigitte at first sight."

Ionia shook his head.

"That can't be... If that were the case, we would have long been in the midst of a scandal."

The idea that Brigitte was once in love with Bruno Henckel, heir to the Marquis of Lagarea, was the lowest kind of accusation.

"The crown prince is the son of Lady Brigitte. In order to strengthen his position, he found himself Crown Princess Emilia from Francoure to compete with Queen Adele. That is also why he created an heir to the throne so early in his life."

"Vi also said that the crown prince is a kindhearted man. Why would he compete against the queen...?"

The headmaster shook his head again.

"The crown prince is deceiving His Highness Prince Gravis. Now that the king's days are numbered...the crown prince's faction will surely make an attempt on His Highness's life."

# Leorino: Julian's Courtship

The betrothal ceremony between Erina Munster and Auriano went off without a hitch. A second ceremony was also held later at the Duke of Leben's estate, attended by the margravine Maia and Leorino's second brother, Johan, as a representative of the head of the Cassieux family. Erina and Auriano's wedding was to take place the following year in a church in the province of Brungwurt.

What the Cassieuxes did not expect as they enjoyed their hectic preparations for the special occasion was the frequent visits of Erina's brother, Julian Munster.

Erina was expected to travel back and forth between Brungwurt and the royal capital on a regular basis to learn the customs of the Cassieux family before her marriage. However, Julian, who should have had no business in Brungwurt, visited more often than his sister.

The purpose of Julian's visits was Leorino.

During the engagement ceremony, Julian was taken by the youngest son of the Cassieux family's beauty, and during his stay, his feelings for Leorino only grew stronger. He had been showing up frequently ever since, trying desperately to get Leorino's attention.

The Cassieux family had been optimistic at first but were now beginning to feel threatened by Julian's increasingly serious attitude. However, because they were unable to do anything about the heir apparent of a duke, Julian visited Leorino whenever he felt like it.

It should have been just another day when Julian appeared with a grin on his face.

He headed to Leorino with enough momentum to overtake the butler who was showing him the way. Leorino, who was having tea on the terrace, released a small sigh at his second visit this month. Julian came carrying some kind of sweets, probably his usual souvenirs from the royal capital.

The appearance of the gorgeous Julian brightened the otherwise staid Brungwurt Castle. Leorino was impressed by the refined way in which this nobleman living in the royal capital carried himself.

"How have you been, Leorino? Without you, the royal capital leaves my heart feeling empty. I can hardly go on living without beholding your angelic beauty."

Julian approached Leorino with a beaming smile, took his hand without hesitation, and pressed his lips to the back of it as if he were greeting a lady.

Leorino had gotten used to Julian's strange behavior by now, but he found his treating him as if he were a lady particularly unpleasant.

"Um, Lord Julian, I believe I'll be repeating myself again, but I would like to remind you that I am a boy. Is that clear? You're more than welcome to stop greeting me like this..."

Even Leorino, who had little social experience, found Julian's behavior odd.

Julian's eyes were filled with admiration, never tiring of gazing at Leorino's face. He was like a collector looking at the finest jewelry, to use a poor analogy. Every time he visited, he would simply watch him for a while. And each time, he would eventually begin heaping praise on Leorino's appearance.

"Oh, Leorino...you are so beautiful. Male or female, I couldn't care less. I have never seen a person as beautiful as you in the capital. You could very well be...an angel or a faerie in the flesh."

After handing him his gift, Julian placed his hand on Leorino's. Leorino made his overwhelming discomfort clear with his gaze, but the young man knew exactly what he was doing and only smiled mischievously as he put more pressure into his fingers.

"Lord Julian, I am terribly sorry, but is there any chance you could release Lord Leorino's hand?"

Julian reluctantly let go.

Leorino felt relieved.

Just as he was about to reach for his cup of tea to calm himself down, Julian once more took hold of Leorino's hands and lifted them to his mouth.

Leorino froze in surprise.

"Leorino, you already know how I feel... I only come to Brungwurt for you. I miss you so dearly."

"Um... Lord Julian, your hands, please..."

Julian knelt before Leorino. The servant behind him was beginning to panic.

"Leorino, I have just asked your father, August...for your hand in marriage."

"What? S-surely you jest..."

Leorino was so surprised that he couldn't hide it if he tried.

"Why would I joke about this? Unfortunately, your father refused. I am, after all, the heir to the Duke of Leben, and you are still too young to know certain things...but I really don't want to give up on you. Please consider marrying me."

Leorino stared at the young man kneeling before him, looking up at him earnestly. Julian looked at Leorino with feverish eyes and an incredibly serious expression on his face.

Leorino was, of course, aware of the favor that Julian was showing him, but he had never been in love before and was still perfectly innocent. However, through Ionia's memories, he understood what it felt like to be in love. In that sense, Leorino had never been attracted to Julian as a potential love interest.

Although same-sex marriages were permitted in Fanoren, it was typical for the eldest son of a noble family to marry a woman. No one had expected that Julian, the heir to the Duke of Leben, would seriously pursue Leorino as a potential spouse, when he could not bear children. Everyone assumed he was only courting Leorino as a short-term love interest.

That was why, wary that Leorino would be chosen for a temporary tryst, a family member or male servant was always present during his meetings with Julian, keeping a close eye on Julian to make sure he did not do anything inappropriate.

"I mean it... I know you're not yet of marrying age and more innocent than anyone. But please do seriously consider marrying me. You deserve to live under my protection."

Leorino asked with his eyes what he meant by that.

Then Julian, with a kind expression, confronted Leorino with the reality of his situation. "Listen, Leorino. You're still innocent. You haven't yet entered society proper... But what about the future?"

"What about the future...?"

"You are the fourth son. You have no title to inherit. And you are far too beautiful. With your beauty and your legs, living alone will be difficult—no, impossible."

Leorino's expression stiffened at these gentle yet cruel words.

"You should live under someone's protection, cherished and safe. I am certain that in time your father and Lord Auriano will come to agree with me."

# Ionia: Beasts Roaring in the Night 4

Ever since that night, Gravis had not returned to Ionia's room.

It had been just the two of them, their secret, intimate meetings that took place every night up until then. It was a brief moment before bed, a time that made Ionia's heart beat just a little faster. And he had ruined it.

He spent the nights alone now, feeling like his heart was about to break into pieces and thinking about Gravis, mocking himself for getting what he deserved.

He missed him.

But he would rather leave things as they were than let Gravis learn the truth about his body and heart, aching for him every night. If he had kept his mind and body immature, they would have likely suffered a much worse breakup. His irreplaceable boyhood was gone, but the loneliness that came in exchange for maturity hid his secret well.

The shadows in the corners of the room grew darker.

His eyes were so accustomed to starlight that the moon felt too bright, and Ionia lay down and covered his eyes with his arms.

A knock echoed through the room. He hadn't locked the door, and the door-knob turned with a clank as someone entered, keeping their footsteps silent. He could tell without looking who it was by the sound of their breathing.

Lucas had entered without permission and quietly closed the door behind him.

"...I didn't say you could come in."

He sensed Lucas smiling slightly at the sight of Ionia, even as he spouted his abuse, his eyes still covered.

"You didn't say no, either, did you?"

"Well, I'm saying no now."

"Ha-ha... Bit late for that."

Ionia slowly lowered his elbows and weakly glared at Lucas.

"...What do you want?"

Lucas slowly approached the bed. He sat down next to his feet. Ionia watched him silently. When Lucas looked at his face, he turned to the window again to avoid his gaze.

The moon was too bright to see the stars clearly.

"His Highness has been making snide remarks at me."

Ionia's eyes twitched at that. Lucas could see the change in Ionia's expression.

"Vi making snide remarks? Hmm... What did he actually say?"

"...He said that you have a significant other."

"Vi would never tell you that."

Lucas seemed to smile at that.

Ionia looked at Lucas again.

He expected to see a wry smirk on his face, but the young man staring at Ionia wore a terribly serious expression.

"You're right; he didn't say that. He scolded me for risking vulgar rumors being spread about you."

"...He did what?"

"'Don't damage Ionia's career by doing anything that might cause rumors. If you're his significant other, then act like it!' I suppose he was referring to the marks I left on your neck. That was a stupid thing to do."

Gravis had been so angry, but now he was thinking of Ionia's honor, even though it meant accepting Lucas as Ionia's lover. Ionia bit his lip at the bitter-sweet thought.

"...What did you think when you heard that?"

Ionia propped himself up on both elbows.

Lucas looked tortured. His face was racked with remorse for his actions.

"I've realized my mistake. I also thought of the pain you must have endured when His Highness found out."

Lucas gently brushed the back of his fingers across Ionia's cold cheek.

"...Did you cry?"

Ionia did not answer, only grabbed his fingers and pushed them away.

Lucas followed his fingers and squeezed them, letting him know his hands were cold.

"You had to lie to His Highness about me being your significant other. You felt like you had no other choice. Am I wrong? ...It was my fault, that night."

"I'm not going to tell anyone about what happened with Vi. Not even you."

"Fine, you don't have to. It's all conjecture on my part."

Lucas's warm fingers let go of his. Ionia's upper body, which he had propped up on one elbow, sank back onto the bed weakly. A large body slowly covered him.

"Do you think I am taking advantage of your weakness?"

Ionia's heart felt nothing when he looked up at the young man's face even as he was close enough to feel his breath. But he did feel heat rising in every part of his body. The body on top of his would have felt that heat.

Ionia looked away. "Do you think I'm cruel for taking advantage of your affection?"

"...How could I ever think of you as cruel when you're making that face?"

Ionia gave a small gasp as Lucas shifted his weight onto him in earnest. Blocking out the sensation of lips trailing down his upturned neck, Ionia continued to speak.

"...Luca. Don't you understand? This is the kind of person I am. I would do anything to stay connected to Gravis, tell any lie, make any sacrifice. I don't care if it hurts you."

"I don't care, either. I don't care if you continue to pursue His Highness

Prince Gravis with all your heart and soul. I fell in love with you just the way you are. I can't help myself."

Lucas brushed the hair from Ionia's forehead and slowly combed it back. His touch was incredibly gentle.

"Luca...I can't give you my heart."

"Weren't you listening? I don't care... Let me be there for you, Ionia. Let me be your significant other. If you need an excuse to be with His Highness, I'll be your excuse. If you want to lie to stay with His Highness, I will be your partner in crime."

Ionia's heart broke at those words. How happy would he be if he could truly love his best friend as his romantic partner. But his heart would not allow it. He had been yearning for those starry-sky eyes for so long, and he would pursue them still.

Lucas's lips gently caught the tear that trickled down his cheek.

Ionia placed his arms around Lucas's neck and pulled him close. Just before their lips met, he murmured quietly: "Luca...please. Be my significant other."

Lucas held the back of Ionia's head and placed his lips on his in agreement.

The young man's lips quickly pulled away after the kiss, but Ionia impulsively followed them and gave them a provocative lick. Lucas's body, spurred on by Ionia's leading behavior, fell upon his.

Ionia could no longer see the night sky from behind his broad back.

The air between Ionia and Gravis remained delicate.

They may have spent a lot of time together on campus, but that was the inevitable result of doing their best to avoid mentioning the events of that night to each other. However, neither of them could distance themselves from the other. Although that was partly due to Ionia's role as Gravis's guard.

Their mutual attachment and unresolved feelings for each other had hardened their relationship.

While this state continued, a two-day and one-night battle drill was to be held in the mountains on the outskirts of the city as an exercise in practical warfare.

It was a large-scale drill conducted with the help of the Royal Army. Students majoring in tactics were allowed to participate in this class from their fourth year. A platoon of thirty men from the Royal Army would play the role of the enemy in a simulated field battle. The students would assume that an enemy platoon had invaded a mountainous area and attacked a watchtower fort and then develop a plan to retake it.

The enemy army would be played by real soldiers. Naturally, there was no comparison between their skills and those of the students. All weapons had dull blades, and physical combat was forbidden. The aim was not to hone individual skills but to learn through practice how to move quickly and in a controlled manner following large-scale tactics and the chain of command.

This year's drill was filled with an unprecedented amount of tension, as the second prince was chosen to participate. It was the first time a royal would participate in combat training—and at the unusual age of thirteen at that.

Prince Gravis was blessed with a strong physique and looked roughly the same age as Ionia and the rest of the older group. But even though he had skipped a grade, he was the same age as the boys who were in their second year at the academy.

The headmaster was reluctant to allow him to participate in the drill. However, Gravis himself strongly wanted to join in. General Stolf also supported his decision. The reason Gravis had skipped a grade to enter the academy was to have somewhere to practice his skills in the first place.

However, the academy could not risk anything happening to a member of the royal family. The Royal Army was also apprehensive about the drill. Therefore, unusual as it was, Stolf, the head of the Royal Army, was put in charge of the exercise and managed it as a whole.

"This drill will be a full-scale mock battle, following a hypothetical raid on a real strategic point. However, it is not a competition of individual combat skills. Make no mistake, each of you must be on your toes."

On the day of the drill, the students straightened their backs at General Stolf's instruction. Marzel was an obvious choice, but even Ionia and Lucas had been entrusted with more important positions than the previous year. Each of them stood in line with serious expressions on their faces.

The Royal Army troops playing the role of enemy soldiers were already hiding in the mountains. This added to the tension. Ionia, in particular, was increasingly nervous, since he would be guarding Gravis outside the academy for the first time.

Gravis would be in command of the student side.

At first, he offered to give up the role of commander to Marzel, who had served as second-in-command the previous year. But it would also be a massive waste to put Gravis somewhere at the end of the line. Everyone who knew the second prince's skill was convinced that he should be in command.

The exercise would take place throughout the day and night, from that point until the next morning.

Ionia approached Gravis, leaned in close, and whispered: "I'm going to protect you, I promise. You can go all out."

Gravis didn't seem particularly nervous.

"In truth, I'd love to be a part of the action with you."

With that, Gravis smiled faintly and looked at Ionia. The two gazed at each other for the first time in a while.

"I hope you'll have my back, Io."

At that moment, Ionia shivered with delight.

In that moment, he knew.

He wanted to be close to Gravis forever.

Closer than anyone else, so close they could understand each other's feelings just by exchanging glances.

Gravis, the commander of the student side, gathered his main comrades in command in a large room in the center of the fort. Ionia was next to Gravis, and among his companions were Lucas and Marzel.

Behind them were General Stolf and several teachers from the academy. The adults would not intervene during the drill unless they deemed it dangerous. But the adults' gazes made the students restless.

"Focus."

Gravis's quiet voice echoed through the room.

The students straightened their backs. Gravis stared into each of their faces, drawing their focus back to himself and helping them regain their composure.

"Treat them as if they were air. You can't be a soldier if you can't focus on what you must do, no matter the circumstances. Is that clear?"

The students were ashamed of their inexperience at the words of the calm and collected prince, who did not act his age at all. But it wouldn't be right to measure Gravis by the same yardstick as the students. At his age, he was already dealing with real problems, strategizing with the top brass of the Royal Army.

Arnim, the most senior student, who had been named second-in-command, made a lighthearted remark to relieve the tension in the room. "To His Highness, a mock battle must seem like child's play."

Gravis looked at Arnim, and the corners of his mouth twitched upward. The students were utterly captivated by the rare smile on his face.

But the prince could not allow them to relax too much.

"No, I am trying very hard to keep us from being toyed with. I am sorry that you must look to me, a younger man, as your commander during this grueling drill."

"What do you mean?"

"I have consulted with Stolf, and he has sent the Tenth Platoon of the mountain troops to play the role of the enemy this time. Those of you who aspire to join the Royal Army will understand what this means."

The students immediately understood Gravis's words. And all of them winced.

The mountain troops, which specialized in fighting in the steep Baedeker Mountains northwest of Fanoren, were made up of one hundred platoons. Each platoon consisted of sixty-two men, including the platoon leader and his assistant. The platoons were numbered from one to one hundred, with the lower the number, the more elite the platoon, operating in the harshest areas.

In other words, the Tenth Platoon was the tenth from the top, which meant that a number of elite mountain warriors had been dispatched to fight the students.

Ionia thought announcing this had been a bad move. The tension among the students had increased dramatically. Some of them turned pale and clapped their hands over their mouths, perhaps feeling nauseous at the thought of what was to come.

He did not understand why Gravis chose to frighten the students.

With a tired look on his face, Lucas complained: "Hey, now… Your Highness, why would you say that? I know you want to get some serious real-world experience, but you could have us all beaten to a pulp."

Marzel followed suit.

"Indeed, no student would dare to go out there knowing that the Tenth Platoon is lurking nearby."

The air in the room changed with their lighthearted words. Gravis glanced appreciatively at the two boys. Ionia admired their quick wits and courage.

"You are the future leaders of the Royal Army. You will need to know exactly what your opponents are capable of and have the courage and good judgment to deal with them." Gravis looked calmly at his companions.

"But Fanoren is peaceful, and conflicts like an invasion on a fortress don't happen often. We will be responsible for people's lives without knowing actual war… But there is no guarantee that we will never face conflict with other countries in the future. What if, one day, one of our neighbors—say, Zwelf— were to suddenly invade?"

Gravis looked around at each of the students. The students listened intently.

"We who choose to become soldiers in a peaceful country do not have many opportunities to experience real combat. This drill is a fantastic opportunity. It is why we have to experience firsthand how difficult real battles can be."

The students' restlessness was gone, and their expressions became firm. They focused on the prince's words.

"This fear we are feeling is just that. That's why I had the Tenth Platoon dispatched. They will attack our fort in earnest. The more difficult this experience is, the more valuable it will be. Is that clear?"

Everyone nodded in agreement.

The sparkle in their eyes was different from before. They all understood the value of this drill and were filled with a sense of tension and elation at once.

"But let's take it easy. The more seasoned the soldiers are, the better they know how to go easy on you. Even if you enter open combat with them, if the students shout 'defeat,' the attack on the individual will end immediately. We can rest assured and learn from them what we can."

Gravis nodded strongly in reassurance.

"The other side is quite accustomed to operating out of sight in the mountains and forests. There is no way we can match them in terms of individual fighting skills. As I mentioned, when it comes to individual combat, you must carefully assess the situation and surrender before you get hurt. If any of your comrades try to do something reckless, you must stop them. Listen, be prepared, and give them hell."

The morale of the students was boosted beyond compare.

Ionia was impressed by Gravis's ability to control people.

"Lucas, don't let yourself go off the rails just because you're fighting someone you rarely get to fight. This is just a drill."

"Marzel, don't just sit in the back because you're a staff officer. Go into the field."

Lucas and Marzel's additional exchange had successfully alleviated the tension.

Everyone laughed. They were in a very good mood.

For a brief moment, Gravis's and Ionia's gazes met. Gravis gave a small nod. It was as if he was trying to make sure that Ionia was within arm's reach.

"In that case, let's talk about the plan. Ginter, please explain how the personnel will be deployed first."

Marzel nodded and began to explain to his companions, pointing at the map.

Ionia had an important mission as the commander's guard. He braced himself to focus on his mission.

Half a day had passed since the start of the mock battle. The sun was setting over the ridgeline, and dusk was slowly approaching the forest surrounding the fort.

The strategy was simple. They were absolutely no match for the Tenth Platoon in terms of individual combat skills, but by taking advantage of their superior numbers, they would drive the Tenth Platoon from the mountainous terrain to the area where their allies lay in wait, which was also where the soldiers would be killed by the students' comrades. The difference in martial prowess was considerable. The only way to achieve this goal was to thoroughly engage in one-to-many battles and destroy the platoon over a longer period of time.

The fortress where the mock battle took place was small, but it was well-sealed and robust. Since the use of large and long-range weapons was prohibited, the building could not be destroyed and breached in one fell swoop. In other words, it was enough to prevent entry from the two gates in the outer wall.

The number of enemies was small. The enemy forces were scattered vertically in the mountainous area, and the students would form a wavelike formation to flush them out along the slope, driving them back.

If the front line was breached, the survivors would join up with the troops behind them and build up the front line in waves again, driving the enemy along the main road leading to the fort. The road leading to the front gate of the fort and the road to the next fort extending from the rear gate were made difficult to breach by high stone walls on both sides. The strategy was to deploy a large number of men in small units along the road to the fort gate after flushing out the enemy soldiers and to kill them one by one along the road.

As the commanding officer, Gravis hesitated about the deployment on the front lines, but he decided to go deep from the front line to the fort by assigning his comrades with excellent combat skills.

It was also significant that Lucas took command of the front line. The

Tenth Platoon would not have expected the students to draw the front line so far from the fort.

The students acting as messengers reported that they had already flushed out and neutralized nearly thirty enemy soldiers before nightfall.

The students were elated, but Gravis kept a stern expression on his face.

"Ginter, how many men were neutralized?"

Marzel checked the list. Next to the names of the students were marked those who had been incapacitated—or in other words, those who were considered casualties and could no longer participate in the drill.

"Twenty-seven. Our forces count just under seventy."

"We will struggle if we do not reduce the enemy's forces by another ten men before the sun sets. They will notice our strategy and attack us in greater numbers... The time to gain distance is over. We will gather our forces closer to the fort before nightfall."

As he said this, Gravis glanced at Ionia beside him.

"Ionia, send a messenger down to the front line. Send Arnim to command the rear gate while redeploying Lucas along the front gate. The rear defenses will be reinforced. However, the general operation will remain the same."

"I understand. Your Highness, may I leave you for a moment? I must send word."

Gravis nodded, and Ionia moved to instruct the various units. Watching him, Gravis gave additional orders to Marzel. "Prepare lanterns for the front line along the roadside as soon as possible. But don't put them above the roadside, only below. They're to get eyes accustomed to light. If their eyes are too accustomed to the brightness, they'll struggle if the fire is extinguished."

Marzel nodded and left the room.

The room immediately grew quiet.

Gravis approached the window and looked out at the fallen who had returned to the fort. The participants who had surrendered wore a white cloth around their necks, indicating their inability to fight.

If the fort could be defended until dawn, the students would win.

It was fortuitous that they were able to cut the enemy's forces in half before nightfall. That was likely due to Lucas's excellence, as he was in charge of the front line.

He was a man of outstanding skill as a warrior and as a commander. He was certain to become a very capable soldier in the future.

He would be a strong backer of Ionia. He was also a man of compassion and good character and would make a perfect romantic partner.

"...What a foolish thought, now of all times."

Gravis shook off the silly thought and focused once again on the drill.

The Tenth Platoon was formidable. Gravis was well aware of how skilled they were in combat. Once the sun set, the students would quickly find themselves at a disadvantage. If they could at least reduce the number of opponents to the remaining twenty before the sun set completely, they would be able to defend the fort until morning.

Ionia returned to the room.

"Three more men were mowed down. We've got about half an hour before the sun sets."

Ionia understood that the commander wanted to cut the enemy's forces by a third by nightfall.

"It's up to Lucas and Arnim now. But everyone is doing very well. It's hard to believe they're students."

"Really makes me wish I could be there."

"You're my shield. Although in truth, I'd like to be there, too."

Ionia and Gravis shared a chuckle. Before they knew it, the awkwardness between them had dissipated.

It was already dark outside.

"We've got one more battle to win before the morning."

The "surviving" students were growing weary from the day-and-night battle. The enemy had only twenty or so men left, and they had less than forty survivors. The difference in battle experience really showed once the darkness had fallen. Even if several of their soldiers set up a trap, they were quickly finished off by a single enemy soldier.

Half an hour to go. Dawn was close.

Only a dozen men remained at the front gate, ten at the rear gate, and about ten inside the fortress and on the first floor of the building. In the command center were Ionia, Gravis, Marzel, and one other person, and the rest were Stolf and the teachers.

"Arnim, the commanding officer at the rear gate...has been hit!"

A dirt-stained messenger rushed in. Gravis looked up. Ionia tapped him on the shoulder.

"I'll go. If you don't mind me leaving your side, that is."

Ionia looked at Stolf, who was standing in the corner of the room. Stolf, who had been silent throughout, gave a small nod. The communication that he would be entrusted with Gravis's protection was instantaneous.

Gravis looked a little disappointed. He wanted to go, too. However, he understood his role as a commander and his status, and he could not risk anything happening to himself.

"Io, don't let the enemy get this far."

Ionia nodded.

"It's your first battle. I wouldn't want to lose."

But just as Ionia was about to leave the room with his sword, a roar shook the fortress.

"...What was that?!"

The central building shook violently. Everyone in the room was thrown out of their stances and put their hands on the walls and furniture.

The windows on the side of the rear gate, which had been dark earlier, were bright. Gravis rushed to the window. To his surprise, the rear gate was engulfed in flames.

"Fire...!"

Everyone was stunned by what had happened... And then the explosions started again, one after the other. They could hear the students in the yard screaming.

"I thought we forbade the use of firearms in the drill!"

"What about the students at the rear gate? What happened to them?!"

"Who did this?!"

The teachers yelled as they ran down the stairs.

Gravis shouted at Stolf. "Stolf, I'm ready to leap!"

"You mustn't. Your Highness, please stay here. This is no longer a drill. This is a genuine attack."

The concern on his face was unmistakable.

"They are likely after your life, Your Highness."

Ionia tensed at these words.

The sound of explosions continued in the distance, followed by the sound of a building collapsing and the cries of students.

Stolf looked at Gravis with a stern expression.

"I will order to stop the drill immediately and send the troops inside the fort to defend it. I will leave, but I will send guards immediately. Until then, I will leave you in Ionia's hands. But, Your Highness, if push comes to shove, please use your Power to escape. Is that clear?"

Gravis clenched his fists.

"You want me to abandon the students and run away all by myself?!"

"Yes, I do. Your life is worth more than anyone else's, Your Highness. Please be aware of that. Choosing between life and death will be an everyday occurrence from now on. You must make the rational decision."

"Stolf! You...want me to prioritize my life and abandon my pride? You want me to abandon my people?!"

The prince was about to grab the general in his rage, and Ionia grabbed him by the shoulders and stopped him as best as he could.

"Vi! This is not the time to be arguing about this!"

Gravis came to his senses and stepped away from Stolf with a hateful look on his face.

Stolf bowed silently and ran down the hall with a speed that belied his age.

"Vi..."

Ionia closed the door and turned around.

Gravis was still standing there, clenching his fists tightly. He was trying to suppress his surging emotions. Ionia put his hand on his shoulder. Gravis placed his hand on top of his and squeezed it so hard it hurt.

Flames flickered outside the window. Noise and screams. Blaze-colored shadows appeared all over the room.

At that moment, they heard the sound of multiple footsteps running up the hallway. Ionia instantly stepped in front of Gravis, sword at the ready.

"Your Highness, Ionia...! I-it's me, Arnim!"

It was the voice of Arnim, who was commanding the rear gate.

Ionia turned around, asking for orders, and Gravis nodded silently. He lowered his sword. Gravis called out to him to come in.

Arnim stood there, his face pale. His uniform was stained with soot, and he looked very tired. Behind him stood an unfamiliar student.

"Arnim...were you okay? Has anyone been harmed by the flames at the rear gate? ...Arnim?"

But Arnim stood motionless in front of the door.

"Arnim, what's wrong?"

Arnim was trembling harder now. Gravis realized what was happening. Ionia reacted immediately and raised his sword again.

Arnim's eyes were filled with despair.

"Arnim... It will be all right."

"...Your Highness, Ionia... I'm sorry... I'm so sorry... *Hic.*"

Tears spilled from Arnim's eyes. The student behind him finally showed himself. He was pressing a dagger against Arnim's carotid artery.

From the door behind him, men with swords and crossbows entered one after another. There were eight of them in total.

The men were dressed in student's drill uniforms, but upon closer inspection, it was easy to see that they were grown men. Wearing the same uniforms as the students must have been a disguise intended to use the mock battle to attack. The explosion at the rear gate must have been the work of these men.

They must have taken advantage of the chaos and used Arnim as a cover to sneak in this far.

"Arnim...don't move. I'll save you, I promise." Gravis spoke to the trembling Arnim.

"You're so naive, Your Highness." The man behind Arnim sneered at Gravis.

"Vi! Get back!"

Ionia immediately brandished his sword and faced the assassins, putting himself between them and Arnim. Receiving a powerful blow, Ionia shouted to Gravis.

"Vi! Leap! Get out of here!"

The assassins' swords were heavy. Ionia felt a sense of danger that he had never felt when fighting other students. Even so, he had been training his swordsmanship so tirelessly for this very moment.

He slashed the man aiming at Gravis diagonally from his side to his shoulder. Only Ionia's and Gravis's swords were sharpened. The man fell over with a groan.

As he received blows from the swords of the men one after the other, Ionia looked back at Gravis and shouted again. "Vi! I beg you, get to safety!"

"No! I'm not running away and leaving you and Arnim to fend for your lives!"

"No! Please! If you'd just run away— Whoa!"

The room was filled with the sounds of men panting and the deafening metallic clang of swords. If Ionia could stall them a little longer, Stolf would eventually return with his soldiers. Until then, he had to protect Gravis's life at all costs.

He was unable to keep the enemy from approaching Gravis. Finally, a man attacked the prince. Gravis fought back.

"...Vi!"

"I'm fine! Focus on the enemy!"

Gravis was also well-built beyond his years and had excellent swordsmanship, but he was still no match for the well-trained assassin in terms of size and skills. Seeing another enemy approaching, Ionia kicked the man in front of him in the stomach, causing the man to retreat, and then slashed at the back of the man fighting Gravis.

That man bent backward. Not missing a beat, Gravis knocked away the man's sword and slashed at both of his arms.

"Io...!"

"Vi... Thank god."

They took out the third enemy together.

Ionia stepped in front of Gravis and turned to face the enemy.

Carefully measuring the distance between them, Ionia frantically thought about how to get out of this predicament.

Five enemies still remained.

At that moment, the man who had been holding the dagger against Arnim's neck suddenly dug the tip of the knife into his neck.

"Arnim...! Stop! You bastard!" Gravis shouted.

"Your Highness. You are truly kind. But you are still a child. You feel pity even for a boy you should have abandoned, and you will end up sacrificing your life for him... And your guard's life, too!"

At that moment, a man with a crossbow shot a bolt at Ionia.

*...He'll shoot!*

"Io!"

At that moment, someone grabbed Ionia's arm from behind. He and that person vanished.

"...What?!"

The men gasped. This was the first time in his life that Ionia had leaped. The instantaneous switch in perspective and the sensation of his insides twisting and turning made him dizzy.

They had leaped next to the door.

"That was close."

"Vi... Thanks."

Gravis gave a small nod. A crossbow bolt had lodged itself deep inside the wall behind them.

"We're going to leap! Io!"

Once again, Gravis and Ionia leaped near the man holding Arnim. At once, they were within the enemy's reach. Ionia was shocked at how reckless Gravis was.

Gravis sprang forth and grabbed Arnim's arm. "Io! Now! Go!"

His body moved on instinct. Ionia's sword cleaved the man holding Arnim.

"Gahhh!"

Arnim was free now. Gravis grabbed Arnim's arm. The next moment, they disappeared.

Ionia almost collapsed in relief. Finally, Gravis had evacuated.

Hoping that he would stay somewhere safe, Ionia turned to the remaining assassins.

"Dammit! The prince has escaped! Find him!"

The assassins must have already known about Gravis's Power. Undeterred by the strange occurrence, they headed for the door to find their target.

The door was behind Ionia's back. Four assassins remained. They were highly skilled, but Ionia wanted to finish them off here, no matter what it took.

After watching one another for a brief moment, the men attacked Ionia once more. A man with a crossbow rushed for the door from Ionia's side, but Ionia blocked his way.

"You're not leaving!"

"Damn you...! I don't care if he's a guard or not, but this kid's in my way! Kill him!"

Ionia, in an all-or-nothing bid, used his sword to repel the crossbow, and closed the gap between them. The enemy flinched at Ionia's recklessness. Ionia instantly focused his Power in his hand and touched the crossbow.

A loud crack echoed through the room.

The man stared at his hands with a startled expression. The crossbow had been smashed to pieces. In that brief moment of distraction, Ionia slashed both of his thighs with his sword. The man grunted loudly and collapsed. Ionia thrust his sword through the fallen man's right hand.

"…He's just like the prince! He has a Power!"

The assassins, who had thought Ionia was merely a bodyguard, suddenly became more vigilant when he demonstrated what he could do.

Ionia was breathing with his shoulders. He knew that his Power had used his life force.

But three men remained. He couldn't collapse until he finished them off.

The men surrounded Ionia.

One man suddenly pulled out a short sword from his pocket and threw it at Ionia's face. The moment Ionia swung his sword and knocked it away, another man threw some kind of powder at Ionia's face.

It was a powerful irritant. He closed his eyes as quickly as he could, but he could not prevent it completely. His vision blurred.

He could see the shadow of the approaching enemy. He adjusted his sword, but he couldn't tell if he was aiming it correctly.

Ionia prepared himself for the approaching likelihood of death.

*…Vi, I'm sorry…*

"Oh no you don't!"

"No way, Vi… What are you…?!"

He heard Gravis's voice, even though he should have escaped.

Ionia searched frantically with his eyes and saw that Gravis had thrust a sword through a man's back.

"Io, are you okay?!"

"…No! Vi, run!"

Ionia's blurry eyes widened in horror.

The enemy was approaching Gravis without a sound.

In the back of his mind, Ionia could hear the voice of the headmaster from that day.

*"His ability becomes meaningless if his body is touched…"* That's right—even if Gravis tried to leap with his Power, the person in contact with his body would go with him.

"I've got him!"

He saw the assassin's hand holding Gravis's arms. He could also clearly see another enemy attacking him from behind.

*I'm going to protect you, I promise.*

"No!"

Ionia yelled and slid his body between Gravis and the man who was about to thrust his sword at him.

He felt a hot impact in his stomach.

"Io...!"

The shock of being stabbed in his side almost made him collapse, but he kept himself upright, threw away his sword, and put his hands on the attackers' bodies. His hands were touching a shoulder and a stomach.

*I'm going to destroy you.*

He never thought about the attackers being human. He just wanted to protect Gravis. With that thought alone, Ionia released all his Power from the palms of his hands.

A sound like a bursting fruit echoed across the room.

Something that was once human had become a red mist that splattered around him. He nearly wretched at the iron smell of blood and viscera.

Gravis and Ionia had been dyed by that mist.

Slowly, Ionia's vision turned dark.

Before Ionia knew it, he was lying on the floor, propped up by Gravis.

"Io! Ionia...! Stay with me!"

"Vi..."

Ionia opened his eyes and desperately stared into the starry-sky eyes. But the strength drained out of his body mercilessly. He could hear Gravis frantically calling his name.

Then a number of footsteps approached. And Stolf's voice.

"Your Highness! Are you safe?! ...What?!"

"Your Highness! ...Ugh!"

The soldiers of the Royal Army gasped at the carnage in the room and clamped their mouths shut.

Through his fading consciousness, Ionia remembered the words of the smiling headmaster.


*"With your Power, you will be His Highness's shield and destroy those who would harm him."*


*Ah, a human shield is exactly what I am. And just as my father had feared, I have now become a murderer.*

With this thought, Ionia lost consciousness.

# Leorino: Spring Is Still Far

August entered the room with a knock.

"Leorino, may we talk?"

"Yes, Father. But...I apologize that you have to see me like this."

Leorino, who had been lying on his bed, rushed to sit up when his father appeared.

August reassured him with a gesture of his hand.

"You don't have to get up. It's your room. You can rest," said his father kindly, but Leorino couldn't simply lay there in front of him. He got up and sat on the side of the bed with his legs tucked under him.

August pulled up a chair from the writing desk and sat in front of his son, who looked somewhat disheveled.

"Are you tired?"

"No... Well, yes, a little."

August gently scooped up Leorino's hands, which were resting weakly on his knees. He softly squeezed the tips of his thin fingers, hoping to cheer him up.

"Leorino, I want to speak with you for a moment."

Leorino knew what his father was going to say. But unable to look him in the eye, Leorino cast his gaze down.

August stroked the backs of Leorino's hands with his thumbs, trying to comfort his youngest son.

"I want to talk about Julian's courtship."

Leorino's hands trembled slightly. August squeezed them once more.

"Before dinner, Lord Julian came to me and told me he asked you to marry him... You must have been very surprised at the suddenness of it."

"Yes... Very much so, I must admit."

August nodded. Leorino slowly began to talk about his feelings.

"...I've been aware of Julian's feelings for a long time."

"I see. Well, he has been showing up very often. And when he does come, he's all over you. He's not very subtle about it."

Leorino smiled at his father's comment.

"Yes, that's right. I thought he was showing me overt favor... But I didn't expect him to ask me to marry him. I had always assumed that Julian, who is in need of an heir, wasn't...looking for a serious relationship with me."

"I see. That must have been very surprising."

"It was. And I...hesitated."

"You hesitated... I didn't think you had taken a liking to Lord Julian. You gave no such indication, so I thought..."

His father was about to begin a terrible misunderstanding. Leorino rushed to correct him, shaking his head.

"Oh, no, I don't feel any particular way about him... It's my future that I'm hesitant about."

"Hundert also reported to me that Lord Julian hurt you with his insensitive remarks. Is that right?"

Leorino shook his head once more. "...He didn't hurt me. I chose to feel hurt. Lord Julian simply stated a fact."

"What fact? That you will struggle to become independent?"

"...Yes."

August stood up, sat down next to his dejected son, and pulled Leorino's little head to his chest. Leorino did not resist. He released a shaky breath and began to speak of the anguish he had been suppressing. "Yes, there is the issue of my legs. I've never gone to school, and I've hardly ever left Brungwurt. I am also aware that I know little of the ways of the world."

There was no denying it. Leorino had only left the castle a handful of times in the past few years.

"I do not have the intelligence to compensate for my lack of experience, nor am I blessed with a fine physique to be a knight of the Imperial Guard, like Gauff. Nor do I have a special Power that could be of service to others, like Mother."

August listened in silence to Leorino's unusually honest words.

"...I'm just a helpless, ordinary child. But even so, I always wanted to live my life with my chin up, never forgetting the pride of the Cassieux family. I may be an ordinary person, but I hope to one day find something I can do, gain experience, and serve my country as a member of the Cassieux family, either in the royal capital or here in Brungwurt... But..."

Leorino clenched his fist and punched his thigh.

It was a sort of self-harm, hurting the leg that had taken several years to finally heal. August couldn't bear to watch and closed his hand around Leorino's fist to stop it.

"But Lord Julian told me that because of this...effeminate face of mine and my legs, it will be impossible for me to live on my own. He said I couldn't live alone without someone's protection..."

Leorino put his hand on his father's chest and pulled his body away. His expression was dark and his eyes desperate.

"Father...am I like a woman who has no choice but to be protected? Am I...an object to be loved like a rare doll because of my face, because of the color of my hair and eyes? Do I only have value because of my appearance?"

"No, Leorino. That's not true."

"Father, you are kind, and you have told me before that every life has value, but... I don't want to have to be protected by anyone!"

"Leorino..."

"I wish I could have been born powerful and strong like my brothers and be able to protect someone. I wanted to be of use to others."

It was the first time August saw Leorino show so much emotion, and his eyes blurred at his son's misery. He could feel the anguish that Leorino had been carrying in his heart.

Julian's casual remark about how Leorino would never be independent and must be protected, with a single blow, shattered the positive attitude that

Leorino, who felt indebted toward his family ever since the accident, had been desperately trying to maintain.

August regretted that he had carelessly allowed Julian to get so close to Leorino.

"I've finally realized how other people—especially *men*—see my face."

"Your beauty is not only in your face. It is your pure heart that we, your family, love about you."

Leorino laughed at himself. "My heart has seen a lot of filth. It's far from pure..."

"Leorino, what are you saying?"

"Father, please be honest with me. In the future, would it be best if I were placed under the protection of a...man of high standing, such as Lord Julian?"

August did not answer immediately.

Julian was right—it would be difficult for his youngest child to survive without a guardian. Leorino, however slender, was still a boy. If not for his leg injuries, he could have learned to defend himself, but that was impossible now. He was unable to engage in any strenuous physical activity.

And above all, Leorino's beauty was so far outside the ordinary that it made him miserable. Even if he had the means to defend himself, he would likely be targeted by the wrong people. He was simply that beautiful.

When Leorino was a child, all August had to do was dote on him. But how long would he be able to protect this beauty, which would shine ever brighter as Leorino matured, when August would only grow old? He couldn't deny that he, too, was concerned about what to do about his youngest son.

He wanted to be honest with Leorino, which left him at a loss for an immediate answer. Leorino looked at his father, heartbroken.

"...I should have been born a woman. If I had been a woman, with a face like this...I could be helpless, and I would not have troubled my father like this about my future. I would have been desired by a man like Lord Julian. I would have married him... I'm certain Mother would have preferred that, too."

"Leorino... That's not how it is at all... I couldn't be prouder to have you as my son, and no one wishes that you had been born a girl instead. We love just the way you are."

Leorino's frustrated remark had hurt his loving father. Leorino bit his lip and cast his gaze down. He was ashamed of his childish behavior. Still, he couldn't bring himself to apologize.

Just as he thought he wasn't going to cry, tears spilled from his eyes. He hated himself more than ever in that moment.

*God, I'm such a girl... Why am I so helpless...? If only I had a body like Ionia's...*

August watched in silence until his son calmed down, Leorino's cheeks wet from the storm raging in his heart.

Leorino soon stopped crying and apologized quietly to his father, who had waited patiently for him.

"Leorino, as I was saying. First, let me ask you what you want to do, not what you think should or should not be done."

Leorino lifted his wet face at his father's words.

"...What *I* want to do...?"

"You have revealed much of your heart to me, so I want to be honest with you... I refused Lord Julian's proposal, but when I heard it, I wavered."

Tears fell from Leorino's eyes once more.

"If you were chosen by the heir of the Duke of Leben, with the awareness that you will not be able to bear children, your future would be secure. Then I could entrust the role of protecting you to someone of equal standing to our family. I thought I could rest easy and simply age in peace."

August chided him for crying, and Leorino bit his lip.

"But I refused. Do you know why? Because you are my son. No boy of the Cassieux family lives by the crowd. Neither will you. No matter how hard physical therapy was, you did it without a single world of complaint, patiently, and of your own will. Because of that, I believe I should ask you what you want to do first."

"...Do I get to choose my future?"

August nodded emphatically. Of course, Leorino had the right to choose his own future.

"But I want to be honest with you. I'm not sure that you'll be able to live the life of an ordinary boy with your appearance, since you took after Maia and even surpassed her in beauty. Lord Julian may be correct in his assessment. But that, too, is part of your destiny."

His father's words were, in a way, an affirmation of Julian's words. But Leorino was able to listen calmly.

"You may not like the way you look, but we love *all* of you: your heart, your looks, and the burdens you carry on your shoulders each day."

Leorino looked his father firmly in the eye and nodded in understanding. His violet eyes were no longer wet and had regained their strength.

"It's *your* life, Leorino. Now, tell your father how you would like to live it. You get to decide."

*How do I want to live my life?*

Leorino had been living with his injuries, and his only goal had been to endure the pain of the day. He didn't have the luxury of thinking about how he wanted to live his life.

He was afraid to even consider it. Thinking about the future only made him anxious. That was why he had lived his life stifling his own potential.

Ionia had the Power to crush anything. Even a strong, healthy human body.

His love was never meant to be, and his Power might have made him miserable, but he was able to protect someone important to him. He got to die protecting his country.

But Leorino had nothing.

He had always despaired at how powerless he was in comparison to Ionia.

*...But if I could wish for one thing, I would like to be useful to Gravis again. I wish I could be by his side again, even if he doesn't know about Ionia and I...*

Right now, that was all he could think of.

So Leorino honestly told his father about his yet formless feelings.

"I don't know what exactly I want to do yet... But if I could choose how I want to live... I want to be able to protect someone, not just be protected, in spite of my body. So...I want to find something that I can do, no matter how small or trivial it may be."

Seeing his youngest son speaking so enthusiastically, even if haltingly, August's heart was filled with emotion as he realized that this boy was also a member of the noble Cassieux family. The blood of the Cassieux family, which protected the territory of Brungwurt to this day, ran through his veins just as well.

"Is that selfish of me? Is it ridiculous of me to want to believe that there is something I can do?" Leorino looked at him with imploring eyes.

August smiled. "You will be eighteen next year, a full-fledged adult."

"Yes."

"And you're aware that in the spring of the same year, the nobles who reach the age of maturity go to the royal capital to attend the Vow of Adulthood ceremony?"

Leorino nodded.

The Vow of Adulthood was a ceremony in which nobles just coming of age declared before the king that they would uphold their duties and serve their country. Auriano, Johan, and Gauff had all attended the ceremony in the capital when they each turned eighteen, of course.

"You must attend the ceremony just as any other adult nobleman. I, however, was planning to take you back to Brungwurt immediately after the ceremony and the soiree... But, Leorino?"

"Yes?"

"You may stay in the royal capital."

Leorino's violet eyes widened in surprise at his father's unexpected words. August laughed, cherishing his honest, childlike reaction.

"If you are looking for something to do, you would be better off in the royal capital than here in the middle of nowhere, where we would be too over-protective and fussy for you."

"Father... Do you mean it? You would allow me to go?"

"I will not allow you to live alone, of course. You will live with your brothers in the estate in the royal capital. Hundert will go with you, and I'll also find you a guard. But other than that, you are free to do as you please. You can look for work or study somewhere."

"Father...!"

"But you have two years. You are far behind compared to the children in the academy... But if after two years, you have not found anything you can do or want to do, or if we find that you are too weak to survive in the capital, we will bring you back here immediately. Do you still want to go?"

Leorino's surprised eyes shone with a strong determination.

Finally, Leorino nodded. Then he bowed to his father, asking for his per-mission. August nodded, put his firm hands on both his shoulders, and shook him roughly, as he would with Leorino's older brothers.

But his slender youngest son wobbled more than he expected, and he reduced his strength in a hurry.

The father and son looked at each other and laughed.

The year would soon be over. When spring came, Leorino would be able to go to the royal capital.

There lived the person he longed to see.

# Ionia: Beasts Roaring in the Night 5

The palms of his hands were touching something warm.

There was a baby in Ionia's arms. He felt the warmth of the small child in both of his hands. The baby was adorable, with red hair and blue eyes.

Ah, it was Dirk when he was little, Ionia's beloved baby brother, who would always smile at Ionia when he held him. For some reason, there was a knife in his little hand.

*...Dirk?*

Dirk struggled to escape Ionia's arms with an adorable smile. Ionia could see the back of a defenseless boy. Someone was holding the boy's arm. Dirk gleefully brandished the knife. Ionia panicked.

*No, Dirk, don't point that blade at him. If you do, I'll have to...*

At that moment, Ionia's vision was tinged with a bright-red mist.

A downpour of red, red, and more red. Crimson droplets trickled down the tips of his fingers and eyelashes. Torn reddish-brown strings fluttered through the air.

The baby in his arms was gone. Instead, there was a canopy of red mist and hundreds of blue eyeballs with red strings dancing in his field of view, all staring at Ionia.

*  *  *

*"Why did you kill me? Why? Why? Why did you shatter me?"*

He couldn't extend his arms. He couldn't move his red-stained body at all. He had shattered his brother.

*Right. I've destroyed everything.*

*Dirk...!*

*"Why did you shatter me? Because you would do anything for Vi? You're a murderer... Murderer... You're a monster who would even shatter a human being if it was for Gravis."*

*"Ahhh, it hurts. Having your body shattered hurts. Murderer, murderermurderermurderer..."*

"...Aaaaah!"

Ionia awoke suddenly, panting.

His heart was beating frighteningly fast. The world was shaking.

"You're all right. Io, it's just a dream."

"Luca... Luca... I killed Dirk this time... He was pointing a knife at Vi. I couldn't risk it..."

"Shhh... It's all right. You're all right. It was just a dream. You haven't hurt anyone. His Highness is safe. It's fine."

Lucas's hot fingertips caressed Ionia's throat over and over. He wrapped his arm around Ionia and pulled him close. The world shook because Ionia's body was trembling.

Ionia was slowly coming back to reality.

Lucas stroked his wet cheeks, whispering over and over again that he was all right in hopes of soothing him. Ionia's eyes widened, and he saw his familiar dorm room. The red mist was nowhere to be seen. He moved his awfully heavy head to look behind him and saw amber eyes fondly watching him. Lucas was still stroking his throat with his left hand.

Had he been shouting in his sleep again?

It had been a year and a half since the assassination attempt in the mock battle.

Since that day, Ionia had recurring dreams of shattering people. And every night he woke up denounced as a murderer. Sometimes he destroyed Gravis, sometimes his friends, and at other times his family. The same way as he did tonight.

A shadow fell on his cheek. Lucas planted his warm lips near the corner of Ionia's eye. Ionia's rigid body gradually relaxed. His ragged breathing slowly regained its normal rhythm.

"Feeling better?"

Ionia nodded quietly. The two remained still for a while.

Ionia had fully come to his senses and apologized quietly. The young man who had given him the warmth he had become so accustomed to over the past two years looked down at Ionia, chuckled, and began moving his fingers.

"...What are you doing?"

Ionia bent backward without a sound as a thick finger gently found its way inside him. He still tender from their earlier encounter.

"I suppose the last time wasn't enough. Shall I tire you out so much that you won't even be able to dream this time?"

"...Agh... Ah... Luca..."

"Want me to stop?"

The stiffness of Ionia's body melted away against his hot skin. It was Lucas who always held Ionia in his arms to comfort him when he couldn't sleep. Ionia shook his head and reached out to pull Lucas's head closer.

They shared a kiss, and their tongues entwined. Lucas's thick tongue lapped at the roof of Ionia's mouth and made the back of his eyelids numb. Lucas began to work his finger in and out a little more forcefully.

The wet sound of his fingers brushing against Ionia's insides echoed around the quiet room. With his other hand, Lucas stroked the firm muscles from Ionia's throat to his chest and caressed his rapidly hardening nipples.

Ionia's sensitive body twitched with each stroke.

A sweet pain filled his entire body. The bloody mist that had dominated his mind until a few moments ago cleared and, little by little, the thoughts receded.

Ionia surrendered himself to the throbbing desire at his waist.

He preferred to be taken, rather than be the one in control. He was especially fond of being taken roughly from behind. Feeling the heat of someone inside him, he felt as if he was melting from the inside and losing himself entirely.

He was lucky. Lucas always helped him forget everything through pleasure.

"Lucas... Enough... I want it now."

"Me too. I can't wait any longer."

Lucas nipped the nape of Ionia's neck, brushing his red hair back.

He tasted of sweat and sex. There was no longer a trace of his nightmares on Ionia's face as he enjoyed the pleasure with his eyes closed.

Lifting his long, beautifully muscled legs, Ionia smiled with relief, his eyes still closed, and he happily followed Lucas's lead and relaxed.

A pitiful, beloved young man who begged with all his being to forget the painful reality and the even more painful dreams. Lucas knew it was his role to fill the void in this young man's heart.

He was his romantic partner in crime who Gravis, with his different status and age, could never be. This was the devotion and loyalty that Lucas could offer Ionia.

Lucas slowly sank his hips back into the body that had had his member in a viselike grip mere moments ago.

The students in the hallway moved out of the way of the young red-haired man with unhidden apprehension. Ionia was used to such reactions and walked past them with a blank expression on his face.

Ionia had little memory of the immediate aftermath of the incident. According to Marzel, the accident at the battle drill had put the lives of many noblemen's children in danger, causing a commotion in the royal capital for a time.

However, a gag order was issued on the assassination attempt on the second prince that took place during the incident and was never reported to the public. Marzel had said this was due to the royal court's fear that it would give other countries an opportunity to take advantage of the situation.

But walls had ears in the academy. Only Stolf and a few teachers had actually witnessed the scene, but before long, people were whispering about the attempt on the prince's life.

It was not until three months after the incident that Ionia was able to return to school. After his return, Ionia's life at the academy changed drastically. He was a hero who fought off assassins and protected the prince, and he was a monster who could shatter people with his bare hands, and not only students but even teachers began keeping their distance.

It was then that he began to have nightmares every night.

But now, a year and a half later, he no longer felt anything.

At the end of the corridor, Lucas, who had spent nearly six years with him, was waiting. The young man had stopped to wait for Ionia and smiled when he saw him approaching.

Ionia would only see this smile for a few more weeks. He felt a small ache in his chest when he realized this.

Lucas would soon graduate from the academy and join the Royal Army. Ionia would be staying in school for another year because of the delay in his studies caused by his injuries.

When he laughed that this was very convenient, since he needed to guard Gravis, who had entered school one year after him, Lucas and Marzel scolded him for making light of his wounds.

Gravis was to attend school until he was fifteen, as planned. After the incident, Gravis's life was repeatedly threatened. Ionia did not hesitate to use his ability against Gravis's attackers.

Nightmares were just nightmares. Every time they came, he had a man to comfort him.

No matter how much blood he spilled, now that his hands had been sullied, they would never be clean again.

At the time of the incident, Ionia's wounds were severe, the one in his abdomen reaching as far as his internal organs. He had lost a lot of blood, and immediately afterward his life had been in danger. He survived thanks to the first aid of Sasha Klonoff, a young military doctor who was present at the drill, and his immediate transport to the royal capital for proper treatment.

When his condition stabilized some two weeks later, Gravis came to visit him in his hospital room in secret.

Seeing the boy for the first time in a while, Gravis looked at Ionia with a pale face. At the time, the guards were on high alert regarding Gravis's surroundings, but he entered the room alone.

Seeing with his own eyes that Gravis was safe, Ionia felt his heart, tormented by anxiety since he had awoken, finally relax.

"...Vi."

He was frustrated that his body wouldn't move like he wanted it to.

Unable to get up, Ionia managed to stretch his hand out, and Gravis knelt by the side of the bed and held his hand.

Ionia felt the precious warmth of Gravis's body for the first time in a while. He was so relieved that Gravis was safe.

But he couldn't have royalty kneeling to him.

"Vi... You shouldn't do that..."

Gravis ignored his words. He raised Ionia's hand with both of his own, pressed it to his forehead, and hung his head for a while. His hands were cold.

Finally, Ionia heard him say in a strained voice: "I'm so glad you woke up."

After a knock on the door, they heard a servant's voice from the other side of the door saying: "It's time, sir."

Ionia was privately disappointed to learn that Gravis was leaving so soon. Gravis gently placed Ionia's hand back on the bed and stood up.

*Don't go. Stay with me a little longer.*

It was their first time alone together since that night.

Gravis's starry-sky gaze met his violet eyes. They could not speak a word to each other.

After he had watched Ionia for a while, Gravis's face lost all emotion once more.

"I have to go."

Right. Gravis was always busy with his royal duties. He was in an entirely different position from Ionia, who now spent his days in bed.

When Ionia nodded, Gravis said in a firm tone: "The incident is still under investigation. I will tell you the full story one day. Get lots of rest and heal."

Ionia instantly reached for his back as he turned on his heel and was about to leave the hospital room. His wounded back. He could see Gravis's wounds, torn between his love for his country and his love for his mother and half brother, respectively.

*Oh, this boy has been hurt so badly.*

*I wanted to protect him... I failed.*

"Vi... Is it hard for you...? Are you all right?"

He called out to his back without thinking. The prince's shoulders trembled as he held his hand on the door.

When Gravis turned back to him, he had a look of fury in his eyes. The prince approached the bed again with heavy steps.

"Why are you always so...?!"

"...Vi?"

"I'm all you care about! I made you into a literal human shield, and still you... You were wounded, you spilled blood for me, but you keep putting yourself last!"

Gravis thrust his hands out to both of his sides and hung over him. Ionia was shocked by the unusually violent gesture.

There was a frenzied emotion in Gravis's eyes. Ionia could only look up at him, mesmerized by his eyes.

The knocking sounded again.

When he glanced at the door, he heard Gravis yell: "Silence!" Instantly, the world beyond the door became quiet.

Ionia was dumbfounded.

"...I forced you to use your Power."

Gravis's expressionless mask finally fell away, exposing the violent emotion beneath.

"I know you've always been afraid of using your Power to hurt people. But you did exactly that in order to protect me."

Gravis mercilessly confronted Ionia with the fact he had been trying not to think about since he woke up.

"All I wanted was to be with you for a few years. I didn't want to involve you in my affairs. But you've shed so much blood, you've been wounded so badly, and you still want to be by my side."

Gravis was now biting his lip so hard that it bled.

That was what Ionia wanted.

"What am I supposed to do? Do I just watch you get hurt...? Or do I say that those wounds belong to me and stay on this path, soaking up your blood?"

Ionia reached out and wiped the blood from Gravis's lips.

"Vi, I want to protect you. That's all I want. You don't need to concern yourself with me."

Gravis brought his face closer. His starry-sky eyes shone brightly.

"Vi...?"

Gravis sealed Ionia's lips with his. Ionia's eyes widened in shock.

"...I've made up my mind."

Ionia could only stare in a daze at the beautiful face pulling away from him.

"I'm still a foolish child who needs your protection... But I've made up my mind. I won't let it end here. I will never let you go, not even after graduation."

"Vi..."

"I will not allow you to leave me. I'm certain you'll shed more blood to protect me. Call me arrogant if you wish. I'm the one making you do it."

"What are you—?"

Gravis's lips pressed tightly against Ionia's once more to keep him from speaking.

The starry-sky eyes snatched away every last bit of Ionia.

"Do you understand, Io? You are not spilling blood of your own will. I am making you do it to protect the helpless, foolish child I am."

With that, Gravis scooped up Ionia's fingers and pressed his lips to them.

"Remember. The blood on your hands, the blood from your own wounds, it's all mine."

Ionia and Gravis would soon graduate from the academy of higher learning together.

Lucas graduated a year prior and joined the Royal Army ahead of Ionia. Ionia had also decided to join the Royal Army after graduation. On many occasions, he had protected Gravis from assassination attempts with his own hands. However, upon graduation, his role as Gravis's guard would end.

If he could keep the prince safe on campus for a little longer, his role would be fulfilled.

But what about his position as Gravis's best friend?

It was rumored that Gravis would assume a key position in the Royal Army after graduation. People were also whispering behind his back that the battle for the succession to the throne would soon be in full swing.

On that day, Gravis told Ionia that all the blood Ionia spilled would be his. From that moment onward, Ionia's blood and devotion would belong to Gravis forever.

However, after graduation, their positions would be worlds different from what they had been. No one could tell Ionia how far he would be able to stay by Gravis's side, even if they both joined the Royal Army.

One day close to graduation, Ionia was summoned to the headmaster's office. Waiting there for Ionia was a person he couldn't have expected.

A middle-aged woman with a dignified appearance sat elegantly on a settee. Her attire and bearing indicated that she was a woman of high standing. Her eyes were dark as she gazed at Ionia, and she looked vaguely familiar. A girl with flaxen hair sat next to her. She must have been a little younger than Ionia.

Two men stood by the door, and two large men in the uniforms of the knights of the Imperial Guard stood by the wall behind the settee. They were quite the entourage. Next to them stood a middle-aged woman who appeared to be a lady's maid and two relatively young women.

By that point, Ionia had some idea of who these women were.

"Ionia Bergund, isn't it?"

Her voice was beautiful and cold. Ionia bowed in the manner he had learned, and the woman nodded at him with an air of nonchalance.

"Come closer."

Ionia obeyed her command and approached the settee. The moment he saw the woman's eyes up close, he gasped. He knelt down and gave her his deepest bow.

"Raise your head."

Starry-sky eyes, Prussian blue flecked with gold. The rare sort of eyes that appeared only in the Francoure royal family.

Ionia's knees trembled faintly.

"You seem to know who I am."

In front of him was the noblest woman in the land, Queen Adele, Gravis's mother.

Why had this noblewoman, who had come from the great Kingdom of Francoure and was praised as a wise queen who protected the reign of the current king, ask to see Ionia, a student and a commoner?

His heart was filled with doubt and anxiety, but he couldn't say anything without explicit permission.

A slender finger reached out and lifted Ionia's chin. Ionia dropped his gaze, trying to avoid eye contact. For a moment, he saw the queen up close, a woman of timeless beauty. She must have been in her midforties but did not look her age at all.

It was clear that Gravis had inherited his good looks from his mother. But his dark hair and large physique must have come from his father, the king.

Looking into Ionia's eyes, the queen murmured:

"...Violet, I see. Not as rare as ours, but a rare color in this country."

There was nothing he could say to those words, so he endured them silently as she held his chin.

Soon the cold fingers pulled away.

Quickly enough to be courteous, Ionia stood upright, keeping a short distance from the settee. He folded his hands in front of him and lowered his gaze in a military-like gesture of reverence.

"I want to thank you for saving the prince from the brink of death on more than one occasion. I have heard from Stolf and the headmaster that you have protected him with your unique abilities. You did very well."

"...I am not worthy of your praise."

The queen showed her appreciation for Ionia's hard work. Her voice was soft but cold, and a shiver ran down Ionia's spine.

"I would like to have a few moments alone with Ionia. Everyone but Helena must leave."

"Your Majesty...!"

The queen's unexpected request caused a commotion.

"...Y-Your Majesty! What are you saying?!"

"That's not safe! You're aware of his Power...!"

What did the queen want to talk to Ionia about that required everyone else to leave the room?

The queen silenced the men's protests with a wave of her fingers. Once more she quietly issued her order.

"Silence. All I need is a moment. This young man, who is so devoted to protecting Gravis, will not harm me, his mother... Am I right, Ionia?"

"...Of course."

He bowed his head, fighting back the pain in his chest at being treated like a threat.

The knights insisted that they could not allow that.

"Then let's keep the maids. Maika here is very strong. He mustn't touch me, in which case... Maika, come here."

The younger of the two maids nodded silently and placed herself between the queen and Ionia. Ionia watched this half-dazed, unable to keep up with the suddenness of the situation.

The men continued to complain for a while, but when the queen glared at them coldly, they gave up, hung their heads, and left.

As soon as the guards left, the room suddenly became larger, and the air grew cold.

A painful silence followed for a while.

The queen turned to Ionia once more.

"Ionia Bergund... I have been meaning to speak with you for a long time."

"...The honor is mine."

About what? About the prince she had mothered, of course.

"The prince seems to rely on you significantly. Stolf told me how you first met. He told me that the prince opened his heart to you during a difficult time, and that he was now...relying on you as his bodyguard."

"...Yes, Your Majesty."

"I've also heard that he wants to keep you around as *more* than just his schoolmate and bodyguard. He wants to keep you close to him as his confidant even after graduation."

Ionia had nothing to say to that.

The queen kept her cold, starry-sky eyes fixed on Ionia as she continued to speak in her icy tone.

"Gravis will soon be betrothed to Helena here."

The flaxen-haired girl smiled at Ionia.

She must have been about the same age as Gravis, and although she still looked more like a young girl than a woman, she was gorgeous, a proper child of a noble family.

"Helena is the daughter of the Duke of Müller. When the prince comes of age, he will marry her immediately."

Ionia wasn't sure if he managed to suppress the trembling in his body.

He had been prepared for this for some time.

Gravis and Ionia were royalty and guard dog, respectively. Their relationship would not change in the future. But why did the queen go out of her way to emphasize that point?

Ionia gritted his teeth, lowered his gaze, and tried desperately to keep his expression firm. If he hadn't, he would have screamed.

But the next thing the queen said made Ionia distinctly shudder.

"But recently in the presence of Helena and I, the prince declared: 'I do not intend to marry anyone, ever.'"

"...What?"

"Considering my son's position, marrying Helena is his best option. The Duke of Müller and Helena are of the same mind, of course. However, my son insisted that he would remain a bachelor for the rest of his life in order to avoid causing any undue disturbances. He says he will watch over the crown prince as he ascends the throne, and spend the rest of his life in the army, defending the country in a different capacity."

For the first time, the queen lowered her gaze for the briefest moment, but she quickly raised her head and looked at Ionia again. Her eyes, so much like Gravis's, stared at him so intensely that it nearly penetrated the deepest part of his brain. She really resembled Gravis so much. The person sitting in front of Ionia was undoubtedly Gravis's mother, the queen of this country.

He never thought he would stand so close to the queen. He thought idly about how far he had come from the blacksmith's shop.

"Ionia Bergund, let me ask you plainly: What is the relationship between you and my son?"

Ionia shuddered.

"I am afraid that I am only a schoolmate and a guard for His Highness the second prince... Nothing more."

"No, there is more. At least, for him. This is my mother's intuition speaking. I may be wrong. But your presence is leading my son astray."

"No, that's preposterous...!"

"No, that boy is lost. He is trying to escape to a place of peace, taking you along with him in the name of 'protecting the country,' neglecting the responsibility he truly has to fulfill for the sake of this nation."

"No, that's... Vi, His Highness is in no way running away! He has been pursuing the choice he thinks is best for the country in his own way."

The queen's starry-sky eyes were filled with cold, dark emotion.

"What do you know of the responsibility of the royal family to this great nation? If this country is weakened as a result of his neglect of his responsibilities, who will take the blame?"

"...With all due respect, what is this 'responsibility' you speak of, Your Majesty?"

"You have been by my son's side all these years. You have spilled blood to protect him. Are *you* of all people asking me that?"

"I..." Ionia bit his lip and looked down.

"What I'm saying is that your presence has become an escape for the prince. He is no longer hiding his fixation with you. Let go of him and distance yourself from him immediately. I also want you to urge my son to propose to Helena. I ask this as a queen and as his mother."

His clenched fists trembled.

This was a misunderstanding. Ionia and Gravis had no such relationship. Gravis couldn't have been fixated on him or trying to escape his responsibilities. Otherwise, why would he have hidden his love from him?

At that moment, the girl who had been sitting silently by the queen's side spoke for the first time.

"Ionia, Her Majesty is truly grateful for your past devotion. You have done very well to protect His Highness as his schoolmate. But from now on, I would like to use my family name to strengthen and support his future position."

Her voice was like the toll of a beautiful bell.

"You will continue to stand in front of His Highness as his shield and protect him. You are a commoner. There is nothing you can do for His Highness's future except to be a shield. As a commoner, you do not have the right to stand by his side. It is I, a noblewoman, who does."

The graduation ceremony ended anticlimactically.

It was originally intended only for the students to receive their diplomas. There was no custom of current students seeing the graduates off. At best, the graduates congratulated one another, but no student had the courage to congratulate a royal like Gravis. Ionia, who had stayed an extra year at the academy, had no close friends.

The two quietly lived through the day and graduated from school.

Ionia returned to the dormitories alone.

After completing the procedures for leaving the dormitory and saying his good-byes to the students, he dispassionately packed his personal belongings in his room. Until he joined the army at the beginning of the new year, he would live at his parents' house in the commoner district for the first time in seven years. He didn't own much, so the packing was over almost as soon as it started.

Memories of his time in this room come back to him one after another.

Their secret encounters before bedtime had been brief, but he and Gravis never tired of talking to each other as they lay together on the narrow bed and joked with each other. This room, where he and Gravis had had their nightly encounters in secret, was a miraculous safe haven. At least until the day Ionia had ruined it and Gravis leaped out of it for good.

Gravis never returned to their no-longer-safe haven. In return for abandoning their innocent connection, Ionia had his love for him cast in the mold of loyalty. He heated it and continued to forge it. At the same time, he made the young man who had been his best friend into his romantic partner in crime.

It was also in this room that he and Lucas had spent many nights drowning in sweat and sensuality, to escape from Ionia's nightmares.

For seven years, Ionia had lived by picking up the pieces of happy memories scattered in the four corners of the room. With these fragments, he removed his desires from his love for Gravis, removed his hopes for the future... And through that, he had been able to hone his loyalty to him. Today those days came to an end.

After his secret meeting with the queen, Ionia received an unsigned letter. The letter was delivered by the young lady-in-waiting who had been called Maika.

Ionia was asked to read the letter on the spot. As soon as he finished reading it, the maid snatched it back and immediately threw it into the fireplace to be burned to ashes.

The letter was written in short sentences: *Do not let the giant star fall. Think on what is best for our country and make the right decision.*

"Do not let the giant star fall," in other words, make sure Gravis ascended the throne.

Ionia had been thinking about this ever since. What *was* the best course for the country?

Gravis wanted to support his half brother, who would become king if he stepped down from the throne succession race that had been set up by the people around him. But at the same time, he could not betray the expectations of his mother, who had followed a solitary path as queen for the sake of the country.

The queen must have known of her son's suffering. Despite that, she still insisted on putting the crown on Gravis's head.

Was it her sense of responsibility as a queen who worried about the future of her country? Or was it the vengeful spirit of a woman who had suffered unbearable humiliation at the hands of her husband?

The queen was right: The best course for the country might have been for Gravis to succeed the throne.

Gravis had denied the crown prince's involvement in the repeated assassination attempts. However, even if it was not the crown prince himself but someone from his faction, could it be possible that he was completely unaware of their actions?

Was he foolish or cunning? Either way, the thought of such a person on the throne explained the queen's concerns.

Was there no future in which Gravis chose to succeed to the throne? What could Ionia do now?

As Ionia was lost in thought, he heard someone call his name from behind.

"Ionia."

He turned around to see a young man standing there, now fully grown, with the body of an adult.

He remembered the soft voice of the boy he was before his voice changed. Now his voice was much lower.

His cold, timeless beauty had sharpened his rounded cheeks, and he was becoming more mature and masculine in appearance. He had also surpassed Ionia in height. It was hard to believe that he had three years left before he became a full-fledged adult.

The only thing that had not changed since they first met was his eyes, still that same indigo with twinkling gold stars. Their pull was immense, but their light was fleeting and so beautiful that Ionia felt as if he could be sucked into them.

"Congratulations on your graduation, Io."

"You too, Vi... Congratulations on your graduation."

Ionia gazed into those starry-sky eyes to his heart's content, knowing that this might be the last time he would ever see them.

"I am grateful for your sacrifice and dedication over the past six years. It was just as you promised me that day. You have been much closer to me than to your significant other."

Ionia smiled quietly.

"You said you wouldn't let me go, no matter how much blood was on my hands."

For some reason, the words just flowed out of him today.

"That's right. I didn't want to let you go. I was grateful to the assassins. As long as they were after me, you would always be by my side. I weighed my life against my time with you, and it was worth it. You were the only one I could trust with my back."

Gravis was also open and honest today. Ionia was so happy to hear those words.

Ionia smiled warmly.

"I doubt that the time you spend with me is worth your life. I know you're joking, but it makes me feel like it was all worth it. I'm glad."

Gravis narrowed his eyes, as if looking at something too bright.

Ionia smiled in that unclouded way that reminded Gravis of the lively, friendly Ionia of his childhood. It was a smile he hadn't shown Gravis in a long time.

"Ionia... I'm not getting married. I came here today to tell you that."

"And here I was going to congratulate you. I really think you should. You would make a great couple."

"I know what Lady Helena told you. Foolishly enough, she had the gall to let me in on it. Yes, I might do so if my engagement to her will buy me more time. I don't care if they say it's despicable behavior. And that's only until I come of age. I will never marry."

Ionia tilted his head as his smile deepened.

"...Why not?"

"Why? *You* of all people are asking me that, here and now?"

The queen had said the same thing.

Ionia was impressed by the resemblance between mother and son.

"Because I need time until my brother becomes king. I hear that His Majesty's illness is not expected to heal. They don't know how many years he has left... That's why my mother is in such a hurry. She wants me to marry the daughter of a duke and have children as soon as possible so that I can strengthen my position before His Majesty's death."

Come to think of it, that girl had declared that she would strengthen Gravis's position with her family name.

"But they have to wait three more years until I come of age. I will never marry. I will never become king, even if it disappoints my mother. Instead, I vow to support the king as his royal brother to the best of my ability, and to protect this country and make it prosper."

"...Why, when your life is at stake? Why are you so loyal to the crown prince?"

"I don't know if all the attacks so far have been ordered by my brother. As long as there is no clear evidence, I want to trust him. If I could show that I am not a threat to the throne and that I know my place, the factions supporting him might cease trying to kill me."

This irritated Ionia.

"You know that's not true. You have never shown any interest in the throne. You have made it clear that you want to be a military man and that you know your place. And yet they keep trying to kill you!"

"My brother's situation is complicated. If they knew I had no ill intentions—"

"You once told me that I was always sacrificing myself for you. But you're just the same. For your country, for the crown prince, for the queen. You've never shown even a hint of ill intentions!"

Ionia finally fought back with emotion.

Gravis then proudly declared: "I told you already that I was weighing your life against mine. I have only one ambition: to keep you by my side for the rest of my life."

"...Don't be silly."

"Fine, let me be silly. I'll do everything I can to buy time until my father's passing and hand the throne to my brother. You must survive until then. Then I will join the army and distance myself from the royal court. I can't give up my right to the throne unless I commit a crime, but as long as my brother becomes king, I'll be free. I can remain by your side as a soldier."

*He'll be free to be with me.*

The prince's words, carried away by the heat of the moment, brought a dark delight to Ionia.

Although their relationship did not blossom into romance, the prince's intense attachment to Ionia remained. The scales of Gravis's heart were ever tilted in Ionia's favor. There was a longing there that could not be contained in the word *love*.

If this was not joy, what was?

At the same time, Ionia could vividly imagine Gravis regretting his decision to abandon his responsibility to the country.

"I'm happy to hear that. I really am, Vi. But what if...I don't want that?"

Gravis's eyes widened at his response.

"You are royalty. Your life is different from us commoners. Is that really the right choice, Your Highness?"

"Don't call me that!"

"No, I think I will. You know what the right choice for this country is. Everyone agrees that you are better suited to be king, but will your heart really be at peace if you abandon that responsibility and choose...me?"

Gravis's eyes clouded with pain.

"...Don't make this hard for me, Io."

"I'm not trying to. I'm saying that as royalty, you need to be mindful of your responsibilities. There will come a time when you will need to choose the best path for this country. I don't want to be a hindrance to you. You don't need to twist your path for my sake."

At these words, Gravis's face contorted in pain.

"You're...fine with me belonging to someone else?"

Ionia impulsively hugged Gravis.

"...I'm fine with that."

Gravis stiffened. Ionia put more strength into his arms. He placed his forehead against Gravis's and closed his eyes.

"I don't care if you belong to someone else, because *I* already belong to *you*."

"...Ionia."

"You don't have to give up anything to have me. Vi...you are free. You are free to choose whatever you want. My blood and loyalty are already yours. What more do you need?"

"...No. You don't belong to me. You belong to Lucas."

Gravis hesitantly placed his long arms on Ionia's back. He nuzzled his forehead against Ionia's neck and pleaded in a muffled voice. "Ionia... I want you. I've always, always wanted you. I don't just want your loyalty, I want everything you are and will be. I want you to be mine...truly mine, forever."

There was more than just attachment in those starry-sky eyes. There were signs of an unfamiliar lust.

For the first time ever, their feelings were mutual.

Ionia had been waiting for a long, long time for this moment, when Gravis would finally desire Ionia with all his heart and soul.

When the new year came, Ionia would join the Royal Army. Graduates of the academy were considered to have already completed their basic training and became officers. It was already decided that he would be assigned to the mountain unit and be put in charge of a platoon. He was to be deployed to the mountains in the northwest immediately.

It was a demanding unit, and he would not be able to return to the royal capital for several years.

He didn't resent being separated from Gravis. He had long accepted his resignation.

He had already received the words he wanted to hear. He had gotten enough.

If marrying the daughter of a duke broadened Gravis's options, he would support that, too.

If Ionia himself stood in Gravis's way, then he would keep himself away from Gravis.

Ionia ran his fingers through Gravis's wavy black hair. Gravis looked up. They gazed at each other from this breathtaking distance.

"Io... I want you."

"Don't be silly. I have a significant other."

"Ionia..."

"But if you want me, you can have me. All of me, just for tonight."

It was *Ionia* who wanted *Gravis*.

This was his final act of selfishness. He wanted the memories, aflame with passion, to channel this overwhelming desire.

He wanted the memories to serve as a spark that would help him hone his loyalty to Gravis even further.

Standing on his tiptoes to overcome the slight difference in height, Ionia kissed the lips of the slightly trembling young man. Gravis's starry-sky eyes widened in shock.

"...I'm okay with anything. You can do whatever you want with me. If that makes you certain."

*That I am yours.*

Ionia pulled him by the arm and slowly pushed him down onto the freshly made bed. Gravis was so surprised, he was speechless as Ionia climbed onto the bed after him, straddling him and placing his hands on the buttons of Gravis's shirt.

"Io…"

"Hush…"

Ionia brought his lips to Gravis's ear and whispered: "Get ready." Gravis shivered. When their gazes met again, Ionia smiled gently.

"You must fulfill your duty as royalty until you are certain that you will not regret abandoning it. Otherwise, you will definitely regret it."

"But then you'll leave me."

"I won't leave you… I will never leave you. Whatever path you choose, you will bring me with you. Just like the day we first met."

The moment he heard those words, the stars in Gravis's eyes lit up.

And so, he asked in a low voice:

"Once I'm ready…can I take you anywhere?"

Ionia nodded.

"You've been struggling for fifteen years, haven't you? Be ready, Vi. You have to be ready to take me with you."

"…In exchange, can I do whatever I want with you, just for tonight?"

Ionia nodded again.

Gravis's supple, muscular hands gripped Ionia's hips tightly. Ionia's breath caught in his throat in anticipation and arousal as Gravis's fingers tightened around his flesh. With a fierce expression on his face, Gravis pushed Ionia onto the bed.

Gravis's presence became everything in the world.

This was the moment Ionia had longed for. His delight numbed his mind.

"And one day, when I'm certain I've made the right choice…then I can choose to live with you?"

Ionia heard his beloved boy's heartrending request through his ragged breathing but couldn't bring himself to respond.

He wasn't even sure if he nodded. He just wanted to drown in the passion he had desired for so long.

At the same time, Ionia had a certain premonition.

This would be the first and last time he would ever lay with Gravis like this. And one day, he would die giving his life and loyalty for him.

The world was covered in snow and ice as far as the eye could see. Three years had passed since Ionia was sent from the royal capital to this mountainous region. In the winter of that year, the entire continent of Agalea was hit by a nearly unprecedented cold spell. Fanoren, located in the center of the continent, also suffered from this cold wave, which quickly became a national crisis. The entire country was covered with snow and ice, making it impossible to harvest crops even in the warmer southern regions. The northern regions were buried under a thick layer of snow, taller than most people. In many places, houses collapsed and livestock died.

Ionia's squad, which was deployed in the mountainous northwestern region, was also working to guard the border under difficult conditions.

When starvation finally set in, a national policy was adopted to evacuate the northern population to less damaged areas, and the rescued inhabitants were sent to the south. The most recent mission of Ionia's squad was to rescue several hundred residents from an isolated area.

In the neighboring country of Zwelf, located in the northernmost part of the Agalean continent, even more people were said to have frozen or starved to death. In the royal capital, both Gravis and Lucas were probably working with no time to sleep.

Staring at the snow-covered world from the top of the fort, Ionia frowned at the cold. Even thick gloves and a fur-lined overcoat could not completely protect him from the subzero temperatures.

The world was white and gray. As he stood alone in this white, silent world, the days spent in the royal capital seemed like a short-lived dream. He hadn't seen Gravis once since the night of the graduation ceremony. The same was true for Lucas.

The year after they graduated, the engagement between Gravis and the daughter of the Duke of Müller was announced. Gravis had said the engagement was just a way to stall for time, but Ionia didn't mind if they really got married.

After being placed so far away, he felt more than ever before his feelings for Gravis overflowing.

*I love you, I love you.* He carried those words in his heart and sent them into the invisible starry sky.

Every time he spoke those words in his mind, he remembered the warmth he and Gravis had shared that day, lighting a fire in his heart. *Even in this freezing land, I can live with just the memory of that day,* Ionia thought.

However, Gravis's marriage, which was to be announced after the Vow of Adulthood ceremony, was never publicly announced.

Then came winter, and the great cold wave with it.


After the most severe New Year's Eve in Fanoren history, spring finally arrived after a long winter. Although the damage in many areas was devastating, Fanoren survived the national crisis without too many human casualties, and positive momentum for recovery began to build throughout the country.


However, a time of great strife came again. The neighboring country of Zwelf suddenly invaded Fanoren without a declaration of war.

Ionia later learned that at the end of the year, the Royal Army and the court had already been aware of the unsettling developments in Zwelf.

Defying Fanoren's prediction that the invasion would come from the Zweilink side, the first battlefield was the mountainous area to the northwest, where Ionia's squad was deployed. The mountain troops, widely deployed in the northwestern mountains, were engaged in small-scale violent clashes with Zwelf's infantry units all throughout the region.

The platoon under Ionia's command was mostly made up of commoners. Five of them, known as the Special Forces, possessed special Powers:

Ionia, who destroyed anything he touched; Edgar Yorke, who could control the wind; Tobias Bosse, who could hear sounds from far distances; Xavier

Erdland, who could restrain his opponents' movements without touching them; and Ebbo Steiger, who had superhuman strength.

Ionia's squad was intentionally assembled for special missions. They were not deployed to a specific area but were active as a special support unit dispatched to areas where the fighting had intensified.

Immediately after the war broke out, Ionia's squad was ordered to temporarily return to the royal capital.

"Ionia Bergund, returning from the front."

Stolf and other important members of the Royal Army were all present in the Supreme Office of the Palace of Defense during Ionia's first return to the capital since being appointed to his post.

Ionia saluted with beautiful posture. After his salute, he noticed that Gravis and Lucas, whom he hadn't seen in some three years, were also there. Gravis was now the chief of staff of the Royal Army, and Lucas was one of his deputy chiefs of staff.

Gravis had completed his Vow of Adulthood ceremony the previous spring and was now nineteen years old. In the past three years, he had completely lost his boyishness, and now his grandeur as royalty and his own ambition gave him a particularly strong presence.

Their gazes met for the briefest moment. Neither Ionia nor Gravis changed their expressions.

The reason why Ionia was called back to the royal capital was to withdraw his unit from the mountainous area in the northwest and dispatch it to Zweilink in the northeast. The mountains were now the main battleground, but the enemy's offensive was half-baked, so this was preparation for the possibility that the enemy would invade Zweilink in the future.

The mountain region was large. While concentrating their forces there, the Royal Army was unable to devote many troops to Zweilink, so Ionia and his Special Forces were selected for the job.

They were in no position to say no to orders. Ionia silently accepted the appointment.

They were to move to Zweilink in three days.

"Ionia."

When Ionia returned to the simple lodging room for officers at the Palace of Defense, Lucas was waiting for him at the door.

After an absence of some three years, his significant other had become a stronger, calmer man. He watched Ionia with a fond smile.

It was as if Ionia was basking in the sun that he had so desperately waited for in that snow-covered fortress. His heart immediately felt warmer.

He invited Lucas into the room, and slowly they embraced. Lucas's body was thicker than before. He could sense the familiar scent from Lucas's chest.

"Lucas...it's been so long. You're looking stronger than ever."

"...It's not easy being popular, you know. I've had many opportunities for flings since you've been away from the royal capital for so long."

They shared some light banter and laughed quietly.

Still in his embrace, Ionia asked: "Will we spend the rest of today together?"

"No... I have another meeting with His Highness after this. Just as you're in the capital, too. It's such a shame."

Lucas complained that he didn't even have time for tea. He was glad he had come to see him for the few moments between meetings.

"Right... I'll be staying at my parents' house tomorrow. I don't know if I'll see you again before I leave."

Lucas sighed.

"It's hard for me to have you at the front. We can't even have sex."

He stroked Ionia's cheek.

Ionia placed his hand on top of Lucas's and pressed his cheek into his palm. Lucas's amber eyes watched Ionia lovingly.

This man's tender feelings had always been a help and a comfort.

*Oh... I do love him. I love Lucas.*

Ionia suddenly realized that, although he could not offer him the full extent of his love, he had indeed given a part of his heart to Lucas.

At that moment, he thought about telling Lucas how he felt about him, but he didn't think he would be able to put it into words.

Ionia smiled in Lucas's arms.

He didn't have to say anything right now. Ionia decided to tell him when they saw each other again and stopped himself from making an impulsive confession.

"What's up? Why are you grinning all of a sudden...?"

"Heh, it's nothing... I'll tell you the next time I see you."

"Oh, I don't want you to go." Lucas hugged him tightly again. Ionia patted him on the shoulder soothingly.

"I'll be fine. With these hands, most of my enemies are no match for me. You haven't forgotten, have you?"

"But there is always a chance. Ionia, if you need me, I'll be there to help you... So be careful. Stay safe."

"I'll be fine. I mean it. You take care of Gravis—His Highness for me."

Lucas was not amused. Ionia laughed at his clearly sulky significant other.

"You always put His Highness first and foremost... What about me? Am I not your significant other?"

"*Now* you have a problem with that? It's fine, really. Protect Vi for me while I can't protect him myself. You're the only one I can ask."

Ionia kissed Lucas on the cheek. Lucas stared into his violet eyes.

"I'll do whatever you say. I'll stay quietly next to His Highness... But, Ionia."

"I love you. Be safe." With these words, Lucas kissed Ionia lightly on the lips and returned to his meetings.

Ionia whispered quietly to his back. "...I'll tell you everything the next time I see you. Lucas, I care about you, too. I love you."

The day before his departure, Ionia returned to his parents' house.

After dinner, Ionia was left alone in the forge. The workshop was dark and submerged in the blue of night, and the smell of iron and charcoal, familiar to him since his childhood, wafted through the air.

This was where it all began.

Ionia's life gained meaning when he met Gravis here.

"Ionia."

He hadn't heard that voice in three years. Somehow he had a feeling that Gravis would come see him this evening.

"How do you always know where I am?"

"I just do. I know where you are."

"And you always call my name from behind."

Gravis tilted his head, wondering if that was true.

"...I missed you." Gravis hugged Ionia tightly. Ionia wrapped his arms around Gravis's back. Gravis looked much more masculine, his body thicker than it had been three years ago.

Ionia wondered about himself. He wondered if he had grown into a strong and dependable man over the past three years. "I missed you, too... Right, what about your marriage to the daughter of the duke?"

"It's been one thing after another with this war and last year's climate disaster. It's no time to marry. If anything, I'm grateful to Zwelf for the reprieve."

Ionia slapped him hard on the back for joking about such serious subjects.

Gravis gave a muffled laugh and then earnestly looked into Ionia's eyes.

"...I had hoped to quickly build up my strength in the army and bring you back to the royal capital. I've been desperately laying the groundwork for the past three years."

"Right."

"But now this war has begun. Stolf and I decided that...it would be most efficient to send your unit to Zweilink, where we're stretched thin."

"My unit would be more effective even with fewer men. Isn't that right?"

"Yes, now that we have the main army in the Baedeker Mountains, if anything should happen to Zweilink, we can count on your men."

Ionia nodded in understanding.

"I've always wanted to have you by my side... But even in times like this, I put the best of the country ahead of myself. Somewhere along the way, I realized that you're going to be an important asset... Do you hate me now?"

Ionia silently shook his head. If anything, he was happy to be depended upon.

Gravis looked around the dark workshop.

"I've brought you this far… From this forge to the front lines of battle."

"I'm glad you were ready to take me with you. Thanks to you, we can fight together forever."

*Isn't that right?* he asked with his eyes, and Gravis looked at Ionia with his eyes glistening with gold and nodded.

"Yes. I brought you this far to be with you forever. When this war is over… I will finally make my choice. When I do, please…choose me, too."

What kind of future awaited the two of them after this war ended?

"I will also protect this kingdom that you want to protect. Leave Zweilink to me. Even if the enemy arrives, I will never let them through… I will protect it to the end."

Ionia wished with all his heart that the war would end quickly and give Gravis a future where he could choose freedom.

He felt he would do anything to achieve that.

Two weeks had passed since he was sent to Zweilink. It happened on a beautiful starry night.

Tobias, with his good hearing, was the first to notice something unusual in the outer fortress. By the time Ionia rushed from the inner to the outer fortress, the fort was already occupied by Zwelf's army. It was clear that Zwelf was being led by an inside man, and the outer fort was no longer retrievable.

Fire arrows were fired one after another from the top of the outer fortress into the middle ground. The plains were immediately engulfed in flames. If the inner fortress was breached at this rate, they wouldn't stand a chance.

In his mind, Ionia turned to Gravis in the royal capital. He was not sure if Gravis could even hear him. But Ionia's voice did reach Gravis.

*"I'm going to save you! You must survive! Just wait for me!"*

These words brought newfound energy to Ionia. He roused his men, and they withdrew back to the inner fort, defeating the enemies in their way.

The battle raged on for several hours. One by one, Ionia's men fell.

If they closed the gates of the inner fortress and holed themselves up, they would be able to buy themselves a few days. They would defend the fort until Gravis arrived.

However, when Ionia and his men finally reached the inner fortress, the gates were still open.

A boulder in front of the gates was blocking them.

If Ionia destroyed it, he would likely reach his limits and die. But he steeled his resolve, determined to do it anyway.

With the support of his men, Ionia mowed down the enemy and reached the boulder.

"Gahhhh!"

Ionia roared like a beast and unleashed all of his remaining Power against the stone.

The boulder shattered with a roaring explosion. Ionia crushed the broken stone into finer pieces. He could feel the source of his Power quickly draining from his body.

His mind began to blur. If only he could crush it a little more, just a little more...enough that the gates could be closed.

His field of vision opened up as the boulder disappeared. Now the gates could be closed. Ionia's blurry eyes caught the shadow of a large army beyond the gates.

*He's here!*

At the army's head, he could see Gravis's pale face and Lucas, supporting him as he looked about to collapse.

Gravis, too, had burned his life away for him.

He had used his Power to his very limit, leaping from the royal capital to Zweilink in one fell swoop with a whole army.

Ionia got to see him one last time before he died.

Seeing Ionia covered in blood and soot, Lucas, his eyes widening, yelled: "IONIA!"

Ionia came back to himself at the sound of that voice.

*No, I can't die yet. There is still work to be done.*

He had to stall for time until Gravis was able to fight. He had to close the gates in time.

Ionia used his remaining strength and shouted to his men.

"...Ebbo! Close the gates!"

"Captain...!"

Ebbo was covered in wounds just like Ionia, and looked back at him with despair. With his superhuman strength, Ebbo could lower the gate by himself.

"Just go! Don't let the enemy through the gates! We've got to protect them with our own hands!"

Ebbo shook his head. "I can't... I won't leave you!"

If the gate was closed, Ionia and the others left outside the fortress would surely lose their lives. Knowing this, Ebbo hesitated.

Exhaling roughly, Ionia shouted once more to his men:

"Reinforcements have arrived! If we can seal the gate and regroup, we win! Go...! For god's sake, go!"

Ebbo's soot- and blood-stained face crumpled as he nodded and ran for the gate.

Xavier used his Power to stop the enemy soldiers who blocked Ebbo's path. He, too, had wounds all over his body.

The men who had no chance of survival used their last bit of strength to help their comrade run through.

Ebbo disappeared beyond the gate. As they waited, the gate began to close.

"Ionia...!"

Lucas kept shouting Ionia's name, and Ionia responded with a scream of his own: "...Victory is ours!"

In front of the slowly closing gate, Ionia used the last of his strength to mow down enemy soldiers. Almost there. Just a little more.

That was when he heard Gravis shout from behind him.

"Io!"

The voice of the man he loved always came from behind.

Ionia couldn't hear much due to the ringing in his ears and the noise around him, but Gravis's voice was clear.

"Io! Stop! Come back!"

He turned around to see Gravis screaming as Lucas held him back.

Gravis lifted his ashen face frantically and reached for Ionia, continuing to scream Ionia's name like a beast.

With a roar, the gates closed.

*Now we won't be defeated.*

At that moment, something pierced Ionia's body.

Looking down, he saw that the sword of Edgar Yorke, who should have escaped, was deeply embedded in his abdomen.

Edgar had a feverish expression on his face and laughed as he stabbed Ionia.

"Ha-ha... This will be the end of you, too... They won't know what I've done."

"...You...you traitorous—!"

Ionia placed his hand on Edgar's stomach and poured all his strength into it. Edgar burst open.

But Ionia had finally run out of strength.

His body could no longer move, and he could no longer tell if Edgar was dead or alive.

He no longer felt the burning heat, the pain of his wounds, or anything at all.

*No. I must tell Vi about the traitor who sold them out to the enemy.*

Ionia continued to scream in his fading consciousness. He wanted someone to carry on his feelings.

Beyond the flames and soot, he saw a starry sky. That was the last thing Ionia saw.

*I love you, Vi. I love you.*
*My blood and loyalty are yours forever.*

# Letter: From Ionia to Leorino

Once again, Leorino had dreamed of that day.

The hand he'd stretched out into the air as he cried was different from the one in the dream. It was a thin, white hand that had never held a sword.

*Yes, I am not Ionia. I am Leorino.*

How many times had he woken up with his pillow wet like this? Every time he had that dream, every time he was reminded of Ionia's love for Gravis, Leorino shed tears.

But today was different. Today, Leorino was shedding tears of anger toward himself.

How could he have forgotten for so long the precious memory Ionia had left behind in those flames?

It was the memory of Edgar Yorke's betrayal. The man who had jumped with Leorino and died in Zweilink. But he had confessed in the end that he had brought their enemies to Zweilink on someone else's instructions.

Leorino clenched his fists tightly over both eyes. That day, Ionia had not killed Edgar with his remaining Power.

In the end, it had been a blessing in disguise. If Ionia had killed Edgar then and there, Leorino would not have learned about the existence of the true traitor who had been controlling him.

Why? How could Leorino have forgotten? If only he had remembered, he would not have wasted the past six years.

At that moment, a knock sounded in the room.

Leorino's full-time attendant, Hundert, entered the room just as he expected his master to wake up. He drew back the curtains, and Leorino squinted at the bright light.

He would trouble himself with the memory of the traitor later.

"Good morning. I see you've awoken."

"...Good morning, Hundert. What's on my schedule for today?"

"The madame was wondering if you could join her and her guests for breakfast."

"Oh, right, the Marquis of Lagarea came last night with Lady Erina."

Right. Last night, Auriano's fiancée, Erina Munster, had arrived at Brungwurt Castle, accompanied by her uncle, the Marquis of Lagarea. Leorino hadn't greeted them because he'd gone to bed early, unable to bear the ache in his legs from the rain.

Marquis Bruno Henckel was a close friend of Leorino's father, August. He had doted on all of August's sons ever since they were young children. He was like family to Leorino.

He was also uncle to Julian Munster, who had proposed to Leorino, and the purpose of this visit must have been to persuade Leorino to accept Julian's marriage proposal.

He should have reproached Julian, the heir of a duke, for attempting to marry a man who could not bear children, but for some reason, the Marquis of Lagarea was enthusiastic about the idea.

Leorino bit back a sigh at the thought that he would be asked again to marry Julian today.

He could not accept Julian's proposal. At least not now that he was trying to find his own way to independence.

"I'll join them, of course. I'm feeling very well today."

"Then let us hurry and get ready."

Leorino nodded, got up, and went to the bathroom to wash his face and brush his teeth. When he returned to his room, Hundert was waiting for him, spreading out his outfit.

Leorino was deep in thought as the attendant helped him get dressed.

Why did the Marquis of Lagarea insist on his marriage to Julian so much?

Even if he was fond of Leorino, Leorino couldn't understand why he was so adamant about it.

Leorino may have been his best friend's child, but why did he want to keep Leorino around so much when Leorino was unable to have children and had difficulty living a normal life due to the disability caused by his injuries?

Since the accident, the Marquis of Lagarea was the only person, other than Sasha, Dr. Willy Jr., and his family, whom Leorino had met several times in the immediate aftermath. The Marquis of Lagarea took advantage of his position as secretary of the Interior to help the family get to the bottom of the Zweilink case.

Leorino remembered that he kindly listened to him when he was still dazed from his injuries.

Right after that, the marquis comforted Leorino and August, who were hurt both physically and mentally, by repeating the same words over and over again.

At that moment, Leorino shuddered at the terrible thought that coalesced in his mind.

*No way, no way...*

The attendant noticed his master shudder with a pale face.

"My lord, what is the matter?"

Leorino forced himself to suppress his trembling and put on a thoughtful expression to the attendant.

"Hundert, get me a brush and paper right away."

"But the breakfast—"

"I'll be quick. Please. It has to be *now*."

Leorino's unusually anxious expression puzzled the attendant, but he had no reason not to follow his order.

He prepared the items on the writing desk as instructed. Leorino wrote the text in a hurry, placed it in an envelope, sealed it with wax, and handed it to Hundert.

"Hundert... I want you to give me this letter after breakfast. If I say anything funny, tell me that I must read it."

"…L-Lord Leorino?"

"Hundert, please. If I *forget* about this letter, give it to me. Tell me I must read it."

He ordered Hundert not to show the letter to anyone until then.

The attendant nodded at his master's words, even as his eyes darted around in confusion.


When Leorino went to the dining room, August and Maia; his eldest brother, Auriano, and his fiancée, Erina Munster; and Bruno Henckel, the Marquis of Lagarea, had already begun eating. It was the same scene as usual.

Leorino gulped.

He apologized for his tardiness and took a seat at the end of the table, trying to look as normal as possible.

Erina, his future sister-in-law, smiled and spoke to him.

"Hello. I am glad to see that you are feeling well today, Lord Leorino."

Leorino returned Erina's calm, youthful smile. Erina's cheeks blushed happily.

"Yes, thank you, Erina. I am very sorry that I was not able to greet you upon your arrival last night."

"Oh, please don't worry about that. The roads were in an awful state because of the rain. We were the ones who inconvenienced you with our late arrival."


Leorino turned to the Marquis of Lagarea and gave a small bow.

"…Uncle, it's good to see you again. I apologize for being unable to welcome you."

The Marquis of Lagarea smiled kindly and waved his hand, insisting that it was fine.

"Oh yes! Lord Leorino, when you go to the royal capital for your Vow of Adulthood ceremony, Mr. Auriano will be with you to represent your father. We have never been in high society together, have we? We will be there to see my family. We'll accompany you."

Erina shyly held Auriano's hand. Auriano looked at his fiancée with a tender gaze and squeezed her hand back.

Leorino watched his brother and sister-in-law in their intimate moment with a smile.

"I'm really looking forward to it" said Auriano. "I'm certain the entire capital will lose their minds at your beauty, Leorino. Isn't that right, Uncle?"

"Of course. We're looking forward to your coming to the royal capital. Julian has not given up yet. He is determined to be the most promising of Leorino's suitors, and he will be second to none."

But Leorino cast his eyes down sadly.

"What's wrong, Leorino?"

"The truth is, I'm still afraid of going outside."

Everyone was surprised to hear this.

Auriano asked why.

"I'm afraid that something like the incident at Zweilink will happen again."

August and Maia were taken aback by his words.

"Leorino, what are you talking about? How could that be?"

"Rino?! Whatever do you mean...?"

Leorino looked at the Marquis of Lagarea.

"When I think of the man who jumped with me in tow—Edgar Yorke—I worry there might be more of his type in the royal capital..."

The Marquis of Lagarea watched Leorino with an expression full of compassion.

"How tragic... You remembered that incident *again*."

Leorino nodded in affirmation. Then he waited for the marquis's next words.

*Time to learn the truth.*

The attendant handed the letter to Leorino when he returned to his room, as requested. But for some reason, his master's beautiful violet eyes widened, and he tilted his head.

"Hundert...who is this letter from?"

Hundert panicked.

Letter: From Ionia to Leorino

It was Leorino himself who had handed him the letter this morning in his anxious state.

"...This is from you, my lord, to be given to you after breakfast."

"What? I wrote to myself? ...Ah, I can't remember..."

Leorino's heart was racing. The handwriting on the letter was clearly his own.

For some reason, he felt the need to read it alone.

Leorino was left by himself after he received the letter.

The ink was fresh, and the only words on the envelope were *To Leorino*, in his own handwriting.

Why had he written a letter to himself? Leorino had no memory of it.

He read the letter, tracing the words one by one.

As he read, his body began trembling violently.

When he finished, Leorino threw himself on his bed and choked back sobs.

Now that he had regained all his memories, he did not want anyone to hear his weakness.

Why?

Why did the Marquis of Lagarea take away Leorino's memories of Edgar Yorke?

A storm swept over his heart.

Leorino became increasingly convinced as he recalled everything that had happened to him. The Marquis of Lagarea had an ability. He must have had the Power to manipulate people's memories.

However, the Marquis of Lagarea did not know that Leorino had inherited Ionia's memories. That was why he was able to recall everything by rousing that memory.

He could not afford to lose those memories again.

The Marquis of Lagarea was likely the only path to the truth.

Leorino would make it his goal for the royal capital. But even as he told himself that, he could not stop the tears from flowing.

He clenched his fists and punched his bed as he cried.

It was the pain of parting from his childhood, the regret of his own naivety that had allowed him to innocently trust others.

Behind his eyelids, he could see Auriano and Erina's heartwarming scene from this morning. It hurt him beyond words to think that his future actions would likely destroy their happiness.

Even so, he could not help but find out.

Because amidst the flames, Ionia had shouted, *"There is still work to be done."*

The conclusion of the letter to himself was signed, *From Ionia to Leorino*.

Yes. This was his last memory and the last wish that Ionia entrusted to Leorino.

That was why Leorino had to reveal the truth.

Even if it cost him an arm and a leg, he would discover the truth.

After all, Leorino was born into this world in order to inherit Ionia's memories and to avenge his death.

# To the Royal Capital

Leorino's life in the capital was rough from the very start. Instead of enjoying his first visit to the capital, he was confined to his bed upon arrival.

The first long carriage trip in his life was tougher on him than he had expected. Although the itinerary had been laid out with consideration for his physical condition, by the time they arrived at the capital, Leorino was unable to walk on his own due to leg pain and fever. Half-dazed, Leorino was picked up and carried into the mansion by his eldest brother. The Brungwurt residence was in an uproar, including Leorino's second brother, who had been waiting for his arrival.

Even Erina, the daughter of a duke, was able to function normally the following day whenever she traveled the distance between the royal capital and Brungwurt. As a man, it made Leorino feel incredibly pathetic.

Before leaving for the royal capital, Leorino was overflowing with ambition.

He wanted to find out the truth about Edgar Yorke's betrayal, but Leorino was still just an unemployed man who had recently come of age. He could not even stand on his own feet, let alone get to the bottom of the matter, and was now stuck in bed, causing trouble for his family.

"Ugh... I hate this."

Leorino exhaled, agonizing in his bed.

It had been two days since he had been confined to his bedroom. The pain in his leg had subsided, but his fever had not yet broken, and he still had not received permission from Auriano, the representative of the head of the family, to leave his room.

There was no use getting impatient. Considering the Marquis of Lagarea's Power, he would surely fail if he acted without a plan. He told himself this to calm his restless mind.

Apart from that, there was something else Leorino secretly wanted to do when he came to the capital. He wanted to visit the commoner district. He wanted to see the house of Ionia's parents, even if just for a glance. He wanted to know if Ionia's parents were still alive and what had happened to his brother.

But reality was not so kind to him. Leorino had not been able to leave his room, and he had not even explored his own house, let alone the commoner district.

Leorino's modest ambition was to get out of his bedroom first.

Alas, he was bored.

"...I can't wait to leave this room already."

While he was fussing about with his feverish body, a small knock sounded in the room. Bored out of his mind, Leorino answered loudly: "Come in!"

He expected a servant, but that was not who entered.

"Hello! It's Sasha, Rino! Long time no see!"

"...Dr. Sasha?"

Leorino was surprised by Sasha's sudden appearance.

He had been planning to see Sasha when he arrived in the capital, but he had never expected Sasha to visit him instead.

Leorino rushed to sit up, but immediately collapsed onto his side helplessly.

"Ah, lie down, please!"

Sasha approached the bed and propped Leorino up. He watched him fondly with his small eyes and smiled at him.

"You still have a fever, don't you? Just lie back down here."

With that, Sasha patted him on the shoulder to calm him down.

Sasha's smile reminded Leorino of the days of his physical therapy when he had endured intense pain. The fact that he was able to come to the royal capital at all was thanks to Sasha, who had helped his legs heal to that point.

Leorino was delighted to see him again and offered him a wide smile on his feverishly flushed face.

"I'm sorry, Doctor. I couldn't welcome you properly. But I'm surprised you're here. I'm really happy to see you."

"Oh, Rino... You've become even more beautiful, haven't you? You look so radiant, I feel like I might go blind."

Sasha was utterly bewitched by Leorino's smile.

Even though he was flushed from the fever and looked gaunt, Leorino was so beautiful that it made Sasha's heart ache. His boyishness was gone, and although he was slender, his physique and facial features were becoming those of an adult man.

If Sasha had been a poet, he would have written thousands of lines of poetry extolling Leorino's beauty. Unfortunately, Sasha was a military doctor who treated the sick and wounded with his skill rather than his words, and he could only gaze admiringly at Leorino, who became more beautiful every time he saw him.

Leorino, on the other hand, wasn't pleased.

Most people began acting suspiciously when they saw him. He was aware that his appearance was the cause, but he had been born with that face and was used to seeing it himself. It upset him that even Sasha, who had seen him countless times in the past, reacted in such a way.

Leorino's practical nature belied his otherworldly appearance. He had gotten to meet Sasha and didn't want to waste a single moment of this opportunity.

*Enough about my looks. I can't make a living off my face. I want a job!*

Leorino did not care about his appearance. He wanted to have a more constructive conversation with Sasha.

Like about finding a job, for example. He also hoped to learn a little bit about how Gravis had been.

"I am very grateful for the unmerited compliments, Doctor, but..."

"'Unmerited.' Please, they're fully merited. I suddenly regret becoming a doctor. I lack the vocabulary, you see. It's a struggle. All because of your beauty."

Leorino nonchalantly ignored him.

"How did you know I came to the royal capital?"

"Well, when I met Johan on business, he told me that you were coming to the royal capital to participate in the Vow of Adulthood. When I heard you had arrived, I decided to come check on your legs for the first time in years. I was surprised to hear that you fell ill as soon as you arrived."

Sasha observed Leorino's entire body with a doctor's eye. "May I?" he asked in regards to Leorino's legs, and turned up his jacket. Leorino agreed to the examination.

Sasha slowly moved one leg at a time to check their condition.

"I know the long carriage ride may have taken its toll on you, but they seem to be moving well, and you don't seem to be in much pain. I can tell that you're still doing your exercises. Very impressive! Try pushing against my hand a little... Yes, they're quite strong. Can you walk now?"

"Yes, I can walk normally. But not for extended periods of time."

"How long can you walk? Have you ever timed it?"

"Yes, my brothers took me to the lake in Brungwurt, and I was able to walk for half an hour, slow as it was. But after that...if I don't rest, I get sore and numb and start to drag my legs a little."

"...I see. Still, that's more than enough. It's the result of your effort and Madame Maia's dedication. You've really worked so hard."

The corners of Leorino's eyes burned. He quickly blinked away the tears.

"Thank you," he murmured quietly.

"I wonder if the fever is caused by a cold. Let's see..."

Sasha asked him to show his throat, and he opened his mouth. Sasha commented on how small his mouth was, inspected his throat, and nodded, then brought his ear to his chest to listen to the sound of his heart. Finally, he smiled and nodded.

"You still have a fever, but I think it's just exhaustion from the long trip."

"That's a relief. My brother wouldn't allow me to get out of bed."

"Hmm? If you eat something nourishing and your fever comes down a little more, you should be able to get up and walk around the mansion as early as tomorrow."

Leorino's violet eyes lit up at Sasha's words. Then, for some reason, he turned to his attendant with a triumphant look on his face, as if to say: *See? I told you.*

Leorino looked at Sasha and Hundert alternately and pleaded with his violet eyes. Those eyes spoke volumes about how much he wanted permission to leave his room.

What was this lovely creature?

The childish air about him was completely gone, but there remained a certain irresistible cuteness about Leorino.

In response to Leorino's silent request, Sasha told the anxious attendant. "He's allowed to leave his bed from tomorrow."

The attendant nodded solemnly

"Tell your brother Dr. Sasha has given his permission, and he will surely allow you to move around a little more."

"Thank you, Hundert! Thank you, Doctor!"

Sasha seemed agonized again.

"Doctor...could you stay with me a little longer? How about a cup of tea?" Leorino implored Sasha with tears in his eyes.

"Of course, not a problem!"

It was a bit of a problem. He may not have seemed it, but Sasha had a good position in the Royal Army. He had work he needed to do that was piling up.

But with Leorino in front of him, Sasha's heart was under his spell. He was usually patient and rarely selfish, but he couldn't help wanting to grant Leorino's smallest request.

Sasha wondered privately if it was possible for someone to be so pure and so devilish at the same time.

"Then by all means, please join me for tea. Thank you, Doctor."

Leorino smiled sincerely. His smile was so bright he seemed to be emitting pure sunlight.

*Rino, this old man can't handle a smile that bright!!*

Sasha pressed his hand to his chest.

Leorino, assisted by his attendant, rested his upper body on the headboard. Sasha received a small desk next to the bed and accepted a cup of tea.

He was indeed a leading aristocrat. *The tea leaves are much higher quality than the tea we usually drink in the Palace of Defense,* Sasha thought with admiration.

"So, Leorino, what did you want to tell me?"

Leorino seemed to hesitate for a while. Sasha waited patiently, wondering if it was something Leorino was not comfortable saying as he enjoyed the expensive tea leaves.

With an anxious expression on his face, Leorino opened his mouth.

"...Doctor, I'm unemployed. I'm willing to do anything, so if you know of a job that could hire me despite my condition, could you put in a good word for me?"

Sasha spat out his tea.

"...Lord Leorino really asked me that. I was really at a loss as to how to respond to such a request from the most sheltered man in the world."

As soon as Sasha entered the office, he began talking even though no one had asked. He asked the redhead adjutant for some tea and made himself at home.

The owner of the office glared at the arrogant military doctor with a look of exasperation. He was a handsome man with a strong body. The man with rare eyes like stars twinkling in the night, whom the office belonged to, was Gravis Adolphe Fanoren, the general of the Royal Army.

Most people would shrivel up in the face of this extraordinary man's power, but the brazen veteran military doctor did not seem at all moved.

The doctor was well over fifty years old, and to him even the ice-cold general was nothing more than a youngster.

"I thought you came to discuss the budget. If you're here to make small talk, get the hell out."

Gravis waved his hand as if to shoo away the military doctor, but Sasha simply shrugged him off and accepted a cup of tea from Gravis's adjutant Dirk.

He sipped the tea, then casually murmured: "Ah, the tea at Rino's house was delectable."

"Doctor, please… If you are going to complain about the tea I brewed for you, then listen to His Excellency and leave, please."

Dirk, the adjutant who had gone out of his way to brew him a cup of tea, complained, clearly offended.

"Oh no, Dirk, your tea is great. But the tea leaves, you see… They're just different there."

Gravis had had enough.

"You'll have to forgive the miserly tea leaves. The Palace of Defense is not the place to sit around gracefully sipping tea. I don't care what it tastes like, as long as it keeps us from day drinking."

"You know, General, for a member of the royal family, you could really use a little more grace in certain areas."

"Sasha…you really should leave now."

Sasha, however, did not seem bothered by the general's ill humor and continued to somewhat rudely slurp his tea.

Both Sasha and Gravis were extremely busy people, but seeing as Sasha had firmly sat himself down with no intention of moving, it seemed he had something serious he wanted to discuss.

Gravis reluctantly asked his adjutant to prepare a cup of tea for him, too. He decided to take a break from work and listen to what the military doctor had to say. He noticed that the adjutant had shrewdly also made himself a cup. Dirk was more than ready to join the conversation.

"…So? What did you want to tell me?"

"What I was just saying."

"So you spat out your tea when the youngest son of the Cassieux family asked you for a job. What about it?"

"Well, I just figured that wouldn't end well. That boy… Well, I suppose he's no longer a 'boy' per se at his age, but in any case, letting Leorino out into the world doesn't bode well."

Dirk tilted his head curiously.

"But he is of age, and while he may be the son of a leading noble family, he is the fourth son, isn't he? Isn't it natural for him to want to find a job?"

"Yes, he's a very decent and sensible young man. But he's also quite unusual, you see."

"Unusual?"

Sasha nodded solemnly at Dirk's question.

"Yes. Put simply, he's extraordinarily beautiful."

"Our general here is also extremely handsome."

"Well, I don't deny that, but it's an entirely different sort of beauty from His Excellency's. You'd know what I mean if you saw him, Dirk. He looks almost like an angel or a faerie—it's overwhelming."

"Wow!"

"The city is relatively safe, but if you let him walk around alone, he would surely be kidnapped in an instant. I'm being serious here. No one would be so reckless as to kidnap His Excellency just because he's handsome, would they?"

"If anyone dared to kidnap His Excellency, I'd rather scout them into our army... But 'overwhelming beauty' sounds great. I'd love to see him."

Gravis was tired of their antics.

"It's true—he was a beautiful child. But is that the appropriate word to describe a boy who is now of age?"

Sasha shook his head.

"If anything, it's more appropriate than ever. I have never seen anyone more beautiful than him, in terms of both face and presence. I'm proud to say that I'm a married man, but I couldn't take my eyes off him for a while."

"Wow, that sounds incredible."

Dirk was impressed for a reason.

The easygoing doctor's wife was a commoner, but in her youth, she had been praised as "the most beautiful woman in the royal capital." When this slender, baby-faced doctor won her over after fending off a host of suitors, the whole of the capital had been in an uproar. Even though she was now in her forties, her beauty was still going strong.

How good-looking could Leorino be that Sasha, who had such a legendary beauty for a wife, would say there was no one more beautiful than him?

"Well, seeing is believing. The general should be able to meet him at the soiree after the Vow of Adulthood. It's been a long time since you've seen him in person. I'm not exaggerating. Oh, wait. I hope the guests won't lose their minds when they see him... No, they probably will."

Sasha seemed ready to talk endlessly about how beautiful Leorino was, so Gravis decided to kill that subject and get back on track.

There was only so long this break could last.

Gravis remembered the boy with that doll-like face lying asleep on his bed, but switched his attention back to his work.

"So the beautiful boy grew into a beautiful man. What of it? Where are we going with this?"

"Oh yes, that's the thing. I was thinking of taking him in."

"...What do you mean?"

"You think I shouldn't? He's an earnest boy, even if a little physically frail."

Gravis immediately shook his head.

"Of course you shouldn't. How can you put such a sheltered, weak thing in a place full of powerful men, and not just the classy ones? Lord August would kill you. You are a nobleman. You should know what it means to have a child of the Brungwurt bloodline in your care."

"Hmm... But he has his wits about him and he's not faint of heart, so once he gets used to his surroundings, I think he would do a fine job. Above all, he has this healing presence about him..."

Gravis shook his head.

"No. It's a shame, but there's also the issue of his legs. Your unit's work is tough enough as it is. He can't work as long as normal men because of his injuries, can he?"

"Well, no, but... I want to help him somehow. In that case, I could put him at the Palace of Defense, instead of the Royal Army."

It was extremely rare for Sasha to want to support someone this badly.

"He promised the margrave that if he can't become independent in two years, the margrave will find him a protector to marry him. He also said, 'I don't want to be protected, so I came to the royal capital to look for a job so I can become independent'... His legs are weak, but he wants to find something he can do... Don't you feel like crying just hearing that? I certainly do."

For some reason, Dirk felt touched by this.

"Leorino sounds like such a sweet boy..."

"If he's so beautiful, I'm sure he'll have plenty of suitors to choose from, even if he's a man. I think he'd be happier being married."

Sensing that Sasha had finally gotten to the heart of the matter, Gravis concluded this bluntly. Surprisingly, Sasha agreed with him.

"I honestly think so, too. If he doesn't get married and find someone to protect him, the people around him will be beside themselves with anxiety. Poor thing. If only he had a different face."

"What do you mean? Isn't his face just extremely beautiful?"

"Maybe it's a hardship you can't understand, Dirk, being unremarkable as you are... If not for that beautiful face, he would be able to live as the son of a noble family, bad legs and all. What's unfortunate for him is that he will be in danger until something horrible happens to his face or he ages out of it. But he's doing his best. He wants to be independent."

"Don't think I didn't notice that jab at me... But I feel kind of sorry for that Leorino boy. You can't be that beautiful and still be happy, can you?"

Dirk furrowed his brow in sympathy. He was fundamentally a very compassionate and emotional man.

"No. He is a very simple boy. Even if he spends his entire life nipping at his parents' heels, a noble family as wealthy as the Cassieux family won't even feel a dent. I wonder if it was the education of the Cassieux family. He doesn't seem to have the awareness that he is the child of a very prestigious noble family, and he doesn't think he can coast through life with his good looks alone. If anything, he says things like, 'I want to get a job,' like a commoner's kid."

"I think I might actually cry..."

Dirk and Sasha were off in their own world.

"He's the kind of boy who would go to work and make money and send his parents his first paycheck, saying, 'I'm sorry for all the trouble I caused you'...

He's so ignorant of the ways of the world in so many ways already. I just can't leave him alone."

"He must be such a sweet boy..."

"Later on, the attendant told me that the eldest son of the Duke of Leben had proposed to him."

Dirk's eyes lit up. "Wow! That's incredible. Julian Munster, the most eligible bachelor of his generation, proposed to him?"

"Yes, his sister married Lord Auriano. Through her, Julian Munster met Leorino and fell in love at first sight, so he kept going all the way to Brungwurt until he finally proposed to him."

"I suppose the heir of a duke marrying a man won't be an issue in terms of succession? Lord Julian must be deeply in love. Leorino is all sorts of impressive."

Gravis was growing increasingly irritated by their conversation. He had no interest in gossip.

Sasha, who had noticed Gravis's genuine irritation, finally decided to get to the point.

"...What I'm trying to say is that I have several concerns, so I want to look after Leorino Cassieux. I have the right to employ him, but he is, after all, the son of the Margrave of Brungwurt and also related to the royal family. I can't take care of him without your permission. I came to ask for just that."

"...Why are you so devoted to this young man?"

The general's question made Sasha tilt his head and think for a moment.

"Hmm... That's a difficult question, but...it's not that I'm attracted to him. If I had to say, it's...his eyes, I suppose."

"His eyes?"

"Leorino has beautiful violet eyes. I don't know how to describe it, but... sometimes his eyes look so wounded. They are the eyes of a strong but wounded warrior who is still going into battle... I'm very familiar with them as a military doctor. They are the same eyes as yours, General, or as the lieutenant general's," Sasha mused. "That's why I can't take my eyes off him, and I want to support him.

"And besides, Your Excellency and I saved his life six years ago. Don't you want to contribute to his future?"

Gravis could understand that feeling.

Realizing that the boy who had been lying there with a pale face, teetering on the verge of life and death at the time, was able to walk, had come of age, and was now in the royal capital made Gravis want to support him.

He felt guilty for not being able to save him.

Gravis remembered the violet eyes of the boy who slipped through his hands by a split second that day.

"I understand the situation...but I can't give you permission right away. The timing's not right, you understand."

Sasha snorted. "Are you concerned about Zwelf, Your Excellency?"

"I am. They may make a move as soon as this year. If that happens, your unit will also be in the field without exception."

Eighteen years ago, there was no future for the man with the same violet eyes.

"Precisely because we saved his life at Zweilink, he should never be taken to the battlefield."

He could not take that boy to such a place.

# The Vow of Adulthood

The Cassieux family, waiting downstairs, were in a temporary trance as soon as they saw Leorino, accompanied by Johan, descending from the second floor.

For the first time in his life, Leorino was dressed in the finest formal attire, and he was very self-conscious about it.

Covered from head to toe in austere attire, Leorino had his usually flowing bangs brushed back, revealing a high forehead. He looked too beautiful for hackneyed words to describe.

"I'm...speechless."

Auriano mumbled this, covering his mouth in a daze, which was met with repeated nods from Maia, the margravine, who had arrived only a week earlier. She was in tears.

"You look marvelous, Leorino. You've come so far... You've really worked so hard."

Leorino smiled at Maia's words.

The people around him sighed in admiration once more at the smile that seemed to beam with veritable light.

Leorino's formal attire was very simple, in accordance with his own wishes. A jacket made of a thick platinum-colored fabric enveloped his beautifully toned shoulders. Simple shoulder straps of the same fabric emphasized the rigid contours of his body, and a thin belt tightened around his slender torso, adding to the fabric that was wrapped snugly around his long limbs.

The fabric had no excessive decoration but was clearly of the finest weave, and it was adorned with delicate platinum embroidery. The folds of his light-purple shirt, which peeked out from the collar covering his throat, and a small brooch in the shape of a winged lion, the emblem of the Margrave of Brungwurt, added a touch of glamour to this modest decoration.

The formal attire was perfectly designed by his mother, Maia, so as not to distract from her son's innate beauty.

"We should get going. It's Rino's big day."

In Fanoren, nobles took their vows and signed their names in the register during the coming-of-age ceremony at the royal palace held in early spring. Commoners took their vows at a church on a weekend somewhere between winter and spring, and signed their names on the commoner's register.

Only after this event was a Fanoren citizen recognized as an adult.

Without being recognized as adults, they could not inherit land, marry, or officially take up work. Therefore, regardless of status, the Vow of Adulthood was the most important rite of passage for the people.

Incidentally, once a person became half-fledged, betrothal was allowed, and a commoner could take up an apprenticeship with an employer or in the family business.

Although Leorino was unable to attend school in the royal capital, he was delighted to be able to attend the Vow of Adulthood ceremony in the royal capital and to be recognized as an adult by the state.

Now he would be able to look for a job in the royal capital with a clear conscience. That was all Leorino could think about these days.

With the servants seeing them off, Leorino and his family boarded a carriage bearing the shining emblem of Brungwurt.

His body felt heavy, probably due to nerves.

"...The formal wear is very beautiful, but it's heavy, too."

Sitting across from him, Auriano frowned at his muttering.

The formal attire worn by the sons of noble families was usually more ornate. Considering the burden on Leorino, the decorations were kept as modest as possible for ease of movement and to reduce the weight, but it was still heavier than everyday clothes.

"You think you'll tire easily?"

Leorino shook his head in response to Auriano's concerned question.

"I'll be fine. I heard that you can sit during the vow ceremony. I think I will manage. It's just the soiree afterward... It will be my first, so I'm not sure I'll be able to stand for long."

His second brother, Johan, smiled reassuringly.

"Good point. We can't accompany you during the vow ceremony, but we will be with you during the soiree, so don't worry. There is a lounge, so you can participate and take breaks whenever you need to. We'll greet everyone, just to be polite, and then we can leave early."

Leorino nodded earnestly at his brother's words.

"All right. That's all I can do anyway, since I can't exactly dance... But I will try not to embarrass Mother and my brothers."

Maia waved her fan gracefully.

"What are you talking about? No matter how you behave, you could never embarrass us. Johan, today Auriano and Erina will be out in public for the first time. I will accompany Erina and introduce her as the next margravine, so please take care of Leorino."

"Yes, Mother. Of course."

"And, Leorino, for the vows, I have rented a room near the Blue Eagle Hall. You will stay in that room until just before the ceremony begins. They will let you know when the time is right. You will enter the room last and sit in the final row."

"...? Why would I do that? Isn't it impolite to enter at the last minute?"

"You have to understand. If you were there alone, it would cause a great commotion. You can't be the only one who stands out on this fine day."

"I will keep to myself. I have no friends or acquaintances in the royal capital anyway... No one should approach me, and I wouldn't know how to speak to anyone anyway, so I'll sit tight."

"You may think that, but reality is usually not as you imagine it to be. For once, listen to your mother."

Leorino could only nod at Maia's command.

Then Johan, sitting across from Leorino, grinned at Maia.

"But, Mother, I'm impressed. You have rented a room in the royal palace for Leorino."

"It's thanks to your grandmother. If anything, she insisted on it, really... You see, she has many contacts in the royal court. Mother has a soft spot for Rino, since he took after her so much."

Maia's mother was the sister of the former king, a former royal who married into the Duke of Wiesen's family. In other words, Maia was a cousin of the former king, and the Cassieux boys were second cousins of the current king and his brother, Gravis.

"The ceremony and the subsequent soiree are important celebrations for all the nobles of Fanoren. Everyone should get some time in the spotlight to keep things as fair as possible, not to mention Leorino alone standing out of the crowd would cause a commotion."

Everyone nodded in agreement.

"Your father said the same thing. That's why we made the outfit so plain. Even so...you're still you. I can already imagine the uproar. I'm so worried."

She pointed at Leorino with her fan. Auriano and Johan nodded deeply at their mother's words.

Leorino had no idea what behavior was appropriate for the occasion. He nodded and decided he had no choice but to listen to his mother.

"Leorino, as soon as you have finished signing your name at the ceremony, leave the hall and come to me. Auriano and Mother will meet up with Sister Erina and go straight to the ballroom, but I will be in the small room by the time the ceremony is over. Is that clear? Don't stop when they talk to you. Get out of there immediately," Johan said.

"Johan is right. Enter the room just before the ceremony begins and sit quietly in the back. You can't avoid coming forward for the vow and the signing but leave the room as soon as it's over. Keep a low profile. That's the best plan. Do you understand?"

Leorino was repulsed by the admonitions of his two older brothers, still treating him like a child. They were utterly overprotective.

"Yes, yes! I understood the first time!" Leorino replied curtly.

"...What's with the attitude? Saying yes once is more than enough. No point in getting huffy now."

Leorino shrugged as his eldest brother scolded him.

But at Johan's next words, Leorino's face stiffened slightly.

"The ceremony is to be officiated by the Marquis of Lagarea. If something unforeseen should happen at the venue, you can count on the marquis. Is that clear?"

Leorino bit his lip.

The Marquis of Lagarea—the man who, for some reason, was trying to cover up the crimes of Edgar Yorke.

There was no doubt in his mind that at the breakfast table, the Marquis of Lagarea had again implored Leorino to forget Edgar Yorke and interfered with his memory. He hadn't seen the man since, but he wondered if he could keep his expression fixed in his presence.

"...Yes, I will not inconvenience the marquis. I promise."

"Rino, what's the matter? Don't bite your lip—you'll hurt yourself. You may be nervous because you are worried about your legs, but there is nothing shameful about being injured. You are a son of the Cassieux family. You should stand proud."

At his mother's words, Leorino's face relaxed.

*That's right. I am a member of the Cassieux family. For the sake of my father, who sent me to the royal capital...and for the sake of Ionia, I have much to do.*

This very day was the first step toward that. It was the first important day that would lead Leorino to find his place in the royal capital and fulfill his goals.

*Take your time... Until I uncover the Marquis of Lagarea's secret, I need to take things one step at a time. Focus on today. Even if my legs become sore, I can't let the pain get the better of me. I have to keep going.*

The carriage bearing the Cassieuxes soon arrived at the main gate of the royal palace. Since the Brungwurt estate was located in the most prestigious district near the royal palace, it was only a short distance away by carriage.

The carriage, bearing the coat of arms of the Margrave of Brungwurt, passed through the main gate without being inspected.

Leorino opened the curtains of the carriage, and for the first time in his life, he saw the royal palace in person. He was nearly overwhelmed by the majesty of it, which was far greater than he could have dreamed.

Leorino stared at the royal palace, ignoring the turmoil in his heart.

*Gravis is somewhere in this palace.*

Leorino's heart fluttered at the thought.

He wanted to see him again, even if just for a glance.

"Now, Leorino, are you ready?"

With a nod, he got out of the carriage. In front of him was a grand staircase, about thirty steps in height.

He felt like he was being tested from the very beginning, but he could not afford to complain.

The first step would be to climb the stairs on his own.

Just before the start of the ceremony, Leorino was led to the Blue Eagle Hall, where the Vow of Adulthood ceremony was to be held. He quietly slipped into the room through the rear door.

He moved without drawing attention to himself, looking down as he had been instructed and keeping his footfalls as quiet as possible.

The ceremony was open to all ranks of the country's recently turned adult nobility, from children of dukes at the top to barons at the bottom.

There were ten seats per row, seven rows in total. Calculating by the number of chairs, some seventy people would be coming of age this year.

Young people in gorgeous costumes sat all around him, looking nervous and excited.

Leorino had never seen so many people of his age before. Most of them must have been classmates at the academy of higher learning.

He had known this but was still saddened by the fact that he did not know anyone in the royal capital.

The young people in attendance were dressed in very lavish, ornate costumes. Compared to their formal attire, Leorino's clothes looked very plain at first glance.

There were only three seats left in the final row. Leorino slid into one of the empty seats, keeping his face down as he had been told.

A woman with reddish-gold hair sat next to him. She was wearing a lovely white dress with light-blue ribbons skillfully sewn onto it and golden flowers embroidered all over.

"Excuse me," he said quietly. The woman next to him replied, equally quiet, "It's all right," but she was not paying particular attention to Leorino.

The Blue Eagle Hall could accommodate some two hundred people standing and was, as its name implied, decorated with wallpaper featuring a series of gold eagle patterns on a blue background. The room was luxurious but somewhat subdued. It was said to be the fifth largest room in the palace and was used exclusively for domestic ceremonies.

All of this knowledge was passed on to Leorino by Johan.

Johan oversaw the budgets of the various ministries at the Palace of Finance. That was why he was intimately familiar with the ceremonies and rituals of the palace.

It was almost time for the ceremony to begin. Just when he wondered if no one else was coming, Leorino heard footsteps rushing behind him.

"Hah, I made it! That was close!"

A young man murmured to himself in a lighthearted tone and sat down next to Leorino in a somewhat rough manner.

Leorino was curious to see what kind of young man sat next to him, but he couldn't see his face.

The young man, perhaps feeling hot, began to fan himself with his palm. Leorino smiled secretly. The young man was, in general, very restless.

Several men in formal attire who appeared to be officials quietly entered through the front door, signaling the beginning of the ceremony.

The recently turned adult young ladies and gentlemen immediately straightened their backs. As one would expect from children of the nobility, who had been trained in etiquette from an early age, they had excellent posture. The young man next to Leorino also straightened his back and lowered his hand in a hurry. At that moment, the young man's elbow grazed Leorino's arm.

"Oh, my bad..."

The young man mumbled a quiet apology, looked at Leorino, and...froze.

*...He's really staring at me.*

Leorino turned his face down farther, feeling the intense gaze from next to him. It wasn't the most socially appropriate behavior, but his family insisted that he didn't expose his face when he was vulnerable.

The young man was still staring at Leorino.

At that moment, the front door opened, and the entrance of the king was announced.

Leorino, still facing the front door, gave a small but sharp motion to the young man next to him, asking him to look forward. The young man came to his senses and turned away.

Leorino let out a relieved breath.

The king entered. The attendees stood up and bowed respectfully.

The Vow of Adulthood ceremony was about to begin. From the stage, a voice called out, "Raise your heads!"

On the stage stood a brown-haired man of medium height and medium build, dressed in lavish clothes, who appeared to be His Majesty the king, and next to him a large, dark-haired man in a gorgeous ceremonial dress.

To his left stood the Marquis of Lagarea, secretary of the Interior, and to his right an elderly man dressed in white who appeared to be a high-ranking bishop.

Behind him stood a number of bureaucrats, and men in uniform of the order of the Knights of the Imperial Guard were standing by the wall.

Leorino gazed bitterly at the Marquis of Lagarea on the stage.

The marquis's face was as gentle and gentlemanly as ever.

Even now, somewhere in his mind, Leorino still believed that the gentle old marquis could not possibly be a traitor. However, no matter how much he thought it over, the marquis was the only man who could have stolen the memory of Edgar Yorke from him.

The events of that morning proved it.

"You may sit down," the Marquis of Lagarea said quietly, and the adult nobles nervously took their seats again.

Leorino kept his face down enough not to appear rude, but when he felt eyes on him from the stage, he involuntarily raised his gaze. His eyes met those of a dark-haired man standing next to the king.

The man stared at Leorino intently, the corners of his mouth lifting slightly. The man's eyes looked like those of a wolf who had found its prey.

*That man is... Prince Kyle!*

He hadn't seen Prince Kyle since Kyle visited Brungwurt for the memorial service.

Perhaps it was the solemn atmosphere of the ceremony, or perhaps it was the passage of time over the past six years, but Prince Kyle looked even more dignified than he had back then. Leorino sneaked another look at the stage. The crown prince's eyes met his again, as if he had been watching Leorino the entire time. Leorino quickly lowered his gaze.

For some reason, the crown prince seemed to be in a very good mood.

The Marquis of Lagarea announced, "His Majesty will give his congratulatory address," and bowed to the man sitting on the throne in the center of the room.

*That man is His Majesty the king...and Gravis's brother.*

The king seemed genial.

When Leorino was Ionia, he had never received a direct audience with the crown prince, Joachim...who was now king. So he had no chance to see, with his own eyes, the image of the half brother Gravis had described or the image of the crown prince that the school principal had hinted at.

Now that he saw the king for the first time, Leorino had the impression of the "moderation" that Gravis described. The king's body, face, and overall presence were gentle, and he did not resemble his half brother at all.

In fact, Crown Prince Kyle resembled his uncle, Gravis, more than his father.

Compared to Gravis's masculine excellence and beauty, the king was quite ordinary. He did not seem to be the kind of man who would plot the assassination of his half brother.

Even from a distance, Leorino could see a hint of white in the king's hair. He would be nearly ten years older than Gravis.

The king delivered his congratulatory address in a calm voice, befitting of his appearance:

"I congratulate you on this momentous occasion. With the vow you are about to recite, you will be recognized as full-fledged nobles of this land. Like your parents and ancestors, you will belong to the nobility of our country and be allowed to exercise your rights. At the same time, you will be obligated to be the foundation of peace and progress in our country. I ask you to dedicate your wisdom, your strength, and your devotion to our country."

All present bowed deeply at the king's words.

Leorino, however, had something completely different in mind.

Gravis did not become king in the end. If the brothers had continued to fight over succession, it probably would have involved all the nobles in the country. But in reality, the crown prince, Joachim, succeeded the throne in due course, and Gravis became a general.

\*   \*   \*

*I wonder what happened after everything eighteen years ago...*

Leorino was eager to ask someone.

"All rise."

Leorino came to himself at the Marquis of Lagarea's words and stood with the other attendees.

"Recite the vow."

At these words, the participants recited the vows they had memorized. The ceremony continued solemnly. After the vow, the attendees again bowed respectfully to the king.

It was at this point that the royals would leave the room.

The bishop would then confer the insignia of the Holy White Eagle, a small white eagle adorned with a ribbon of blue flowers, a sign that one had become an adult member of the nobility. The ceremony would be complete when everyone signed their names in the register in their own hand.

"His Majesty the king and His Royal Highness the crown prince will now take their leave."

Then, suddenly, the crown prince said, "No, I will stay and present the insignia on behalf of the bishop in celebration of the promising young people who have reached the age of maturity."

The abrupt change of plans caused a stir on the stage.

The king took one glance at the crown prince with a confused expression, but left the room without saying anything.

The Marquis of Lagarea heaved a sigh.

"Starting from the first row, you will all come forward to receive your insignias from His Royal Highness the crown prince."

At these words, the young people stirred. Starting with the front row, the attendees were called by name, had insignia smaller than the palm of their hand pinned to their chests, and then walked to the side to sign the register of adults before returning to their seats.

Finally, Leorino's row was called.

The Vow of Adulthood

"Next, Antonia Elizabeth Klaus, daughter of the Count of Arhen."

The woman with reddish-gold hair next to Leorino stood up with a beautiful posture. She was even smaller than Leorino.

At last came Leorino's turn.

"Next, Leorino Viola Maian Cassieux, son of the Margrave of Brungwurt."

As soon as Leorino's name was called, the attendees were astir. Leorino was afraid of what their reactions might mean.

They wouldn't know Leorino, but most of the children of the nobility around his age knew one another. The fact that the fourth son of the great Cassieux family, whom no one had ever seen or met before, was attending the event had been drawing attention for some time.

Leorino gathered his courage, looked up, and began to walk toward Kyle.

With each step Leorino took, the attendees' murmurs soon turned into a ripple of silence as they held their breath.

Only the crown prince watched with a grin as the attendees, one after another, were stunned by the sight of Leorino up close.

Kyle smiled happily as Leorino approached. Leorino nervously bowed in front of Kyle and quietly waited for him to put on his insignia, completely unaware of the shock he was causing.

Kyle skillfully pinned the insignia to his chest.

He was able to step down from the crown prince's presence without issue. Finally, Leorino let out the breath he had been holding.

Finally, the name of the young man next to him, the one who was the last to enter the room, was called.

"Next, the son of Viscount Hafeltz, Kelios Eugen Keller."

Leorino returned to his seat with his face down, as he had been told to do. He could still feel the gazes of the entire audience on him. He wished he could run away.

*Don't make a scene... Keep your head down...*

But in the end, Leorino's concern was all for naught.

Immediately after the Marquis of Lagarea announced the end of the ceremony, the crown prince, Kyle, called to Leorino in a charming voice from the stage: "Leorino Cassieux. Come here."

All eyes turned to Leorino once more, curious about what was going on.

"Allow me the right to take you to the soiree after this."

The crown prince's bombshell announcement caused another wave of excitement in the hall.

Leorino, forgetting his family's advice, stared at Kyle onstage, dumbfounded.

The crown prince, with a mischievous look in his eyes, watched Leorino with a smile that showed he knew exactly what he was doing.

# The Crown Prince's Excuse

Leorino sat, dispirited, in the small room reserved for him by the Cassieux family.

He had done his best to follow his family's instructions to keep his head down, but his efforts had been undone by an event none of them could have predicted.

On the couch across from him sat the dark-haired crown prince, who had caused the incident. Beside him stood the Marquis of Lagarea with a sour expression.

"Your Royal Highness, what have you done?"

Johan protested to the crown prince, doing his best to keep his voice down.

Under any other circumstances, it would have been unthinkably rude for a man of Johan's status to object to the crown prince himself. However, Kyle was close to Johan in age, and they were on relatively friendly terms.

Kyle shrugged at his friend's angry stare.

"Johan, this is no joke. I'm being rather serious here... That reminds me, Leorino. It's been a long time. Do you remember me?"

Leorino was still puzzled, but he nodded honestly.

"Yes, Your Royal Highness. I greeted you when you arrived in Brungwurt for the memorial service... Um, about what you said earlier..."

Kyle looked at Leorino's troubled face and put on a kind expression.

"We didn't get to talk much then, did we? I heard about your struggles after the accident. But your gait is very steady. You must have worked very hard on your recovery. I wish to talk with you a little longer. We won't have a chance to talk once the soiree begins."

At Kyle's words, Leorino bowed his head.

He couldn't hide how red his face had become. Seeing this, Kyle smiled again.

"Even back then, you were an eye-catchingly beautiful boy, but...you're so gorgeous now. It's incredible. When I saw you at the ceremony, I could hardly believe my eyes. I wondered if this beautiful creature was a figment of my imagination or a trick of the light. Truly, your beauty has no equal in all of Fanoren. Am I right, Marquis of Lagarea?"

"I will not deny that Leorino is one of the most beautiful young men on the continent... But, Your Royal Highness, you are taking this joke too far. Even in a gambit against us, I never thought you would involve Leorino. August will be furious when he learns of this."

The Marquis of Lagarea sighed that his head already hurt at the thought and put his hand on his forehead. Kyle looked uneasy for the first time when he heard the margrave's name.

"Hmm... Not even I will be able to withstand the anger of the Margrave of Brungwurt. What shall we do?"

Johan was caught up in the "gambit against us" the Marquis of Lagarea had mentioned.

"What do you mean by 'gambit'? What do you mean by 'involve Leorino'?"

The aging secretary of the Interior let out a sigh as the wrinkles on his face deepened.

"His Highness is trying to use Leorino's beauty as an excuse to escape responsibility."

"...Lagarea. Watch your language. You forgot some crucial information."

"Don't waste your breath on empty threats, Your Royal Highness."

"Marquis of Lagarea, what was the crown prince's intention in his statement? Since Leorino is involved, we have the right to know."

Leorino had no idea what this meant, but all three adults were looking at him with threatening expressions.

"As the crown prince of this country, His Highness has the duty to sire an heir. However, His Highness the crown prince still stubbornly refuses to marry—or even to look for a fiancée. His Highness must have thought he could buy some time by making it seem as though he had fallen in love at first sight with Leorino's exceptional beauty. The crown prince, who has never been swayed by any beautiful woman, had no one better qualified than Leorino to claim that he had fallen in love at first sight."

Johan trembled with rage. "...What a horrible thing you have done, Your Highness. Leorino was supposed to start his life in the royal capital quietly, but now you've dragged him into the middle of a scandal and made him the target of strange rumors at court, without ever giving him a choice in it!"

Kyle glared at the Marquis of Lagarea, indignant. "Do you doubt that I fell in love at first sight with Leorino? I mean it when I say that I want him. Six years ago, I asked August for his hand in marriage, and I was refused."

The marquis was unmoved. "I hope you won't use that nonsense as a plausible excuse. It is undeniable that Your Highness's shortsighted expression of interest in Leorino in public may have linked Leorino's existence to the issue of royal marriage. If things go wrong, Leorino will be the subject of rumors as soon as tonight's soiree."

Realizing the truth of the crown prince's statement, Leorino turned red with shame. It made him sad to think that because of his face, he had been once more used against his will by someone with ulterior motives.

Kyle immediately saw through the quiet anger that Leorino wore on his face.

"...I see I've offended you. Leorino, what I said earlier was not entirely calculated. It is true that I wanted to talk to you. But it was a careless remark. I'm sorry I got you involved in my issues."

Although he did not bow his head, Kyle frankly admitted his mistake and apologized, despite his status as the crown prince. His clear eyes somehow resembled those of Gravis.

Leorino simply said, "Thank you," and accepted the apology. He did not know how to respond.

Secretly, he bit back a sigh.

His energy had been sapped by the stress and the unexpected turn of events, and he found himself feeling sluggish.

At that moment, a knock sounded in the small room, and a servant announced that it was almost time for the soiree to begin.

"It may be rude to go against His Highness's word, but I will still accompany Leorino. Consider this a message from Brungwurt," Johan said, holding Leorino's shoulder.

The Marquis of Lagarea objected with a frown. "Johan, I understand where you are coming from. But that would ruin His Royal Highness's reputation. Besides, Leorino is likely to be accused of ignoring His Highness's wishes... What an ordeal."

Leorino could only wait and see what the adults would decide.

"Johan, is it your duty to take Leorino to the venue?"

Johan nodded at the crown prince. "Yes, we will join our mother, brother, and sister-in-law at the venue."

"Then I will do the honors for you. I will hand him over to you immediately at the entrance of the venue. I wanted to talk to Leorino for a little while, for entirely personal reasons. And I'll refrain from talking to Leorino once we're there... How's that sound, Lagarea?"

"That should do. If anyone asks questions, we can simply say that His Highness and Leorino met six years ago and that His Highness was kind enough to escort him to the venue because he was concerned about his injuries. So, Johan, we will wait for you at the venue. Your Highness, please escort Leorino there. Please keep a respectful distance."

Leorino stood up at the same time as the adults.

Johan hugged Leorino's shoulder with concern.

"I'll await you at the venue, Leorino. There's been a change of plans, so His Highness will be escorting you... Your Highness, Prince Kyle, please don't do anything to Leorino. My brother is truly ignorant of the ways of the world. If anything happens to him..."

"It's fine; I get it. I really am sorry about this. I just have to make sure that people have no cause to spread any indecent rumors about Leorino. I swear to keep my distance, as if he were my brother... Well, I suppose we really are distant relatives. You can trust me, Johan."

"I never did trust that nonchalant attitude of yours..." Johan sighed, asked him to take care of Leorino, and left the room with the Marquis of Lagarea.

Leorino was left alone with the crown prince. Though of course, an attendant and a knight of the Imperial Guard stayed behind.

"Leorino, once again, I'd like to apologize for my actions. You look a bit pale. Are you tired?"

Leorino shook his head.

"The Marquis of Lagarea said that Your Highness used me as an excuse to avoid marriage. Why is that?"

Kyle raised one eyebrow at Leorino's frank question.

But Kyle did not scold him for his rudeness, perhaps to atone for involving Leorino in the first place.

"You don't beat around the bush, do you? ...I suppose I'm just not in the mood for it—that's the primary reason. But you could also say that I can't go through with it until I'm certain."

"Can't go through with it...until you're certain?" Leorino tilted his head, not understanding what he meant. Kyle smiled at this. Kyle's expression somewhat resembled that of Gravis. They were supposed to be uncle and nephew, but he resembled him more than he did his father, the king. Leorino thought this might be the reason why he could not bring himself to hate him even though he had just learned he was being used.

"I mean the legitimacy of the crown."

He still didn't understand what Kyle meant.

Kyle looked at Leorino tenderly and held out his hand, offering for them to go. Leorino took it.

The crown prince raised one eyebrow again, perhaps out of habit. He looked at Leorino with interest and pulled him close. Leorino had no choice but to follow, pulled by the hand on his hip.

He then heard a small sigh, and the crown prince placed his hand on Leorino's head.

"Can I help you?"

Leorino looked up to see that the amused expression on the crown prince's face had faded, and he was staring down at him with a worried, exasperated look.

"...Have you never been told to be more cautious around men?"

"Yes, I was told to keep my head down. I'll be careful."

The guard behind them cleared his throat.

The crown prince looked at Leorino with a pitiful expression and murmured: "Not what I meant."

The royal palace of Fanoren consisted of twelve palaces and two grand gardens.

The royal palace was said to be the most majestic on the Agalean continent. It consisted of the Palace of Administration, a four-story building with some nine hundred rooms that was situated across the front garden leading up to the main gate. It was also flanked by six palaces for ministries—the Palace of the Interior, which governed national and civil affairs; the Palace of Finance, which controlled the budget; the Palace of Defense, which handled domestic and international defense; the Palace of Heaven and Earth, which governed national religion; the Palace of the Supreme Court, which protected the law; and the Palace of Foreign Affairs, which handled ceremonies and foreign affairs, as its name suggested.

Behind the Palace of Administration was the palace that served as the residence of the royalty. Opposite the Palace of Administration was the inner palace, where the family of the king resided. Farther in, there was a vast inner garden, which was dotted with the palaces of the queen dowager, the king's brother, and the crown prince.

Together with the palaces for the royal family, which were now closed, the twelve palaces were collectively called the "detached palaces."

The Divine Confine, where the soiree would be held, was the largest ceremonial hall in the country. It faced the courtyard on the side of the palace and was about a fifteen-minute walk from the Blue Eagle Hall. Leorino had also learned this from Johan.

Leorino walked in silence, recalling such nonsensical information in his bid at escaping from reality.

"Ah, look around, Leorino. Everyone is losing their minds over your beauty. How exhilarating."

Contrary to the crown prince walking next to him, who seemed to be enjoying himself, Leorino was walking with his eyes downcast.

He was trying his best to hide behind the tall crown prince and his guards, but it was a futile exercise on his part. With this entourage, he couldn't *not* stand out.

"Leorino, why are your eyes downcast? Your beauty is our national treasure. Show it off with pride."

"No, I'm sorry... I'm afraid I can't do that."

Leorino realized it was rude, but he could no longer afford to look up.

The crown prince sounded amused, but his face, looking down at Leorino, had an expression of concern on it

Leorino, however, did not notice his anxious gaze. A serious problem was slowly coming to Leorino's attention.

As soon as they left the room, the crown prince noticed that Leorino could only walk at a slow pace. The crown prince did not say anything and matched Leorino's gait, but he could not deny that this put him in a position to show off their fancy procession.

Despite the crown prince's concern, Leorino's legs were already beginning to complain of a dull ache from the unprecedented overuse and nerves. Leorino moved his legs frantically. If he was not careful, he felt he would trip over his own feet.

*They're starting to hurt. But I have to keep going... If I fail here, I'll bring shame to His Royal Highness the crown prince.*

When they finally arrived at the Divine Confine, Leorino exhaled loudly in relief.

The crown prince whispered to him, in a voice so quiet that no one else could hear, that he had done well. He must have had an inkling of the state of Leorino's legs.

Leorino nodded in gratitude. He could tell that the crown prince's concern was genuine. He really couldn't bring himself to hate him. The crown prince may have appeared arrogant at first glance, but he was in truth a sensitive and caring person.

"Leorino, look. Auriano seems to be very angry with me."

By the door, Johan, Maia, Auriano, and Auriano's wife, Erina, were anxiously waiting for Leorino.

The crown prince chuckled at how overprotective they were.

The entire Cassieux family greeted the crown prince with the utmost respect.

Auriano had a small furrow between his eyebrows. He advanced before the crown prince and Leorino and took a deep bow with a courteous smile. "Thank you, Your Royal Highness, for showing the unfamiliar Leorino around. It has been a long time since you met in Brungwurt, hasn't it? I hope you had a chance to talk about old times."

Maia joined with a smile and a graceful bow.

"My husband had also instructed Leorino to thank Your Highness for your hospitality. We are honored that you have given him the opportunity to speak to you yourself, Your Highness."

The crown prince whispered again in a voice only Leorino could hear: "Your family is truly overprotective."

"Margravine of Brungwurt, Lord Auriano. Thanks to Leorino, I was able to refresh my fond memories of those days. I am relieved to hear that the margrave is in good health. Leorino, thank you for catching me up."

What a farce.

But this was just a little performance to let everyone know that the crown prince wanted to know more about Brungwurt and had chosen Leorino for the task, and that he was not interested in Leorino personally.

To finish the scene, Leorino spoke as he had been instructed.

"I am happy to be of service to Your Highness, despite my young age."

Leorino was unacquainted with high society, but even he was aware of the nobles who were listening to them with great interest.

They seemed to surmise that the sudden offer to Leorino was something that the Cassieux family had already anticipated from the start, and he sensed the tension surrounding them slightly relax.

*Who could have thought social interactions took so much skill...?*

Leorino sighed in relief, thinking the adult world was a difficult place to navigate. However, Kyle, who looked as if he was about to leave, suddenly grabbed Leorino's hand. Leorino was surprised.

"Your Highness?"

When he looked up, he noticed the crown prince watching him with kind eyes. He moved his face close to Leorino's, but not close enough to feel particularly intimate, and whispered in his ear.

"...There's too many onlookers today. When I said I wasn't joking, I meant it. I'll see you again."

The crown prince immediately let go of Leorino's hand and walked away with his guards toward the throne.

*...Wh-what was that all about?*

Auriano must have heard the crown prince's final whisper.

"For crying out loud... Is that man trying to ruin all our efforts?" He huffed in a scandalized tone. "Leorino, were you all right?"

"Yes, Auriano. I am sorry for the trouble I have caused you."

He was so relieved that all his strength suddenly left him. However, when he noticed Erina, who was watching him anxiously alongside Auriano, Leorino smiled at her sweetly.

"Erina, my dear sister, how are you? You look very beautiful today. Congratulations on your debut."

"I'm very well, Leorino, and thank you. Lord Auriano has been so worried about you. I'm so glad everything is all right."

Erina was dressed in a youthful orange dress, looking like the perfect bride. She smiled comfortably. "Leorino, you're dazzlingly beautiful as always."

Erina had finally gotten used to Leorino's good looks after living with him and now was no longer nervous around him. She was as comfortable with him as with the rest of the family. He was very grateful for that, but it didn't change the fact that she still complimented Leorino's looks with a little girlish twinkle in her eye.

"Leorino, you look a little pale... You must be tired. Do your legs hurt?"

Johan placed his hand on Leorino's elbow in concern. Leorino shook his head and denied it, but Maia's and Auriano's faces both became clouded, though not enough for the people around them to notice.

They could see that Leorino was quickly running out of stamina. However, in high society, one could not afford to show weakness. They could not let the people around them notice that Leorino was not feeling well so early in the night.

The king's congratulatory address and toast were to be followed by individual speeches. The family members, anxious to see whether Leorino would be able to stay upright until then, exchanged meaningful glances.

Loud, magnificent music sounded, announcing the entrance of the royal family to the audience.

"Oh my. Let's move. Johan, watch over Leorino."

The entire Cassieux family hurried to a place befitting their rank and prepared to receive the royal family. Soon after, the royalty entered one by one. The nobles greeted them with the deepest bows.

The moment Leorino saw a certain tall man in the line of royals, all but one thought disappeared from his mind.

The man he had always wanted to meet was right there.

Loose black curls. Perfect masculine good looks.

Gravis had become an adult man, much more mature than Leorino remembered, with the sort of masculine charm befitting of that status. The full regalia of the general's military uniform suited him perfectly.

*Oh... Vi... Vi, I've missed you so much...!*

Leorino gasped quietly and staggered.

Johan immediately offered him his arm, but Leorino shook his head and refused. "...I'm all right. I can still stand."

The Cassieux family nodded in unison at Leorino's courage

"Rino, we believe in you."

"That's right. Show us your mettle as a man of the Cassieux family."

"Thank you, Mother, Brother... I will be fine. I cannot afford to stumble here."

He would endure any amount of physical pain if only he could see those starry-sky eyes again, even just one glance from up close.

Leorino continued to watch Gravis on the stage with a twinkle in his violet eyes.

Leorino's appearance caused a storm of excitement in the audience.

"Ha-ha, look at that. It's like the ground is opening up before us."

Captivated by Leorino's beauty, the guests made way for him one after another. Johan smiled at the sight.

"It's easy to walk with you by my side."

Auriano nodded in agreement and whispered so that only his family could hear, keeping a serious expression on his face. "That's never happened to me at a soiree before. I never thought a brother of mine could be so useful."

"Oh, Lord Auriano, you mustn't say that. Someone might think you mean it." Erina laughed pleasantly at her husband's casual remark.

Leorino's kind brothers were all trying to ease the nerves of their youngest brother. Leorino's heart was filled with gratitude. And to think that even Auriano, who was even more serious and brusque than his father, would joke about it. Leorino couldn't help but laugh out loud. His smile, like a flower blooming open, drew a gasp from those around him.

Johan gave him a small nudge with his elbow, and Leorino's mouth stiffened in a panic. However, when Leorino hid his expression, the delicate shape of his face stood out as if it were a work of art. This time, he could hear sighs of euphoria escaping from the lips of the nearby guests.

"Leorino, you shouldn't smile so overtly in public. Be dignified and resolute."

"Yes, Mother. I apologize."

Leorino sighed to himself.

He was too inexperienced to know the appropriate behavior in such situations. Leorino raised the corners of his mouth just a little, as he had been taught, but tried to keep a firm expression, not to show his emotions to the best of his ability.

Maia smiled behind her fan and nodded. "Yes, that's it. You're doing very well."

"Leorino, you look so elegant. Be confident." Erina also smiled at him encouragingly.

Leorino bowed his head, careful to keep his expression fixed. The thought that he would soon be able to greet Gravis gave him all the energy he needed.

"Oh..."

The line advanced, and Leorino looked at the seats of the royal family. He involuntarily let out a disappointed gasp.

Gravis should have been onstage when the audience began, but he was now gone.

"What's wrong, Leorino?"

Auriano turned and looked at Leorino with concern. Leorino replied that it was nothing, but his voice sounded clearly disheartened.

*I wonder why he left... I would have liked to see him up close, if only for a brief moment...*

The disappointment deflated his spirits. The pain in his legs, which he had driven away by sheer force of will, returned.

Feeling faint, Leorino cast his eyes down. Then the dignity of his stance faded, revealing his true fragile nature.

A discerning eye would not miss this change in Leorino. Those who had, until then, watched him with a reserved gaze began to look at Leorino with hungry eyes, as if they were staring at prey.

It was his mother, Maia, who immediately took notice of these scoundrels.

"Leorino, you mustn't do that. Lift your face."

Maia struck her fan against her palm with a crack and squeezed her youngest son's elbow. Her warm Power flowed into his bloodstream and throughout his body. The tender vitality flowing from his elbow eased the pain a little, and Leorino came to his senses.

*Noble* was unfortunately only a descriptor of one's status, not their character. Lowlifes who would take advantage of the weak and vulnerable existed everywhere. If he showed any weakness to such people, he would quickly fall prey to their desires.

"Yes, Mother, I apologize."

Leorino himself was not aware of this change. But he knew that if he remained with his eyes downcast, he would bring shame to the proud Cassieux family.

He put his strength into his core once more.

*Right... I can't let something as small as not seeing Vi up close get to me so much. That's not what I'm here for. Keep it together.*

When he regained his resolute attitude, Maia nodded at her youngest son in approval.

The audience with the king and other royalty was a time of endurance for Leorino. In the end, the king's brother didn't make an appearance onstage, and Leorino's heart ached with disappointment.

Tonight's soiree was a celebration of the vows of adulthood of the noble sons and daughters. Leorino was the first to be congratulated. However, the queen was awestruck by Leorino's beauty and praised him endlessly, which made it difficult for him to leave her presence. The king, not quite as amazed as the queen, was also admiring the beauty of the youngest son of the Cassieux family to his heart's content.

Leorino felt very ill at ease with this. It was as if he wasn't a person at all but a work of art, a decoration.

The crown prince, who was standing behind them, looked somewhat restless, glaring at the nobles behind Leorino as they passed by the Cassieuxes.

The king and queen also generously congratulated Auriano and Erina on their marriage. After all, it was the union between two of the most powerful noble families in the country, the Margrave of Brungwurt and the Duke of Leben. For the court of Fanoren, this was a matter of great interest.

The Margrave of Brungwurt rarely left his territory and was not directly involved in the political situation at the capital, but apart from the Royal Army, he was the only nobleman with a powerful military force in the country.

The Duke of Leben, on the other hand, was known for his neutrality and moderate views. He was the wealthiest and most prestigious nobleman in Fanoren, owning the third largest estate in the country, after the royal palace and the Brungwurt estate, in the suburbs of the royal capital.

Auriano and Erina's marriage was a union of wealth and power between two such powerful nobles that even other countries took notice. From the political perspective, it would not be an exaggeration to say that this marked the birth of an influential power second only to the royal family.

However, their marriage was approved only because neither of the two families could find any candidates of similar status and because the successive heads of the families were known for their mild temperaments and lack of political ambition.

Furthermore, there was a certain agenda at work in the connection between the two families that would affect the fate of the country, but no one other than the heads of the two families knew it yet.

The two were the focus of much attention, but the sight of Erina happily following her husband with her cheeks flushed and Auriano tenderly caring for her made it clear to everyone that their marriage was not a mere political ploy.

Due to these circumstances, the audience of the Cassieux family took an unusually long time. The entire family endured the intense stares from everyone in the hall. Their only concern was the state of Leorino's legs after kneeling for so long.

Finally, they were dismissed. Leorino, who remained on his knees respectfully the entire time, managed to stand on his own, even as he staggered slightly. The whole family was relieved to see Leorino in such a state.

From that point on, the audience went smoothly.

After the audience, congratulatory music and the national anthem were performed for the sons and daughters who had reached the age of maturity.

Finally, the soiree turned into a social event.

"...Hah, it's finally over! Leorino, you did so well!"

Johan exclaimed over his brother's hard work. Auriano and Maia nodded emphatically. Leorino was simply relieved that the whole thing ended without incident.

From this point on, the only person accompanying Leorino would be his second brother, Johan. Auriano would go pay courtesy calls as the next head of the family, while Erina, the next margravine, accompanied by Maia, was expected to greet the other ladies.

Maia showed her appreciation for her youngest son. "You've worked very hard. Once you've stayed in the hall long enough to still be considered polite, please go home early with Johan."

"Yes, Mother... I must thank you, my brothers, and my dear sister-in-law, Erina."

Leorino nodded toward his family, saying that he would be fine.

Watching the boy with concern for a while, Auriano and the rest of his family soon headed into the hustle and bustle of the glamorous soiree to fulfill their respective duties.

Leorino watched their backs, feeling empty on the inside.

*I want to go home right now.*

Leorino was exhausted.

# The Encircling Net

The soft breeze of the spring evening blew in through the wide-open windows, cooling the heat in the hall.

Against the backdrop of a fantastic garden lit by a bonfire, candlelight filled the room with its brilliant flicker. Lavishly dressed men and women, young and old, were enjoying the banquet, laughing and talking the night away.

Vivid colors fluttered and shimmered at the edges of Leorino's vision. To his eyes, it seemed less real and more like something straight out of a dream. Everything was different from Brungwurt, which was full of nature, simple, and solid.

*I really am in the royal capital.*

"Leorino, you did really well today. How are your legs?"

Johan's words brought him back to reality.

Leorino nodded without thinking. He was too tired for coherent thought.

Perhaps the relief of having successfully accomplished what needed to be done had completely deflated him.

"Thank you, Johan… I wish I could say they're fine, but to be perfectly honest, I could really use some rest."

Leorino finally let himself complain. His face was pale.

Johan discreetly led Leorino to a wall. He rubbed Leorino's back tenderly.

"Do you want to go to the lounge?"

Leorino nodded frankly. His body was just about to give out, but protocol dictated that he stay in the hall a little longer. He should take a break and come back to keep himself from appearing unsightly.

It was hard to tell on the surface, but Leorino was more nervous and exhausted than he appeared. He had never seen so many people before and had never been away from home for such a long time.

This was partly because the family had been so overprotective, and he was not allowed to experience the outside world on his own. The only place Leorino had ever been on his own was Brungwurt Castle and its courtyard. And even then, he was always accompanied by his full-time attendant. He had no more experience than a half-fledged child.

His only saving grace was that he had the memory of Ionia as an adult, but Ionia had lived in a small world without having established proper human relations. Nor did he have any experience in the social circles of the nobility.

In the end, Leorino would have to face this phase in his life on his own and overcome it one experience at a time.

For Leorino, this day had been a long time coming.

"Lord Johan, how good to see you. Won't you introduce your beautiful brother to me?"

Suddenly, a voice called out to them from behind. When they turned around, they saw a man in his midthirties, dressed in gaudy clothing, standing there.

Leorino, wondering who he was, observed the man as politely as possible, and the man stared back at him with passion in his eyes. Leorino got the distinct impression he would not like him.

He found the strength to mend his expression.

Johan casually changed his position to hide his brother from the man's gaze. He put his hand on his chest and bowed to the man. Leorino did the same. The bow was an indication that they were dealing with a nobleman who Johan recognized as being of a higher rank than himself.

The man's exact status was soon revealed.

"…Marquis of Schwein, well met. My brother may have reached the age of maturity, but he is still an immature boy, ignorant of the ways of the world… You would not enjoy making small talk with him, I assure you."

Johan indirectly refused to let Leorino exchange greetings with him. It seemed that Johan was wary of this Marquis of Schwein for some reason.

Leorino was concerned about his brother's attitude, but he focused on keeping his expression firm.

The man shook his head with an exaggerated gesture.

"Why, he's an adult now. Wouldn't you say he's one of us? …Please, what's the worst that could happen? No need for charades. I simply want an introduction. Or do you think I don't deserve one?"

Johan fought the urge to click his tongue in disgust.

He was so concerned about Leorino's health that he neglected to observe his surroundings, and he had fallen into the clutches of the worst kind of man.

The Marquis of Schwein was a playboy of the worst kind, known for doggedly pursuing both men and women. However, despite his reputation, he held a significant position in the Palace of Heaven and Earth and had a lot of power. Because of his wealth and good looks, he had many cronies, both male and female. These cronies had as little restraint as he did, and there was no end to the scandals that followed them.

Such a man had set his eyes on Leorino's beauty. This was bad. But to cause a fuss at this juncture would be to put Leorino's future in jeopardy.

Johan decided to leave immediately after exchanging greetings.

Leorino had an anxious look on his face as his brother whispered in his ear: "Greet him briefly. As soon as you're done, I'll take you to the lounge. Just have a little more patience."

Leorino nodded. Johan urged him to step forward.

The man took this as consent; he grinned, leaned in closer, and offered his hand. Leorino hesitated, but finally shook his hand.

"It's a pleasure to meet you. I am Karl Hermann, the Marquis of Schwein."

"I am Leorino Cassieux. It's a pleasure to meet you."

Just as Leorino was about to let go, the marquis squeezed his hand so hard it hurt and pulled him close.

"Ah!"

When Leorino looked up, perplexed, the man was looking down at him with his penetrating gaze, from so close that he could nearly feel his breath.

"...My god, how beautiful you are up close. Never in my life have I seen anything as perfect as you... A true miracle of creation."

Leorino was dumbfounded at the nerve of the man.

"You insolent—! Marquis, please take your hands off my brother right this instant!"

Johan glared at the Marquis of Schwein with a fierce expression and got in between them. The man cackled without offense and finally let go of Leorino's hand.

"...Ha, you are very overprotective of him, aren't you? Well, given his beauty, I suppose it's no wonder."

At the man's words, the usually cheerful and amicable Johan turned indignant.

Leorino did not understand what the man was trying to do. He was frustrated with himself for not being able to read behind the insinuations and teasing and respond appropriately.

"That's enough." Johan urged Leorino to leave, but before they knew it, they had been surrounded by men.

The Marquis of Schwein had called them, and the men who had been staring at them from a distance now surrounded them, all wanting to talk to them.

Johan quickly pulled Leorino close and glared at them intensely. Leorino shot them a stern gaze that seemed to warn them to stay away from him. He didn't know the intent of the men's suggestive glances. But he did know he hated to be looked at like some rare object.

Still, the men remained undaunted, watching Leorino with a dangerous gleam in their eyes. Even the Marquis of Schwein was smiling wickedly.

*  *  *

*Why... Why are these men...?*

To the more experienced men, Leorino's warnings must have looked like a kitten baring his claws in a desperate attempt to intimidate them. He may have behaved haughtily, but his naivete and innocence were as clear as day. If anything, his show of courage made him look all the more adorable.

Leorino hadn't even realized he was cowering in fear. The men's excitement reached its peak as he helplessly clung to his brother.

"Oh... You're a real marvel, aren't you...?"

"Dear Johan, please introduce your brother to us as well."

"Look at those eyes!"

"...His skin, his slender waist. Incredible..."

He and Johan couldn't bear the vulgarities thrown at him.

Johan could no longer hide his anger. He grabbed Leorino's arm and ordered the men to let them pass.

The more reasonable among the men retreated at Johan's undeniable wrath, but the foolish ones remained unmoved, still staring feverishly at Leorino. They even had the nerve to hold out their hands and begin introducing themselves. Leorino was frightened and confused, wondering if he had done something wrong.

It was then that he heard a voice: "Leorino!"

It was Julian Munster, Erina's brother and the next Duke of Leben.

Upon recognizing him, the men surrounding Leorino backed away.

Pushing himself through the crowd, Julian approached him gallantly, with a gentle smile on his handsome face, and took Leorino's hand in a friendly manner.

"I'm so glad I found you here... Leorino, you look as beautiful as always. Congratulations on your coming of age."

"...Lord Julian."

"Welcome to the royal capital. I've been waiting for you, my angel."

Leorino heaved an involuntary sigh of relief at the appearance of a familiar face. Thanks to Julian, the tension between him and the men surrounding him vanished. Leorino looked up at Julian with gratitude.

Julian must have already guessed what was going on. He glanced around quickly and glared at the men with a cold expression, like a true heir of a powerful noble.

"I never thought anyone could be so rude to you… Looks like some people need to learn their place."

His severe, cold expression was the polar opposite of the kind smile he offered Leorino.

Having faced Julian, the men loosely broke their siege with guilty looks on their faces. Only the Marquis of Schwein seemed amused at Julian's behavior.

"…So that's how it is. I've heard rumors about the young man whom Julian was head over heels for. I hadn't thought *this* was the boy you were making advances on."

Julian ignored his words, keeping his expression fixed, and smiled at Leorino, holding out his hand.

"My mother would like to see Lord Johan and you. Will you come with me?"

Any offer to escape this baffling, unpleasant situation was beyond welcome. Deciding that a meeting with his in-laws, the Munster family, would be a valid reason, Leorino nodded.

He knew it was impolite not to give Julian a proper answer, but for some reason, his words caught in his unusually tight throat.

Julian seemed to notice this.

"Well then, gentlemen. We'll be off."

Julian took Leorino's hand, saving him from the men encircling him.

"I'll see you soon," the Marquis of Schwein called to Leorino's back. He was watching Leorino again with that piercing gaze.

"I'm so glad you found us, Lord Julian. It was my fault. I had no idea that man had his eye on us. It is thanks to you that we escaped unscathed."

"Why, this is nothing. If anything, I am glad that Leorino made his debut at the soiree and this was the worst it got. It might have been partly thanks to His Royal Highness the crown prince keeping them in check."

"His Highness was keeping them in check?"

"Oh yes, everyone is talking about it. I heard that His Highness approached him personally. During tonight's audience, from where he stood onstage, His

Royal Highness was clearly discouraging anyone giving Leorino insolent glances. Haven't you noticed?"

Leorino looked up at Julian.

Julian, too, gazed at him with tender eyes, as if bewitched.

Leorino had already rejected his marriage proposal once. Why was Julian still so kind to him, as if nothing had changed?

Pondering such absurd questions, his mind dulled by exhaustion, he tripped over his own feet.

"...Oh my. Leorino, are you all right?"

The adults supported him from both sides.

"...Lord Julian. I hate to disappoint the Duchess of Leben, but Leorino is very tired. I want him to rest. I must take him to the lounge."

"Of course, I understand." Julian nodded without seeming offended.

"Depending on how he's feeling, I think we may leave for the night, early as it may be."

"Of course, my mother doesn't need to see him today. As long as Erina is in the royal capital, there will be another opportunity. You're right—he's looking awfully pale... Leorino, you did very well today. You must be very tired."

"No, I... Yes... Well..."

He couldn't think of the right words.

Perhaps still reeling from the situation he just escaped, Leorino was unable to keep up appearances and returned to his natural state, looking completely at a loss.

He seemed so frail at that moment.

Johan and Julian looked at each other and nodded, thinking it would be difficult to force Leorino to stand in the hall any longer.

"Lord Julian...we'll take our leave here."

"Of course. In that case... Leorino, I'll look forward to seeing you again."

Leorino could only stare at Julian silently.

Julian stared back at Leorino with his utterly charmed gaze and whispered: "Leorino, I know this is not the place to say this, but I haven't given up on you yet."

Leorino's eyes widened.

"Lord Julian... But I..."

"Hush now. I don't want to upset you any further. I'll leave you be. Now, go get some rest."

Julian smiled at him one last time, said his good-byes with a beautiful bow, and left.

Leorino, now completely exhausted, managed to slip discreetly out of the hall with Johan's help.

"Leorino, make yourself comfortable and rest. I'll be right back after I talk to Auriano. Lock the door and don't open it until I arrive, all right?"

"Yes... Thank you, Johan."

Leorino occupied one of the lounges near the ceremonial hall and, with Johan's help, plopped down on a chaise longue.

"It must have been very unpleasant for you to be pestered by that brute. I'm so sorry I couldn't protect you."

"No, I'm... I'm so sorry I couldn't do anything right, when I keep saying how I don't just want to be protected by others."

Johan gave Leorino a pat on the head, praising his efforts.

"You heard what Julian said, didn't you? You're doing so well. You were so resolute in front of His Majesty. You had the best possible debut. We are so proud of you. Have some faith in yourself."

"...All right. Thank you."

Johan nodded and left the room, reminding him to be sure to lock the door.

The lounge was very quiet.

There were only a few chairs and a display shelf against the wall. A small candle cast a soft shadow.

The bustle of the soiree was far away.

Leorino slightly slumped into a position that was easy on his legs and feet.

Once he sat down, his whole body felt terribly heavy. From the waist down, he felt a dull ache. The area from the left knee down was particularly numb. He finally realized how much he had stressed and overworked himself throughout the day.

He knew he had to lock the door as Johan had instructed, but he couldn't seem to get up. Still, remembering the discomfort of being surrounded by men, he realized he needed to keep himself safe. Encouraging his aching legs, he locked the door and finally found himself able to relax.

His confusion and impatience gradually faded away, and his troubled mind slowly calmed down.

At last, he could calmly ruminate on the day's events one by one.

Leorino finally understood the meaning of his family's advice. This was not Brungwurt, where he was born and raised. This was not the safe home where everyone had watched Leorino grow up from a young age.

Many men's eyes clearly showed a wide variety of interest in Leorino. Perhaps those baffling, unpleasant gazes were the proof of other men's strange interests, as his family had often warned him.

Even when he had been Ionia, he was often subjected to uncomfortable stares. But even though he had been met with gazes of apprehension and disgust, they had never clung to his skin like this.

It was because he had been born with this face.

This was likely just the beginning, and he felt he would experience this more often in the coming months. But if he was going to live in the royal capital, he would have to accept it sooner or later.

*And yet I... I couldn't do anything... I'm so pathetic...*

Leorino felt horrible.

He knew he couldn't show fear, but he couldn't stop himself. Being surrounded by a large group of men whose eyes roamed all over his body finally made him show his weakness.

What would have happened if Julian had not come along? As he remembered the sincere gaze of the young man who had rescued him from his predicament, Leorino's heart was once again filled with mixed feelings.

Julian was a gentleman beyond reproach. He was kind and good-natured, and there was no fault to be found with either his looks or his status. If only

Leorino could accept his protection, there would be no one more suitable to take as a husband.

However, Leorino knew that even Julian saw him only as something to protect.

Perhaps it was his face that made the men think of him as if he were a woman. But he didn't want to be treated like a woman. He didn't want to be an object of protection.

He wanted to fight.

Leorino wanted to be strong. He couldn't help thinking about how he could stand on his own feet as a respectable man.

"I wish I could have seen him..." He sighed without thinking.

He missed Gravis.

Six years ago, Gravis had saved his life at Zweilink. But his memories of the incident were blurry at best.

Once Leorino was able to sit up in bed once more, he wanted to know more about what had happened. However, August did not tell him anything, perhaps fearing that reliving the incident would make his son suffer.

Leorino wanted to get a closer look at Gravis as he was now.

He would keep Ionia's memories in his heart, never revealing the truth to anyone.

He didn't think anyone would believe something so impossible. If a man as frail as him were to show up and say, "I was Ionia in my previous life," all anyone would get from that would be disappointment.

He didn't care if he couldn't be there for Gravis.

He just wanted to accomplish the only thing he could do for him. That was to uncover the truth about the betrayal at Zweilink, a secret now known to Leorino alone.

The stars were already twinkling in the night sky.

Leorino, attracted by the starry sky, opened the glass door leading to the balcony, then stepped outside.

Perhaps it was the bright lights, but there seemed to be fewer stars than in

Brungwurt. Still, they were enough to remind him of the eyes of the man whom he so hopelessly pursued.

Stairs on either side of the balcony led directly out into the courtyard. The cold night air was pleasant, even as his legs continued to ache.

To his left, he could see the flicker of the soiree bonfire. The area to his right was dense with trees, giving it the appearance of a forest. This must have been the garden that led farther into the inner palace.

That was when he heard footsteps on the gravel. Leorino looked in the direction of the sound and froze in fear.

"…I knew it. It's so good to see you again, princess of the Cassieux family."

There stood the Marquis of Schwein, whom he was sure he had left at the venue, with an unfathomably ominous grin, the light of the bonfire illuminating his back.

Leorino was too shocked to speak.

"Who would have thought such a precious gem would choose to leave the safety of its treasure chest, when it's so utterly defenseless? …Didn't your guardians tell you to lock the door and stay inside? Hmm?"

With his penetrating gaze, the man placed his foot on the steps leading to the balcony where Leorino stood.

Leorino immediately ran down the opposite staircase.

The man's face was out of sight on the opposite side, but his excited, loud laughter echoed in the quiet evening darkness.

"There's no use running, princess."

A chill ran down Leorino's spine.

The Marquis of Schwein had deliberately come here looking for him. Leorino didn't know what the man wanted to do. But the malicious intent with which he was approaching Leorino was palpable.

There was no time to hesitate.

All Leorino was given was the few dozen steps splitting the balcony.

"…Please, I'm not going to hurt you. We're just going to play a little."

The sound of the man's feet on the stairs. The man's voice drew nearer.

*My body can't run…!*

Leorino moved his painfully numb legs like his life depended on it, diving deeper into the courtyard, into the darkness of the trees.

*I have to get out of here before he can catch me...! Legs, move... Please just keep moving!*

The grove's thick foliage kept the moonlight from reaching the ground. This was fortunate for Leorino. His platinum hair and outfit were reflective enough to reveal his location if the light hit him for even the briefest moment.

In the darkness, he moved little by little from one thick trunk to another, doing his best to protect his feet, as he hid over and over.

Leorino did everything in his might to conceal his panting.

The grove in the courtyard was well-maintained, the ground perfectly flat, offering no place to hide. His only allies were the darkness and the thick trunks that hid his body. But he did know how to kill all signs of his presence. He knew how to hide in a dark forest.

But with *this* body, the knowledge would do little if he couldn't move as he intended. He could barely see at night, and his legs were beginning to cramp, losing function with each step. He had no weapon to fight back with and little physical strength in his arms to begin with.

Only the darkness could save him now. All he could do was save his strength and hide behind the trees, concealing all signs of life.

"Where are you? Come out, dearest. No point in hiding."

The voice of the man chasing him seemed to draw farther away, but then it came from startlingly close by.

"Come out, come out, wherever you are... Pretty, pretty princess."

The man must have been thinking Leorino was as good as his. He did not hide either his footsteps or his sneers.

Leorino desperately listened for the man's footsteps and the sounds of him brushing against the branches, trying to establish his exact position.

Then, without missing a beat, as the man seemed to draw farther away, Leorino moved under the shade of another tree. He could only repeat this process.

Little by little, Leorino was driven deeper and deeper into the courtyard.

Leorino never expected to outrun a healthy adult man.

All he wanted was to buy himself some time.

Johan must have returned to the lounge by now. If Leorino could buy enough time, if he could just keep running, his family would surely go looking for him.

*Johan... Anyone, please. Please let someone notice...*

"...Give in already! You can run, but you can't hide!"

The man was losing his patience for his prey, who continued to flee with unexpected persistence.

Leorino was quickly running out of stamina.

He was so exhausted, his left leg was dragging. When he shrank back and hid behind one of the largest trees, Leorino found himself unable to move.

His legs felt weak, and his body shook. His foot caught on something, making a rustling sound.

Leorino clung to the trunk and did all he could to stay upright. His heart was pounding so hard, he worried the man might hear it. He clutched his chest and held his breath.

"I heard you. Hmm? This way?"

The man's footsteps were approaching him now. A chill crawled up Leorino's spine as he heard the sound of heavy breathing. Johan might not make it in time.

*Help me...! Someone, notice...!*

"Ha-ha-ha, there. I knew I heard a noise over here."

In his heart, Leorino shouted the name of the man who was ever at the forefront of his mind.

*"Vi...!"*

# Embraced by the Winter Woods

After leaving the soiree early, Gravis had finished his business at the royal palace and returned to his own detached palace.

As the king's brother, Gravis was obligated to attend official functions. Tonight's coming-of-age celebration soiree was one of those. But by showing up, he had fulfilled his duty.

He did not have the time to be greeted by an endless onslaught of nobles. As the head of the Palace of Defense and the Palace of Foreign Affairs, he was tasked with an impossible number of duties.

As socializing was not one of them, he avoided it to the greatest possible degree.

His palace was a relatively small one among the detached palaces. Even so, in addition to a ballroom that could accommodate around a hundred guests, there were four ceremonial halls of various sizes and a large dining hall for formal meals. However, most of them never saw the light of day.

As soon as he appeared in his room, his valet arrived. It was Theodor Anhalt, from the family of Count Moreau, who had served him since they were children. He was a stern and neurotic man, but also deeply loyal to Gravis and therefore trustworthy.

Whenever Gravis returned home, Theodor was quick to notice and make an appearance.

"Welcome home, Your Highness. I see you slipped out early again."

"I don't have time to sit around celebrating fledglings leaving their nests... But I'm sure you'll recall I sent Alois to my uncle in Francoure. Has he sent word yet?"

"No, not quite yet. But it is Lord Alois we're talking about. He knows what His Highness is looking for. I am certain he will return with the king of Francoure's answer in the very near future."

Gravis nodded.

Theodor placed his hand on Gravis's shoulder to remove the cloak from his military uniform. At that moment, his master's muscular shoulders suddenly jerked, and the valet withdrew his hand.

"Sir...?" Theodor tilted his head at his master's unusual behavior as Gravis stared into the void. "...Your Highness? What's wrong?"

"That voice again..."

Gravis continued to stare at nothing with a fierce look on his face.

"Your Highness...?"

"This... This cry. It's...Leorino!"

"...Your Highness! Where are you—?"

The next moment, Theodor's hand grasped thin air.

Gravis had leaped.

Theodor was used to his master's sudden disappearances, but he couldn't help feeling curious about the name the man had murmured.

"Who is 'Leorino'...?"

Before Gravis's eyes stood Leorino, looking terribly pale and exhausted.

He must have been surprised by Gravis's sudden appearance. His violet eyes were wide-open. The moment Gravis saw those violet eyes, he remembered the events of six years ago.

The angelic boy had been shivering, spilling tears, caught in the arms of a delirious soldier on the edge of a wall of the fort. The small body slipped through his outstretched hands and fell beyond the wall. The regret of not having been able to save him had been clinging to Gravis's heart ever since.

But over the past six years, the boy had grown up. And so beautifully that his sight almost made him dizzy.

How could he have forgotten such a dazzlingly beautiful creature?

"...You called me again, Leorino."

Leorino was still too stunned to speak. He might not even recognize Gravis.

"Do you know who I am?"

Leorino answered in a trembling voice. "Vi... Your Highness, Prince Gravis...?"

"That's right."

"H-how...?"

"Your calls somehow always reach me...though I don't know why."

At that moment, a man's voice came from behind Leorino.

Leorino's slender body was trembling as he turned around with a horrified expression.

Gravis immediately understood the situation.

He knew from Sasha that Leorino was attending tonight's soiree.

Judging by the circumstances, he must have been targeted by the wrong man. He must have been chased around and had to flee all the way to the back of the courtyard by himself.

*What on earth are his guardians doing?* he wondered in anger. The adults were beyond foolish to take their eyes off such a beautiful young man for even a moment.

Leorino was hanging on to a tree trunk in an unnatural position. He looked exhausted. He likely could hardly keep himself upright anymore. Gravis remembered that Leorino was still suffering the long-term effects of the injuries to his legs. He was amazed that Leorino had managed to run this far.

Leorino was trembling. He must have been very scared, Gravis thought sadly.

"...You did well. Come here."

Gravis held out his hand.

Leorino, who had been watching his back, jerked at the sound of Gravis's voice and looked at him. Gravis spoke again to reassure him.

"It's all right. Come now. Come to me."

His voice was so soft, it surprised even Gravis himself.

Leorino's thin, white fingers hesitantly reached toward him. As soon as his hand left the trunk, his thin body staggered.

"...Ah!"

Gravis immediately caught him and gently held him in his arms.

"You're all right now. You did all you could."

He stroked his small head. He pulled him into his cloak, completely covering his thin body. Now no one could hurt him anymore.

His thin body was still trembling.

"Your legs hurt, don't they?"

Leorino nodded silently.

"Let's take you to Sasha."

His violet eyes looked up at Gravis with anxiety.

A faint ache filled Gravis's chest.

Leorino's thin body fit so strangely and comfortably in his arms.

"I can hear you... Oh...? Ah, Your Royal Highness... What brings you here...?"

The Marquis of Schwein's legs appeared from the trees behind Gravis, and Gravis fixed him in place with his fierce gaze.

The boy's thin back shuddered at the man's voice, and Gravis softly stroked it. Concealing his small head, he whispered: "...You're all right. I will make sure the man who did this to you will be punished... Don't think you will walk away unscathed."

The last words were meant for the pale man who stood there, stupefied.

Gravis held Leorino's body firmly in his arms and leaped toward the Palace of Defense.

Leorino felt like he was dreaming.

*How did I end up here...?*

He wished he could even a glance of Gravis.

At the soiree, he did indeed spot the familiar figure of the man among the seats of the royalty. But when it was Leorino's turn to greet the royal family, Gravis was already gone.

He had half given up hope of ever seeing him up close again... So why was he now being embraced by Gravis at a distance so close that his breath almost mingled with Gravis's?

The first time he ever felt the warmth of a man's body, Leorino shuddered.

Compared to the ice-cold air surrounding him, Gravis's body was extremely hot.

His heart was pounding so loudly that Leorino could hardly produce a coherent thought.

*...Vi is holding me.*

Gravis placed his hand on Leorino's waist, supporting his unstable body as if he were handling a delicate broken object. His hands were so large that he could hold Leorino's waist with one hand.

From Gravis's chest came a fragrance like that of a winter forest. The moment Leorino smelled it, he suddenly felt like he was Ionia again.

*Ah, it's Vi's scent...*

Now that Leorino saw him up close, he noted that Gravis had matured into a perfect adult man, with the sort of masculine charm befitting of that status. His body was more muscular and fuller than Leorino remembered.

Dressed in formal attire, Gravis was dazzlingly beautiful.

In the back of his mind, Leorino knew that the man in front of him was Gravis. However, Leorino now felt an instinctive fear toward him that he had never felt in his dreams as Ionia.

In his memories, they were almost eye level, but now Leorino's forehead barely reached the man's shoulders. This height difference scared him. He felt as if he was in the arms of a strange man, and his body froze on the spot.

Up until the moment of their encounter, Leorino had thought that if he were to meet Gravis again someday, he would feel the sort of fondness and affection he had felt for him back when they were best friends on equal terms.

But what he felt now was something else entirely. Their difference in size and age completely overwhelmed him.

He was painfully aware of how different he was from Ionia in every possible way. Even though he shared Ionia's memories, he realized that in the end he was nothing more than Leorino Cassieux.

Leorino was confused by the gap between his memory and reality.

"Can you stand?"

The voice brought him back to his senses. He had been in the dimly lit courtyard just a moment ago.

*...Where are we?*

Before he knew it, he had been brought to an unfamiliar location. He looked around the utilitarian room. It seemed to be an office.

"You don't seem surprised."

"What...?"

The leap was unexpected, but Leorino's mind had not yet caught up with the situation, and he had completely forgotten to pretend to be surprised by Gravis's Power, which he was *supposed* to be experiencing for the first time.

An amused look flashed in Gravis's cold eyes. All because Leorino did not look surprised by the man's unusual ability.

His violet eyes were single-mindedly focused on Gravis.

Lucas was right. Leorino's eyes were just like Ionia's, whom he had lost forever eighteen years earlier. No, they were *Ionia's* eyes. That unique indigo with a hint of dawn. He never thought that identical eyes to Ionia's could exist in this world. Those precious violet eyes that he saw in his dreams to this day were moving, glistening with life right where he stood.

But no. This young man was not Ionia.

His origins, his appearance, his everything was different from Ionia.

He was a completely different person from his best friend, who had protected Gravis with his Power and loyalty until his death.

He was so helpless, he could never be him.

He might have known Gravis, but all he could do was freeze up when suddenly brought to a strange place by a man he had never properly met before. It could be that he didn't know how to resist a man's advances, but he was likely too trusting in the first place. Sasha was right; at this rate, some brute would get his hands on him in no time.

For some reason, the thought of someone having their way with this violet-eyed young man irritated Gravis beyond belief. He had only saved him in the garden through force of circumstance. But before he knew it, he began to feel like he couldn't let go of Leorino.

Gravis had often been teased for being the ice-cold general, but now a strange feeling stirred in his heart. It must have simply been the boy's helplessness that birthed this immense desire to keep him safe.

*...Sasha wasn't exaggerating after all.*

Gravis decided to scare him a little, putting some strength into the hand around his waist and pulling him close forcefully. If this taught him to be cautious around men, good. They would tend to his legs and send him back to the venue immediately. That had been the intention, at least.

But Leorino's feeble body fell into Gravis's arms more easily than he had expected.

The slender young man gasped in surprise. "Huh...?"

Leorino was clearly bewildered. His expression told him that he had no idea what to do as he looked up at Gravis in a daze, his violet eyes open so wide they looked ready to pop right out of their sockets.

*I didn't think he was* this *unguarded.*

Gravis chuckled. Leorino's thin, supple body fit snugly in his arms. Leorino had little to no muscle, making him feel like he belonged in his embrace.

Gravis felt a faint buzz of heat in his abdomen.

*"Protective instincts," my ass. What in the world is wrong with me?*

"You're unbelievable... You really are," Gravis muttered to himself, and chuckled again.

He slept with both men and women whenever he felt the urge, but only ever one-night stands to avoid any complications. No one had moved him emotionally per se, but the partners he impulsively chose were usually well-built, red-headed young men. He never thought that at the age of thirty-seven, he would feel so touched by a young man who, his extraordinary beauty aside, looked like a child who had just come of age.

Still, he couldn't let such a pure and innocent young man fall prey to some playful flirtation.

"Sasha is right. You'd be kidnapped in an instant."

Leorino rushed to press his hand into the man's chest, trying to put some distance between them. Gravis wasn't putting much strength into the arm around his waist, but Leorino's weak arms could only pull him away by a fistful.

Leorino felt humiliated as a man.

"Y-Your Excellency... Please let go of me."

But his wish was not granted.

Gravis placed his large hand on the back of Leorino's head. His long fingers threaded into Leorino's hair and pulled, revealing Leorino's fair neck.

Leorino couldn't take his gaze off the starry-sky eyes that were slowly getting closer and closer. At this breathtaking distance, he heard Gravis's low, smooth voice.

"What do you think would have happened if you had stayed in that courtyard, unable to move?"

"Ah... What?"

"You should be resisting the advances of a man at all costs, even at this very moment."

How could he resist when Gravis was holding him like this?

Just as Leorino looked up at Gravis with a deeply troubled, almost pleading expression, he heard a loud clang, as if something had been dropped behind them.

A muscular, red-haired man was standing there, a box of documents and its contents scattered at his feet, pointing at them and trembling.

"Keep it down, Dirk."

"Your Excellency...? I thought you were attending the Vow of Adulthood soiree tonight. And... What is this? Who is that dashing person?"

Gravis looked down at Leorino.

It was true that everything about Leorino made him look very dashing.

The adjutant seemed to have arrived at some conclusion.

"...Y-you can't be serious!"

"You've heard of him. This is the youngest son of the Cassieux family. Is Sasha still here? If not, tell whoever is on the night shift in the medical department to bring him some painkillers."

Dirk was still bewildered.

His superior, who was supposed to be at the soiree, was holding an impossibly beautiful young man.

Such an unusual scene was unfolding in the barren office.

The young man looked up at his superior with a somewhat puzzled expression. "Your Excellency...um, could you tell me where we are?"

"My office in the Palace of Defense."

It was no wonder Sasha had said he looked like a faerie or an angel. He was too gorgeous for words.

Dirk shuddered in horror at the thought. "No way..."

*No way... No way, no way... Don't tell me he just brought him here...?*

Dirk's bad hunch was more accurate than he could have imagined.

"Um, Your Excellency... Thank you very much for saving me. But I'm certain my family is worried about me, so I would like to go back to the soiree now."

"No. First, you have to be able to use your legs. Dirk, call Sasha immediately... Hey, Dirk? Dirk!"

Dirk finally screamed: "...Y-you! How could you kidnap a son of the Cassieux family?!"

Gravis had extracted this precious gem of a young man from the soiree without telling anyone, after all.

Gravis briefly explained the circumstances that led him to bring Leorino here. Leorino himself described to them how he had ended up being chased by a man.

Dirk finally calmed down.

"Hah, I see. So you just sheltered him here. I can't exactly fault you there... Hmm. In any case, Lord Leorino, that must have been very difficult on you."

"It was. He should get some rest, Dirk."

"Yes, sir."

Gravis gathered Leorino in his arms and carried him to the settee.

Leorino was told to get comfortable, but before he could change his position, Gravis took the liberty of raising his knees and laying him down. Just throwing his legs up on the settee would have helped, but this was rather overbearing.

Next, the redhead took the pillow from a nearby chair and handed it to his superior. Gravis took it silently and stuffed it under Leorino's back. His upper body sank into the soft pillow.

As Leorino's eyes began darting all over the office, the redhead immediately offered him a glass of water. Gravis told him to drink it, and Leorino listened, taking a sip of the cold water. The cool sensation of the water running down his throat released the tension from his stiff body.

The men watched in silence as Leorino let out a sigh of relief.

Being taken care of by such brilliantly coordinated men made him feel like a little child.

Unable to take it any longer, Leorino cast his eyes down. "Thank you very much…"

He had rehydrated his throat, but he suddenly felt so nervous that he couldn't speak properly. Leorino drooped, worrying if they thought he was too rude to even properly say thank you.

But the redhead, who heard his quiet voice, offered him a friendly smile.

*Is he the Dirk I know? …He can't be, can he…?*

He felt like the man resembled David, Ionia's father, whom he remembered from his dreams. The man would also match Dirk's current age. Leorino was so curious about the man's identity that he stared at him as if he wanted to devour him with his eyes.

The adjutant, feeling the beautiful young man staring at him so intently, blushed involuntarily.

"Um… Lord Leorino? It's a little embarrassing to be watched like that… you know, ha-ha-ha…"

"…I-I'm sorry."

He had been rude. He saw the man scratch his flushed cheek and apologized in a hurry.

"Does he bother you, Leorino?"

"Please, sir. It's unseemly for a man to be jealous because his subordinate is getting the attention of a beautiful young man… Wait! This is not the time for this, sir! Return to the soiree and inform the Cassieux family that you brought Lord Leorino here! Now!"

Right. His family must have been very worried. His disappearance must have become a major incident by now.

Leorino rushed to sit up. But Gravis's long arm lightly pressed down on his stomach, keeping him down.

"No. You need to rest."

"He's right. Lord Leorino, you should rest until Dr. Sasha arrives. Please, I'll go get Dr. Sasha. Your Excellency, head to the palace, please!"

"…Why don't you go?"

The settee on which Leorino was seated was wide enough for three large men to sit side by side. The man who sat himself down by Leorino's feet had a pointed look in his eyes. But the adjutant, accustomed to his superior's cold treatment, remained completely unfazed.

"I can't! I'll have to get dressed, and once I'm there, I'll have to mediate... It'll take forever. Whereas you would be in and out and get through to them in a heartbeat. Am I wrong? Please just go! It's scandalous for us to look after the Cassieux family's son without their permission."

"...Fine. Then you stay here. I'll send Sasha over, so don't leave Leorino alone. And don't let anyone in except Sasha."

"Yes, sir. Ha-ha, I suppose we're executing a Fialtewand? Looks like Your Excellency finally understood what Dr. Sasha meant."

The adjutant laughed at his superior's excessive caution in Royal Army terms. He joked about entering a state of alert that completely shut out any intrusion—the Fialtewand, also known as the Fifth Wall.

Completely ignoring his cocky second-in-command, Gravis stood up.

Leorino couldn't help but admire the perfect figure of the handsome man standing there, looking impossibly good in the formal attire of the Royal Army.

No matter how old he got, Gravis was still a beautiful man.

*I wonder if this is the last I'll see of him tonight...*

He was disappointed with himself for not being able to have a proper conversation with him. That was when Gravis noticed Leorino's anxious gaze and crouched in front of the settee.

He gently stroked Leorino's cheek with the back of his fingers to comfort him, and Leorino's golden lashes, slightly darker in color than his hair, trembled slightly. Leorino's violet eyes lit up and darkened once more. It was as if a golden butterfly was opening and closing its wings as it perched on a violet, Gravis thought to himself, enjoying the beautiful image. The corners of Gravis's mouth turned up slightly.

"Don't worry. I won't leave you alone, and this man won't do anything to you. You are safe here."

Leorino shook his head. "Will I...be able to see Your Excellency again today?"

He looked anxious. His needy eyes were adorable.

"Yes, I'll be back."

Leorino smiled at his words, as if reassured.

Gravis stroked Leorino's cheek once more. His fingers were cold and hard. There was no smile on his severe, tight face, but his eyes did indeed show concern and tenderness for Leorino.

Starry-sky eyes and slightly teary violet eyes watched each other.

*He's so close... Am I dreaming?*

"...Uhhh, so whatever it is you're doing right now, could you perhaps get a room...?"

When Leorino remembered himself, he found the red-haired adjutant watching him with his arms crossed, blushing and looking rather uncomfortable.

"I-I'm sorry."

"What do you mean, 'get a room'?"

Leorino tilted his head, wondering the same thing.

"...Perhaps it's better that you're not aware of it. I mean, I'm not concerned with you, Lord Leorino. But, Your Excellency, at your age... Wait! Go, Your Excellency! Get out of here! They must be losing their minds over there even as we speak!"

Gravis got to his feet, exasperated.

"You're so rude," he said, and disappeared.

"...Hah, he finally left. Now the Cassieuxes will know you're here."

Leorino felt a sense of kinship with the adjutant, who now looked back at him and smiled. He really appreciated how the adjutant didn't behave differently around him even after seeing him up close.

"I sure hope things haven't gotten too bad over there... Well, I'm sure Dr. Sasha will be here soon. Get some rest until then."

"Thank you... And I'm sorry for troubling you at this late hour."

The adjutant shook his head to reassure the self-conscious young man.

"No, it's no problem at all. And I got to see something rare, so it's all right."

"Something rare?"

"Oh yes. The general is usually a cold man, his heart below freezing, you know. Partly because of his beautiful face, he's incredibly intense and fearsome... But he's so kind to you. I've never seen him so gentle." The adjutant shook his head again. "Doesn't that man know what he's doing?"

Dirk may have been joking, but Leorino argued quietly, not wanting Gravis's kindness to be doubted. "That's not true... Vi has always been kind... The general, I mean."

He recalled Ionia's memories. Gravis had always been a very compassionate man by nature, even if he rarely showed emotion. Tonight as well, he came to Leorino's aid as soon as he learned of his predicament, just like he had six years ago. When Leorino remembered it, he felt like crying with joy and relief.

When Dirk heard Leorino's rebuttal, he blushed for some reason and started mumbling to himself. "Oh... Yes, ah-ha-ha... Why am I getting so embarrassed?"

*Right...! I need to know!*

Since they were finally alone, Leorino had to seize this opportunity and find out for sure.

"Um, I think I should introduce myself properly. My name is Leorino Cassieux, the fourth son of August Cassieux, the Margrave of Brungwurt. I'm pleased to make your acquaintance."

"Wah, you're right. I haven't introduced myself, either. My apologies. I am Dirk Bergund. My rank in the Royal Army is lieutenant colonel. I am the second-in-command of General Gravis Fanoren. Pleasure to meet you."

"Second-in-command... Lord Dirk Bergund..."

*Ah... It really is Dirk... He was still a child back then. Now look how big he's gotten!*

"Oh, no 'Lords,' please. I'm a commoner, so please just call me 'Dirk.'"

"Commoner..."

Dirk looked somewhat concerned by Leorino's reaction.

"Oh, uh, does that bother you? ...Hmm, that's not ideal. I could call someone else to chaperone you instead..."

"No, no! Not at all...!" When Leorino realized that he had been mistaken for a bloodline purist, he quickly shook his head. "Um, I'm... I'm really, really glad you're here with me, Lord Dirk."

*I'm so glad...! I can't exactly tell him I'm Ionia, but I'm so glad I got to meet him in this life...*

Leorino had always wondered what happened to Ionia's family in the royal capital after Ionia died. He had no idea that Ionia's younger brother, who was just a boy when Ionia died, had grown up to be such a fine man, even serving as Gravis's second-in-command.

Their ages were reversed now, but Dirk had grown up to be a bighearted and good-natured man. Although not as muscular as Gravis or Lucas, his toned physique was practical and strong, and his arms appeared to be well-trained.

Leorino looked at Dirk with tears in his eyes.

"Ahhh... I don't want you to misunderstand, but you're more powerful than you think." Ionia's little brother, who had grown up so fine, was now blushing and covering his mouth for some reason. "But thank you...I think? But, Lord Leorino, as I said, please don't 'Lord' me."

"Right. Well then, Dirk... Mr. Dirk! Please call me 'Leorino,' too!"

Leorino looked at Dirk intently with tear-filled eyes and smiled sincerely.

"Hnng..."

Receiving a direct blow to his heart, Dirk produced a sound like a bird being strangled.

"Ha-ha, oh boy... Going on a first-name basis right after we meet... That might be a bit much..."

"…Is that a no? I'd like to get to know you better."

The beautiful young man who could easily be mistaken for an angel had a twinkle in his eye.

Leorino raised himself up and patted the settee, urging Dirk to sit next to him. Of course, Dirk couldn't just accept the invitation.

"…Please. Please just call me 'Leorino'…!"

Leorino's beaming grin was so adorable that it made Dirk dizzy.

*Dammit, how am I supposed to say no to him…?!*

*So that's what he meant by "overwhelming"!* Dirk suddenly remembered Sasha's words.

Gravis first leaped to his room in the royal palace. From there, he quickly made his way on foot to the Divine Confine.

As he grew older, Gravis's Power only grew stronger. Alone, he could leap several times to the neighboring Kingdom of Francoure and back. On this day, he had already made several round trips to the Palace of Defense, the detached palace where he lived, and the royal palace, but traveling such short distances would not wear him out.

However, since leaping directly into a crowd could cause accidents, when leaping to the royal palace, he first used his room as his base and then moved on foot as far as possible.

As he approached the Divine Confine, the Imperial Guard and the attendants he passed in the corridor were all panicked and tense.

A significant number of the Imperial Guard had been dispatched. This meant that someone must have already ordered them to search for Leorino. The Marquis of Lagarea or Kyle must have acted at the request of the Cassieux family.

To avoid disrupting the atmosphere of the soiree, the Imperial Guard were laying low, acting as an extension of the security. However, the number of personnel deployed was unusual. Soon the guests would notice and be in an uproar.

*Dirk was right. If the commotion had grown too loud, the boy's reputation would have been needlessly tarnished.*

He approached the Imperial guards gathered in the hallway. The sudden appearance of the general made the guards tense, and they responded by lurching upright.

"General! Is everything well?"

"Are you allowed to leave? I have a couple of things to ask of you."

The younger Imperial guard looked at his older colleague. The elderly Imperial guard had served at the palace for many years and was familiar with Gravis.

"Yes, sir. How may we help?"

"There must be someone from the Cassieux family of Brungwurt in the hall. Do you recognize the face of Auriano Cassieux or Johan Cassieux? … Good. I want you to bring them to me discreetly."

"Yes, sir, but…what do we tell them?"

"You can mention my name. Tell them I have what they are looking for stored in a safe place."

At these words, the Imperial guards gasped. Gravis was pleased with their perceptiveness.

He pointed to the small lounge nearby.

"Is that room empty? …Good, then I'll wait there. Bring them in."

The Imperial guards nodded.

"Did Kyle give the order? Then inform Kyle as well. You know what to tell him."

"Yes, sir. 'Cancel the treasure hunt,' is that right?"

It was incredibly convenient how truly little he had to say to be understood. Gravis was pleased with the Imperial guard's response.

The two guards left to deliver the messages to their intended recipients.

The remaining Imperial guard led Gravis to the small room he had just mentioned. After checking inside, he gave a small nod to the general.

"The room is vacant, sir. You may enter."

Gravis thanked him and slipped into the room.

Until the knock sounded in the small room, Gravis thought about the young man he had left in his office.

The moment the gates closed at the border fortress on that day eighteen years ago, Gravis's heart had closed as well. The tender emotions that had shattered with the death of the man he loved were long gone.

Or so he thought.

Until today, when he was reunited with Leorino.

The only man Gravis had been willing to entrust his back to was no more. He died right in front of him, on the other side of the burning fortress, without ever returning to his arms.

He was a young man who, had Gravis not met him, would have been able to live out his life peacefully as the son of a blacksmith. It was unquestionably Gravis who had driven Ionia to his death.

Gravis had been responsible for the death of the only man he had ever loved.

The remaining vestiges of his love for the young man were slowly fading.

For the past eighteen years, Gravis had been in despair, and his heart was beyond empty.

And yet he found himself surprisingly moved by the young man who had nothing in common with Ionia in terms of birth, appearance, or personality.

Perhaps it was his rare violet eyes that made him so.

It reminded him of Lucas, who had six years ago feverishly told him that Leorino had the same eyes as Ionia. Now that Gravis had seen those eyes up close, he could understand why Lucas was so obsessed with Leorino.

That was how special those eyes were to the two men.

However, other than those special violet eyes, Ionia and Leorino were polar opposites with no other similarities.

Leorino's beauty was even keener than Sasha had described it.

It was not just his appearance. His entire demeanor portrayed innocence, fragility, and an odd sort of helplessness for an adult. He was a pitifully beautiful and defenseless young man.

With that appearance and personality, it would be difficult for him to live as an ordinary man.

Dirk, Gravis's second-in-command, had ridiculed his unusual fussing over Leorino when he said he *"finally understood what Dr. Sasha meant."* What Dirk didn't realize was that his words accurately captured Gravis's change of heart.

Like Sasha, Gravis found himself beginning to think about Leorino's future. He was filled with this immense desire to protect him. But instead of finding this troubling, it felt right, somehow.

He had no intention of stopping this mysterious stirring in his heart for the moment.

"...Whatever might this mean?"

Before long, a knock sounded in the room. It was the elder Imperial guard from earlier. Then came two brothers of the Cassieux family. The crown prince, Kyle, was with them.

Gravis turned to the men, all of whom had severe expressions on their faces.

"I see Kyle has come with you. This won't take long."

"I didn't expect to see you here, Uncle. We've lifted the search order for now... But let's hear what you have to say."

Kyle smiled cynically at his uncle with his usual boldness.

On the other hand, the Cassieux brothers were terribly nervous.

Their youngest brother, who was supposed to be resting in the lounge, had disappeared without a trace, and they had been going crazy with worry for the past hour. Johan, the second brother, was particularly shaken, feeling responsible for ever taking his eyes off Leorino.

After searching the entire premises and realizing that their brother was nowhere to be found, they finally turned to the crown prince. Kyle immediately decided the situation was an emergency, and just as he began his search with the Imperial Guard, he received a message from the king's brother that he could not have expected.

Under what circumstances had Leorino found himself in the care of his uncle?

Auriano and Johan were unable to speak when faced with the sheer might of the king's brother. Sensing this, Gravis began the conversation.

"It's good to see you again, Lord Auriano, Lord Johan. I apologize for calling you here."

His low, smooth voice, with a hint of unexpected gentleness, relaxed the tension between the Cassieux brothers.

"It has indeed been a long time, Your Highness… May we ask about the message you sent us?"

Gravis nodded firmly to soothe Auriano's grief-stricken expression.

"It's quite straightforward. Your youngest brother is in my care. I want you to rest assured."

The brothers' relief was palpable.

"Thank you…"

"But, Your Highness…! Where is Leorino right now?!"

"Johan…calm down. You mustn't speak like that." Auriano reprimanded his agitated brother.

"It's fine—you must have been worried. He is tired, but he is safe. Sasha is looking after him now."

"So Leorino is in the Palace of Defense, sheltered by His Highness and with Dr. Sasha?"

"Yes. He is in my office as we speak. I have instructed my trusted second-in-command to let no one but Sasha in. I can guarantee Leorino's safety."

Auriano and Johan were relieved to learn that their brother was with Sasha. But the thought that he needed to be examined by Sasha made them once more worry about what had happened to him in the first place.

"How did our brother end up in Your Highness's care…? You don't mean to say something happened to him…?"

"He's fine. He has not been hurt."

They both sighed in relief at Gravis's words. They had no reason to doubt the words of a man hailed as the Matchless Hero. Above all, there was no reason for Gravis to lie.

Kyle, who had been listening to the conversation between his uncle and the Cassieux brothers, looked somewhat relieved and asked: "How did Leorino end up with you, Uncle?"

Johan nodded. "Exactly. Leorino had been in the lounge. But in the span of a few minutes, he just vanished… Where in the world was he?"

Gravis's expression immediately turned grim.

"...When I found him, he was deep inside the courtyard. He couldn't move."

"Wh-what...?"

"The poor thing must have overworked his injured legs. He was shaking so badly that he couldn't stand on his own and was clinging to a tree in pain. I took the boy with me, thinking I should let Sasha take a look at him, but... I apologize for not informing you, his guardians, first."

Stunned by this knowledge, Auriano bowed deeply to Gravis. "How could I ever thank you enough for helping that child in such a state? Your Excellency... Thank you so much."

"But why was he there in the first place, especially considering his legs?"

The air surrounding Gravis turned threatening at Kyle's words.

"It was Karl Hermann... That bastard. Leorino was running from him."

"What? The Marquis of Schwein?"

"You don't mean...! That brute was *still* after Leorino?!"

The others looked at Johan, who seemed to know what was going on. Johan bit his lip in frustration.

"What do you mean by that, Johan?"

"...We were surrounded by the Marquis of Schwein and his cronies at the venue due to my negligence. Schwein had taken an interest in Leorino, and kept following him around, looking at my brother with an obscene gaze the entire time."

Auriano's expression turned sour.

"How could you let this happen when you were there with him?"

"I apologize, Brother. They surrounded us in an instant. It was my fault. I couldn't afford to make a scene, considering Leorino's reputation, and as I was pondering the situation, Lord Julian appeared and successfully rescued us. I was certain we were in the clear..."

"Fine, the point is Schwein was interested in Leorino. But the lounge was locked, wasn't it? How did he get to Leorino?"

Gravis answered that question. "From the balcony. Leorino had thoughtlessly opened the glass door to breathe the night air and was ambushed by the man who was waiting for him on the other side. He said the marquis almost caught him, but he went down into the courtyard and ran for his life."

"That boy... How reckless of him."

"I thought we had made him well aware of the danger he was in... I'm sorry for the trouble we've caused, Your Excellency. We failed to educate him."

Kyle reassured the Cassieux brothers as they apologized to Gravis for their brother's thoughtless behavior.

"He's not a woman. I think that no matter how many times you tell him to keep himself safe, he won't understand what it truly means. The man who has gotten the furthest with him is Julian Munster, correct? He's a gentleman, so I doubt he's ever touched him, especially with the margrave around. But the truth is, Leorino didn't even seem wary when I pulled him close."

"Wh—? Your Highness! You pulled him close?"

"I was simply curious. I had no ulterior motive. But he was completely unguarded. I don't know if he considers himself a full-fledged man now that he has reached the age of adulthood, but he is no better than an infant in the royal capital when he is so unguarded."

Auriano and Johan sighed deeply.

"I hate to hear it, but Your Highness is right. We brought him to the royal capital at his insistence, but he has never been outside by himself before. We're painfully aware that we should have first taught him common sense."

"He also needs more self-awareness, with that appearance. Why is it that such a beautiful boy is so unaware of his good looks?"

Auriano answered reluctantly.

"That's because...something happened when Johan and I were attending the academy in the royal capital. He was almost kidnapped twice when he was very young. He may not remember it, but Gauff and a childhood friend of his had gotten injured in his stead, and... Our parents have been extremely protective of him ever since."

Johan continued.

"Since then, they have never let him out of Brungwurt's territory. Six years ago, when he was half-fledged and our mother and father were finally thinking of giving Leorino some social experience...he was seriously injured in that infamous incident. He's been confined to the estate ever since."

"Still, he's so beautiful. I'm sure he's been admired by all kinds of people in his life... Is he perhaps not the brightest?"

"No, that's not the issue. He really just has no experience. I am ashamed to say that I can count on one hand the number of people Leorino has met in the last six years, outside of family and servants. When he met Lord Julian last year...he finally realized that men find him attractive, but the only unmarried nobleman he has met so far is Lord Julian. He hasn't experienced anything that would make him cautious."

The royals looked at each other. They couldn't imagine such a life.

"...That's a rather warped upbringing for a noble."

"...Yes, sir, we realize this. Our parents are aware of it and regret it. By now I see that we should have taught him more about the ways of the world. Even if it had been difficult for him to walk around with his legs, we could have done something about it, such as inviting guests to Brungwurt to give him some social experience."

The brothers were distraught.

"...You may be surprised to learn that he has never been on his own, even within Brungwurt. He has only ever been allowed to walk freely in the castle courtyard at most. Even then, he was always accompanied by an attendant."

The two royals were indeed surprised by these words. Even a royal princess had more freedom than that.

"He hadn't even had a chance to leave our estate before he fell ill after arriving in the royal capital... It's no excuse, but for that boy, today is truly the first time he's been out in the royal capital. And this is the first time he's been away from his family for such a long time since the accident."

Kyle rubbed his temples in exasperation.

"So he's been unimaginably sheltered. Of course he'd have no self-awareness whatsoever. How could you have taken your eyes off him for even a second?"

Gravis nodded at Kyle's words.

"You should be protecting him until he gains enough experience to make judgments on his own. That is the role of a guardian."

Auriano bowed deeply.

"You are correct, of course. I can't apologize enough for the trouble I have caused you. And I would like to thank you…for saving my brother's life twice, once six years ago and once more tonight. I cannot thank you enough."

Gravis denied it.

"Six years ago, I couldn't get there in time. I couldn't save him, even though I was right there in front of him, and I'm partly to blame for that serious injury… It's a shame, but his legs will never function normally again, will they?"

"That's correct. He has no trouble walking normally, but Dr. Sasha thinks this is the best he's going to get. It's hard enough for him just to stand and walk for long stretches of time like he did today, but he probably pushed himself too hard in the courtyard… I'm really glad that man didn't catch him."

Gravis spoke words of encouragement to the brothers, who were relieved but heavyhearted nonetheless.

"Don't worry. He's clever. He's not as helpless as he seems."

"…What do you mean, Uncle?" Kyle asked.

"He knew he couldn't outrun the Marquis of Schwein because of the state of his legs, but he could buy time until someone in the family noticed his absence and came looking for him. He didn't run around recklessly, but instead hid himself behind trees, looking for the man, moving quietly, and repeating the process, and that's how he managed to escape for nearly half an hour."

"…Huh, that was quite prudent of him," Kyle admitted, impressed.

Gravis nodded. "Isn't it? He understood the state of his legs and did everything in his power to keep himself safe. I'm sure that as he gains more experience and learns more, he'll be able to do better. Yes, opening the door and going outside unprotected was his mistake, but when he returns home, you should first praise him for his efforts to escape on his own."

Kyle did not miss his uncle's unusual behavior. He looked at him as if to say, *Oh?*

"...Why, what an interesting thing to say, Uncle."

"What do you mean?"

Gravis looked at his nephew with suspicion. Instead of answering his question, Kyle asked one of his own.

"Uncle, is it possible you have taken an interest in Leorino? In *that* sense, I mean."

"...As if. What are you talking about?"

Kyle looked at Gravis with amusement as Gravis flatly rejected his question. Although they were barely related by blood, the uncle and nephew shared a very similar aura. They were also very similar in their boldness.

Auriano and Johan wisely kept quiet and observed their exchange. However, they were taken aback by Kyle's next words.

"See, I *am* interested in him in that sense. The only issue is that he's of the male persuasion... But, well, it's not out of the question, depending on how I feel."

"What...?!"

"Your Royal Highness, what do you...?"

Kyle laughed at the Cassieux brothers.

"I mean that I might marry your little brother."

Gravis chided his nephew for his antics. "Kyle, you should know better than to joke about this."

"Same-sex marriage is not forbidden in Fanoren. Legally, it wouldn't be an issue. It's just that there has been no precedent among royalty in the past."

"Don't scare them off with your nonsense. It's not a very funny joke, especially after their brother has just been chased around by a man."

"I suppose you're right. I am sorry, Auriano, Johan. But it is a real possibility. You are of Brungwurt, after all."

Kyle may have been fond of Leorino, but he didn't have the eyes typical of men in love. Gravis wanted to know why he was so eager to joke about this.

Gravis turned to face his nephew.

"...What the hell are you on about, Kyle? If you have something to say, then say it. Don't use him as a pretense."

"Oh, I just think that if I won't be able to succeed the throne, then you should become the next king, Uncle."

At that moment, the intense wrath radiating from Gravis sent chills down Auriano's and Johan's spines. Dark, starry-sky eyes glared abhorrently at his nephew.

"...Kyle. That's enough. You've gone too far, even for a joke."

"I'm serious to a fault, Uncle... That goes for Leorino and for the issue of who the right to the throne of this country should go to."

"Kyle, enough!"

The uncle and nephew, who looked very much alike, glared at each other for a while.

It was Gravis who looked away first.

"...I'm going back to the Palace of Defense. I'll have Sasha check up on him and then send him directly to the Brungwurt residence. Do you have any instructions for Leorino?"

Kyle shrugged in disappointment, and the men of the Cassieux family released relieved sighs.

Auriano and Johan had many questions about their exchange, but their brother was their first priority.

"Your Highness...! Um, if possible, could you please take me to Leorino with you?" Johan asked with an earnest look on his face.

But Gravis shook his head.

"I'm afraid I can't do that. You work at the Palace of Finance. That would be a violation of the Dritereich. I cannot allow you to enter my office without formalities."

Johan bit his lip as he recalled the rules of the royal court.

In each of the seven palaces of the government of Fanoren, there were areas called Dritereichs, which were off-limits to those who belonged to other palaces without permission. In the case of the Palace of Defense, this included Gravis's office, the offices of the top officials, and the secret archives. Only three members of the royal family were authorized to enter the Dritereich of any palace—the king, Gravis, and Kyle.

"Leorino went through something horrible, all because I took my eyes off him. I can't just sit still, and... I'm sorry."

Johan bowed his head.

"I promise you that I will return him to the Cassieux family without harming a single hair on his head. Don't you believe me?"

"Of course I believe you. I... I'm truly grateful. Please tell my brother, 'I'm so glad you're safe. We'll be waiting for you at home.'"

"I will," Gravis replied, and disappeared from the scene without another word.

The room fell silent as soon as the king's brother left. As if to ease the air, Kyle murmured to himself again.

"Well, I guess that settles it... Inform the rest of your family to keep them from worrying."

Auriano and Johan bowed deeply to the crown prince.

"Thank you for everything, Your Royal Highness. We apologize for the great inconvenience we have caused you."

Kyle waved his hand.

"No, it's nothing. I'm just glad the boy is safe. We'll have to think about Schwein's punishment sooner or later... Well, I'm sure my uncle has something in mind already."

Kyle, who was about to head for the door, murmured, "Right," and turned to them.

"When we leave this room, forget everything my uncle and I said earlier. Have I made myself clear?"

# The Great Misunderstanding

Dirk's forehead was sweating profusely despite the cool spring evening.

He was used to seeing flawless beauty on his superior. Dirk prided himself on his high tolerance for beautiful men, but perhaps because he was usually surrounded by fierce, intimidating men, he was having trouble establishing the right distance between himself and Leorino, who was so vulnerable and friendly.

Dirk finally succumbed to Leorino's innocent pleas to sit next to him, but to maintain an appropriate distance, he sat down on the very end of the settee across from Leorino.

Whenever Leorino offered him a friendly grin, he felt restless.

*Ugh, you can't do this to me... He's so beautiful, it hurts. I'd rather take the dark, cold smiles. Your Excellency, please come back soon...!*

"Um, may I ask you one more question, Mr. Dirk?"

"Whoa, um, y-yes. What is it?"

Dirk, who had been absorbed in his own thoughts, replied in a hurry, and once again a smile bloomed on Leorino's lips.

*Hahh! Stop that already!*

"I don't mean to be indelicate, but... Mr. Dirk, how did you come to be the second-in-command of Vi—of His Excellency? Did you not belong to any unit and suddenly find yourself working at the Palace of Defense?"

Dirk, who had been admiring him as a rare and truly beautiful boy, was blindsided by his question.

This young man, who did not look like he would know anything about fighting, may have known more about the Royal Army than Dirk had assumed. His reasoning for this was that the 'sudden assignment to the Palace of Defense,' as Leorino referred to it, was extremely rare for a first posting in the Royal Army. Leorino must have been quite knowledgeable about the Royal Army to know that.

Dirk recognized Leorino's listening to him with a gleam in his eyes as a boyish admiration for the Royal Army. *He seems so out of this world, but he is still a boy,* Dirk thought with a smile.

"Um...did that question bother you?"

"Oh, no, not at all. I just thought it was an interesting question. It's not really a secret, but I graduated from the academy of higher learning and enlisted as an officer."

"You went to the academy of higher learning? You too?"

"Is that the interesting part?"

Dirk blinked at Leorino's reaction.

"No, it's just... I couldn't attend, so I was so envious that I...got a little excited."

"I see. Oh, because of your legs..."

"Yes, well, I interrupted you. I'm sorry. Please continue."

"Oh, sure. I am on duty at the Palace of National Defense. Of course, I was not the second-in-command to the general from the beginning. My first assignment was to the General Staff Office."

"Wow! You must be very smart to have been assigned to the General Staff from the start."

Dirk seemed to have a pretty promising career ahead of him. Although the Palace of Defense had more commoners playing an active role than any other palace, it was still evidence of considerable excellence.

Leorino was truly proud of Dirk.

Perhaps because he only remembered Dirk as a boy, he did not feel as if he was a brother to the fine adult man in front of him. However, even though they were not related by blood in this life, he still felt closer to him than he did to most people.

*I never thought I'd be able to talk to a grown-up Dirk like this... I'm so glad I came to the capital!*

"Ha-ha, Leorino, you know a lot... But I'm not particularly smart. I just like to collect and analyze data in detail, and when I was a student, I did a lot of research on past wars... Well, it just sort of happened. I was in General Staff for nearly five years. For the past six years, I have had the honor of being appointed as the adjutant to His Excellency the general."

"Really? That's a big promotion."

Dirk returned Leorino's praise with a shy smile.

"I'm very grateful for the assignment. There was another senior adjutant for four years, and I studied under him, and finally I was appointed as the chief adjutant the year before last. There's one more adjutant outside of me."

"Wow! That's great, Mr. Dirk..."

"Ah-ha-ha, we're really talking about me a lot. Thank you."

Leorino listened to Dirk's story with a gleam in his eyes the whole time. Dirk couldn't stop thinking it, but his smile was so cute that it almost made him dizzy.

Dirk felt restless again. He did not mean to be conceited, but he felt as if he was being treated with special favor. However, there was nothing amorous about it; he simply felt Leorino had taken to him well.

But what had he done to make Leorino like him so much when they had just met? No, he hadn't done anything in particular. In that case, was this beautiful young man always this friendly with everyone? If so, he really needed to learn more caution.

Dirk inclined his head but continued talking.

"The truth is, His Excellency has been looking out for me for a long time. Well, when I was first offered the position, I thought he was just trying to make amends, so I said, 'No, thank you,' and declined."

"Make amends...?"

"Oh. Ummm..."

*Shit*, Dirk's awkward expression seemed to say.

*Gravis...making amends to Dirk? ...But why?*

Leorino stared at Dirk, waiting for him to continue. The red-haired adjutant began reluctantly. "It was a long time ago, but my older brother was actually His Excellency's guard when they were students. My brother, he...he was killed in the war eighteen years ago."

"...Oh."

"I don't blame His Excellency, though. At the time, His Excellency came to my father to apologize over and over... My father was so upset, now that I think about it, he could have been arrested for disrespecting royalty, but he really cursed him out in the beginning."

Leorino's expression stiffened.

"After that, His Excellency kept looking out for me and my family... It's a terribly humbling thing for a commoner to be taken care of by His Royal Highness the king's brother... I assumed that my promotion was his way of atoning for his sins."

Dirk scratched his head.

"...So that's what you meant by 'make amends'...?"

"Yes. But I was wrong. His Excellency wouldn't let me live that down. He even asked me: 'You think I'm foolish enough to choose a second-in-command so willy-nilly?'"

Dirk smiled.

"I was happy. He even told me, 'Something as meager as a promotion could never compensate for your brother's death.' So I agreed, and here I am, serving as his second-in-command."

"Wow..."

"It's true that he was looking out for me, though. But once I began working, he worked me to the bone... I mean, I received strict but warm guidance, and I realized that, oh no, I wasn't getting *any* special treatment here, which was a relief, but... Wait, what?!"

Dirk was taken aback by the state of the young man sitting across from him.

"Leorino! What's gotten into you?!"

Leorino had suddenly started crying, fat tears rolling down his cheeks with no end in sight.

Dirk rushed to the young man and peered into his face.

In the next moment, Dirk was so shocked that he forgot how to breathe.

"...No...way...?"

Dirk reached for Leorino's face before he could think better of it. All issues of appropriate distance and etiquette went out the window. It was a fully unconscious action.

Violet eyes wrapped in platinum-colored lashes. This special hue, like a spoonful of dawn plunged into indigo. They were Ionia's eyes, the very eyes of his older brother, who died eighteen years ago... He'd recognize them anywhere.

"No... Your eyes... My brother— He..."

Leorino's eyes widened at Dirk's murmur.

"Leorino, you...may think me strange for saying this, but...your eyes are just like my dead brother's."

"...D-Dirk..."

Dirk had cupped both of Leorino's cheeks at some point and was gazing into his eyes as if he wanted to devour them.

"They're my brother's eyes... You... How...?"

Leorino stared back at him, tears streaming down his face.

More than ever before, he was filled with nostalgia and longing for the man in front of him. The young man in his memories seemed to shout:

*Dirk... You're completely right. I know it's not the same, but...your brother is here...*

More tears spilled from his large eyes. Leorino gently laid his hand on Dirk's.

"Rino! I heard everything! Are you all right?!"

At that moment, the door to the office was thrown open without as much as a knock.

"Oh…"

The three men froze in place.

Sasha remained rigid for a while, then took on a fearsome expression before their eyes.

"…Dirk. What. On earth. Were you doing?"

"Huh?"

Dirk inclined his head.

*No, I was just talking to Leorino, and…somehow I made him cry, and when I looked closer, his eyes were violet…*

"…Whoa!"

Before he knew it, Dirk had found himself fully leaning onto Leorino. Not only that, he was holding his small face in his hands, and his own face was only a breath away from his. Viewed from the outside, it was a conspicuous position that could be mistaken for a close attempt to steal the young man's lips.

"Give me one good reason not to perform an early autopsy on you. How's that sound?"

"Oh my god! No, this is—! This is a misunderstanding! Doctor, you've got it all wrong! I haven't done anything!"

Dirk rushed to jump away from Leorino and straighten his back. Sasha slowly approached him.

"…Misunderstanding? Then why is Leorino crying?"

"Huh?"

Dirk looked down at Leorino once more. His cheeks were covered with clear tearstains.

Leorino's beautiful, pale face broke into a weak smile, as if he were trying to hold back the pain.

"Thank you, Dr. Sasha. I'm so…relieved that you came."

Depending on the interpretation, his statement could be extremely misleading.

Dirk turned pale.

He was going to be killed.

He was not sure who would kill him, his superior or the doctor, but either way, he was a dead man.

Sure enough, Sasha's gaze was perfectly firm.

"Lieutenant Colonel Dirk Bergund! Stand fast!"

"Yes, sir!"

Sasha's rank in the Royal Army was that of a colonel.

Dirk stood at attention at the doctor's order.

Sasha approached the settee, glaring suspiciously at Dirk with his perfectly straightened back, then knelt down in front of Leorino and addressed him gently.

"Rino? Did he scare you? Are you all right?"

The remains of Leorino's tears had not yet dried, but the sight of the familiar doctor made him smile sweetly with relief.

"Yes, I'm fine. Maybe a little scared."

Dirk, on the other hand, was panicking.

*Oh no... That'll absolutely give him the wrong idea...*

"Right, I know it may be difficult to talk about, but what did Dirk do to you?"

Leorino inclined his head at the question.

"What? He didn't do anything I didn't ask for."

"I see... Wait, what?! You're not being serious, are you?"

"Oh no, he did all sorts of nice things to me."

Sasha looked back at Dirk in disbelief. Dirk wanted to shake his head as hard as he could at Sasha, but he did his best to hold himself back.

*Leorino! No! We were talking! Tell him we were just talking!*

Until the order was withdrawn, he had to maintain his posture. Dirk broke out in a cold sweat.

"Rino... I'm going to ask you one more time. Dirk didn't coerce you? You asked him to do it?"

"Yes. I insisted on it. Dirk was so gentle with me and did everything according to my wishes, even though this was our first time meeting. Yet still I cried before he could even finish..."

*For the love of god! How are you making this worse...?!*

Once again, Sasha turned back to Dirk with a stiffness that should have made a creaking noise. His eyes clearly said, *Why did he choose someone as plain as you?*

Dirk could hide his agony no longer.

He wanted to cry.

Dirk's superior chose the worst possible moment to return through a rift in thin air.

Dirk had been looking forward to his return so badly, but not like this, never like this.

"Leorino, why are you crying? ...Dirk, Sasha, what happened?"

Dirk prepared to die with a distant look in his eyes.

Gravis had returned to his office in the Palace of Defense.

As he did, Leorino, who had obviously been crying; Sasha, who was kneeling in front of him with a grimace; and Dirk, who for some reason was standing at attention, all turned around at once.

*What is this?*

Each of them greeted Gravis with indescribable expressions on their faces.

"Leorino, why are you crying? ...Dirk, Sasha, what happened?"

Gravis walked over to the settee and held Leorino's chin with his finger. Leorino's large eyes were wet and his cheeks tearstained. Gravis ran his fingers over Leorino's cheeks to be sure. The tearstains were still moist.

"What happened while I was gone?" he asked, in a quiet voice so as not to scare Leorino. Feeling awkward, Leorino tried to escape the man's fingers. But Gravis would have none of it.

Leorino's smooth, fair cheeks were incredibly soft, hot, and wet.

Gravis frowned. Leorino did not seem to be aware of it, but he was feverish.

Leorino cast his eyes down at a loss, as if the staring contest at point-blank range had become unbearable.

"Um, Your Highness... Oh, um, please let go of me."

"Leorino, don't look away. Tell me why you were crying."

Gravis put the slightest bit of pressure into his thumb. Leorino's face flushed even harder when he caught his gaze.

"Uh... Ummm..."

"Don't stutter. You're a boy of the Cassieux family. Speak up."

When Gravis scolded him, the young man bit his lip. He stared up at him with strength in his eyes. He seemed to have developed a rebellious spirit of sorts.

Even as Gravis considered it a good sign, Leorino's minor resistance was so charming that he smiled, the corner of his mouth rising for a change.

That only seemed to annoy Leorino.

"...I'm not crying."

"You're not? You're on the verge of tears even as we speak. You're a Cassieux. You mustn't lie."

"I'm not lying... I was just moved."

"While talking to Dirk? What was so moving about whatever he had to say?"

Leorino stared into the void.

"Ummm... The part where he had a successful career despite being so young..."

"What? He's not that young; he's older than you. And when has Dirk ever been successful?"

Sasha, unable to watch this disjointed exchange, offered Leorino a helping hand.

"Sir, why don't you ask Dirk instead? Dirk, who quite literally fell for Leorino's charms."

A mysterious sound emanated from Dirk, still standing at attention.

"Fell? What are you talking about?"

"Allow me to spell it out for you. Dirk lost himself to Leorino's charm and did something naughty."

"What…? No, that's not—!" Leorino jumped up at the military doctor's outrageous statement. Finally, he realized Sasha's great misunderstanding. "Doctor! No, he didn't do anything n-naughty to me!"

"Is that so? Are you sure? You were *this* close, as if your lips were about to touch, and I mean *thiiis* close, like he was really going for it."

Sasha raised both hands in the air, imitating the attempted assault he thought he saw.

Leorino denied this with a bright-red face. "You have it all wrong! He didn't do anything like that! Mr. Dirk would never do such a thing."

Leorino turned to Dirk before he could think better of it.

The red-haired adjutant was looking at him with an inscrutable expression, still standing at attention. But when his gaze met Leorino's, his eyes smiled at him.

Gravis observed the three of them in silence. At times like this, it was impossible to tell if Sasha was being serious or messing around, so he couldn't fully commit to his version of the story.

From what he could see, Leorino did not seem particularly frightened of Dirk. On the contrary, he was desperate to defend him.

Leorino's peerless beauty aside, there was no way his second-in-command would do something to him. All in all, Dirk was a reasonably calm man.

But the fact of the matter was that Leorino had been crying.

Gravis walked up to his subordinate.

"…Dirk. At ease."

"Yes, sir."

Dirk responded to his superior's order but did not allow himself to relax.

"I know you would never do something as insolent as what Sasha is describing to someone in my care."

Dirk relaxed slightly.

"…Yes, sir. Thank you."

"But it's also true that Leorino was crying."

"...Yes, sir."

"Your Highness! ...It wasn't his fault! I just got emotional."

Gravis ignored Leorino's voice. He then called his subordinate's name. "Dirk."

Dirk correctly read the meaning of his superior's intention. It meant, *We'll speak later.*

Dirk still did not understand why Leorino had suddenly started crying in the middle of the conversation. But there was no point in keeping secrets from his superior. He decided that it would be best to tell him exactly what had happened.

Dirk agreed to explain things later with a glance. Gravis nodded in approval.

"...Sasha! You forgot the entire reason we called you here. Examine Leorino."

"Oh...! That's right! I'm sorry, Rino!"

Sasha changed his expression to that of a doctor examining his patient.

"...I'm going to take a look at your legs. Let me take your shoes off."

Seeing Leorino nod, Sasha took Leorino's feet and removed his shoes with a careful hand.

Sasha put his hand on the sole of Leorino's left foot and slowly flexed his knee, using his other hand to support Leorino's calf.

"...Urgh."

When he bent his knee past a certain point, Leorino's body shuddered.

"Ah, I'm sorry. Does it hurt when I do...this?"

He then took hold of Leorino's ankle and twisted it slightly. This time Leorino moaned and closed his eyes tightly.

His clenched fists were shaking.

"...When I twist it, is the pain unbearable?"

"Yes... It really hurts past a certain point."

"You can handle a lot, so if you say it hurts, it must be really painful... Hmm, yes, I think you overworked yourself a little bit today... Let me check the other leg, too. This one hurts at the joint, right?"

With that, Sasha suddenly pressed at the joint in his right leg. Leorino groaned in pain again.

"…Y-yes."

"Ah yes. Right, you've overworked your left leg pretty badly, but the right one should be fine. Since you were protecting your left leg, your right one got pretty sore, too. Hmm, let's see. Two or three days of rest should do it."

Leorino nodded. He was very familiar with his own legs. He had some idea of the state they were in.

Sasha smiled, stood up, and took out something that looked like medicine wrapped in thin paper from the bag he had brought with him.

"Dissolve it in hot water and bring it back to me, will you?" he said before handing it to Dirk.

Before long, Dirk brought him a tea-colored drink that looked like a medicinal infusion.

"Here. It contains painkillers and antipyretics. Drink it. Rino, you may not realize it, but you're already feverish."

"Ugh… Okay."

Leorino got used to drinking this infusion back when he had initially gotten injured. Still, being used to it didn't make it taste any better. Leorino furrowed his brow deeply as he sipped the medicine.

Gravis, who had watched the scene play out in silence until then, asked Sasha: "Will he be all right?"

"He'll be fine. He overworked his left leg, and he's in poor shape, but rest is all he needs."

"Good… Leorino, that's pretty good news, huh?"

Leorino finished the infusion with a heavy exhale and nodded toward Gravis.

"Yes, thank you."

"…Rino, don't let Mr. Hundert rub your body today. No baths, only wiping yourself down. You won't need a brace for your leg, but you should rest until the pain goes away. I'll give you some ointment and painkillers."

"Yes, Doctor… I'm sorry for causing you trouble in the royal capital."

"Oh, it's all right. Now that you're here, I can check on you whenever. I will find some time to pay you a visit tomorrow."

"Yes, sir."

"See, this would be impossible if you were in Brungwurt. Not everyone can be like our general, zipping from place to place in seconds like it's nothing."

Sasha gently stroked Leorino's head and jokingly pointed at the general. Leorino followed his finger, staring at Gravis until he let out a small yawn and began blinking rapidly.

Gravis asked Sasha with his gaze. The doctor gave a small nod. Apparently, the medicine also contained a sedative. Sasha must have decided putting him to sleep was the best choice.

"Sir, may I borrow your cloak?"

Gravis nodded. Dirk quickly moved behind his superior and removed the cloak fastened to his shoulders. He handed it to Sasha, and the doctor deftly wrapped it around Leorino's body. Dirk helped.

Leorino was cozily wrapped in the fine cloth, only his face sticking out. He seemed to become drowsier by the minute. His eyelids were heavy.

He seemed too childlike to be an adult.

Gravis approached the settee and got to his knees in front of Leorino.

The general, a member of royalty, was kneeling. The adjutant and the doctor were stunned speechless.

Leorino shook his head over and over, trying to focus on the man's face, but he couldn't seem to overcome the drowsiness.

"Your Highness Prince Gravis... General... Your Excellency?"

"Call me whatever you like."

"...Yes, Your Highness... 'Your Excellency' is hard to pronounce... Thank you for saving me."

Gravis gently brushed back the bangs stuck to Leorino's forehead. Watching this, Sasha and Dirk gasped at the unusually tender gesture coming from Gravis.

"I'm glad I made it in time, for once."

"I...must have really made my brothers worry..."

"They're fine. They said they would be waiting for you at home. When you wake up, you'll be home. Relax."

The Great Misunderstanding 347

Leorino's slowly drooping head rested against the cloak he was wrapped in up to his neck. He buried his face in it.

"His Highness... It smells like His Highness..."

The murmur was so adorable that Gravis chuckled.

Letting him fall asleep, the adults kept silent.

Soon, Leorino's platinum lashes were completely downcast, and they could hear his quiet, slow breathing.

Asleep, he looked like a china doll, even more innocent than when awake.

"There he goes... Ah, he's already running a fever."

Seeing him sound asleep, Gravis lifted him, keeping him covered with the cloak. He cradled his light body and rested his head where it fit best.

"I'll take him back to the Brungwurt estate. I won't be coming back here tonight... Dirk, Sasha, I appreciate your help."

"Yes, sir... I swear, I really haven't done anything questionable." Dirk relaxed and finally spoke in his usual lighthearted manner.

"You can tell me about it later. By the way, Sasha, are you certain Leorino will be all right?"

"Yes, he's fine. He just pushed himself too hard. I think he really tried his best to escape, judging from the state of his legs. I said he might cause a stir, but I didn't expect him to have such a rough debut... Poor boy."

Sasha gently stroked Leorino's head as he slept in Gravis's arms.

"Sasha...you were right."

"...? What does that mean, sir?"

"I can't leave him alone."

Sasha smiled smugly. "I know, right? So will you reconsider my offer?"

Gravis nodded.

"Let's see... Perhaps after he learns a little more of the world."

With those words, Dirk understood that Gravis had decided to look after Leorino.

"Sasha Klonoff, I will accept your offer. Leorino Cassieux will be allowed to stay in the Palace of Defense under my authority."

# Sleeping Angels, Turning Futures

Leorino's ego had been injured far worse than his body.

"My lord, you must cheer up. Your body will not recover at this rate."

"It's all right, Hundert... I'm so hopeless... I want these memories to disappear and take me with them."

How many times had they had this exchange already? Hundert's master would lay disheartened in his bed before pressing his hands to his face and fussing about and repeating the cycle again.

Leorino had been acting like this ever since he awoke.

"I may not know what happened, but I have heard from Madame Maia that you greeted the royal family at the coming-of-age ceremony and the subsequent soiree with great dignity and firmness. What is there to be ashamed of?"

"Yes, well...that part went fine, I suppose, but... Hundert, I want to be honest with you; my legs were actually very, very sore. But I still managed to accompany His Royal Highness the crown prince and go through the whole audience without stumbling."

"Isn't that more than enough?"

Leorino looked dejected again. He covered his face with a pillow and mumbled in a muffled voice.

"But then I did the...stupidest, dumbest, lousiest... Ahhhh!"

"But that wasn't your fault, my lord, was it? It was all because of the scoundrel who set his mind on your beauty. I heard that you dealt with him well."

"Not at all! ...I was just running around... And then Vi—His Highness rescued me. I finally got to meet him, and I couldn't even properly speak with him."

"I see. You feel you were rude to His Highness."

"Yes. I feel bad for Mr. Dirk, too. I didn't mean to cry... But I did... And then His Highness came back and told me to behave like a proper member of the Cassieux family... Ugh."

Hundert had no idea what this meant, but it seemed that the king's brother had taken good care of his master.

"I am very grateful to His Royal Highness for saving you once again, my lord."

"Hundert, were you listening to me? That's not the issue. I fell asleep—I don't even know when—and he carried me here, and... I was just snoring away without ever properly thanking him... How do I live with that?"

"You weren't snoring. You were sleeping as soundly as a babe."

"Ugh... A baby... That's even worse. I'm a son of the Cassieux family. What am I even doing...? I'm an adult now. I don't deserve to be in this house anymore... Hundert, you've served me very well over the years. Thank you."

Hundert pulled the pillow away from his brooding master's face.

"Ah...! Th-that's so mean...!"

"It is not. What is this nonsense you're spouting? Agonizing won't change the past, my lord. That is no way a boy of the Cassieux family should behave."

"Ugh... You're *so* mean."

"I am not. Please, it's just your fever. Let's be positive and work on your recovery so that you can leave your bed soon. Health should be your utmost priority. You can worry about all of that once you're better! ...Now, drink your medicine, please."

Hundert scolded his master, who was clearly acting childish. Hundert placed his hands around his master's back and lifted Leorino into a sitting position. He then stuffed the pillow he had just taken behind his back as a backrest. Now that Leorino was sitting up, he handed him a cup of medicinal infusion.

"Drink, please."

"All right. But the doctor's medicine is so bitter... And, Hundert, you're so mean... You said I'm not like a man of the Cassieux family, as if I don't already know that..."

Leorino was still suffering from a fever due to his overexertion. Perhaps caused by the excitement from his first long outing, he seemed unaware of his condition and continued to talk in circles all day.

Leorino was only this whiny when he was physically unwell. He was usually patient and well-behaved, and rarely acted selfishly. His attendants had little to complain about their master.

Recently, however, he had begun showing this childish side to Hundert alone, who had taken care of him since he was little. The servant found this endearing and was happy to have his master's complete trust.

"Dr. Sasha said that if the pain seems to have subsided, we should help your muscles relax. I'll give you a massage right away. After that, you can wriggle and writhe as much as you please, like a true boy of the Cassieux family."

Leorino took a sip of the medicinal infusion and frowned.

"Ugh... I hate this. But I'll do my best... Just don't force me..."

The medicine Sasha prescribed contained both painkillers and sedatives. Hundert had been giving his agitated master the infusion since last night in an effort to get him to rest regularly.

"Once you finish it, please get some more rest."

"All right. I wonder if I can talk to Auriano once I wake up. Is he home today?"

"I believe he and the young madame are having dinner at the Duke of Leben's today. They should have time tomorrow. I will ask the attendant about Master Auriano's schedule."

Leorino nodded meekly. Hundert helped him once more and laid his thin body back on the bed.

"Hundert... I would like to go out once I'm feeling better. I want to look around the royal capital, meet people, attend soirees properly, and learn how to conduct myself so I can fit in better."

"That's a wonderful idea. Speaking of going out, the commander's second son will be escorting you starting from this afternoon."

"Josef is coming? I suppose Father did say he would provide me a guard. So he meant Josef. But why now? Why didn't he come with us?"

Josef was the second son of Lev, the commander of the Brungwurt Autonomous Army. He was three years older than Leorino and a trusted childhood friend of his.

"My lord, he has been studying under the Royal Capital Garrison for the past month, thanks to Master August, to learn about the geography and security of the city. This will allow him to protect you whenever you go out, my lord. He is the best swordsman in Brungwurt, after all."

"...I see. Josef isn't even used to being in the royal capital. I feel bad for forcing him to join the garrison on such short notice."

"Josef was rather pleased with the experience."

"Right... Well, I do really appreciate it... I'll thank him when I see him..."

Leorino yawned. Hundert pulled on the canopy drapes to darken the bed, and soon after, he heard his master's slow breathing as Leorino fell asleep. At this rate, the pain in his legs would be gone by tomorrow or the day after at the latest, and he would be able to leave his bed.

The old attendant sighed deeply, glad that his master had not been hurt. Auriano had explained everything that had happened to Leorino at the soiree. Hundert recalled the night two days prior, when his master arrived home in the arms of His Royal Highness the king's brother.

The servants waiting for their master's return, eagerly awaiting to hear of Leorino's spectacular debut, paled as soon as the family carriage arrived. Leorino was nowhere to be found.

Maia and the rest of the family entered the drawing room with somber looks on their faces, and they kept sitting down and standing up restlessly without even changing their clothes. Johan paced around the room like a beast in a cage, and Auriano kept telling him to calm down.

Hundert gathered his courage and asked where Leorino was. Auriano frowned, simply replying that he should be home soon.

*Leorino would be coming home alone? How?* More questions swirled in the attendant's head, but he could not question his masters.

When Hundert's anxiety was reaching a fever pitch, a large man suddenly appeared at the front door.

There was no warning, no sound of a carriage.

The doorman shrieked in shock. The servants moving about in confusion by the entrance jumped at the sound of his scream.

The man, whom they recognized at a glance as a nobleman, was carrying a large package wrapped in a black cloth in his arms.

The servants were stunned speechless in surprise and dread.

"Call Auriano."

Casually calling for the head of the family by his first name, the man boldly entered the mansion without asking permission.

The man, illuminated by the lights, was a little older than Auriano and overwhelmingly perfectly handsome.

"Lord Leorino!" The scream of a lady's maid echoed through the room.

Upon closer inspection, the man was holding Leorino in his arms, wrapped in a black cloth, his eyes closed.

Perhaps stirred by her scream, the members of the Cassieux family came running out of the drawing room.

Auriano and Johan looked relieved, bowing deeply to the man.

"Your Royal Highness…! Thank you so much!"

The servants were once more taken aback.

It was His Royal Highness Prince Gravis, whom they had seen at Brungwurt Castle six years prior.

Hundert's mind went blank at the sudden appearance of the royal. Just like six years ago, the man was carrying an unconscious Leorino. The servants instantly fell to their knees and bowed their heads.

"Sorry to keep you waiting."

"Your Highness… Leorino… Is he…?"

"Sasha has drugged him. He's asleep. Here... Don't wake him up."

"Of course... Thank you. This way."

Johan extended his hands, and the king's brother placed Leorino in his arms. Leorino was still sound asleep from the medicine. He did not wake up at the movement.

Maia looked at the king's brother with tears in her eyes, then fell to her knees.

"Your Highness Prince Gravis... How can I ever thank you enough...for once more saving Leorino from danger?"

"Madame, I realize this must have been a difficult day for Leorino and for your entire family."

"Yes, sir. Truly, I'm so..."

When Maia tried to thank him again, Gravis held up his hand.

"It's fine. Worry not. Your sons have thanked me enough. Did you hear the details of what took place in the courtyard?"

Maia nodded with a stiff expression.

"Sasha said he should rest for two to three days. Also, no bathing or massaging tonight," Gravis relayed.

"Yes, sir."

Gravis took Maia's hand, and she shrank back in fear. Maia pressed his hand to her forehead and bowed once more.

Gravis nodded and turned on his heel.

But then, as if remembering something, he spun around and called Auriano over.

Auriano approached him immediately. Gravis brought his lips to Auriano's ear and whispered something. Whatever it was, it blindsided Auriano.

"Your Highness... But that's...!"

"It was Sasha's idea. He said he will come tomorrow to check on Leorino. If you're available, you can ask him then. Farewell."

"P-please wait. Your Highness, doesn't this cloak belong to you? We must return it."

The king's brother had used his cloak to cover Leorino's body.

Wrapped in the dark cloth, with only his small white face poking out, Leorino was fast asleep. At this sight of defenselessness, the gaze of the king's brother suddenly softened.

"Have that delivered to the Palace of Defense... Ah, but...I've got an idea."

"Sir? An idea...?"

"Once Leorino feels better, he can come and return it himself. Consider it a lesson in social skills. You really need to give him more exposure to the outside world."

The king's brother smiled in a way that didn't feel right on his cold face.

The next moment, the powerful figure who had dominated the space suddenly vanished before Auriano's eyes.

The lady's maids shrieked.

But that was inevitable. All of them were startled to a greater or lesser degree. For those unaware of the royalty's unusual abilities, the series of events they just witnessed had been too sudden and absurd.

What remained were the members of the Cassieux family pondering the fate of Leorino, asleep in his second brother's arms, with frowns on their faces, and the servants who were still unable to grasp what had happened in their confusion.

Johan asked his eldest brother nervously, "Auriano, what did His Highness tell you?"

The elder brother covered his mouth with his hand, answering in a muffled voice: "...He may have found Leorino a job."

"What?"

Maia and Erina were taken aback.

"What does that mean? Auriano, is that really what His Highness Prince Gravis said?" Maia asked.

"...Oh my. Darling? Where would this job be?" asked Erina.

For once, Auriano was at a complete and utter loss. He stared at Leorino's artificially induced sleeping face in Johan's arms.

A hush fell over the room.

The usually calm Maia was the first to snap.

"Auriano! Don't be so coy. Say it!"

"His Highness said he will take care of Leorino at the Palace of Defense..."

Not even the scream of shock that echoed through the Brungwurt estate could awaken the youngest son of the Cassieux family.

He had no way of knowing that his future had already been decided.

# The First Outing

Immediately after the coming-of-age ceremony, the Brungwurt residence was flooded with invitations, much to the chagrin of the butler.

Invitations to deepen friendships with Margravine Maia, who rarely left her province, and the newlyweds, the next margrave and margravine, while they were in the royal capital, were numerous.

But that was nothing next to the veritable mountain of invitations addressed to Leorino personally.

"This is why I can't stand the royal capital."

Maia was in charge of handling the invitations. Erina, her daughter-in-law, was sitting next to her, watching and learning from Maia's judgment.

After the butler's initial selection, there were about fifty invitations left for Maia to decide on. Maia deftly handpicked them, leaving about thirty invitations, and returned the rest to the butler.

Ten were invitations to her eldest son and his wife.

"I will double-check with Auriano, and if there are no issues, we will accept them."

"Yes, ma'am."

The following ten were invitations to Maia, mainly from other noblewomen.

"Erina and I will attend these ones. Please accept the ones that fit both our schedules."

"Yes, ma'am."

Maia began carefully examining the remaining invitations to Leorino.

"This invitation is from the Countess of Archen. The countess was a schoolmate of mine, and the previous countess is a close friend of my mother's. Let's attend."

"Yes, Mother."

"I believe the Countess of Archen has a daughter. It will also be a chance for that young lady to make connections. Are you familiar with the daughter of the Countess of Arhen?"

"Yes, she was four years younger than me, but...I have spoken to her several times at the academy. Oh... That would mean she's the same age as Leorino. She would have reached the age of maturity this year."

"In that case, we could take Leorino with us."

"Yes, Mother. But should we? Won't Leorino be bored at a tea party with so few young ladies and gentlemen?"

"Well, you are only twenty-two years old yourself, you know. You're still plenty young." Maia laughed.

Erina's cheeks flushed. "Mother, please. I am already married. I can no longer behave like a maiden."

Maia smiled at her daughter-in-law's pure spirit.

"You can still act like a maiden. My husband is still in good health, and until Auriano takes his place, you should be able to do as you please."

"Thank you. But I have been in the royal capital for some time now, and I've had plenty of time with people my own age... I'd like to learn social skills as a Cassieux lady under your watchful eye, Mother."

"Thank you. I am very pleased to hear that. Auriano has truly found himself a perfect spouse. You're still a maiden after all. And I'm so happy to finally have a daughter."

Erina's cheeks flushed once more at her mother-in-law's praise.

"But, Mother, if you want Leorino to accompany us, wouldn't it be better to take him to a place where the younger generation is more likely to gather?"

Maia shook her head.

"No, I would prefer to begin with a more relaxed setting with older people, like the one we are inviting him to. He needs to learn how his appearance is perceived by people outside his family and how to avoid unwanted attention."

"I suppose you're right…"

"Immediately taking him somewhere with young ladies and gentlemen wouldn't end well. We wouldn't be able to handle it on our own."

"That's also true… I'd be sick with worry without my husband or Johan accompanying us."

"We have to think of his dignity, too. It would hurt his pride as a boy if he had to be escorted by his brothers all the time. For him to gain confidence, he needs to gain experience on his own so that he can feel comfortable without them. That's why a tea party attended by many calm elderly people should be about right."

Erina nodded.

"…When I first met Leorino, I was shocked to see that such a beautiful person could really exist in this world. Not only his appearance, everything about him was so…angelic. I hardly remember what I said to him at the time."

Maia laughed, recalling her reaction.

"Oh yes. I'd never seen a noble family so flustered."

"Even now, I feel so moved every time I see him. Now that I know him better, he really is just a normal, gentle young man, but…his beauty is downright criminal. I worry about him. I'm afraid that…something like the recent incident might happen again."

Erina, too, had been informed of how Leorino had almost been assaulted by a man in the palace courtyard.

The women looked at each other and sighed deeply.

Maia asked a lady's maid for more tea. As soon as the maid left, Erina spoke up once more.

"And how should I put this…? Too many things have been happening around Leorino… And that worries me, too."

"What do you mean, Erina?"

"First and foremost, my brother. We hesitated to tell you this, Mother, but my brother has quite the reputation in the royal capital. My brother had his pick of all the maidens in the capital and even of foreign princesses, and yet... neither I nor my parents could have predicted he would become so infatuated with Leorino."

"Yes, well... We didn't expect that Lord Julian would seriously ask Leorino to marry him. My husband was surprised to hear that he had gone directly to the Duke of Leben and settled the issue of inheritance."

"But it's not just my brother. On his first day in high society, Leorino caught the attention of the crown prince... And Lord Johan even told me he was surrounded by many gentlemen at the soiree. And then that courtyard incident... Then His Royal Highness saved him and then suddenly privately approached us, saying he would take care of Leorino at the Palace of Defense..."

"...You're right. That was one very long day for that boy."

"That's the issue. It was just one day. Leorino hasn't even done anything. And yet..."

"You mean to say that he might lead the gentlemen astray."

Erina nodded. "We're talking about the most powerful men in the country... It feels wrong to say this about an adult male. But I do worry about him."

Maia sighed deeply.

"...My husband and I have been concerned about that very thing as well. That boy thinks he came to the royal capital to look for a job... He naively thinks that if he works hard enough, he'll actually get one. I hate to say it, but I don't believe he needs a job at all."

Maia and Erina may have been ignorant of the ways of the world, but they were still much more adept at worldly affairs than Leorino. They were well aware Leorino would likely never live like an ordinary noble boy.

"I would much prefer he spend time in Brungwurt than get involved in the dangerous affairs in the royal capital."

"Then why did you allow him to move to the capital?"

"...My husband had his reasons."

"Reasons?"

"I can't go into details right now. You'll learn everything in due course. All I can tell you now is that it'll depend on the situation and that we will take measures as soon as possible."

The conversation was cut short when the butler entered the room with a knock on the door and a cup of tea.

"...In any case, we won't be able to send Leorino back to Brungwurt for a few years. The boy will have to remain in the royal capital. So let's carefully choose the social circles Leorino will partake in. We hope you will help us in this matter, Erina."

"Yes, Mother."

"In a few weeks, we will return to Brungwurt... We must help him gain at least a little life experience before then."

Completely unaware of his mother and sister-in-law's concerns about his future, the freshly recovered Leorino was in his room, carefully stroking a beautifully wrapped package. The package contained Gravis's cloak, which Leorino had been wrapped in the previous night. It had been carefully cleaned by the servants.

Leorino's face tightened as he declared to his guard and attendant: "Josef, Hundert. I am now going to return the cloak I borrowed from His Royal Highness."

"Sounds great, young master. But did you get permission to leave the house from Lord Auriano or Lord Johan?"

A slender young man with sand-colored hair stood beside Leorino. He was Josef Lev, the second son of Commander Lev, who had recently become Leorino's guard. He was three years older than Leorino.

He had rather feminine features, but what helped him appear masculine was the scar that ran faintly from his temple to his cheek. Combined with his threatening steel-blue eyes, he exuded an aura of danger.

Perhaps because he had known Leorino since he was little, he was accustomed to Leorino's beauty. They had been childhood friends, and his casual way of speaking was proof of their relaxed relationship. Their friendship transcending their statuses was accepted with the sort of generosity characteristic of the province of Brungwurt.

"Yes. I should have gotten permission...right? Hundert."

Leorino twisted his head. Josef looked to the attendant, questioning him with his eyes. Leorino clearly didn't have an answer. Hundert, his full-time attendant, knew all about such trivial matters.

The old attendant nodded. He had received permission to leave.

Seeing this, Leorino excitedly moved to pick up the package on his own. Hundert rushed to lift it instead.

"My lord, we have a carriage ready for you. You can take it out anytime you like."

"A carriage... It has our coat of arms on it, doesn't it? It would be one thing if it were Auriano, but it feels inappropriate for someone like me to take it to the Palace of Defense... I know! Let's hail a cab somewhere."

Josef sighed in exasperation. "Young master, where did you get the idea of hailing a cab? This is the noble district. No cabs pass through here."

"I see. Then let's go on foot. Oh no, I suppose it's too far... Hundert, Josef, what do I do? At this rate, I'll never return the cloak."

The servant reassured his panicking master. "Let's take the carriage. There's nothing inappropriate about your taking the family carriage, my lord."

"Then why don't we take the carriage to the gates of the royal palace, and from there, we will walk to the Palace of Defense. Can we do that?"

"I don't see why we couldn't. It's a little far, but once we're inside the palace, walking shouldn't be an issue."

Leorino nodded enthusiastically.

He was filled with anticipation and excitement for his first personal outing.

Leorino was elated when Auriano told him that Gravis had said he should go return the cloak himself. He might be able to see Gravis and Dirk again. He was happy that Gravis chose to give him that opportunity. Leorino hoped that he could keep up this momentum and make a start on his other plans.

Josef held out his cloak to him. "Here, your hooded cloak. Please keep it on. We can't have the young master showing his face in public."

Josef dressed Leorino in the cloak and fastened the buttons at his neck. He pulled the hood over Leorino's head and adjusted the angle several times. When Josef finally mumbled "Okay," Leorino decided he was ready.

They followed the attendant downstairs.

"I wonder if His Highness will be there. I'll be visiting unannounced, so I might not be able to see him."

"That's true. Well, if he's such an important figure, you can't really blame him."

"I know. If he's not there, I will leave the cloak in the hands of his second-in-command, Mr. Dirk, and return home."

"All right, young master. Please do not stray from us, do not act alone, and if any threat appears, follow my instructions at all costs."

"Of course. I promise I won't act alone."

Josef nodded in approval. He loved to act self-important around Leorino.

"Josef, I'm too old to be called 'young master,' so please don't call me that anymore."

"All right. I'll call you 'Lord Leorino' from now on."

Enjoying the light banter with his childhood friend, Leorino waited for the carriage at the entrance, which was when Maia and Erina came to see them off.

"Mother, Erina, how do you do?"

"Leorino, are you going to see His Highness Prince Gravis?"

"Yes, Mother. I am going to return the cloak I borrowed and thank him for his aid the other day."

Maia smiled at the excited look on Leorino's face. But there was also a hint of concern in her eyes.

"Have you sent word to His Highness? Isn't it impolite to visit him without warning?"

"No. It would also be impolite for someone like me to send word and demand his time… If I don't get to see him, I will leave the cloak with someone else and return home."

"I see. Stay safe."

"Yes, Josef will be with me, so I should be all right. Thank you for seeing me off."

Leorino nodded emphatically and got into the carriage. But then he turned around as if he had suddenly remembered something.

"Mother, I may be late getting home!"

"...? And why is that? The royal palace is just around the corner. It shouldn't even take you an hour to complete your business."

Leorino smiled wryly at his mother, who was tilting her head in confusion.

"I'm aware. Since I'm already going out, I think I'll stop by the employment agency on my way home."

Maia blinked.

"What...? What did you just say?"

"I'm job hunting. I'm feeling better now. I should start searching for a job in earnest."

"Job hunting..."

"Yes. Haven't you heard, Mother? There is this employment agency that serves both commoners and nobles."

"Employment agency..."

"Yes! I will look for a job there. Maybe they have some apprenticeship I could do."

"Apprenticeship..."

Finally, Maia began to stagger. Erina rushed to support her. "Mother!"

"Mother...! Are you all right?"

The next moment, the guard bonked Leorino on the head.

"Ouch! ...Josef! Wh-why...?"

When Leorino held his head and turned around, Josef was glaring at him with an angry look on his face.

"Absolutely not."

"What?"

"What were you thinking? We are *not* going to the employment agency!"

"Why?"

"Think! You've never been in the royal capital in your life. You can't just suddenly start looking for a job!"

Josef's harsh voice echoed through the garden. Leorino gasped.

The guard ran his fingers through his sand-colored hair, then grabbed Leorino firmly by both shoulders and locked eyes with him.

"...Young master!"

"...Y-yes!"

Leorino stood at attention at the intensity of his guard.

"Now! Is this the first time you're going out alone in the royal capital...?"

"I-it's my first time, sir."

Leorino was, for some reason, being deferential.

"Good. First, you need to complete your first errand. You can worry about looking for a job after that."

"...Y-yes, sir."

"If you can't run an errand, don't even dream about finding a job! Is that clear?"

"Yes, sir!"

"All right, let's go!"

Having talked Leorino out of his plans, Josef pushed his back, forcing him into the carriage. Hundert, who had been watching them in a daze, rushed to get into the carriage with his package.

Josef nodded to Maia and Erina, who were still speechless.

"I will make sure he returns home after completing his errand."

With these words, he got into the carriage himself.

The guard at the Palace of Defense observed the cloaked young man and his companions with suspicion.

The white cloak on the young man was of the highest quality, and his bearing seemed refined as well. The guard could not see his face well, but he seemed to be a young nobleman. He was accompanied by an elderly man, who must have been his servant, dressed in his uniform, and a young man wearing a sword by his belt, who appeared to be his bodyguard.

The Palace of Defense was, by its very nature, not a place for civilians to visit without business. Most outsiders were either from the other palaces or visited after sending word in advance. Naturally, anyone who did not have an appointment would be asked about their identity.

"Who are you and what is your business at the Palace of Defense?"

The young man began to explain the nature of his errand in a clear voice.

"My name is Leorino Cassieux. These men are my attendant and my guard. Today, I have come to return something I recently borrowed from His Excellency the general. Is there any chance I could, um...see His Excellency today?"

The Cassieuxes were the family of the Margrave of Brungwurt, the guard recalled. However, the guard was not familiar with the genealogy of the noble family. He was not certain if the young man was a son of the Cassieux family, and he rejected the request.

"I apologize, sir. You cannot see the general without a prior appointment."

The young man's head, hidden by his cloak, seemed to droop a little. But he looked up again, nodded in understanding, and motioned to the servant behind him. The servant stepped forward, holding up his package.

"In that case...could you please leave this with the adjutant Mr. Dirk? If you, um, tell him that Leorino Cassieux delivered it, he should hopefully understand."

The guard wondered what was inside the bulky package.

"May I inspect the package for safety reasons? We can't allow anything suspicious slipping by."

"Ah yes. Of course. Please go ahead."

The young man received the package from the servant and presented it to the guard.

The guard opened the carefully wrapped package. Inside was a cloak of the finest quality. It appeared to be almost black, but upon closer inspection, the fabric was a deep blue like the night sky. He probed the folded fabric with his palm, but there seemed to be nothing suspicious hidden inside.

"Is this...the general's cloak?"

"Y-yes, sir."

Judging by his voice, the young man must have been still a boy, so how in the world did he come to borrow a cloak from the general of the Royal Army?

"Excuse me, but where did you get this?" inquired the guard out of sheer curiosity.

The cloaked young man seemed flustered. "I... Um..."

Then the sandy-haired young man who had been standing behind him spoke up.

"Your job is to inspect the package. It is none of your business how my master came to borrow this from the general." He admonished the prying guard.

The cloaked young man flinched and looked behind him.

"Josef! ...You're being rude!"

"How am I rude? It's far ruder of him to leave you standing here, young ma—Lord Leorino, insolently prying into your private business."

"That's his job. That's what he's supposed to do... Um, I apologize for my guard."

The palace guard was clearly offended, but the young man glaring at him had a point. He had no right to demand such information.

If this young nobleman had been close enough to the general to borrow his cloak, keeping him standing at the entrance and questioning him could cause problems for the palace guard later down the line.

He decided to pander to the young man a little, just in case.

"I understand. Deputy Bergund may be able to meet with you even without an appointment. Shall I call him?"

"Is that all right? Then yes, please!" The young man replied in an excited tone.

"...So you could have called him from the start, and you played coy instead?"

"What—? You...!"

"Please, Josef! ...I'm so sorry. He didn't mean that."

The palace guard regained his composure, seeing the young man bow apologetically.

"You'll have to wait here. Is that all right?"

The cloaked young man nodded, to which the elderly attendant behind him raised a humble objection.

"I apologize, but do you have a waiting room or something of the sort? I cannot bear to leave my master standing for too long."

"Hundert, I'm fine. I'm sorry. We'll wait here... If that's not an issue, of course."

"It's not an issue, but it is a bit conspicuous... But to prepare a guest room right now would be—"

The sandy-haired young man released a small sigh. "Such a huge palace, and you can't even prepare a room or two for a few unexpected visitors...?"

The palace guard had had enough. "What was that? What's wrong with you? Where the hell do you think you are?!"

"Lord Leorino has blessed you with his presence. Don't you find it rude to make him stand around waiting for you?"

"Josef! ...Please just stop speaking." The cloaked young man chided the blond man glaring at the guard.

"What's all the fuss about?"

At that moment, a voice reached Leorino's ears, alongside the sound of footsteps.

The moment he heard the low voice, Leorino shivered.

He had often heard that voice in another life.

When he turned around, he saw a large man with hair golden like the sun walking through the entrance, accompanied by several soldiers.

The guard saluted the man. "Welcome back, Lieutenant General."

"Is there a problem? ...Who are these gentlemen?"

Amber eyes scowled at Leorino and his men. The man had not yet recognized him.

"Sir! They are here to deliver a package to His Excellency the general. This is Leorino Cassieux."

As soon as he heard the name, the lieutenant general's eyes widened.

"...Leorino Cassieux...?! Leorino, is it really you?"

With a quickness that belied his huge frame, the man quickly closed the distance between them. He grabbed Leorino by the arm and pulled him closer. The force of the pull caused the hood to slip off Leorino's head.

"...Ah!

"...Leorino...!"

Their eyes met for the first time in six years.

When Leorino's face was exposed from the shadow of his hood, it caused a stir around him.

But Leorino and Lucas were caught only in the other's gaze.

"Leorino…"

*Lucas… Luca…*

Seeing the man's face at this breathtaking distance, Leorino noticed it was as manly and strong as in his dreams. But there was also no denying that eighteen years had come and gone over his former lover.

The man would turn forty this year, and like Gravis, inspired the sort of awe only a man of his age could inspire.

Only Ionia's memories remained stuck on that day eighteen years ago.

Leorino was speechless in the face of the man he seemed to know so well yet who felt like a complete stranger.

Lucas was similarly dumbfounded, staring at the young man in his arms. He finally relaxed his hold but did not release Leorino.

"…Do you remember me?"

"Remember…? Of course I do, Lieutenant General. It's been a while."

Leorino came to his senses and, with a small, panicked jerk, tried to put some distance between himself and Lucas.

But the man's hands on his arms would not budge.

Unable to greet him properly, Leorino furrowed his brow.

The man rubbed his thumbs on Leorino's thin arms as if to soothe Leorino. The touch sent a small electric shock down Leorino's spine.

"Then you'll remember I told you to call me 'Lucas.'"

"…I can't. That would be inappropriate."

"Call me 'Lucas.' 'Luca' is fine, too… I did hear you were in the royal capital. Oh, how I've missed you."

The people around them were speechless at the young man's beauty now that it was exposed from his hood, but they were even more baffled by the lieutenant general's behavior toward the young man. The lieutenant general, who was always so calm and composed, was clearly excited, his eyes bright, as he pulled the young man's slender body to his, looking as if he was about to embrace him.

Leorino hated every second of it.

In no world was this appropriate. The people around them must have begun questioning the nature of their relationship by then.

But Lucas was completely oblivious to his surroundings. "Oh... You were quite the sight six years ago, but now that you're fully grown, you've become dazzlingly beautiful."

Leorino was horrified by his words. The trauma of being targeted by men at the soiree was still fresh in his mind.

"Lieutenant General...! Please let go of me."

"Call me 'Lucas.' Ah, but...your violet eyes are just as they used to be."

Leorino stiffened.

"Let go of me... Please... Lord Lucas."

Hearing his name, Lucas smiled with satisfaction.

"That's better. So what do you want in the Palace of Defense?"

Leorino had no reason to lie. He answered honestly.

"I've come to deliver something to His Highness Prince Gravis."

"Deliver what exactly?"

"Um... Could you please let go of me first? Please."

The man refused to honor Leorino's pleas.

He had wondered about the same thing six years ago, but had Lucas always been so forceful? Or had he changed over the past eighteen years?

"Lord Lucas. Lieutenant General, Your Excellency... Pardon me, but it is a private matter I would rather not discuss."

"You can't even tell me what you're delivering?"

Why was Lucas so concerned about his business with Gravis? Leorino had no idea what the man was thinking.

He twisted away slightly in refusal. Worrying he could be in danger, a hint of fear appeared in his voice. "Please let me go. Lord Lucas!"

He was seriously resisting now.

That was when he heard a faint sound of metal scraping against metal behind him.

The next moment, Lucas pulled Leorino to his chest with full force.

"...? What—?"

Lucas held down Leorino's head, but he still looked up desperately at the man's face, far above his own. Lucas was glaring behind Leorino with a fierce gaze.

"...What the hell do you think you're doing? Who are you?" Lucas was glaring at Josef.

Leorino twisted in his strong arms and looked behind frantically. He saw Josef's hand on the hilt of his sword, revealing a sliver of the blade from its sheath.

"What—? Josef! No! You can't pull out your sword here!" Leorino admonished, turning pale.

In the Palace of Defense, it was forbidden to draw swords except in times of emergency. Anyone who violated this law would be severely punished, member of the Royal Army or not.

*And...if Josef draws his sword...*

If he allowed Josef to draw his sword, and something went wrong, someone could die. With a sword in his hand, Josef could kill any opponent with a single blow. Although his appearance didn't suggest it, back in Brungwurt, he had been celebrated for his exceptional swordsmanship skills.

Beyond that, Leorino knew. Lucas was merciless with his sword against those who dared oppose him.

"...Let go of my master. Can't you tell he doesn't like that?"

Lucas's face turned ferocious.

"...You have some nerve to try to pull your sword on me here."

Josef did not back down, even as Lucas stared him down with his fierce gaze.

*What do I do...? I must do something! It's my fault it got to this in the first place...*

Josef was not only committing a crime, he was also about to turn his blade on the lieutenant general of the Royal Army. If he fully unsheathed his sword, he could even face capital punishment.

"No! Josef, let go of your sword...! Let it go!" Leorino yelled. This triggered Lucas's entourage to slowly bring their own hands to their swords.

"You ruffian! How dare you disrespect the lieutenant general?!"

"Where the hell do you think you are?!"

Josef made nothing of their threats. He only kept staring at the man holding his master with his severe gaze.

Lucas glared back at the young man with piercing eyes.

Tensions were stretched taut.

"Josef...! Put your sword away! Please!" Leorino sounded like he was about to cry.

At his master's scream, Josef finally released the hilt. But he did not stop glaring at Lucas.

"...Please get your hands off of Lord Leorino."

"Hah, you're pretty bold despite that pretty face. I can respect your readiness to protect your master at all cost. But I can't approve of your drawing your blade so close to Leorino. What if he got hurt?"

"I would never hurt Lord Leorino."

Leorino looked up at the man holding him and pleaded desperately.

"Lord Lucas, I'm so sorry! It's not what you think... Josef was only trying to protect me."

Lucas looked down at Leorino.

"...You think that will suffice?"

"I'm so sorry, sir. He has only recently arrived at the royal capital! He doesn't know the customs of the Palace of Defense! So please...!"

"Fine. If you insist, we'll forget this ever happened. But!"

The man interrupted Leorino's desperate pleas with force.

"...Ah... Ugh!"

The man suddenly lifted him off the ground.

"...I'll give you a chance to atone for this man's sins. You'll be coming with me for a while."

He lifted Leorino up by his waist, one hand pressing the back of Leorino's head against his shoulder. Holding Leorino with his strong arms, the lieutenant general turned on his heel.

The faces of Leorino's attendant and guard paled at this.

"You son of a bitch! Let go of my master!"

Josef brought his hand to his sword again. Lucas turned around to scoff at him. "Do you want your master's sacrifice to be for nothing? Then draw your sword. And be ready to regret it."

Josef bit his lip and held back.

He immediately tried to run after him but was blocked by Lucas's entourage.

Lucas's deep voice echoed through the entrance to the palace.

"Schultz! Deliver Leorino's package to one of his men, Bergund, or anyone else. Make sure it arrives safety."

"...Yes, sir. Of course."

Despite his answer, Schultz, Lucas's second-in-command, was puzzled by this sudden turn of events.

Schultz was the son of a count, and knew the name uttered by the guard and exactly where Leorino came from. He did not know what his superior officer intended to do with the young man in his arms, but the boy was no ordinary nobleman. If anything were to happen to the youngest son of the Margrave of Brungwurt in the Palace of Defense, the consequences could be severe.

He could not help but address his superior.

"Lieutenant General. That gentleman is Brungwurt's... Is this really all right? And what about these men?"

"Leave them be. I will forgive the swordsman for what he has just done, for his master's sake."

"Put Lord Leorino down! You won't get away with this!" Josef yelled in indignation.

Lucas stopped in the middle of the stairs and glanced back at him. "I will return your master to you soon enough without as much as a scratch... I've finally found him again, my precious jewel."

# A Cage of Mad Love

After the lieutenant general left, only a perfectly still silence remained. It immediately became clear how the pressure of his ambition had filled the space to the brim.

While no one else dared move a muscle, Lucas's second-in-command, Schultz, was squaring off against the young man biting his lip.

The young man lashed out at Schultz. "What the hell has gotten into the lieutenant general...?!"

"That's 'His Excellency' to you, you lout."

Schultz did not answer his question. Perplexed by his superior's unusual behavior, he wanted to know the answer himself.

"Is that gentleman Leorino Cassieux of Brungwurt?"

"He is. We just came here to deliver something. And then your lieutenant general... His Excellency showed up out of the blue and snatched him away. What will you do if something happens to him?"

"The lieutenant general said he would return him to you without a scratch... And he's not one to break his promises."

"How can you know that?! He...held him down so hard that Leorino couldn't speak, and then he picked him up!"

"It was your thoughtless behavior that brought this on in the first place. You should first reflect on your foolish actions, which led to your master being taken away."

The young man bit his lip again. Then, from behind him, an elderly man who appeared to be Leorino's attendant stepped forward with a pale face.

"I am sorry to trouble you, but I would like to ask the lieutenant general for his forgiveness. My master is very frail, and his body is not strong enough to endure such rough treatment."

"Yes, Lord Leorino has bad legs. If you aren't careful with him, he will break."

The cocky guard aside, Schultz felt bad for the servant who spoke so earnestly of his master. But Schultz couldn't stop his superior from doing anything.

"...I apologize, but I'll need you to wait here."

The attendant cast his eyes down sadly.

Schultz ignored the pain in his chest and extended his hand to the dazed guard.

"...Is that the package Leorino Cassieux wanted delivered? Give it here. I will take it to Lieutenant Colonel Bergund."

"Y-yes, sir!"

Schultz received the package from the guard and was about to turn on his heel when he was grabbed by the arm.

"...Wh-what is wrong with you, you boor?!"

The sandy-haired guard was right behind Schultz. He did not let go of Schultz's arm even as Schultz tried to shake it off. He had a very strong grip for such a slender man.

"Take me with you to this Mr. Bergund."

"What? Who do you think you are—?"

Josef's eyes flashed. "Yes, I messed up this time. I'll have plenty of time to reflect on it later... But right now, I need to get back to Lord Leorino as soon as possible. I'm sure the general's second-in-command can help in some way."

"What? Bergund has no authority to challenge the actions of His Excellency!"

"Still. He could tell the general what happened. The general had ordered Lord Leorino to deliver his belongings after all."

So Leorino had come to the Palace of Defense on the general's orders. Schultz's brow furrowed as he realized this fact only made things worse.

"If something should happen to the general's guest, it would be your superior who would have to answer for it, wouldn't it?"

Josef hit a sore spot.

Schultz was beginning to doubt himself.

"...You're one smooth talker, aren't you?"

"I'm just desperate—that's all. And I'm worried he might hurt Leorino... You saw what he did. He was so excited, his eyes were practically glowing. That wasn't normal."

Schultz was at a loss for words. He considered it.

The lieutenant general bounding up the stairs with Leorino Cassieux in his arms was out of the ordinary—that much was true. He also did secretly want to intervene, but it would be difficult for Schultz, who always faithfully followed every order. But what if this young man, unburdened by manners, made a direct appeal to Bergund?

"...Fine. Follow me. But listen—you need to know your place. This is the Palace of Defense. If you do anything like that again, you will be detained and punished."

Josef nodded with a serious face.

Before Leorino even got a chance to resist, he had been picked up and taken to a room upstairs.

He desperately attempted to escape by pushing against Lucas's arms, withstanding the shaking of the man running up the stairs, but he was unable to create even the slightest opening between him and the man.

When the hand holding the back of his head finally let go, he swiveled his head around and looked the place over in a panic. It appeared to be Lucas's office.

It was smaller than Gravis's office, but it was still a very decent room.

He could no longer afford to worry about how he might come off. Leorino pounded his fist on Lucas's muscular chest in protest.

"Please let go of me! I refuse to be treated like this!"

"What's that? Weren't you going to atone for your guard's insolence?"

"I do apologize for his behavior. If there must be a punishment, I will receive it. But I don't deserve to be treated like this."

The wall of muscle in front of him did not budge no matter how hard he punched. Lucas gently grasped his wrist and restrained him.

"Stop. You'll hurt yourself."

His hands were so big. The man easily grabbed both of Leorino's hands in one of his own. He was holding them gently, but there must have been some trick to it, because Leorino couldn't move his arms at all.

*How is he so strong...?!*

As he frantically twisted his wrists, the wall of muscle in front of him began to shake irregularly. He glanced at him to see Lucas looking down at Leorino's struggle and laughing.

"You may have the same eyes as Ionia's, but...you're much weaker than he was."

Leorino's anger was instantaneous and intense.

"Please put me down! Put me down right now! ...Th-this is *so* inappropriate!"

Furious, Leorino kept struggling. He kicked up, flapping his legs. He didn't care if he hurt his freshly recovered legs. He didn't care if he would be punished for his rudeness.

"Stop!"

No longer laughing, Lucas lifted Leorino with the arm around his waist and locked his other arm around the back of Leorino's knees. Leorino's legs were now immobilized.

"...Don't. You'll hurt your legs."

Leorino was so helpless, he felt frustration burning in the corners of his eyes.

He knew better than anyone that he wasn't born into a warrior's body.

He had known that Lucas could add two and two together. Considering his violet eyes and the fact that he was born the morning after the Zweilink tragedy, he suspected that he was the reincarnation of Ionia.

And he had been right. Leorino Cassieux came into the world with the memories of Ionia Bergund. He had never heard of anyone having memories of a previous life. If that could be called "reincarnation," that's exactly what it was.

And on behalf of Ionia, he would uncover the truth behind the secrets hidden in his memory. He had made it his destiny.

But Leorino was *not* Ionia.

He was just a helpless person, desperately trying to move forward and live his own life, searching for anything he could do to be useful.

*I hate this... I hate this...!*

He had to accept that he was powerless. Leorino was more bitter about his own weakness than anyone. Still, he did not deserve to be mocked for it.

Leorino struggled even harder now that he was restrained. Lucas panicked at that. When Leorino struggled as he held him vertically, it was difficult to restrain him without injuring him.

"Leorino, don't! Stop!"

Lucas took a few steps and gently lowered his body into a chair.

He held both of his shoulders soothingly.

"Don't struggle, all right? You'll hurt yourself."

Lucas got on his knees, placing his hands on the chair's elbow rests, loosely trapping Leorino's thin body. Leorino was breathing so hard his shoulders moved, staring at Lucas with rage in his eyes.

Lucas's fingertips reached for him, as if entranced by his eyes. When he tried to touch his temple, Leorino turned his head away.

"Please don't touch me."

Out of the corner of his eye, he caught a glimpse of regret in Lucas's amber eyes. Leorino's chest ached.

"I'm sorry."

Leorino said nothing.

"I was so happy to see you again that I forgot myself… I apologize for how rude I've been."

Leorino continued to stare at one wall of Lucas's office. If he didn't, he felt he would be overcome with emotion and break into tears.

"…I'm sorry for being rough with you. Did I hurt you? How are your legs?"

Leorino finally looked at the man then. Lucas had finally awakened from his trance and was concerned about him. In that sense, he was still the gentle man Leorino remembered.

The indignation and confusion that had been brewing in his heart began fading. But the resentment from having his agency ignored and being restrained still lingered.

When Leorino looked away again, the man's face twisted with sadness.

"I'm sorry."

*If you're going to make that face, you shouldn't have done it in the first place… Stupid Lucas!* Leorino swore in his mind, which helped.

He focused on his limbs. He didn't feel any pain anywhere. He looked at his wrists and saw no bruises where he had been grabbed. He had been unable to move at all, but the man had used skill, not strength after all.

"…It's fine. I'm not hurt."

Lucas's eyes relaxed. He poured a glass of water from the pitcher on the desk and handed it to Leorino.

"Here. Drink. I'm sorry I can't make you a cup of tea. My second-in-command is not here."

"Thank you… I'll have some."

Leorino accepted the glass and rehydrated his dry throat.

Watching him drink, Lucas laughed again, and Leorino wondered what he was thinking. When Leorino questioned him with his eyes, the man laughed out loud, looking even more amused.

Leorino bit his lip in shame, wondering if he had done something wrong again. Lucas rushed to defend himself. "I'm not trying to make fun of you. I'm sorry. I'm just impressed with your upbringing… Thanking me so politely after everything I'd done to you."

"What…? I…don't see why I shouldn't thank you. You thank people if they pay you a kindness, no matter how rude the person who offers it is."

He replied with the best sarcasm he could think of. Lucas must have found his answer amusing, because he smiled again.

"And you don't even suspect what might be in the water."

"Wh-what's…in it…?"

He stared at his half-drunk glass in a panic.

It tasted and smelled like regular water.

Lucas chuckled.

"Of course, there's nothing in it. But you shouldn't let your guard down so easily, especially when you're alone with a man. You wouldn't want someone to drug you."

The man's advice upset Leorino again.

*If you suspect that I'm a reincarnation of Ionia, you could at least treat me like you treated Ionia. I don't see why you need to act as if I'm some defenseless woman.*

Staring at Lucas, he kept a stern expression. It was as if Lucas was making fun of the differences between him and Ionia. It was frustrating, and Leorino hated every second of it.

"Please don't treat me like a woman. Appearances aside, I am a boy. I know how to handle myself!"

"You drank water offered to you without a second thought. Are you really in any position to say that?"

"Th-that has nothing to do with it. I have no reason to doubt your character, Lieutenant General. I believe you to be a man of honor and integrity."

Lucas threw up his hands in surrender.

"I can't argue with that. I'm sorry for teasing you."

An awkward silence fell between them.

"More important, may I know the reason you brought me here? I will apologize as many times as it takes for the behavior of my guard. As far as punishment is concerned, my family will humbly accept it."

"Like I said, we'll forget anything ever happened. I just wanted to ask you a personal question."

Lucas sat down in the chair across from Leorino.

"...What is it that you want to ask me?"

"Why have you come to the royal capital?"

Leorino's violet eyes widened at the unexpected question.

"...Will you marry Julian Munster? I know he proposed to you."

"...How did you know that?"

"Oh, everyone's been talking about it in the royal capital. The heir to the Duke of Leben spoke directly with the duke in order to marry a person of the same sex. There was much talk about who had won the heart of the most eligible bachelor of his time. Munster frequently visited Brungwurt. It doesn't take a genius to connect the dots... So how about it? Will you marry him?"

Leorino fiercely shook his head.

"I will not! Marry him? Please... I would never. But I don't see why I should tell you about my private life, Lieutenant General."

"I see... Well, I'm sure Munster hasn't given up on you yet. So, why did you come to the royal capital? ...Have you, perhaps, remembered something?"

Lucas was once again looking at Leorino with a feverish gaze.

Leorino immediately cast his eyes down.

"I came to the royal capital to look for a job."

He didn't want to lie. But he couldn't tell him the truth, either.

"Huh... Is that why you came to the Palace of Defense?"

"No, sir! I only came here to deliver something I borrowed from the general..."

"Oh yes. What did you borrow from His Highness?"

Leorino had no way to dodge the question.

"A cloak... I borrowed it on the day of the soiree and have come to return it."

"Right... The Vow of Adulthood. But His Highness is much larger than you. It could only serve you as a blanket at best. How did you come to borrow a cloak from the general of the Royal Army? What happened?"

The man's blanket comment was far more accurate than he could have known.

Leorino did not have a good answer to Lucas's questions. Why should he have to tell Lucas that he had almost been assaulted by a man or that Gravis had come to his rescue and had brought him home?

"...Fine. As soon as you arrived at the royal capital, you met His Highness Prince Gravis and me. Moreover, you came to the Palace of Defense... Do you know what this means?"

Leorino had no answer.

"No. What are you trying to say, sir?"

"...Do you remember the name 'Ionia Bergund'? Does anything come to mind...?"

Too many things came to mind.

The gaze piercing him from the chair across from him hurt. The man's expectant expression made his chest feel tight.

"Don't you feel anything when you look at me? Nothing when I ask you to call me 'Luca'?"

Leorino still didn't want to say it.

He knew that Lucas was looking for Ionia Bergund.

"I don't feel anything. Not six years ago...and not now."

"I see," Lucas mused but continued watching Leorino with eyes searching for the truth.

Lucas had changed somewhat after all.

The sunny cheerfulness of those days had faded, replaced by darker passions.

"Sir, do you really believe I am the reincarnation of...that Ionia Bergund you speak of?"

"Yes."

Lucas's voice was full of conviction.

"But...why?"

"Why, it's just a hunch."

"A hunch. Honestly... How can you decide I'm someone else because of a hunch?"

"I didn't say you were someone else. I think Ionia lives inside you. From the moment I looked into your eyes, I was convinced that he had returned to me in a different body."

"But you're wrong... I am Leorino Cassieux."

"Leorino..."

"Yes, I am Leorino, son of August Cassieux. I am not Ionia Bergund!"

A silence fell between them.

"...How many times must I say this? I am not Ionia Bergund. Please let this be the last time we speak of this."

"...So what you're saying is, you don't know *me*?"

The man looked more threatening now.

Leorino stood up, frightened.

He bowed his head to the silent man.

"...If that is all you wanted to discuss, I shall take my leave now. My servants are waiting for me."

He headed for the door, scolding his legs for trembling.

All he knew was that he couldn't stay there any longer. He had to get back to his life as Leorino Cassieux before Lucas could corner him.

He placed his hand on the door. Suddenly a large, hot palm covered Leorino's slender fingers.

"...!"

Leorino shuddered as a hot breath fell on his neck. A shiver ran down his entire body.

*No... No...*

"Don't you remember me...doing *this* to you...?"

He felt a scalding-hot sensation on his neck.

"...What...? S-stop!"

Lucas's lips dragged across the exposed nape of his neck.

Trembling with fear, Leorino desperately tried to pull his hand free. But he could do nothing. When the other hand surrounded him, he could no longer move.

The man's breath tickled his ear.

The smell of green grass enveloped Leorino.

"Don't you remember...? That night we were like this..."

"Stop... Please stop! Sir, please..."

Hot lips traced his neck, and where they stopped, they closed around his smooth fair skin and sucked.

"...N-no, please, no!"

Leorino arched his back and resisted the urge.

The memory of that night brought Leorino back to the past.

"Remember what we were... Remember who I was to *you*."

The man's heat covered his slender body.

"Ionia," Lucas whispered. The voice calling the name of the dead man awakened Leorino's memories.

# Where the Heart Lay

Keeping up with the soldier's fast gait, Josef was overwhelmed by the sheer size and grandeur of the Palace of Defense. The most opulent building Josef knew was Brungwurt Castle. But the royal palace was on a different level entirely. The dazzling splendor of the palace symbolized the very power of the Fanoren royal family in the country. With every step that brought him deeper into the palace, Josef, a commoner, felt more intimidated, his heart sinking.

Josef was a headstrong man, but he deeply regretted putting his master in this predicament with his own foolish behavior.

Walking quickly, he slapped himself on the cheek to bring himself back to his senses.

"...All right!"

That was all it took to dispel the overwhelming aura of the royal palace.

He would have time for all the regrets in the world later. Josef now had to focus on finding a way to rescue his cherished master from the arms of the lieutenant general here in the Palace of Defense.

Schultz turned at the sharp sound but did not mention anything when he saw Josef's faintly reddened cheeks.

"Um, Schultz. What's going on? And who is this man?"

Dirk asked Lieutenant General Brandt's adjutant, pointing to the young man who was clearly a civilian.

"Ouch...! What do you think you're doing?!"

The young man suddenly gripped Dirk's finger with surprising force.

"It's rude to point at people. I am Lord Leorino's guard."

Dirk was so taken aback that he wiggled his finger in an attempt to shake him off.

"Fine. I'm sorry I pointed at you! But, um? You're Leorino's...guard? And?"

The young man, however, stubbornly refused to let go of his finger.

"Mr. Dirk, I have a favor to ask you."

"Fine! I don't know what's going on, but let's just calm down, young man. And let go of my finger already!"

"You're a pretty strong man, aren't you? I don't want you to just pick up the package and leave."

"I'm not leaving until you explain to me what's happening, and I'm on the same level as Schultz. I'm not particularly powerful, either!"

"Huh. Well, that's okay."

The young man finally let go of his finger. Dirk finally got his finger back.

*Ow*, he thought, and glared at his colleague, who was watching the scene with exasperation.

"...Schultz, why is this young man, who claims to be Leorino's guard, so far inside the Palace of Defense with you? Please, can you help me make sense of whatever's going on?"

"I'll explain."

Josef immediately raised his hand, but the soldiers standing on both sides stopped him before he could try.

"No, you won't."

"You've said enough for now."


Schultz briefly explained the situation to Dirk. The guard next to them wore a serious expression. He must have been very worried about Leorino.

"...I see. So the lieutenant general took Leorino somewhere, basically kidnapping him. Do you know where he went? To his office?"

"Yes, I can't think of any other place."

Dirk tilted his head.

"...Have Leorino and the lieutenant general known each other? Why would he take him away?"

"From the way they spoke, it seems they had met before. But I don't know why the lieutenant general took him with him. But His Excellency was... How should I put it...?"

Josef, who could no longer stand it, interrupted.

"He picked up and carried Lord Leorino away with frightening strength. He wasn't acting normal... It was like he was so obsessed with Lord Leorino that his eyes changed."

"...Huh, I see."

Chewing on this information, Dirk observed Leorino's guard.

The slender young man must have been a very skilled fighter, from the way he carried himself. Still, judging by his smooth skin, he must not have been much older than Leorino. If it were not for the faint scar on his temple, his feminine face would look far gentler and more demure, even now as he bit his lip in frustration.

However, the nerve with which he had grabbed Dirk's finger out of the blue was completely unbecoming of a guard to a young nobleman.

Dirk was intrigued by this sandy-haired young man.

"So can't you do something about it, Mr. Dirk?"

The sandy-haired young man stomped his foot, looking annoyed at Dirk's apparent refusal to do anything.

Dirk's face turned serious as he realized that if this young man was going to be Leorino's guard, the first thing he would have to learn was manners.

"We can't stage an intervention into the lieutenant general's actions if that's all we have. I don't believe His Excellency Brandt would hurt Leorino. You agree with me, which is why you are hesitating, Mr. Schultz."

"I..."

Leorino should return unharmed because the lieutenant general had promised them as much. Knowing Lucas's character, Dirk shared Schultz's opinion.

But if he was so certain of this, why did the straitlaced adjutant bring this young guard to Dirk under the guise of delivering a package?

"...In any case, my order was to deliver this package to you. My job here is done."

"Right... So you're going to insist that it's this guard fellow alone who's making a direct appeal to me."

"...I'll let you make that choice."

Dirk laughed at Schultz's stiff reply.

This answer made everything clear.

The lieutenant general had been acting so strange that his second-in-command wanted Dirk, and by extension, the general himself, to intervene.

Indeed, the only person who could stop the lieutenant general at this point was Dirk's superior. In other words, the man in control of the Palace of Defense.

*Okay, little guard. You made the right choice by following Schultz.*

Dirk smiled and nodded.

"The general did indeed order Lord Leorino to deliver this package himself. I will inform His Excellency at once that he has just completed his request."

Josef was flustered by Dirk's sudden statement, not understanding what it meant. But the next moment, he gasped. "So you'll..."

"Oh yes, I'm certain His Excellency the general will want to thank Lord Leorino *in person.*"

Dirk implied Gravis's intervention. Schultz relaxed his shoulders slightly.

"Right... Then I'll leave you to it."

"I don't get it. Does that mean you're going to help?"

Dirk smiled, not offering a clear answer. Certain things could not be said out loud. But what did Josef know of worldly affairs?

"So you *are* going to help. I owe you, Mr. Dirk! When I get paid, I'll treat you to a nice meal. Tell me how I can stay in touch with you."

Seeing Josef thank him so earnestly but so tactlessly, still clearly not understanding the meaning behind his words, Dirk felt all energy drain out of him.

Dirk returned to his office. He reported the situation to his superior.

"What do we do, sir?"

Gravis stared silently at the package on his desk. The package contained the cloak he had wrapped Leorino in on the night of the soiree. Leorino had come to deliver it himself, just as he had promised.

Gravis could just imagine Leorino nervously talking to the palace guard. At the same time, he considered his adjutant's proposal.

He had known Lucas for nearly thirty years. He knew very well what sort of man Lucas was. He would never hurt someone as frail as Leorino.

However, the fixation Lucas had shown toward Leorino at the frontier six years prior had been unusual. As Gravis recalled the dangerous passion in Lucas's eyes, looking at Leorino as if he were the second coming of Ionia, his intuition told him that he mustn't leave them alone together.

The report from his second-in-command only further fueled his concern.

"He had carried such a frail young man away. Even if nothing happens to him, if he were to complain that 'The lieutenant general did something to me,' his reputation—no, the honor of the entire Royal Army would be in tatters."

"That's not funny, Dirk."

"That's because I'm not joking. If the margrave were to learn of this, we could be starting a war with Brungwurt. Leorino's family is, after all, the only noble family in the country with the military power to oppose the Royal Army."

The adjutant's concern was perfectly valid. Even aside from their military power, the Cassieux family was the one and only noble family that the Fanoren royal family could not afford to slight.

"Fine. I'll go to Lucas's office," Gravis said, and stood up.

He made it sound as if he had been influenced by Dirk's words, but he had half made up his mind to intervene from the moment he heard what had taken place.

"...What are my plans after this?"

"Yes, sir. Your next meeting will begin in about half an hour."

"Then delay it by another half hour. No one is to enter this room for a while... That includes you. You are not to enter until I give you express permission."

"Yes, sir."

The moment Dirk nodded, his superior disappeared.

In the bright room, Leorino was in the shadows, hidden by the massive frame of the man leaning onto him.

He shook his head frantically, trying to shake off the heat torturing his neck.

"No! ...Sir, let go of me...! Please, I'm scared...!"

Lucas flipped him over, forcing Leorino to look at him.

"Ah...!"

Leorino's back hit the door with a thud. He stopped breathing.

Lucas's gaze pouring onto him from above, his hot breath began approaching him.

"Call me 'Luca.' Oh, Ionia... How I've missed you."

"No...!"

Lucas hugged Leorino tightly with his hot body.

"Ever since that day, when you died in those flames for Gravis... Do you know how much I...how much I...?"

The moment he heard Lucas's muffled voice, Leorino could no longer hold back his tears.

*This man has been waiting for* him *this entire time.*

Lucas had spent the past eighteen years looking for any trace of Ionia he could find. The man who had always been so kind and cheerful had transformed his love for Ionia into this dark, sinister passion.

It broke Leorino's heart. It hurt too much to even consider.

*But... Luca... I'm sorry. I am not Ionia. I am Leorino Cassieux.*

Leorino had already realized.

No matter how many of Ionia's memories remained in him, aside from his yearning for Gravis, Ionia's heart was gone.

Before leaving for Zweilink, Ionia had something he wanted to tell Lucas.

Ionia wanted to tell Lucas of his love for him, the love he had quietly nurtured behind his unconditional feelings for Gravis.

But that heart had belonged only to Ionia.

Cruelly, Leorino was Ionia and was *not* Ionia at the same time. He could not respond to Lucas's feelings.

"...I'm sorry..."

He couldn't stop his tears.

Lucas's thick fingers gently wiped them away.

"...What are you apologizing for, Io?"

Even as Lucas held him to his chest, Leorino kept shaking his head in refusal. His tears scattered.

"I-I'm not...Ionia... I'm s-sorry..."

"No, you are Ionia. Look at me."

Lucas grabbed him by the back of the head and forced him to look up.

"I...couldn't care less who you really are."

"...! Luca..."

Despair seared through Leorino's brain.

What had gone wrong?

Had Leorino done something wrong? Or had it been Ionia's fault?

Was he still somehow responsible for warping Lucas's mind to this extent?

"...No!"

Lucas's lips came closer. Trembling with fear, Leorino shut his eyes tightly.

He was scared. Scared and anguished.

He felt like his heart was about to burst.

*I'm sorry... I'm so sorry... Luca...*

Leorino had almost lost himself to his despair when suddenly someone's warm hand covered his tearstained face.

"That's enough, Lucas."

The arm thrust between Lucas and Leorino gently but adamantly pulled Leorino back to safety.

The next moment, Leorino was embraced by the smell of the winter woods, the safest thing he had ever known.

Lucas was dumbfounded.

As he sluggishly looked up, he saw Leorino, whom he had just been embracing, now in Gravis's arms. The thumping of his heartbeat in his neck still darkened and narrowed Lucas's vision.

"Do you understand what you have done, Lucas?" Gravis asked sternly.

*He's mine… I've been waiting for him this entire time… Mine…*

A blade of reproach sliced through Lucas's dark thoughts.

"Lucas Brandt! Stand fast!"

When Gravis's harsh voice issued the order, the military man's nature reacted on instinct. Instantly, he folded his arms behind his back and stood at attention.

"Look me in the eye, Lucas Brandt."

Gravis watched Lucas with glacial fury.

The two men glared at each other in silence for a longer while.

As Lucas looked into the eyes shining like stars in the night sky, the violent emotions swirling in his heart seemed to fade away into nothing.

Finally Lucas came to his senses.

"Have you calmed down?"

Standing at attention, he was forbidden to say anything at all. The order was not intended to demonstrate the authority of the orderly. It was a kind of ritual encouraging the person assuming the posture to reflect on their actions.

Lucas was reflecting on his own behavior during his moment of passion. He was dismayed to see the state of the young man protected by Gravis's arms.

Leorino looked, for all intents and purposes, like a victim of assault.

His platinum hair was tousled, and his cloak, still hanging around his neck, was on the verge of slipping off. The shirt around his neck was roughly disheveled, and the skin peeking out from his collar showed several marks Lucas had left on him.

He must have been terrified of being manhandled by a man several times his size. He was still trembling in Gravis's arms. His pale face was wet with tears that still spilled from his eyes, and his eyelids were swollen and painful to look at.

At the sight of those hurt violet eyes, his lips trembling as he bit back his sobs, Lucas's chest felt tight.

*"I'm sorry... I-I'm not...Ionia."*

Through his vain resistance, Leorino had kept apologizing to Lucas. He no longer understood why Leorino felt the need to apologize. But the apologies had only spurred Lucas on. *Tell me you're Ionia. Be Ionia for me*, he had thought.

If Gravis had not stopped him, he likely would have claimed the young man's body where they stood. If he had done so, if he made that violet-eyed man his once more, he felt that Ionia would return to him. If that wasn't horrible enough, he had told him that he couldn't care less who Leorino was. He let his desires run wild and tried to own Leorino's body, if nothing else. Leorino's pitiful state was the result of an outburst of his feelings for Ionia that had been building up over the past eighteen years.

*What... What have I done...?*

When he saw that reason had returned to Lucas's eyes, Gravis quietly commanded:

"At ease."

"...Yes, sir."

Lucas kept his hands folded behind his back. He didn't trust himself about what he might do otherwise. He felt like slitting his own throat for his loss of reason and the guilt he felt toward Leorino. The fists behind his back were trembling with anger at himself. However, he had no choice but to endure this humiliation.

Lucas hung his head, feeling he didn't have the right to express remorse.

"Do you have anything to say in your defense?"

"No, sir. Lord Leorino Cassieux has the right to accuse me of violent misconduct. I will humbly accept any punishment."

"Leorino, what do you want to do? You have the right to denounce this man and demand that he be punished by the Royal Army."

Gravis looked down at the young man still trembling in his arms. Leorino, who had been watching Lucas with melancholy eyes, shook his head at Gravis's question.

"...There's no need... Please don't punish the lieutenant general."

Lucas's face crumpled.

Gravis asked Leorino once more.

"Why? He brought you here against your will and tried to force himself on you."

"...No, he didn't hurt me."

"No...not *physically*. But you *feel* hurt, don't you?"

At Gravis's words, large tears spilled once more from Leorino's violet eyes.

"I—I... I..."

His trembling lips failed him, and he broke into a small sob.


Gravis held his slender body.

"You can relax. You're all right now."

At this, Leorino could no longer hold back his sobs, clinging to Gravis's chest as he broke into tears in earnest.

Gravis gazed silently at his subordinate, who wore an anguished but remorseful expression.

"Lucas."

"...Yes, sir."

"I thought we discussed this before. Ionia is gone. No matter how much we may see of him in this boy, Leorino is *not* Ionia."

"...Yes, sir."

Lucas was racked with guilt.


"Leorino... I am so sorry. I will never do such a thing again. I can't apologize enough."

Lucas squeezed out the words with a pained expression.

Leorino raised his tearstained face and looked at Lucas with his violet eyes. His beautiful dawn-colored eyes, a mirror image of Ionia's.

The moment their eyes met, Lucas's heart stirred with yearning so intense it nearly drove him insane.

But Lucas had been wrong.

"Lord Lucas... Luca."

The men were blindsided by the name Leorino used. Leorino himself didn't seem to notice.

"I'm sorry...I couldn't be Ionia."

The men gasped at his words.

Leorino himself saying he was not Ionia left Gravis feeling relieved and disappointed at the same time. He realized that he had held the same hope as Lucas that Leorino was the reincarnation of Ionia.

It was only natural. It was the fault of the maddening feelings that had, for years, nestled inside the two beasts who lost the man they loved forever. But at the same time, their obsession was proof that they were ignoring Leorino, a boy who was doing his utmost to live a fulfilling life.

"...Leorino, I'm sorry."

Gravis apologized.

Lucas couldn't help reacting. "Your Highness! Why are you apologizing for *my* misconduct?"

Gravis was in the position to mercilessly denounce his subordinate for so carelessly losing control of himself and assaulting a young man who had just barely come of age in his office.

"Why... Why are you apologizing?"

"Lucas, I can't blame you."

"Why...?"

"Because I'm just as guilty as you. I can't forget Ionia, either. I live my life in pursuit of his shadow."

The slender body in his arms shuddered at these words for some reason.

Gravis continued speaking to Lucas.

"...I'm just like you. I, too, would sacrifice anything to have Ionia back in my arms, even right now, at this very moment. I would lay down my life if I had to."

"Your Highness, I..."

"Wouldn't you? I dug up his grave many times in my dreams. I'd do anything to bring him back to life. So to say that I don't feel anything at all when I look into the eyes of this boy and see they're just like Ionia's would be a lie."

Leorino's trembling grew more intense.

Gravis stroked his small head soothingly.

"...It's all right, Leorino. We won't ask you to be our Ionia... But..."

He looked quietly at Lucas again.

"Lucas, I know what that obsession feels like. So I can't blame you. I'm just as guilty as you are. If push came to shove, maybe I would have done the same thing."

"Sir! But with Leorino, I nearly...!"

Gravis stood Leorino up and knelt in front of him.

"Leorino, we got you involved in our obsession, and I apologize for that."

Leorino clutched at his chest and endured the pain. He couldn't stop his tears from flowing. His heart ached beyond words from the moment he heard Gravis speak of his feelings. Leorino's heart was violently shaken by the eighteen years of love and obsession the men had experienced.

It might have been easier to just confess.

*Say it. Confess*, a voice seemed to whisper.

He had once been Ionia Bergund—and he could have the same relationship with them once again.

But at that moment, the value of Leorino's existence would disappear. And when the men returned to their senses, they would be disappointed at how frail Leorino really was.

They would be going in circles.

Gravis couldn't take this a second longer. He stood up and took Leorino's slender, quivering body in his arms again.

He nodded toward Lucas.

"I'm taking Leorino with me."

"...I can't apologize enough."

"Leorino is willing to forgive your crimes, but don't think I'll forget what happened here."

"I understand. I will accept any punishment. And I will issue an apology to the Cassieux family."

Leorino interrupted their conversation quietly.

"...Please keep this matter between us. I don't want my father or brothers to find out and blow this out of proportion."

Even aside from this, a soldier of the Royal Army had once inflicted a wound that would never heal on Leorino. Not even the mild-mannered margrave would forgive them this time.

Gravis gratefully accepted Leorino's offer to spare Lucas's life, even as he thought Lucas didn't deserve it.

"Leorino's magnanimity has kept you alive."

Lucas bowed his head at the words.

"Lucas, you must be wondering why I'm so calm. How I can remain so composed in front of this boy."

"Yes, sir..."

"You once asked me how you and I are different. It is because I am no longer entitled to think that my feelings for Ionia are as true as yours."

The two men's gazes met.

"I often dream that perhaps there really was a way to stop that tragedy before it happened, and I try to think about what we could have done differently... But when I wake up, nothing ever changes."

Ionia had died in those flames.

"Every time I wake up, I regret that it was my fault that he died, that it was because of my failure as a commander. But my regret will never be enough to atone for my sins."

"Your Excellency..."

Lucas squeezed this out an anguished voice. But there was nothing more he could say.

"I am royalty. I am responsible for Fanoren. Ionia sacrificed his life to defend this country that I must protect. I must be satisfied with that."

"Sir...!"

"You and I are different. I was only his best friend... And I must be satisfied with that. No matter how strongly I felt about him."

In Gravis's arms, Leorino had been listening to his confession with tears streaming down his cheeks.

"Ionia gave his life to close those gates that day. And this boy was born the following morning. Do you understand? August had said it himself. This boy is a symbol of the hope that Ionia left us...the hope he gave this entire kingdom. He is the future of this country."

Gravis placed one hand behind Leorino's knees and picked him up. Finally, he looked at Lucas, who stood there in blank amazement.

"So, Lucas, look at the boy for who he *is*. Look at him, at the brilliance of his own life as Leorino Cassieux."

# Sinful Lips

This was the second time Leorino had been brought to this office.

The Palace of Defense was an opulent building, but the office was, by its very nature, a very simple room. Aside from its size, it was not much different from Lucas's office.

Gravis sat down on the settee, Leorino still in his arms. Being sat in the man's hard lap, Leorino looked to be at a loss but accepted what the man was doing. He lowered his hood, revealing his small, tearstained face. His red, swollen eyes were darting around, unable to focus. He was miserable and painful to look at.

But even in this state, he was beautiful.

The decorations of his military uniform looked painful against Leorino's soft cheeks. Gravis undid the buttons of his jacket and leaned Leorino's little head back against his shirt.

Wiping Leorino's damp cheeks, still fresh with tearstains, he heard a small sniffle.

"...You're quite the crybaby, aren't you?"

Leorino's trembled against his chest. Was he trying to say he wasn't crying?

"I'm sorry for Lucas. I want to apologize to you again for what he did."

"...I keep causing Your Highness trouble."

The young man in his arms sagged pitifully.

"You have nothing to apologize for. You did what I told you to do; you delivered my cloak. I was hoping it would do you some good to learn some social skills, but it seems I was wrong."

"I failed to deliver on our promise."

"No, I never thought Lucas would do something like that."

For some reason, Gravis sighed softly. At the weary, somewhat self-mocking sound, Leorino timidly looked up at the man.

"Oh, I was just thinking you have a particular affinity for finding misfortune everywhere you go."

The man gently stroked the area under Leorino's eyes with the back of his fingers.

"I'm sorry... I shouldn't have said that, considering what Lucas did to you."

Leorino's eyelashes, sticking together because of his tears, quivered. Gravis ran his fingers across them, untangling them. His fingertips became damp.

Leorino rested his cheek against Gravis's chest. Gravis gently rocked him as he would with a child.

"...I consulted with the palace guard and decided to leave the cloak with Mr. Dirk and go home."

"I heard. You did well."

Leorino nodded stiffly.

"I thought your family was overprotective, but after seeing you get into this kind of trouble, I can understand why they wouldn't want to let you out of the house. I feel I can't take my eyes off you for one second."

Leorino cast his gaze down and apologized once more.

"Are you afraid of me...? Being this close, I mean."

Leorino thought for a moment, then answered that he wasn't.

The tension in his body had disappeared the moment they entered the room. It was filled with Gravis's scent. So he wasn't afraid. If anything, it made him want to completely yield himself to Gravis. He wanted to be trapped in his arms forever.

"Ever since the day I met Your Highness... I have never feared you, and I don't fear you now. In fact, I feel very safe."

"I see." Gravis smiled. "It must be difficult, being so unguarded."

"Sir...?"

"Don't look at me like that. You've finally realized it, haven't you? You drive men crazy."

"But Lord Lucas thought I was Ionia... Whoever that is... That's why he did what he did."

Leorino's face crumpled again.

"No, Leorino, *you* yourself drive men who should know better at our age crazy."

"But not you, Your Highness. You're always kind to me and..."

The man rested his chin on Leorino's head. The firmness of his jaw startled him. Leorino instinctively ducked his head.

Gravis's chuckle resonated in his skull.

"You heard me. I have the same urges as Lucas."

"...Does Your Highness also wish I were Ionia?"

"Maybe so... No, that's not right."

Gravis silently pondered it for a brief moment and then laughed quietly.

"I can't seem to take my eyes off you."

Leorino gasped as Gravis's beautiful bony fingers trailed down his neck. The skin Lucas had toyed with was extremely sensitive.

"Did Lucas do *this* to you?"

"...This...?"

"You have a mark...right *here*."

With that, Gravis pressed on a spot on his neck. From there, a strange numbness trickled down his spine and seized Leorino's heart.

"...Your Highness."

"I'll ask you again. Leorino, are you afraid of me?"

"I-I'm not afraid of you... Your Highness."

The corners of Gravis's mouth lifted.

"That's not good enough. I've told you this before. You should be afraid of me, too."

Leorino felt Gravis's low voice on his forehead. Slowly, the man's face came to rest on his neck.

"...Ah."

"...I can't have another man marking this fair skin of yours."

A heat tickling the little hairs on his neck pressed hard against the spot Gravis had just traced with his finger, leaving a sharp pain like a spark, then disappeared.

"That's better."

At the sound of Gravis's satisfied voice, Leorino's heart lurched in his chest with a painful thump.

Leorino didn't understand what had just happened.

"...Why?"

"Just because. Now I'm just as guilty as Lucas for hurting you."

Leorino was shocked by these words.

*How awful...*

This man had shifted the blame to himself by overwriting the proof of Lucas's misconduct.

Leorino's violet eyes filled with tears.

He glared at Gravis as best he could.

"You didn't have to do that. I won't tell anyone about Lord Lucas."

Gravis was blindsided by his high-pitched protest.

"What, did you think I was trying to shoulder Lucas's guilt?"

Leorino nodded, but just as he was about to let out a sob, Gravis pressed a finger to his lips and heaved a small sigh.

"How do you arrive at such strange conclusions? I would never leave a mark on you for such a reason."

"...Fine, then wh-why?"

Gravis laughed.

"...I knew you were unfamiliar with this sort of attention, but for god's sake... Whatever will I do with you?"

"Ah."

Gravis pulled on the back of Leorino's head, exposing his throat.

Gravis's perfect beauty was only a breath away now. His austere lips were smiling slightly. Leorino lost himself in his starry-sky eyes.

"Lucas was just about to...do *this* to you, wasn't he?" Gravis whispered in his low, smooth voice. "But he didn't."

Leorino swallowed audibly. Struggling to breathe, he quietly gasped.

"You've never allowed anyone in *here*, have you?"

Gravis pressed his thumb to Leorino's lips. Leorino released a quiet moan as he stroked the sensitive contours of his lips. With a small smile, the large man leaned in.

Leorino was enveloped in Gravis's gentle twilight shadow.

The man's fingers slowly slid across the back of his head. Just when he thought Gravis put some force into his fingertips, the next moment he gently pulled Leorino in, slowly sealing their lips.

"...Hnn."

Leaving a soft sensation on his lips, Gravis's masculine beauty quickly pulled away.

"...Is this the first time you've been kissed?"

Still in a daze, he nodded reflexively.

The man who had just stolen Leorino's first kiss pulled back the corners of his lips in satisfaction.

"Now you know I wasn't covering for Lucas. Not these marks...and not this, either."

"Ah..."

The man brought his lips to Leorino's exposed neck once more and sucked lightly at his skin.

"I just wanted to overwrite this mark...and I wanted *this*."

His insolent lips took Leorino's once more. It all lasted only an instant, his touch light as a feather.

"...I just wanted to be your first. That's all. Do you understand now?"

Leorino's eyes widened—he was speechless.

He worried his lips had melted right off.

He touched his lips with his fingertips. They were a little wetter than usual, but otherwise nothing had changed. He gently probed the puffy area with his tongue.

"I know you're not aware of what you're doing, but that's very provocative. I told you. You're a danger to me, too. Besides, those violet eyes of yours... They really are identical to his."

Timidly, Leorino looked up at the man.

Gravis seemed to see someone else in Leorino's eyes.

Leorino knew who it was. A man who was larger and stronger than Leorino and who had won Gravis's and Lucas's immense trust and friendship.

He ardently wished that Gravis would look at Leorino himself. He was heartbroken that the man held no feelings for him now.

But Leorino knew he was the coward here. He was too afraid of disappointing the man to tell him he was the reincarnation of Ionia. He wanted to have his attention because he was Leorino, not because he had once been Ionia. He was disgusted by how pathetic he was.

"Ionia was Dirk's older brother?"

He wished for Gravis's attention for who he was, but at the same time, he wanted Gravis to tell him about Ionia. He knew it didn't make any sense.

"Yes. I regret what I have done to Dirk's family. Ionia was a commoner, the son of a blacksmith. But when he met me, his fate shifted. In the end, it was my fault for sending him to the battlefield."

Leorino shook his head before he could help it.

"...Who was...Ionia to Your Highness?"

It was the one thing he wanted to know most—and the one thing he didn't want to know at all.

When he looked up at Gravis hesitantly, he noticed Gravis was also watching him.

"Who was he? Good question. If I had to say, I think he was my destiny."

"Destiny..."

"That's right. I don't know why, but he was the only person I ever wanted to be by my side. And I half forced him into a situation where he had to be."

Leorino felt melancholy, knowing it wasn't just Gravis who had brought Ionia to that school.

"He had suffered to protect me."

Leorino shook his head without thinking once more.

"...Don't you think he was happy to serve you?"

Gravis's eyes widened at Leorino's words.

"I don't know. But he was the only man who helped me carry the burden of my fate. Ionia was the only man I trusted with my back."

Gravis placed his hand on Leorino's head.

"I told you that I experience the same sort of obsession as Lucas."

"...Yes."

"After Ionia died, I was driven entirely by my desire for vengeance. After the war, I honestly couldn't bring myself to care about anything. It was as if my future had died that day at Zweilink."

Leorino recalled Gravis's words to Ionia on the day of their parting, back when Gravis was nineteen years old.

*"When this war is over...please...choose me, too."*

Right. Eighteen years ago, Gravis had said that to Ionia: *"When this war is over..."*

He had not known that the next time they would meet would be to say good-bye forever.

"But Ionia's father rebuked me. He said, 'My son defended this country for you. So live and fulfill your duties.'"

Leorino closed his eyes.

"I think he was right."

The man looked down at Leorino and smiled bitterly.

"My life is like a shadow of its former self. So while I might not be as intense as Lucas is, suddenly...your existence complicates things. Looking at you makes me restless."

Leorino asked the question that had been on his mind.

"Your Highness, if...Ionia were here, would you act like...the lieutenant general?"

Gravis nodded without missing a beat.

"I think I would. And this time I wouldn't let him go for one second."

Leorino was glad he had not confessed on impulse. It would hurt him too much to disappoint Gravis.

"I'm not Ionia..."

"...Yes, I know."

"I may have the same eyes, but I am not him."

"I know."

Gravis put some strength into his arms and rocked Leorino's thin body reassuringly. But this did not comfort Leorino.

Leorino cast his eyes down and stared at his hands.

They were too helpless to belong to a man.

Lucas had grabbed him with ease, and Leorino hadn't been able to do anything to resist.

*I hate this...*

"I can't do anything. I can't wield a sword. Frankly, I can't even run. There was nothing I could do earlier, either... You'd have to be joking to think I'm anything like Ionia."

"Leorino."

"I don't have the right to call myself a man. I can't fight. There is no Power in my hands anymore."

At that moment, Gravis's body stiffened.

But Leorino, lost in his own thoughts, did not notice.

"So I—"

"Leorino." A low voice called his name, interrupting him. When he looked up, the man's gaze had changed.

"...Did you just...?"

At that moment, a knock sounded in the office.

They both gasped at the same time.

After safely handing Leorino over to his servants, the adjutant returned to his office and reported to his superior.

"Sir, I have delivered Leorino to his carriage."

Dirk tilted his head at his superior, who was so deep in thought that he seemed not to have heard his subordinate's report.

"What's the matter, sir?"

The man remained silent and continued to stare into the void with a stern expression on his face.

A spark of suspicion had begun to smolder in his mind.

# A Sweet Abyss

The moment he glimpsed his master's neck, Hundert gasped at the mark he found there. The attendant paled, imagining the worst possible scenario.

"My lord... Did they...?"

"No."

Leorino denied the attendant's suspicions.

Hundert's expression turned stern. He was usually very mild-mannered, but he, too, hailed from Brungwurt. He would not remain silent when his master was harmed.

His master's beautiful face, hidden by his hood in the carriage, showed dry traces of tears.

"...Hundert, I beg you, don't say anything."

"...I am informing Master Auriano."

"No! Please, Hundert."

"My lord. It is a matter of great importance to Brungwurt if you have been dishonored."

"No. No one has done anything to me. So don't say anything to my father and brothers."

Hundert was surprised by the uncharacteristically strong tone of his master's voice.

But Hundert was his full-time attendant.

"Then I shall inspect your body. Otherwise, I will tell Master Auriano."

Leorino hesitated for a moment, but the servant's unyielding attitude made him nod reluctantly.

They silently made it into the bathroom, and as usual, the attendant helped him undress, taking off his garments one by one. Before long, his smooth, milky, porcelain skin was exposed before the attendant's eyes. Leorino spread his arms a little and urged the servant to check.

"…Is this enough? There's nothing there, is there?"

His slender, graceful limbs, extending from his beautifully taut shoulders, showed no traces of sex. Aside from the crimson mark on his neck, his body was as pure and charming as always.

His nipples were a fair shade that seemed to melt into his skin, and so were his genitals, surrounded by some downy hair, looking soft and smooth as usual.

Leorino exhaled, seeing the attendant's relief after he cursorily examined his entire body.

"Please turn around."

Leorino's cheeks took on a darker shade for the first time then, and he hesitated, but he finally listened to his servant, obediently turning around and placing his hands on the wall.

"…Like this?"

"Yes. Excuse me."

Hundert spread Leorino's small, soft buttocks and looked beyond them. His master's nethers remained their innocent shade of light pink. Leorino was still chaste.

Hundert finally breathed a true sigh of relief then and removed his hands from Leorino's fair flesh.

"I noticed nothing out of the ordinary, thank you."

Leorino was accustomed to exposing his skin to his attendant since he was little and didn't even flinch at the full-body inspection. For the two of them, it was a routine, unremarkable act.

"If anything were to happen to you, my lord, the master's wrath would be immeasurable."

"I don't doubt it…"

The attendant reminded the dispirited Leorino:

"Brungwurt has the power to turn on Fanoren. As a member of the Cassieux family, you must never forget this."

"...I know. I'm sorry for worrying you."

"I will not tell your brothers about the mark on your neck. I will not ask how it got there, either. But only this once. Can we agree on that?"

"Yes. Please and thank you... No one has done anything to me. Are we clear?"

The old attendant nodded at his master's words.

His master was now a full-fledged adult and was able to think and make decisions on his own. He likely wanted to avoid causing friction between the Royal Army and Brungwurt because of his personal affairs.

"...I don't want to cause His Highness Prince Gravis any more trouble."

Leorino's cheeks were slightly flushed. There was something faintly sexual about Hundert's master tonight.

Nodding at his master's request to use the hot water, the attendant began preparing Leorino's bath.


Leorino announced that he did not want dinner and instead retired to his bedroom early.

He curled up on his bed like a cat and buried his face in his pillow.

He had kept himself together as best he could until he got home. The same was true of his earlier exchange with Hundert.

But now that he was alone, the feelings he had been suppressing finally boiled over. He let himself cry as much as his body demanded.

Eventually, his tears dried up, and he was left feeling completely empty.

Leorino was finally able to calmly reflect on the day's events.


He had met with Gravis and Lucas. As he recalled both men, a storm raged in his heart.

If he were to be honest, he had been truly scared when Lucas assaulted him. The size and strength of his body genuinely frightened Leorino.

What Lucas had wanted was Ionia. Not Leorino. It was violence molded in the shape of love that disregarded Leorino's personhood. Being faced with that had hurt him the most.

But in the end, which man had taken more from Leorino?

Lucas, driven mad with his love for Ionia, who had said, "*I...couldn't care less who you really are.*"

Or Gravis, and the passion his lips had brought him, who had said, "*I just wanted to be your first.*"

Movement and stillness. Light and darkness. The polar opposite men had both taken something of Leorino's innocence.

The time he had spent at the mercy of the passion of two grown men was indescribably unnerving, as if he were a leaf carried by a storm. The heat they lit up in the depths of his body against his will was still confusing Leorino.

But which man had lit up that heat?

Leorino rolled from his catlike posture to his side. He held his upper lip, the same one Gravis had stolen a kiss from, between his fingers. The heat that trickled down to his abdomen at that moment somehow never went away.

*Vi touched me here... With his lips...*

The touch had been as soft and brief as a feather brushing across his lips, but despite Gravis's cold, firm appearance, it had felt scalding hot. As Leorino remembered it, his body grew hot.

*I...wish he had gone further.*

In his dreams, Ionia had exchanged passionate kisses with the men.

Leorino wanted Gravis to teach his current body the pleasure of entwining tongues. He gently took his thin finger in his mouth and gingerly stroked his tongue.

"...Mmm...ugh."

That was when he felt something deep in his abdomen tighten.

"Nn... Ah!"

The bath should have washed it all away, but the spots on his neck the two men had teased were still throbbing. Rolling his finger across his tongue, he gently traced his neck with the fingers of his other hand.

"Mmm..."

The spot where Lucas's ferocious heat had burned him. The pain like a spark that overwrote his mark. Even these memories, now overwritten by Gravis's sweet darkness, had become a faint spice that made Leorino's body feel hot.

"Vi... More, please give me more..."

He couldn't think of anything.

All he knew at the moment was the cry of his own body.

He wished those lips would seek him, not Ionia. He wanted to be ravaged by those beautiful thin fingers, by those cold yet hot lips.

He was disgusted by the base desires he didn't even know he had. But he couldn't do anything about it now. He had to relieve this heat alone.

His young body gave in to the intense lust he was feeling for the first time in his life. He had become hard before he realized it, and he loosely grasped himself over his clothes.

"Ngh..."

It felt good.

He couldn't resist touching himself. His slender fingers searched for pleasure and stayed where they found it. Both the finger in his mouth and the fingers around his groin made him feel good.

"Vi... Vi..."

The sight of Leorino, alone on his bed, clumsily indulging in the lewd act, would have been dizzying in its obscenity if anyone had been watching. His fair skin was stained a light crimson, and his finger-sucking lips were swollen and red in a way that would be impossible to hide.

His supple body, writhing coquettishly atop the sheets, moved in irregular sensual waves. His restless puppylike gasps bounced off the canopy.

Releasing his grip from his fully erect shaft, Leorino timidly reached behind him. The moment his fingertips made contact, his toes curled. For the first time in his life, Leorino was overcome by an uncontrollable surge of sexual desire.

Like Ionia, he wanted to feel a strong man deep inside him. He wanted Gravis to take him, body and soul. He wanted to feel Gravis erupt inside of him.

Leorino was desperately recalling the hazy memories of Ionia's sex life and imitating whatever he could.

His tight entrance was throbbing with pain, and he was beginning to worry that he might hurt himself.

"Ah... Ah..."

But his body had never been with a man and struggled against his probing. The disconnect between the urge controlling his mind and his body, which knew nothing of sex, drove Leorino mad.

He couldn't do anything about the pain at the moment. He was quite unfamiliar with the intricacies of pleasuring himself in that way. He had no choice but to return to his front, this time slipping his hand beneath his undergarments and touching it directly. He rubbed himself clumsily as the slick sensation gingerly flowing from his tip coated his fingers.

It was a skill-less motion that only satisfied the desire leaking out from the inside, but slowly his manly instincts took over, increasing the pace of the movement that brought him pleasure.

It was not because Ionia's feelings were occupying his heart. Leorino himself was attracted to Gravis. Gravis was nineteen years older than Leorino now. He was a man of a higher status. He was also the man Ionia had once loved. But every time Leorino saw him, he couldn't help the way his heart ached for him.

These were his own feelings. Feelings belonging to Leorino alone.

He would have never crossed paths with him otherwise.

But through some miracle, as soon as he had arrived in the royal capital, he had gotten close enough to feel the warmth of the man's body twice already. And today he learned the heat of his lips.

Leorino licked his own lips, hoping to somehow recreate the heat of Gravis's lips on his.

"No, that's not right..."

Whining impatiently, Leorino lightly curled his tongue. He was so eagerly seeking the tongue of the man in his fantasies that he exposed his slender, smooth throat to the evening air.

He was nearing his climax.

Beyond the point of release awaited sweet despair and disappointment in himself.

Leorino threw himself into that sweet abyss.

Panting heavily, he stared at the evidence of his desire in his palm. Dripping down his hand was the proof of his greed, of wanting to be much closer to Gravis. Pushed over the edge by this desire, he fell into several contradictory conclusions.

He could hear a voice telling him to confess that he'd had Ionia's memories. For eighteen long years, Gravis had longed for him so much. This time, there might exist a future in which they walked hand in hand.

On the other hand, Leorino realized that he was still different from Ionia. The only man whose attention he desired was Gravis.

He wanted the right to stay by his side as Leorino—even as he realized what an impossible desire that was.

Leorino was left unarmed in a place where desire, expectation, and fear blended into one. Each thought was as strong as the other and equally confusing to Leorino. His heart continued to waver.

But it was Leorino's current truth. He was just a powerless person, filled with contradictions, putting up a struggle—that was his reality.

*"Look at the boy for who he* is. *Look at him, at the brilliance of his own life as Leorino Cassieux."*

Those words were his only guiding light through the chaos of the future.

*Yes. The only thing I might be able to do for Gravis. I already have the courage to accomplish it... I'll do all I can.*

He had to grow up.

He was certain he would find himself running into walls in frustration many times in the future. Even so, he would not turn away from reality—he would find meaning in his life as Leorino.

For that sake, Leorino decided to first face his own weakness.


The day after their visit to the Palace of Defense, Josef visited Leorino's room to apologize for his blunder. However, the moment he saw his master, Josef was so shocked that the apology he had prepared vanished from his mind.

Seeing Josef standing there in a daze, Leorino laughed quietly.

"What's the matter, Josef? ...Come, you can sit down."

"Young master... Did—? I mean, my lord..."

Overnight, Leorino had become someone whom Josef could not recognize. There was nothing different about his appearance. As always, he was a beautiful man with his miraculous beauty and an ephemeral aura.

However, there was something different about him that had not been there yesterday.

"Lord Leorino... What happened yesterday?"

"I told you in the carriage—nothing happened."

"...But..."

His master's golden, feathery eyelashes turned toward the ground. Josef gasped.

He pulled his gaze away and questioned the attendant standing behind him with his eyes. Hundert only silently shook his head. He must have noticed the change in his master as well.

Leorino, Josef's childhood friend and now his master, had always been a somewhat fickle, otherworldly young man.

Overnight, he seemed to have been reborn into a human being with all the rawness brought on by living.


Josef finally noticed.

The contours of his master's cheeks were smooth but not juvenile. His shoulders were beautifully firm, his neck as straight as a waterfowl's, and his limbs graceful. There was nothing masculine about him, but neither was he childlike nor feminine.

He was not an angel, nor something equally fanciful. He was a young man who was becoming an adult. But even so, he was so overwhelmingly beautiful that Josef found himself unable to speak.

His perfectly smooth skin, his pale eyelids, and every hair on his head were so clear and vivid that they captured the gaze of everyone who saw him. Every time Leorino moved, color and light seemed to pour out of him.

*He's so beautiful...*

"Josef, sit down."

"...R-right."

Leorino's calm voice brought Josef back to his senses, as if waking him from a dream.

"I want to talk about what happened yesterday in the Palace of Defense."

"Right."

"I like you, Josef. You were my only childhood friend back in Brungwurt. You played with me when there were no other children close to my age, other than my brothers. I was so happy when I learned that you were going to be my guard from now on."

"And yet I... I'm really sorry about yesterday...young master."

Josef threw his hand over his mouth. He still could not get out of the habit of calling Leorino "young master," and Leorino smiled at him.

"We're both new to the royal capital and ignorant of the ways of the world."

"...Yes."

"So until we learn all the customs and rules, we need to be more cautious. All right?"

"Yes, sir. I understand."

Leorino chuckled. *What an enchanting smile*, Josef thought with a start.

"I can't believe it. Josef, you've always acted like one of my brothers. I never thought you'd be telling me 'Yes, sir.'"

"I've had my share of reflecting to do."

Josef's slender face turned red at his master's teasing.

"I need to ask something of you so that you can stay by my side from now on. You can't pull your sword on people like that. Please act with discretion."

"Yes, sir…"

"Josef, you're so headstrong, and I worry about you, especially the way you speak to your superiors. Now that we will be meeting members of high society, I need you to be more careful. This is not the Brungwurt we know so well… Do you understand?"

"Yes… I came here today to apologize. I was trying to help you, young master, but I only caused you trouble. I'm sorry."

Leorino offered him a pained smile then, as if he had remembered something. But Josef, whose head was in a deep bow, did not notice.

"…Mr. Hundert gave me a full dressing-down after that… I'm sorry that… my actions put you in harm's way, young master. I'm a horrible guard."

"I appreciate your sincerity. I'll be counting on you as always."

"Lord Leorino…"

Leorino smiled again and grasped Josef's hand in his own. Josef could feel the heat in his slender fingers. The warmth of his master's body reminded him that Leorino was flesh and blood, which somehow made Josef's heart ache and his chest feel very tight.

"I want you to assist me so that I can live in the royal capital."

"Lord Leorino…?"

"I want you to be my sword, Josef."

His thin fingers squeezed Josef's hand.

"I finally understand how helpless I am. I thought I could get by on my own, but…I couldn't."

"…? What do you mean by 'get by'?"

"I need strength. The strength to fight."

"…What are you trying to fight, my lord?"

Leorino only shook his head.

He seemed to have no intention of answering Josef's question. Only his beautiful violet eyes spoke to Josef with their sincere gaze.

His eyes were shining brightly.

"I should know better than anyone the cruelty of offering your life to someone. How horrible of me… But…"

Josef's head was full of questions.

"Josef, will you stay with me? No matter what path I walk down?"

Josef immediately nodded.

"I will follow you wherever you might go. I swear I will protect you, Lord Leorino. I will be your sword."

Leorino's eyes widened. His violet eyes glistened.

"Thank you... We may run into danger. Do you still wish to proceed?"

"I don't mind. That's my job. And have you forgotten? I'm strong."

"Yes, thank you... I'll protect my heart by myself. So you don't have to coddle me. You just have to protect this helpless body of mine."

The strange feeling Josef had the moment he entered the room was no illusion. *Something* had definitely happened to his master yesterday at the Palace of Defense. An event that greatly transformed him on the inside.

And because of that event, his master was trying to shed his childishness. He was trying to become an independent adult. Perhaps the first step in this process was to admit his own weakness like this.

Josef made up his mind. He would never call Leorino "young master" again.

That was the moment Josef decided that Leorino would be his master for life.

An immense desire to protect him grew in Josef's heart. But it was not the feeling of an older brother figure watching over his childhood friend. It was a mission he was willing to stake his life on.

Leorino was the master and Josef was his guard, each fulfilling their respective destinies. Leorino asked Josef if he was ready for that. And Leorino had expectations for Josef.

"I want to do better, too... And I'll start by watching my language."

His master offered him a dazzling smile and laughed. "Yes, start with etiquette."

When Josef heard that clear laugh, a smile appeared on his face.

"Let's both do our best in the royal capital, Josef."

"Yes, sir. Lord Leorino... I will do everything in my power to protect you."

# Distant Thunder

"Welcome back, Alois. You have come a long way."

"Yes, sir. Thank you for your patience."

Alois, who had been dispatched to the Kingdom of Francoure as Gravis's personal envoy, had finally returned to the country.

Like Dirk, Alois was Gravis's adjutant. Alois's mother was a noblewoman from Francoure, so he, too, was fluent in Frankish. For this reason, he frequently served as Gravis's special envoy.

This time, Alois was sent to Francoure by order of the general to share information on Zwelf with their ally. Gravis had gathered his other adjutant, Dirk; Lieutenant General Lucas Brandt; and Brandt's adjutants, Schultz and Acker, in his office to hear what news Alois had brought from Francoure.

"Your Excellency, have you received the missive I sent?"

"Yes, I've read it. Everyone here is aware of the situation. So what did my uncle decide in the end?"

The "uncle" Gravis was referring to was the king of Francoure, the brother of the queen dowager, Adele.

"Sir, he has no doubt that Zwelf has signed some kind of contract with Gdaniraque."

Except for Gravis, all the men groaned, grim expressions on their faces, at this information.

Gdaniraque was a relatively small country located northeast of Fanoren. Nevertheless, they could not afford to ignore it, due to its geographical location in a narrow strip of land adjacent to the great powers of Zwelf, Fanoren, and Francoure. In practice, it was a mercenary state whose main export was military power, with ties to an organization of the large, strong warrior peoples of the north.

Gravis did not change his expression, only urged Alois to continue.

"And my uncle believes this on what grounds?"

"Sir, according to the chancellor, Francoure's secret police learned that between last fall and this year, General Zberav of Zwelf visited Gdaniraque on three occasions. Since then, two of the main roads leading from Francoure to our country via Gdaniraque have been regularly closed off by Gdaniraque."

"How has Francoure responded to that?"

"Sir, Francoure has sent an official messenger in protest. However, Gdaniraque has been noncommittal on their reasoning and has not given a definite reply. It seems they are hoping for a reaction from Francoure."

Lucas deeply furrowed his brow.

"Does that mean Gdaniraque is acting at the request of Zwelf, trying to separate Francoure from our country?"

Alois nodded at Lucas's question.

"If the roads through Gdaniraque were closed, that would leave only two other roads between Francoure and our country. Both of these routes are very roundabout. It would certainly be an obstacle for any reinforcements sent from Francoure."

"Vandarren... That clever bastard."

Lucas's manly face twisted as he spat out the name of the king of Zwelf.

"Vandarren has been purging all the moderates, and it's been how many years since he went from being the disinherited crown prince to the new king? ...Nearly three, huh. That might have voided the treaty, but Zwelf has been paying us reparations for fifteen years until then. Do they really have the money in their treasury to pay off Gdaniraque?"

The men pondered Lucas's words for a moment.

"Dirk, what's east of Gdaniraque?"

"...? Oh, I see."

Dirk immediately clapped his hands at Gravis's quiet question.

"You mean they've started spreading it around the area?"

"I'm sorry, I'm not following you. What do you mean, Dirk?"

Schultz asked this to Dirk.

"Iron. The only iron deposits on the continent are in Zwelf, our country, and a few mines in Francoure. Zwelf, destitute from postwar reparations, has only one means of earning foreign currency, and it's iron... In the past six years or so, Zwelf has ceased their iron exports, haven't they?"

"And? Aren't they keeping it to manufacture weapons in case of war?"

"That, too, but as the lieutenant general just mentioned, they need foreign currency. Without it, they wouldn't be able to pay off Gdaniraque, a mercenary state. Remember what His Excellency said."

"...Oh god."

Schultz finally understood. Dirk nodded.

"The Gdanis Sea, east of Gdaniraque, is home to the Jastanya Islands. There is little information about that region on the continent, but it is a multiethnic country, plagued by conflict for ages. That's likely where they're getting their funding by unscrupulously distributing iron, the material for weapons... Sounds plausible enough, doesn't it, sir?"

Gravis nodded appreciatively at his second-in-command, formerly of General Staff fame.

"Most likely. It's possible that by going through Gdaniraque, which excels at weapons manufacturing, they are exporting iron ready for battle. Gdaniraque also stands to gain from that deal."

Gravis's answer made them all groan.

"...Zwelf's got it all figured out. It would be conspicuous to make any moves within the continent, but to turn their attention to the conflict in Jastanya, where the national policy is ambiguous at best, with the help of Gdaniraque... Alois, has there been any other real harm done to Francoure?"

"Yes, sir. There have been several clashes in the very port of the Gdanis Sea."

Gravis nodded. He wore no distinct expression, but his eyes were piercingly bright.

"Then we're right. Zwelf got the funds to work with Gdaniraque. And we can be certain that they contracted them."

An oppressive silence fell over the office.

"Lucas."

There was a threatening gleam in Lucas's eyes.

"Yes, sir."

"Eighteen years have passed since the last war. Fortunately, our country has not suffered any major conflicts since. Many of our soldiers in the field likely do not know anything about warfare. Summon the commander of every unit. Make sure they can hold their own in a real battle."

"Yes, sir."

The two men looked at each other and nodded.

"Start with the mountain troops in the northwestern part of the country and Zweilink. And deploy troops along the trade route to Francoure to ensure security at all times. You can reinforce your forces if you see the need. Obtain funds for the reinforcements from the Palace of Finance via Ginter. I trust you to handle it from here."

"Yes, sir. How much time do you think we will have to prepare?"

Gravis turned his eyes to Dirk.

"...Dirk, when do you expect them to attack?"

The adjutant had been in General Staff until his appointment as Gravis's second-in-command, and he began analyzing the information he had gathered and the news his colleague had brought.

"As early as this fall. Perhaps we should treat this with more urgency. They should wait for the snow to melt, so next spring may be more likely."

"And how do you reason?"

"For one, the military strength of Zwelf. Even if we estimate more than we did initially, it will be, at most, two-thirds of our military strength. King Vandarren is no fool. He would never attempt a second war if his military was lacking. And he wouldn't use Gdaniraque only to stall Francoure. They must want them to participate in the war against us. On the other hand, Gdaniraque is a mercenary nation, and its principal value is money, but as expected, they must be prudent about making an enemy of our country and Francoure, two of the biggest nations on the continent."

Dirk explained this eloquently, with his finger on his chin as if talking to himself.

"...And the king—or rather, the chief of Gdaniraque is, to my knowledge, a very wicked and greedy man. He will try to negotiate with Zwelf by raising the price. My second reason is that even if their deal was sealed, they would not choose to go into the mountains in winter, considering they would have to build up their armies and make further preparations. Hence, they should declare war next spring. However, if they somehow secured some special funding, it is very possible they could attack as early as this fall."

Gravis nodded.

"That's an accurate assessment. You should work with the chancellor and General Staff while you're at it to gather evidence. Alois will work with Francoure. We must prepare by the fall."

"Yes, sir."

The general, now tenser than before, fixed his dark, starry-sky eyes on the other men.

"You must be ready. If Zwelf is to attack with the help of Gdaniraque, this time the first spark will fall on Zweilink."

Once the others had left, Gravis ordered Dirk to call Sasha.

"Sir, I heard you wanted to see me...? Oh, Alois, you're back from Francoure. Welcome back."

"Dr. Sasha."

Sasha stood in front of the desk. "So what can I do for you?"

"Sasha, I'm leaping to Brungwurt. I have something I need to discuss with the margrave."

"Ah, I see Alois had some news for you... But why are you going there personally, sir?"

"It's a long way from here. It's more efficient to go there myself. That is what I intend to do for the time being."

The clever Sasha immediately guessed the reason why Gravis was leaping to the frontier.

"I see... So I guess it's finally happening. And I'll be swamped with work again. I really wish you'd treat your elders better."

Grumbling in displeasure, the military doctor showed a kind of resignation and a brazen defiance.

The next moment, however, he was surprised by his superior's words.

"In addition, I will tell the margrave that we will take care of Leorino at the Palace of Defense. You should arrange a meeting with his eldest son as soon as possible and convince him. I already mentioned it to him the other day."

"Um, Your Excellency? I did ask for that, but...! You were so prudent before. Isn't this a bit sudden?"

But Gravis did not feel the need to explain himself. He looked at Dirk as if he had suddenly remembered something.

"Why was Leorino crying that night?"

"Hah... Hmm, I'm still not sure myself. I don't remember telling him anything in particular that could make him cry."

"Explain again what you were talking about."

Dirk recalled his conversation with Leorino.

Back then, he had gotten in trouble because Sasha had misunderstood the situation and assumed Dirk had made Leorino cry by doing something inappropriate to him.

"I remember I told him that after I graduated, I joined the army, was assigned to General Staff, and a few years ago I was appointed as His Excellency's second-in-command. Then, before I knew it, Leorino was crying these big fat tears."

Sasha tilted his head.

"What, that's all you were talking about? But what about Dirk's personal history would make him cry?"

"Right? ...My question exactly."

Sasha's doubt made perfect sense. Dirk scratched his head in confusion.

"What else did you talk about?"

"Let me think... Oh yes. I told him about my late brother and how he used to be His Excellency's guard when they were students."

His superior's black hair swayed slightly. Dirk felt the change in his expression and quickly apologized.

"...I'm sorry, I shouldn't have done that."

"No, I don't mind. So did Leorino say anything?"

"No, nothing. He just kind of...cried."

"...I see."

Dirk recalled the moment.

Yes. Dirk had been struck by the dawn-colored eyes that looked just like his late brother's, like a ray of dawn suspended in the indigo.

He glanced at his superior.

Dirk had noticed. He had rarely heard his superior mention his brother, but after spending so much time with him, he could tell.

His brother's presence had been special to Gravis. Gravis was still clinging to his brother in a way that could not be described as mere regret. His brother's presence was still engraved on his heart.

But how was Gravis's most recent decision and the reason why Leorino had cried that night connected? Even the discerning Dirk couldn't tell.

So he had to ask.

"What does Leorino's behavior that night have to do with the decision to send him to work at the Palace of Defense at this time?"

The general had always been world-weary and never showed much emotion, but he had been acting strangely ever since the young man appeared in his life.

After a moment of silence, Gravis answered: "Anyway, the boy will stay with us for a while. Did you hear that, Sasha? I'm counting on you."

"Wait, please. We should tell Leorino first."

Gravis stared into thin air with his dark, glowing eyes.

"No need. Whatever his intentions are, I've decided to keep him in my sight."

"...Sir!"

"This is an order. You are to obey it."

# Secrets of the Old Castle

Gravis leaped to Brungwurt.

Just like on that day six years ago, he was taken to the study, where he waited for August, the head of the family.

It was a simple and sturdy room with no superfluous decorations.

Compared to this, the royal palace was far gaudier. But the brighter the light, the darker the shadows. For Gravis, the royal palace was the place where he was born and raised but not somewhere he could relax.

This old castle, made of stone and wood, had an immensely subdued atmosphere, which Gravis found comforting. The honest and unpretentious appearance of Brungwurt was similar to the temperament of the Cassieux family. And to Leorino.

Leorino's beautiful appearance would be suitable for the majestic splendor of the royal palace, but having actually spoken to him, Gravis knew his looks belied a simple and honest disposition that had little to do with pretense. Gravis felt strangely at ease with him by his side.

In any case, the castle was very old. Gravis felt the history it carried far more than the royal palace. It was rustic and solid, and looked like it had survived many wars. It was a large castle, too large, even to serve as a home to the lord of the land, built like a fortress with high walls on all sides.

It was therefore not surprising that Brungwurt Castle was not originally a home. It was the royal palace of the former Kingdom of Brungwurt, which Fanoren had invaded and annexed two hundred years prior.

Until some two hundred years ago, back when the Agalean continent was still rife with small nations, the family that now called itself the Cassieuxes had ruled this area. But the Kingdom of Brungwurt was destroyed in a war against the royal house of Fanoren.

At the time, the king of Fanoren did not treat the Brungwurt royal family with disrespect. However, he did strip them of the Brungwurt family name, instead bestowing on them the family name "Cassieux," derived from the name of a local wild plant called "cassia," and conferring on them the title of "marquis."

However, the locals, who had adored their monarchs for generations, strongly opposed the renaming. The king, fearing a rebellion, eventually allowed the name of Brungwurt to remain in their title.

Ever since, the region had become the main battleground for territorial disputes with neighboring countries. The Fanoren royal family, struggling to defend the area from the distant royal capital, consequently turned to the Cassieux family, who knew their lands well.

In exchange for granting the Cassieuxes autonomy and allowing them to build their own autonomous army, the king ordered them to become the main defenders of the northern border. The Cassieuxes loved the lands of Brungwurt dearly and willingly agreed to these conditions, if it meant they could return to the land they had once ruled.

Since then, the Cassieux family had confined themselves to Brungwurt, changed their title from "marquis" to "margrave," and maintained an autonomous army to protect the land for generations.

Although they did not receive the title of "duke," due to a lack of blood relations to the royal family at the time, the title of "the Margrave of Brungwurt" in Fanoren was treated as almost equal to or even higher than a duke, due to their royal bloodline, which spanned further back than any other noble family in the country.

The Fanoren royal family had cleverly maintained an inseparable relationship with Brungwurt by regularly marrying into the family, taking political considerations to prevent Brungwurt from becoming independent or rebelling against the Crown.

It was by chance that August, the current head of the family, fell in love at first sight with Maia, the daughter of a duke's sister who had married into the royal family. But even without that chance encounter, August and Maia could have been forced to marry.

Maia was the cousin of the former king. She was a princess with a strong royal bloodline. If she had not married August, she would have likely been married off to some royal family.

In fact, several princesses of royal blood were mentioned as potential wives for Auriano, the eldest son and the next margrave. But the Cassieux family turned them down due to their close proximity in blood to Maia. As a result, Erina Munster, the eldest daughter of the Duchess of Leben, who was related to the royal family for several generations, was chosen to marry Auriano.

Thus, with a high degree of political consideration, the relationship between the Fanoren royal family and the Cassieux family had been maintained to this day. Marriages with the Fanoren royal family were held every few generations. For this reason, the bloodline purists secretly called the Cassieuxes "the other royal family."

Looking over the walls of the historic castle without truly looking at them, Gravis pondered the relationship between Brungwurt and the royal family.

And then something occurred to him.

There was another bloodline that was related to both the current Fanoren royal family and Brungwurt.

The lineage of the Marquis of Lagarea.

Gravis's half brother, the current king, Joachim, was born to a cousin of Lagarea who had been adopted by the marquis from a relative. Erina, who married into the Cassieux family, was the daughter of Lagarea's sister, who married into the family of the Duke of Leben.

Was that really a coincidence?

*And he's also a good friend of August's, isn't he?*

It was not something one could conveniently arrange, but still, the Marquis of Lagarea had a strong connection with both of these families, to a curious degree. Just as Gravis was about to further reflect on the Marquis of Lagarea, there was a knock on the door.

"Come in."

August Cassieux, the head of Brungwurt, appeared. Tall and strong, his body showed no signs of decline. His hair, however, was already streaked with gray, betraying his approach to old age. Seeing him once again, Gravis realized August's three eldest sons really were carbon copies of their father. On the other hand, his youngest son, Leorino, fully took after his mother.

August quickly bowed. Gravis did not expect August to behave in a formal manner in front of him.

"I'm sorry to keep you waiting, Your Highness."

"No, it was I who paid you a sudden visit. I was lucky you were in the castle."

When Gravis asked him to sit down, August nodded and sat down across from the general.

"...If you have gone out of your way to see me, does that mean things are finally...?"

August broached a topic with no preamble.

Gravis, too, skipped his introduction and got to the core of the issue.

"Yes. Unfortunately, it seems the time will come again."

"When exactly, Your Highness?"

"We are gathering intelligence as fast as we can, but for now we are expecting it next spring, perhaps earlier. We want to be ready to face them in the fall. I want you to be prepared for everything."

"Yes, sir. I have been prepared for three years now."

"I appreciate it. There is one more important thing I must tell you."

August's fading blue-green eyes flashed. His eyes still had plenty of strength and drive.

"Zwelf has made a deal with Gdaniraque. At the moment, they are only interfering in the trade route between Francoure and our country, but it is possible their mercenaries will join the war."

August nodded.

"If that is the case, they will most likely begin with Zweilink."

"Most likely."

August's face showed no sorrow or fear.

"We have been preparing in secret. By early autumn, our preparations should be nearly complete." August stood up and asked, "Would you like to see our progress, sir?"

At these words, Gravis raised his eyebrows.

"May I?"

"Of course. Let me show you."

The Brungwurt Autonomous Army rarely revealed its military capabilities. Given its autonomy, even the Royal Army had no right to interfere. Taking advantage of the generous offer, Gravis got up and followed the margrave.

They mounted their horses and rode out of the castle and into the Brungwurt Forest. No one was accompanying them, but Gravis could feel the occasional presence of people. Soldiers must have been stationed at regular intervals.

After about half an hour's ride, they entered a thick forest and suddenly found themselves in a clearing.

"Wow..."

There, three large one-story buildings had been constructed, carved out of the forest behind a rocky outcrop. A dozen or so soldiers saluted August as soon as they saw him.

Leaving their horses with a soldier, August led Gravis to the armory.

A loud noise came from the armory. The doors opened to reveal a vast amount of armaments, protective gear, and large weapons, so neatly arranged that even the Royal Army could not compare.

"…My god."

Gravis gasped. Slowly, he stepped into the armory. The cool, dark room echoed with the heavy footsteps of two men.

"This is the armory and reserve of our army. In addition to this one, there are four other locations of this size in the province. Please do not expect me to inform you of their locations. It took us three years to build up our equipment to this level… We have also increased the number of our soldiers. This should give us the strength to fight with pride."

Gravis marveled at what the margrave had accomplished.

"…You've done well for yourself. We are glad to have you on our side. Your level of preparedness is extraordinary, August."

August laughed in his low voice at the praise.

"I'm glad we managed to arrange the marriage of my eldest son in time. If they can have a child by next spring, we couldn't ask for more as a family… But, well, that will be up to the heavens. There's only so much I can expect."

"And Lord Auriano is aware of all this?"

"Of course." August nodded. In his eyes, the deep trust and pride he held for his brilliant heir was clear.

"He has learned enough from me. Once the war begins, Auriano will take command with me. He is to return with Erina shortly."

"And Lady Erina?"

"I have not told her yet. Auriano will not be able to leave Brungwurt, so we will give them six months together. And whether or not she bears a child, Erina and Maia will return to the royal capital in early fall. I have already promised the Duke of Leben to do so."

Gravis stopped.

"You have been talking with the Duke of Leben as well?"

"Yes, I have. Allow me to confess to Your Highness. When we were offered the hands of several princesses related to the royal family as candidates for Auriano's bride, I turned them down for one other reason besides their proximity in blood to Maia."

"That being?"

"Their fortune. In fact, we had our eye on the Duke of Leben's fortune—and therefore Erina Munster. But if the Cassieux and Munster families were to be united through marriage, the people in the capital would be very wary of a rebellion on our part. That's why we declined the offer of marriage with the royals on the grounds of blood relation. We were very fortunate that Erina's name, which I had my eye on, came up in the form of a recommendation without our having to make an offer. And this is how we used the dowry Erina brought us..."

Gravis laughed at the old man, who looked around the armory with a satisfied look on his face.

"They say you have no interest in politics, but when you get serious, you go all out. You are a clever man. The royal court has played right into your hands, hasn't it? You have earned your title as the head of Brungwurt."

"You mustn't misunderstand me. It is not out of self-interest. I have never dreamed of rebelling against Fanoren. We have invested everything we could in our lands to prepare for the next war. We simply needed more money to build up our army."

"I understand. But how could the Duke of Leben take you up on your offer?"

"I knew the Duke of Leben well through Bruno. He is a wealthy and generous man, and he, too, understands his duty as a nobleman."

August's words reminded Gravis of the mild, white-haired duke. He was a moderate man who had always remained neutral and had never been a member of any faction. He had built up an enormous fortune and had never slighted anyone.

"I went to see him myself three years ago, after the treaty with Zwelf was breached...right around the time we were selecting Auriano's potential bride. I met with him in secret so that the royal court would not speculate what I was after. We had a heart-to-heart then."

"That's when Leben took you up on your offer."

August nodded solemnly.

"Leben could tell we were on the precipice of war. He was determined to stand together against the coming national crisis. We received his eldest daughter, and he gave her a significant amount of money in the form of a dowry. Although, all we could give in return was our bloodline."

The Brungwurt bloodline was worth just that much. Gravis nodded, thinking it was a fair price to pay.

"In the end, Auriano and Erina get along well, and as a parent, I am relieved."

Gravis gazed into the solemn face of the experienced head of the family. They watched each other for a moment, until finally Gravis smiled.

"I'm aware that I'm barely even part of the royal family... But thank you for telling me."

The wrinkles around August's eyes deepened.

"If Your Highness is barely even part of the royal family, then so is everyone except His Majesty the king. If I may, I trust Your Highness. During the last war, you recaptured Zweilink with the strength of a god of judgment and protected Brungwurt, and by extension this country, from the oncoming enemy."

"I only did what I was expected to do. Back then, I honestly would have destroyed anything in the name of the cause. I can't say whether my actions had the lofty convictions of a man like yourself."

When Gravis laughed bitterly, August shook his head with a serious face.

"Nevertheless, it is thanks to Your Highness that this country still enjoys peace as the greatest power on the continent."

"It is not thanks to me. It is thanks to all the men who fought for it."

"That is also true. But there is another reason why our family trusts you."

Gravis raised his eyebrows.

"And that is?"

"You have saved my youngest son twice. The first time in Zweilink. The second time in the royal capital. I will forever regret letting him go to the royal capital. I have built up a lifetime's worth of debt for that. I thank you for everything."

Gravis had a sudden epiphany.

"Leorino said he came to the royal capital to look for work... Now I see. You let him escape to the royal capital before the war, didn't you?"

August neither denied nor affirmed.

"In truth, I had intended to immediately marry him off to Julian, the son of Leben."

"You had...?"

"Leben had been blindsided by his eldest son's sudden declaration that he would be 'marrying a man,' which was unbecoming of an heir... But he finally gave up after seeing Leorino at the wedding and realizing that his eldest son's infatuation was inevitable."

August laughed in a low voice, remembering the event.

"I was hoping that Leorino would come to like Julian, of course, but he was so innocent and didn't take to Julian's seduction at all. Quite the contrary, he cried and asked me, 'do I have no choice but to be protected by a man?'... When I pressed him about it, he said, 'I want to be able to protect someone, not just be protected,' like a true boy of the Cassieux family. So we let him go to the royal capital."

"...Leorino told me that you refused Julian Munster's proposal."

August shook his head.

"We haven't broken off the engagement yet; it's simply on hold. Leorino is the only one who doesn't know it."

Gravis said nothing.

"It wouldn't be easy to let that frail child escape once war broke out. Just traveling to the capital put a lot of strain on his body. But concerns about the war aside, I asked Julian to take things slowly in the royal capital and let things proceed at Leorino's pace."

For some reason, Gravis felt an immense surge of irritation toward the cunning margrave. He immediately clenched his teeth in an attempt to bite back the feeling.

"If anything should happen to me and Auriano, Brungwurt will be destroyed. It would not be easy for Johan and Gauff to regain our territory and rebuild. Still, they're good boys. They can live their lives as ordinary men. But Leorino cannot. I worry that no matter how hard he tries, he will never be able to live on his own."

In his mind, Gravis saw a beauty that was too ephemeral and graceful for a man. The moment he took his eyes off him, the young man could be captured by devious desires.

"I told the boy that I would give him two years, but in fact I thought it would be…until the war began. I thought it would be another two years before Zwelf was ready to fight, but… That bastard's country somehow got the money to hire Gdaniraque mercenaries, didn't they?"

"…Yes. But I can't give you the details."

August nodded in understanding.

"In any case, thanks to Your Highness's information, I know there won't be much time to spare. I feel sorry for Leorino, but I intend to have him and Julian engaged by early autumn."

"…You do?"

Gravis gnashed his teeth harder.

Leorino would marry Julian Munster. Gravis knew that, rationally speaking, it would be the best path for Leorino.

But for some reason, just thinking about it was unbearable.

He recalled the faint heat he felt when he touched Leorino's small, trembling lips. Leorino had trembled like a little bird in his arms, his eyes wet with the surprise of having his lips claimed for the first time.

What was the feeling that stirred in his chest as he gazed into those teary violet eyes at that moment?

He had finally met someone who once again awoke the soft, hot, deep emotion that he was convinced had long withered away into nothing.

That person would belong to another man forever.

Someone other than himself would make both that soft body and that honest soul their own.

"…That will not do."

The words slipped out of Gravis's mouth before he could stop them.

August tilted his head quizzically.

"It will not do? And why would that be?"

"I came here today to tell you one other thing. Your youngest son will be employed in my Palace of Defense."

August's expression changed.

"…You must be joking, sir."

"I am not. I want to give Leorino a job he can do under Sasha."

"I appreciate your consideration for his will to work, but I'm going to marry him off to Julian as planned."

"You will not. That is…the only thing I cannot abide."

The men glared at each other.

"Why do you think I sent him to the royal capital in the first place? You want him to join the Royal Army when we're about to be at war?"

August's harsh words had Gravis shaking his head.

"I would never send Leorino to the front lines. Hell, I won't even let him leave the capital."

"Then why? And if something were to happen to his family, who would protect him?!"

"I will protect him," Gravis declared.

August was blindsided.

"I *will* protect him," Gravis said, looking at his hands.

He recalled Leorino's warmth as he held him in his arms.

He wanted to protect him. But just as strongly, he wanted to have him all for himself where no one else could see him. Yes. He felt the same fierce urge to possess Leorino as he did when he first met Ionia.

Why and when had he become so attracted to him? They had met only a handful of times. But the thought of that young man leaving his hands filled him with unspeakable distress.

"Your Highness… It can't be."

August gasped as if he had noticed something in Gravis's unusual behavior.

"I will protect him. I'm placing him in the Palace of Defense for that very reason."

"Your Highness… Prince Gravis… You must not."

"I promise to protect him from any and all threats."

"Your Highness… Why are you so concerned with that boy?"

August's immediate rejection only served to frustrate Gravis beyond belief.

"Why? No particular reason. He's an adult. He doesn't need your permission."

Gravis's cold eyes flashed darkly, and he began to intimidate the man in front of him. Sweat beaded on August's forehead.

"Your Highness, please listen to me!"

"…! What the hell is going on?!"

"Your Highness Prince Gravis!"

The men's angry voices cut through the air.

A rattling sound came from the entrance, and the men came to their senses. A soldier, apparently having heard the shouting, called out from a distance: "Are you all right?"

August insisted that everything was fine, and silence returned to the armory.


"…Your Highness Prince Gravis. Are you aware of what you are saying and with what expression?"

August sounded somewhat weary, and Gravis raised his eyes.

"…Aware of what?"

"It sounds to me like Your Highness is refusing to let go of him."

"…Is that what you think I'm doing…?"

August was staring at Gravis with a strange look of pity on his face.

"Am I wrong? It sounds to me like you are saying that you don't want to let Julian—or anyone else, for that matter—have him… Anyone but yourself."

Gravis stared at his hands.

"I don't want anyone else to have Leorino…?"

August pressed on sternly.


"You and Leorino never had the chance to get to know each other well enough. Are you not only attracted to his appearance? Do you not lust after my son?"

"No! No, I do not! I just…"

Leorino had said it himself. He was powerless. He said his hands had no Power.

Was that just a metaphor or some kind of sign?

*  *  *

*...Am I like Lucas? Do I desire that trace of Ionia?*

Was that all there was to it? Did he really want what little remained of Ionia? Or did he just want to keep Leorino on hand to confirm his suspicion?

He didn't know.

He just wanted to learn the truth.

Maybe he just wanted the coincidence to be an inevitability. Maybe it was an obsession, like Lucas's born from his yearning for Ionia.

But if Leorino turned out not to be the reincarnation of Ionia, could he let him go?

"What I feel for Leorino is..."

Was the feeling that welled in him as he held Leorino in his arms not affection?

The same thing he had felt when he met Ionia at the blacksmith shop.

He wanted to keep him by his side forever. An unacknowledged yet immense urge to say, *He belongs to me.*

At that moment, Gravis finally realized his true feelings.

At his age, Gravis was dismayed at just how obtuse he had been.

He didn't care if Leorino was not the reincarnation of Ionia. He only wanted Leorino.

"I'm sorry, August."

His voice was full of bitter self-mockery.

"...What is the reason for this apology?"

August's voice was equally bitter.

"I won't let Leorino out of my sight."

"As his father, I cannot allow that. Please give up on him. You are royalty. You cannot protect him by giving him your name like Julian!"

August shook his head, his face pained.

"Do you understand? You are not in the position to be involved with Leorino alone."

Of course. The war with Zwelf was about to begin, and at this critical time, it would be crazy to fixate on a single young man.

"Your burden is far too much for him to carry. If you care for him, please let him go. Pray for his happiness from afar!"

The father pleaded desperately.

"I know. It's possible I will join the battlefield myself. I should probably leave him under Julian Munster's care. I know that's the only reasonable choice. But..."

The crease of Gravis's brow furrowed in anguish.

"I hate the thought of him belonging to another man. If you think I'm too old to have such feelings, laugh all you want."

"Your Highness..."

"If praying for his happiness is love, then I suppose I don't know what love is."

August glared at the man with fury in his eyes.

"...Do you wish for a war with Brungwurt, sir?"

"Not at all. I only want to protect him. I swear I will not force him into anything."

Gravis shook his head.

"...But if his heart ever favors me, no matter how slightly, then I will never let him go again."

Deep within the man's heart, the door that had kept his emotions locked away creaked open. The scratch caused by that friction was proof that he had fallen in love once more. The feeling he hadn't felt in years was bittersweet.

Gravis looked August squarely in the eye and told him clearly: "If I can win his heart, then he will be mine. You don't get a choice in this."

He wanted to take that irreplaceable young man and lock him away in his hands.

He wanted it beyond words... Beyond all reason.

*Continued in the next volume*

# Let It Snow

Ionia woke up to the smell of damp air.

It wasn't quite dawn yet, but it was already light outside the window. It was the snow that had fallen while he was asleep that made it so. The bright-white snow illuminated them through the curtainless window.

The left side of his body was warm. Ionia tilted his head, gently, so as not to wake him, to look up at the young man sleeping soundly next to him. They had passionately embraced each other all through the night. Now the young man's face was so peaceful as he slept quietly next to Ionia. His face, with its long eyelashes downturned, was more childlike than usual.

Seeing his sleeping face for the first time, Ionia couldn't help but smile.

*Vi...*

Gravis had held Ionia in his arms and had not let go, even as he'd fallen into a deep sleep. His right arm was under Ionia's neck, and his left was wrapped around Ionia's waist. The young man's hot body was too comfortable for Ionia to pull himself away.

Ionia's body felt pleasantly heavy after having received Gravis's all night long. His lower body felt especially numb, as if they were still in the act.

He wondered how long they had been embracing.

By the end, they had both collapsed onto the bed, covered in sweat, drifting along the edge of consciousness. He had no memory of what happened after that.

＊　＊　＊

Ionia raised an arm to investigate the spot that had been ravaged all through the night. It was still soft and wet with fluids that could have belonged to either of them.

Ionia laughed at his own body's lack of discipline. What he had just experienced must have been very pleasurable. His body reacted even to his own fingers, ready to open up and take Gravis in once more. He felt a tinge of shame at the lewdness of his own body, but more than anything, he felt satisfied.

*How indecent of me...*

Taking the lead was not Ionia's area of expertise. Of course, he felt pleasure when a man caressed him, but he felt far better being explored from the inside.

It was Lucas who had made him this way.

But it was not his significant other who had held him tonight. Ionia felt neither guilt nor remorse for this.

While tracing his tender areas, he realized he desperately wanted to be entered again, and so he put his middle finger to task.

It was much warmer and wetter than usual. The sound his body made was all the evidence he needed that Gravis had finished inside.

"...Mmm... Ah."

He no longer had any doubts that Gravis had received his bedchamber education. There had been no hesitation or confusion in their hasty act. Gravis had deftly loosened Ionia's tight flesh, cleared the path inside him, and then took him like a storm.

Ionia went deep and then deeper still.

Ionia indulged himself, remembering the sensation of being taken so roughly, so deeply, and so sweetly. He was a bit sore from all the rubbing, but he felt good just playing with himself.

*I wonder if Vi felt good, too?*

Had Gravis not been disappointed with his body? Was Ionia able to please him?

The proof of their passion would disappear eventually. Just like the snow falling beyond the window. The rapture they had experienced would remain in their hearts for a while, but it, too, would melt away someday.

But this memory would remain forever.

Ionia had been holding on to this feeling ever since they met on that day when Ionia was eleven years old, thinking that it would only be for today, only for tonight, but it had finally arrived at a conclusion.

The despair and delight of this moment was indescribable.

*...I love you. I love you. I will always love you.*

Ionia lifted his head, which was resting on Gravis's chest. He wiped away the tears he found there.

He gently slipped out of Gravis's arms. He wrapped his fingers around Gravis's now soft body part. Sliding down his naked body, he slowly brought his face to Gravis's thighs.

"Mmm... Io...?"

Without a word, Ionia took Gravis's length into his mouth. At the same time, he began gently massaging his balls with one hand.

"...Io... What are you...?"

When Ionia laced his tongue around the tip in his mouth and sucked on it gingerly, Gravis quickly grew turgid.

"...Io, you..."

Ionia was soon unable to fit even half of it in his mouth.

His breathing became labored, but the sensation of having his mouth filled to the brim was too satisfying to relent.

Gravis was becoming more aroused by the second. He was still in a state where his instincts won over his rational mind. He dreamily stroked Ionia's head, ruffling his hair, as Ionia devoured him below the waist.

Ionia loved Gravis beyond words, seeing him at his mercy, indulging in the pleasure he was giving him.

Gravis grew larger and larger still, and before he knew it, tears were spilling from Ionia's violet eyes.

Ionia could hardly breathe from love and pain alike.

He couldn't hold back any longer.

He relieved his fingers of their task of cradling Gravis and began to tease his entrance again. In and out, in and out, the delicate softness of his body craved something more.

"Ah... Unf... Ahhh..."

The pleasure working its way up his back finally forced him to pull his mouth off of Gravis's shaft.

As he inserted another finger, and then another, Gravis grabbed him by the hips.

That was when he realized that Gravis, who was observing Ionia's obscene display with a scorching gaze, was now fully aroused.

The golden stars twinkling in his eyes could not have been brighter.

"Io...honestly... How could I resist after seeing you like this...?"

Ionia smiled seductively, pleased to hear Gravis's lustful murmur.

Ionia pleaded with the flushed young man before him: "So, Vi...could we...go again? It's not morning yet... So..."

"...Of course. Get on top...and stay there."

Gravis's hand urged him to straddle his stone-stiff member.

Ionia slowly lowered his hips.

Since he'd had Gravis inside him for most of the night and further pre-pared himself with his fingers, Gravis's impressive length slipped in without issue. Ionia's inner walls twinged with delight at the hardness of him.

"Ahhh... Ah... Oh... Ah, you're so good..."
"Haah... Io... Io..."

Ionia, always one to do his best work from inside, brought Gravis over-whelming pleasure. The sheer pleasure of it blurred his vision.

Ionia's hole, nearing its limit, squeezed Gravis at the base. His ravenous inner walls massaged Gravis, the warm, wet flesh threatening to swallow him whole. Gravis's liquid passion sang in perfect harmony with Ionia's warmth and grip. The sweet sensation near mimicked a hole men did not typically possess, but the feeling was unmistakable.

When the thought occurred to Gravis that it was Lucas who had made Ionia's body so lewd, an intense jealousy stirred in his chest.

As if to take out his resentment on him, Gravis pinned Ionia's hips in place and thrust into him with mounting vigor. Ionia moaned, his taut body bucking.

Gravis learned all of Ionia's most sensitive spots during their first round. And making use of his girth, he worked over Ionia's tender areas once more, pushing his tip deep inside again and again. In response, Ionia's flesh only swelled further, becoming the perfect vessel for pleasure.

Ionia moved his hips on instinct, reveling in the rapture Gravis granted him.

"God... You're so good... Vi...! Ahhh... Ahhh... Agh... Hnng!!"
Taking advantage of Ionia moving his hips on his own, Gravis sat up and brought him into a position where they were face-to-face. The movement allowed Gravis to effortlessly drive himself even deeper.

Ionia's legs trembled.
Holding Ionia's undulating hips against him, Gravis licked one swollen

nipple exposed before him and rolled the other with his thumb. Ionia began moaning almost loud enough to scream.

"Ahhh, ah, Vi, not there... Together, hah. Wait..."

"...Why? I thought you liked it when I licked you here..."

Ionia reached out with both hands and clung to Gravis's neck, still being regularly thrust into from below.

"I'll finish...soon, too soon... No, Vi, not yet..."

Ionia's spasming flesh brought Gravis a frightening amount of pleasure. He had never felt such overwhelming bliss, not with any man or woman.

Gravis felt himself grow even harder inside Ionia.

He wanted to lose himself to the pleasure and explode inside him, but he held back.

*I love you, Io. I love you. I want to spend the rest of my life with you... Give me just a little more time...*

If it weren't for the three-year age difference.

If it weren't for the difference in status between a royal and a commoner.

But that would be an excuse.

Gravis hated his own indecision and inability to choose a future with Ionia.

It was he who had put their future into question. Gravis knew that he was the one who was uncertain about the future he wanted to grasp.

Their hot skin intertwined with the other so tightly that they could no longer tell where one ended and the other began. Ionia closed his eyes tightly, feeling the comfort and urgency of it all.

Gravis's rough breathing tickled his ear.

"Io...open your eyes. Look at me."

Violet and starry-sky gazes met. They both glimpsed into the other's soul, both crying and screaming on the inside, not wanting to let go of the other.

*I want his eyes to burn me to death. I want to always...always stay with him like this.*

"Io... I..."
"...Don't say it... Vi. Just kiss me. Don't say anything. Just keep going..."
Just like this. Just their bodies, melting into each other.

Gravis pulled Ionia's head closer, bringing him to his lips. The moment their lips touched, they devoured each other with reckless abandon.

*I wish this could last forever. Just this, forever.*

Above and below, they were one in every way that mattered.

Their hot bodies intertwined, and they continued to indulge in the pleasures of their flesh without ever tiring of the other.
Only tonight could they wholly and fully belong to the other.

Let the snow pile up outside the window.
Let it make this time last forever.

The more snow fell, the more memories of this night would be imprinted in both their bodies and minds.

Until their dying breaths, this heat would continue to warm their hearts forever.